I0602597

MARRY ME, MARQUESS

LADIES LEAST LIKELY

MISTY URBAN

OLIVERHEBERBOOKS

All rights reserved.

No part of this publication may be sold, copied, distributed, reproduced or transmitted in any form or by any means, mechanical or digital, including photocopying and recording or by any information storage and retrieval system without the prior written permission of both the publisher, Oliver Heber Books and the author, Misty Urban, except in the case of brief quotations embodied in critical articles and reviews.

PUBLISHER'S NOTE: This is a work of fiction. Names, characters, places, and incidents either are the product of the author's imagination or are used fictitiously. Any resemblance to actual persons, living or dead, business establishments, events, or locales is entirely coincidental.

Marry Me, Marquess Copyright 2024 © Misty Urban

Cover art by Dar Albert at Wicked Smart Designs

Published by Oliver-Heber Books

0 9 8 7 6 5 4 3 2 1

CHAPTER ONE

LONDON, 1798

The library was the only safe place in Westrop House.

Until the girl pursuing him slipped inside.

She was a Ponsonby, he thought. Or was it a Sysonby? Some sprig of a lesser branch, a young daughter yet unmarried, a deplorable situation the family wished desperately to remedy.

On the surface, there was nothing objectionable about her, and nothing Leo, for his own part, objected to.

It was the state of marriage to which he objected—or, more precisely, the state of being shoehorned into marriage, penned like a bull in the pasture by connection-hungry mamas, the worst of which was his own maternal figure. The one person who ought to have had his best interests at heart was, instead, colluding with the enemy.

Leo had no doubt that his doting mama was the traitor who'd told the girl where to find him. If she hadn't drawn out a map of the house, with Leo in the library as the X marking the buried treasure, no doubt Lady Mary had marched the chit to the door, pushed the wooden portal open, and shoved his pursuer inside.

Could she have found it, Leo had every expectation her

ladyship would have pocketed the key and marched away, confident that, in a few moments, she would have a marriage to announce to her assembled guests. Who would she elect to discover him and the girl in supposedly compromising circumstances? The girl's mother? A doyenne of *le bon ton* known for being a high stickler and a moral guardian? Would her ladyship herself do the deed?

Gideon Leonidas Paxton Westrop was not a bull, and he refused to be treated as one. He'd put the library key in his pocket when he snuck away from his mother's *soiree* and into this room, five minutes ago.

The floor-to-ceiling drapery at the sash window offered refuge, but he'd not made his retreat in time. The girl's eyes slitted like a red kite spotting an animal it could digest.

"Your lordship," she said coyly, wafting his way like a spray of apple blossoms. Leo disliked apple blossoms; they made him sneeze.

"No lords here," he demurred. "I am titleless."

She halted her forward motion, confusion pulling together her violently plucked brows. "But you will be heir to the marquess."

Dear God, the dirt hadn't even dried on Rupert's grave and Leo's mother was auctioning him off like a stallion at stud. Her cry had been heard throughout the house when the black-edged letter arrived. Leo still wondered if it had been, in fact, a crow of triumph.

If she hadn't prayed for his cousin's death, Leo felt quite certain her ladyship had skimmed over Rupert's name in the daily list of requests she presented to the Almighty. She was too pious to have consulted a witch, and too conscious of her mortal soul to actively hasten a man's death. She'd worn mourning for her valiant nephew, but there was no doubt that the Battle of Île Saint-Marcouf and the death of Lieutenant-Colonel Rupert

Westrop had pulled the curtain back on Lady Mary's dreams. Let her son, her worthless eldest child, inherit the marquessate of Waringford, and Mary Bailey Westrop would consider herself requited for all she had suffered in her life.

Now, if only her errant son could be made to wed the girl she'd chosen for him, thus shoring up the fortunes of a persistently impoverished family, her dreams could come to full and luxurious fruition.

Too bad Leo didn't share that dream.

"As I am not in the direct line of succession, I am not a candidate for a courtesy title," Leo explained. "And I could perish in advance of my uncle, you know. The men in my family are notoriously short-lived. Almost as if we're under a curse. A plague upon our house, possibly."

The girl chafed her lip, which had been pinkened with color. "Are you sickly? Ill?"

Should he lie? It would go better for him if he could simply lie. "Not to my knowledge," Leo admitted, regretting his scruples.

She started toward him, her skirt drifting about her legs. She was rail thin, and the muslin gown hung like a pillar from the ribbon snugged under her breasts, pushed into display like two plums in a pouch. Her hair clung in shaped curls to her forehead, peaks in pudding. Every part of her followed the lines of the latest fashion.

Leo had little appreciation for fashion.

"Have you a *tendre* for someone else?" she thought to ask.

Again, he wished he could lie. His father had been a cheerful prevaricator of the first degree. Why had Leo inherited his mother's moral streak instead of his father's gift for mendacity? The Fates were indeed capricious.

"My affections are currently unengaged."

Leo retreated behind the massive oaken desk. At least she

couldn't throw herself into his arms with the furniture between them.

He shot a glance of desperate longing at the door. How much longer before the sword of Damocles fell upon him? Could he hope for salvation to open the portal, and not a mama kindling with righteous wrath?

"Then there is no reason you shouldn't engage *me*," the determined damsel said. He understood the rapid movement of her eyelids was meant to be provocative. The effect was rather to the contrary.

"I am not unconscious of the great honor you do me, mademoiselle, but I am not free to offer my hand to anyone at this time," Leo said with all the dignity he could muster.

Hell's gate, he was playing the woman's part. And the kite was swooping, rounding the far corner of the desk.

"I have four thousand pounds," she said sweetly.

Leo curled his fingers around his favorite quill. He had no intention of stabbing anybody, of course. He was a pacifist. It was why he'd never been able to enter any of the professions his family would have respected. Military. Foreign service. Standing for MP.

"Four thousand pounds of what?"

She blinked in confusion this time. "My dowry, of course."

"How very fortunate for you."

"My family has money. You have a title. I think a match between us is written in the stars, milord."

There was that title business again. Leo frowned. "Do you even know my name?"

More blinking ensued. "Gregory."

He stroked the feathers of the quill, oddly stung by her ignorance, yet also vindicated. "No."

"Gabriel?"

"Wrong again."

"It doesn't matter if—"

The nightmare began. The library door inched open. Ponsonby lunged across the desk.

"By all the graces of heaven! My dear Empyrea, what has happened to you? Mr. Westrop, what have you *done?*"

Leo, furious, sweating, still clutching his quill, cast a despairing look toward the door and the two mamas framed within it, one the girl's mother, trembling with outrage, the other his own parent, smirking with triumph.

"I haven't done anything," Leo said.

He took a step backward. The girl lay stretched across the desk, crumpling the sketches he'd put there earlier in the day. Her skirts hung from her knees, her shoes dangling in the air, little roses daintily affixed to the satin.

"Ow," she said, blinking as the hard edge of the top no doubt cut into her midsection.

"She fell," Leo explained.

"She has fallen indeed!"

He could only presume this was the Ponsonby matriarch. Leo tried to remember if she had a title of any sort; he didn't have these ranks and orders of precedence imprinted in his head, like his mother did. The matriarch laid a hand to a bosom swelling with indignation.

"Mr. Westrop, I would have thought you, of all people, a gentleman! I presume an offer will be forthcoming immediately?"

A haze descended across Leo's vision, hot and prickly. His breath came in short pants, a cornered bull in truth. Here came the lead to snap through the ring in his nose, and off he'd go, bellowing and digging in his hooves, but he'd go all the same. He had never brought shame upon the Westrop family, and he never would. His father had done enough of that for three generations.

"An offer for what?" An angelic voice, the sweetest thing Leo had ever heard, broke through the rising tide in his brain. "He really hasn't done anything."

She sat in a chair facing the empty fireplace, and with the fire screen beside her, he'd looked past her when he entered. Admittedly, the driving thought in his mind, other than hiding from his mother, had been his new notion that the burial chambers of the barrow might lie to the northeast instead of the southwest, given the size of the mound and the orientation of the surrounding stones.

Leo watched in awe as a young woman rose from the armchair, shutting the book in her hands.

The candle on the table beside her cast a nimbus about her, setting her white gown aglow. The lovely gold embroidery sparkled like stardust. Modest sleeves ended in a little ruffle, and lace along her neckline covered most of her bosom, a pity. Her gown too had that ridiculous high waist, but he detected curves, a proper woman's curves, beneath it.

Lips a normal lip color, as if she'd been eating the raspberry pastilles laid on as refreshments, and her cheeks were a natural pink, not rouged. Glorious hair, not cut short but caught up in thick round swoops, the color of the first yellow fieldcaps in early spring, circled her head like a crown. She was a goddess come to life.

"Who," Leo's mother said shrilly, "are *you?*"

"Lady Mary. Mrs. Ponsonby." The angel performed a small, stately curtsy. Her cheeks showed a dimple. *Dimples.* "I am Lillian Gower."

A moment passed in which everyone in the room stared at her. She set down the folio-sized, leather-bound book, aligning it neatly with the inlaid wooden edge of the table.

"Of the Leveson-Gowers?" said Ponsonby senior in reverent tones.

The angel shook her head. A small daisy fluttered amid her tresses. "Only distantly related. Very distantly, I'm afraid."

"Oh." Lady Mary sniffed. "Then you're no one."

"No, milady."

"You were in the library all this time?" Ponsonby junior hauled herself to her feet and attempted to straighten her dress. She had mussed his papers in her ill-planned attack, but she made no attempt to tidy those.

"I have been present throughout the interview, yes. Your mother will be so relieved to know that Mr. Westrop did not compromise you in any fashion. Not so much as an inappropriate remark."

Ponsonby junior turned the color of a ripe currant. Senior narrowed her eyes.

"Then why was she sprawled across his desk in, might I say, a most undignified posture?"

"I believe she swooned, madame."

"My daughter," said Mrs. Ponsonby with a stabbing glare at both young women, "does not *swoon.*"

Ponsonby junior, who looked as if she had been considering that very contingency—and calculating whether her trajectory might bring her anywhere near Leo's arms—straightened her spine, abandoning the option of collapse.

"Ah," said Miss Gower, and that dimple danced in her cheek. "Then perhaps she indeed fell."

Leo's mother and Madame Ponsonby looked around the room, then at one another. At Miss Gower, who remained steadily composed under the scrutiny, and then, with suspicion on the part of Mrs. Ponsonby and sour disappointment in the aspect of his mother, the women turned toward the door.

"Empyrea, come," Ponsonby senior commanded, and the junior trotted out the door after her dame, chin held high, sparing nary a glance for the scene of her humiliation.

The library fell quiet. Outside the window, a horse whinnied in the square. The candle bobbed in a sudden draft. The books dozed quietly on their rows of shelves, and Leo, inhaling, smelled geraniums. Rose with a hint of lemon, and an earthy undertone that hinted at some sturdy, leafy vegetable, robust and nourishing. The scent steadied him, though his heart maintained a drumming beat as he regarded the agent of his deliverance.

"I feel I arrived in the cart at the guillotine to find the executioner has abandoned his task. Does this mean I am free?"

"Of Empyrea, at least. Will there be others?" Miss Gower raised a brow that had not been violently plucked, but was rather a lush, dark brown. "Good grief. To have to live up to the expectations of *that* name."

Hers was Lillian. He rolled it around in his head, luscious as a fine wine, a name with scope and heft but an alluring softness at the edges.

"Try Gideon."

Her large eyes were a vivid Delft blue, and Leo had the oddest sensation that the edges of the room were sliding away. They stood within a vast space, an endless firmament holding only the two of them.

"A mighty warrior, wasn't he? From Judges. God's hand against the—who was it, the Midianites?"

An angel who knew her biblical history. "A timid farmer who threshed his grain in a winepress and didn't believe the angel who came to him." Leo set the quill in its stand. "He tested God several times before he finally accepted his calling."

"Don't we all," Miss Gower murmured. "How many times have you tested your mother?"

"This is the first, but she's showed her hand. Now I comprehend the depths of her determination."

"To have you married?"

"To have me titled." He tidied the papers on his desk.

The corners of Miss Gower's delectable mouth quirked up. He wondered if she knew how devastating that dimple was. "Isn't it customarily the wife who acquires a title at marriage?"

"Ah, but you see, my uncle is the marquess, and he has only daughters. My cousin the heir is now gone—"

Leo paused to swallow the knot in his throat. Miss Gower did not look alarmed at his momentary loss of self-possession. Instead, her eyes glimmered and her mouth turned down at the corners, as if she understood his grief.

"My condolences on your loss," she said quietly. "I read about the battle. Five hundred British forces fought back a French fleet ten times their size."

"And five men died." With Rupert, confound the luck, being one of them. Leo cleared his throat. "My uncle has lost his wife and so hope of another son, and unless he sets his daughters to the business of producing heirs, the title will come to me, God forfend. My mother believes that if I make a speedy match of which he approves, my uncle will formally acknowledge me as the heir presumptive and thus fulfill her lifelong wish of seeing at least one of her sons make something of himself."

She smoothed a wrinkle on her evening glove, which drew Leo's attention to her rounded arms and the satin skin showing between glove and sleeve.

"There's something so macabre about planning the succession, isn't there?" she remarked. "It's all predicated on the death of someone you are likely disposed to care about. The king is dead. Long live the king."

He smiled. "Grand men have always cared a great deal about the disposal of their inheritance. Didn't the ancient Mesopotamian kings start planning their tombs from the time of their coronation? So did the Egyptian emperors, they say."

"You seem to know something about tombs." She bent, and

the motion gave him a splendid view of the breasts nestled into the scoop of her gown. Not plums. More cantaloupe sized. He was still staring when she rose, holding out a piece of parchment.

"They *are* tombs, aren't they? These barrows in your drawings."

"I'll know if I'm ever allowed to excavate one. I'm waiting on permission."

He wasn't about to bore an enchanting young lady with news of his stalled plans. Instead, he looked past her to the book she'd placed on the table. "And you seem to know something about—" He caught his jaw before it dropped. "The botanical discoveries made by the Forsters as they traveled with Cook to the South Seas." That book was in Latin.

Her eyes twinkled. "They made some quite extraordinary finds. Plants that exist nowhere else, as far as we know."

The twinkle recalled him, her eyes glimmering as if the candlelight danced within their blue depths. Was he addled in the upstairs? They were in the library of his house. They were alone. She was a young unmarried woman.

"Good Lord. Have I compromised you?"

Her brows lifted. "Not to my knowledge."

"Yes, but we're alone. Exactly what Ponsonby hoped to achieve."

"Then I will remedy that oversight directly and betake myself back to the soiree. I suppose I ought to look for my cousin, since I am ostensibly her companion."

This time the dimple *and* the twinkling. He narrowed his eyes at her. She had to know what she was doing. It was like coming at him with whip and blade. How was a man supposed to stand strong against such weapons? The bosom, the eyes, her mouth, her bosom, and the scent of geraniums tugging the lid off his brain—

Was his mother that clever, to stage a dramatic siege as a decoy and plant the real danger in the corner, like a drink of poppy ready to lull him into submission? If Miss Gower held the chains, Leo might very well put his own leg in the shackle.

He shook his head to clear the fancies. "*You* are a chaperone? Where are your parents?"

"Away, excavating with Mr. William Cunnington at Stonehenge."

He gaped at her, well and truly stunned. "You're one of *those* Gowers?"

"Yes, but I would be the one not allowed to go with, because of my cousin." She pouted, and the noose settled around his neck. Leo didn't even flinch.

"I must speak with you, though not here, more's the pity." He cast a look about the softly glowing library, the perfect setting for a tête-à-tête with a delicious, dimpled angel. "Return to the drawing room and I shall find you, and hope my mother will not force me into dancing before we might converse." He bowed, gesturing toward the door. "You lead the way, Miss Gower, and I will reappear after a suitable interval."

"Or remain hidden in the library, and I will not be here to protect you next time."

"God forbid I shall need further protection, but if I so require, I shall seek you out all the sooner. Run along now and pretend we are respectable."

She pursed her lips, pink as a sweet pea blossom. But a few steps forward would put him in a position to drop a kiss upon those lips. She might have detected the flash of hunger on his face, for a blush the color of a wild rose climbed her cheeks. She was nothing but a collection of wildflowers, and if he ever had the opportunity to bury his nose in her silken surfaces he could browse there for hours, growing drunk as a bee on pollen.

He stepped back, struggling for control over the thrum of

blood in his body. Did Miss Gower launch herself at him, she would meet with a far different reception than the one he had granted Ponsonby. Better if she didn't know the power she held.

She could depend on him to follow her. He was holding his own damn nose out with its ring, and, whether she knew it or not, she held the lead. Her parents, known and respected antiquarians, could be the key Leo needed to finally pull his own expedition together. He would not let Miss Gower out of his sight for long.

CHAPTER TWO

H e wouldn't seek her out. Lillian told herself not to be a widgeon.

Mr. Westrop was only being gallant in the moment. She had extricated him from a touchy situation; he was relieved, which accounted for the intent way he had regarded her face. And, even more intently, her bodice.

He had been impressed by the breasts, but they, and she, would be forgotten the moment she departed the room.

It was too bad of her to venture to the library in the first place, located on the floor holding the family chambers. But the Marquess of Waringford had been on the subscriber's list for a folio copy of the Forsters' volume on the botanical specimens they'd discovered in Australia. And when Lady Mary sent invitations to a soiree at Westrop House, where the family resided when in town, the temptation had been too strong to resist.

She couldn't regret her foray. Mr. Westrop, with his well-fitting coat and his fascinating sketches of barrows, was the most intriguing man she'd met all season.

Lillian floated through the public rooms in search of her cousin, pretending she wasn't watching for someone else. Lady

Mary had opened the entire first floor to guests, the dining room devoted to cards, the drawing room to music. The double staircase in the foyer spiraled up from the entrance hall below, built on the grand scale of earlier centuries, a monument to how long the Westrops had been a family of note. No doubt every girl in these luxurious rooms had been assembled in hopes of interesting the new marquess-to-be.

Good heavens—the thought stung like a bee, slowing her feet—Aunt Giles couldn't be reaching that high, could she? Hester, like Lillian, was only the grandniece of a baronet. It would be like a duke marrying a vicar's daughter. Or an earl marrying a milliner.

Aunt Giles sat behind a card table in the dining room, playing quadrille. Everything about her, including the ostrich plume in her cap, frowned in disapproval as she spotted Lillian. It must be hoped her aunt wasn't losing money, as standing Aunt Giles' gambling debts made Sir Lloyd cross, more cross than when Lillian's father requested funds for archaeological expeditions.

The refreshments table bore platters of almond pralines and bonbons. Lillian let a coffee-cream bonbon dissolve in her mouth as she surveyed the room. Hester wouldn't be here unless ordered; she bored quickly of card games, unable to keep straight the most basic rules, though she would play nine men's morris for hours if Lillian complied.

One of those *Gowers?* There was no mistaking the emerald light that sprang up in his silver eyes. But what possible interest could Westrop have in Lillian?

None. He was not looking for her, nor she for him. At any rate, he was not occupying the small hall at the top of the stairs, where a Louis XV giltwood sofa stood between two short pillars holding the busts of ancient Roman orators and knots of people stood caught up in conversation, flirtation, or debate. Hester wasn't in the hall, either.

Above the sofa, a florid oil painting depicted a nearly naked man in a vaguely classical setting menacing a pale woman whose breasts spilled from her gown. The rape of Tamar or Lucretia or some other poor terrorized woman. Lillian moved her gaze away. Best not to wonder if Mr. Westrop looked like *that* beneath his beautifully tailored coat and cream-colored breeches.

Hester stood at the back of the parlor that had been turned into a music room, browsing a tray of refreshments on a sideboard lacquered in silver. The raspberry pastilles had acquired companions of chocolate, almond, and lemon. Her cousin and pastilles both; Lillian headed her way.

"I don't suppose you know what this one is?"

Hester held out a purplish red pastille. Her cousin dispensed with conversational gambits she found pointless, such as greetings, common courtesies, and idle questions about one's health, family, or the weather.

"I should guess barberry. It may be tart, Hex."

Hester popped the treat in her mouth, waited a moment, then puckered her lips with a scowl. "Sour. Try one."

Lillian laughed. "Oh my, this is terrible. Try it," she teased.

"What? What did I say?"

"Nothing. You're a darling. I will try the sour, but only because I plan to have three chocolates next." Aunt Giles could neither see nor scold, and the sweet would tame Lillian's belly. Her encounter with Mr. Westrop had set off some jangling of nerves with which she was unfamiliar.

Lillian was the steady one among the Gower women. Aunt Giles frequently suffered nervous prostration; Lillian's mother, Alida, was prone to flights of fancy; and Hester, though placid as a sheep, could not be relied upon. Lillian was the one her mother called upon if a worker had jumbled the archaeological tools in their box, the one her aunt turned to if a member of the staff was being pert. Lillian was the only person Sir Lloyd trusted to handle his library.

"Well, don't eat them before I get to try one of each," Hester said.

Hester didn't mean to be catty; she didn't have a cruel bone in her body. She was seventeen, five years younger than Lillian, and had the body of a developed woman, but her intellect was approximately that of a child of six.

Lillian did not think her cousin's mind would ever mature to match her physical age, but she wasn't allowed to discuss it with anyone, because Aunt Giles pretended her daughter was like every other young English debutante. Lillian's mother was not around often enough to really know Hester, and Hester had not discerned any lack in herself. The one benefit of being left out of her parents' expedition to Stonehenge—the *only* reason Lillian hadn't made an unholy fuss, or hired her own transport to the site after her parents left her behind—was knowing that, in London, she could help Hester navigate the social currents that were utterly foreign waters to her.

The singer concluded her piece and Lady Mary shooed her away, claiming the space between the sash windows that looked out onto the square. The performer, pale and slim as a catkin in her white dress, slouched to the side with a sulky expression, but did not wander far. Every eye on the room turned toward their hostess, or rather, her companion, for her son stood beside her.

He looked a coffee cream bonbon himself in his dark cloth cutaway coat. The tails shaped his lean form, the row of bronze buttons down the front adding breath to his chest beneath the embroidered waistcoat. His cravat was not so high that one could miss the strong jut of his jaw, but the cascade of white ruffles on his shirt added a soft touch to the smart attire. His dark brown hair was wavy and tousled. Either he'd run a hand through it, or he'd spent an hour with his valet and curl papers to achieve the à la Titus style.

His expression was markedly flat, but Lillian sensed a leashed temper in the set of his mouth. His gaze swept the room as if he were a predator marking his competitors. Or a hawk seeking a way out of the mews.

Studying Mr. Westrop, Lillian missed the opening of Lady Mary's speech. It held a note of triumph.

"—after a long, *very* long wait, I am so pleased to announce that my son, Gideon, has finally affixed his affections—"

He winced. He didn't like the name Gideon.

"—a match that will bring both of our families great joy, as she is a young lady of impeccable reputation, greatly admired by her peers—"

His eyes narrowed into slits and his jaw tensed. He was furious. Lillian paused with the pastille in her hand, her stomach a covey of pheasants taking flight. How, in the brief time since she'd left the library, had he become betrothed?

"—as well as her mother being a great personal friend of mine," Lady Mary went on, enjoying the rapt attention of her audience. She was either unaware or uncaring of her son's reaction, the lowering of his dark brows, the tight line of his lips. His sharp gaze landed to the left of her, and Lillian turned to look.

Near the doorway, Mrs. Ponsonby fairly shivered with joy, a triumphant anticipation overtaking her face. Beside her, Miss Ponsonby looked first annoyed, then alarmed, and then, as the direction of Lady Mary's speech became clear, victory shone over her features.

"—and the delightful young lady is none other than—"

"Madame." Westrop stopped his mother with a hand on her wrist. *Madame*, not mother. "I don't suppose you will let me have the floor?"

Her ladyship's look of confusion would have been comical if Lillian didn't have the sneaking suspicion that she was pitching her son into a trap. Mrs. Ponsonby squeaked, pressing forward, the feather in her headdress atremble.

Mr. Westrop cleared his throat. "I have, indeed, this very evening, made an offer to the young lady of my choice."

His roving gaze landed on Lillian and paused there long enough that the curious eyes of every other person in the room turned to Lillian, too.

Her throat went dry. She couldn't stand here holding a pastille going sticky in her glove. Not knowing what else to do, she popped it in her mouth, her cheeks warm with embarrassment. Had he *wanted* Miss Ponsonby and Lillian had gotten in the way? But why was he looking at her like this? His expression was bland, courteous, but behind it, Lillian detected misery. And a plea.

"In fact, I have just come from speaking with her in the library." He swallowed.

Lillian's mouth puckered as the barberry juice hit her tongue.

Lady Mary burbled. "You did—" She cut off her cry when her son lifted his hand.

"I made my offer then, but she has not yet given her answer."

"Who?" Lady Mary demanded.

His gaze didn't lift from Lillian. He was indeed a hawk, and she the hare frozen by his gaze. Her mouth, and her stomach, turned inside out.

"Miss Gower?" he called, and her name rang like a bell through the room.

A screech echoed in Lillian's ears, and she hoped it wasn't her making such a sound. She swallowed the pastille, a sour path scorching through her insides. "I beg your pardon?"

He held her gaze steadily, and she saw his desperation writ clear. He was begging.

"Would you do me the honor—the very great honor—of accepting my suit?"

She stood frozen as he moved toward her and the crowd parted, their wondering eyes moving from him to her and back again. It was a large room, but he'd crossed it before Lillian could fit two thoughts together. All that filled her vision was the plea in his eyes.

"I've surprised you, I know." He reached her. He was quite tall. He lifted her hand, sticky with the sugar coating of the pastille, and placed a kiss on the back of her glove. The print of his mouth scorched like a cooking fire.

"Miss Gower. I would have chosen more discreet circumstances, but now we all must know your answer. Will you knit your life to mine and make me the happiest of men?"

It was a trick. She saw it now. The teeth of the man trap were descending about him, and he wanted to bring her between him and descending annihilation. He was drowning, and she held the rope that could save him.

He squeezed her fingers. His grip was tight, yet oddly, he did not hurt her. It *was* a trap. If she stepped into the noose with him, everything she wanted for her future might disappear.

And yet, with him holding her hand, she was certain she would be safe.

She could read his eyes. *Trust me. Help me,* his eyes said.

That was her lot, was it not? Lillian the helper. Lillian the soother. Lillian the calm and steady. Lillian, the eye of the storm, who sacrificed what she needed so another might have their wish.

"Very well." The words emerged a whisper around the pinch in her mouth. The knot in her stomach might never unravel. "Yes, Mr. Westrop, I suppose I'll marry you."

CHAPTER THREE

He didn't mean it, of course.

Lillian reminded herself of this as the swirl of congratulations, astonishment, and demands for answers rose around them. Westrop held her hand as if they were an affectionate couple in truth. She was much too limp to pull away, and more importantly, were he not holding onto her, the bones of her knees might dissolve. The top of her head had already fizzed away, her thoughts champagne bubbles floating around the chandelier over their heads.

Hester, at her side as the crowd of well-wishers pushed forward, continued to suck on pastilles. Her eyes lit with excitement—Hester loved drama—but Lillian also knew that her cousin would take in the heightened emotions and in short order become nervous and agitated. They couldn't stay here long, but with a wall of curious guests hemming them in like stiles in a pasture, she didn't see a path to escape.

"Westrop! Didn't even know you were on the hunt for a shackle. Could have turned out any one of my gels for you, had you asked."

Lillian tried to place the older man. Aunt Giles knew her noble families down to the third generation, but Aunt Giles was in the card room. They'd be sure to hear her screech of horror when she learned what Lillian had done.

A lady wearing a jeweled turban and a court-length train on her gown sniffed. "Don't be rude, Highcastle. We're to congratulate the young couple." Her lips thinned as she surveyed Lillian. "You're the one staying at Gower House?"

"Yes, Your Grace." Highcastle. A *duchess* had addressed her. Lillian mentally pinched herself. She couldn't wait to tell her mother.

Which wouldn't be until who knows when. They'd likely stay at Stonehenge until the first frost, and when they returned, her parents would be too busy cataloguing their finds and preparing their notes to take any interest in Lillian's social escapades in London.

"Give over, Medora." Lillian found herself pinned by the sharp stare of Lady Cranbury, ancient and vastly terrifying, a woman who had ruled her corner of London's *haut ton* since well before Lillian was born. Probably since before Lillian's mother was born.

"You're Lloyd's niece," Lady Cranbury said, raking Lillian from head to toe with her gaze.

"Grandniece, yes, milady." Lillian tried to recall Lady Cranbury's rank—earl's wife? Baron's? If a knight, of which order? She never knew how deep to curtsy. Besides, with Westrop holding her, she'd pull his arm down with her and tilt them both off balance. She chose instead to dip her chin in courteous acknowledgment.

"And your parents are the ones who play about in old ruins."

"Yes, milady."

"Well." Lady Cranbury's sniff was much like Lady Highcastle's. There must be a distinct whiff ladies of high society employed to express their disdain. Westrop's wife would need to know that sniff, were he to become the marquess. A marchioness would need to know a great many things.

Lillian's chest cramped, the pastille burning its way down her gullet.

"That explains it. All you antiquarians run in the same train, don't you?" Lady Cranbury said to Westrop.

"I have not yet met her parents, madame. Miss Gower captivated me solely on her own merit," Westrop replied.

The lady's gaze swung back and forth between them, like St. George's dragon, deciding which challenger she would first annihilate with her fiery breath.

"I wasn't aware you were courting her," Lady Cranbury said, apparently outraged that Westrop could have been wooing without her permission.

"It was quite sudden," Lillian managed. "A surprise even to us."

Westrop glanced at her, a slant to his eyes, and Lillian read him again: a flash of humor at her jab, and a flash of worry. That she would betray him? His fingers tightened around hers. She liked that far more than she ought to.

"Have you set a date, then?"

"We've yet to work out the details," Westrop said in a silky tone. "You must allow me a moment to simply savor my good fortune, madame."

Lady Cranbury sniffed again. "I don't see a fortune in *that* family," she said, but the rest of her complaints were to be aired elsewhere as Ponsonby senior elbowed her way into the group, her face as tight as if she'd been stuck by a pin.

"Mr. Westrop. I hope you know that my Empyrea was

simply lost in this grand house when she wandered into the library. You won't take it against us for interrupting your—suit."

Her baleful glance made Lillian's stomach knot further. *She knew.*

Mrs. Ponsonby knew Westrop's mother had been about to trap him with a staged betrothal, and she knew Westrop had ducked beneath the harness and outmaneuvered her.

"We accept your apologies, madame. And your felicitations," Westrop said.

"Oh, of course. Felicitations, I'm sure."

Empyrea, following her mother's lead, stared at Lillian. Her expression of sheer puzzlement was one Lillian had been familiar with all her life: what was *this* thing doing here? No fashion, no address, no family, no fortune, no beauty of face to recommend her, and a figure decidedly opposite the svelte silhouette now in vogue—how had *she* snagged the interest of a marquess-in-waiting?

"Lillian Tiamat Ovidia Gower." Aunt Giles sailed into view like a Spanish galleon dominating the horizon. "*What* ridiculous tales have you been spreading?"

She halted, and Lillian stifled a laugh at her aunt's expression as she comprehended the situation: Westrop at Lillian's side, well-wishers surrounding them, Lady Mary still at the front of the room, stabbing Lillian with a burning stare. Aunt's gaze fell to their clasped hands and her mouth hinged open.

"I beg your pardon that, as Lillian's chaperone, I did not ask your permission," Westrop said. His tone was cordial, his words measured. He was a match for this more than preposterous situation. Lillian wondered what, if anything, could overset him.

She also guessed that he didn't know her aunt's name, or their precise relationship, but he was hazarding a guess. The man was perceptive, unlike the ordinary examples of his sex.

Lillian was accustomed to being overlooked, like a potted

plant or pillar that was part of the garden scenery. When Westrop gazed down at her with a fond expression, however, she felt the exact opposite of overlooked. She felt *seen*.

As if he might detect every flaw, every crack showing the strong emotion roiling beneath her pleasant façade. She had gambled her reputation, her entire future on this man—and why? Because he looked at her with a plea in those gray-green eyes, and she let the rope settle about her neck like a lamb led to slaughter.

"I suppose you also think it strange I did not ask her parents' permission either," he continued. "I admit to having been a bit—swept off my feet."

Now, that was doing it too brown. Lillian cast him a quelling look.

No, fond; she must appear fond to keep up the ruse. "That is true for the both of us, sir."

A corner of his mouth quirked up, and that emerald light flashed in his eyes. He was a man of sense, for all that he'd just done something desperate. She could trust him.

Lillian had learned to rely on no one but herself.

"Hester." Aunt turned to her daughter. "Tell me what has been transpiring here."

Hester put a hand over her belly and blew out a puff of air. "Oof. I ate too many pastilles, and now I feel sick."

Aunt whirled back to Lillian. "We must depart at once. And you might explain yourself in the carriage."

"I can drive Miss Gower home, madame." Westrop held her hand as if, once he let go, the ruse would be broken and his shield would drop, leaving him defenseless. He shot Lillian a questioning look. "We have one or two things to talk about."

She frowned, nodding. Like why he had chosen *her* to spike his mother's matrimonial wheels, and what on earth they were to do next.

Whatever he was about, it wasn't an interest in Lillian's own person. She mustn't be fooled into thinking this was about her. He simply needed another body beside his under the testudo, the turtle-like shield wall the Romans used to defend their foot soldiers. He wanted someone else in his castle during the siege.

"Lil. I don't feel right," Hester complained.

"I'm coming, Hex." Lillian held Westrop's eyes, communicating her intent. *I'm leaving. You're on your own. Yes, there is some explaining to do.*

He lifted her hand to his lips again. "I shall call upon you tomorrow, then. At Gower House."

He'd been paying attention. He was paying too much attention now, catching the way her eyes flared and her breath hitched when he leaned close. He smelled of citron and olive with a hint of tobacco as an undernote. Lillian adored olives. She'd eat them with every meal and tea were she allowed.

"Till tomorrow, sir," she said. How demure should an affianced bride be? Ought she flirt? Flutter her eyelashes? Sigh wistfully? If she'd spent more time reading romantic novels instead of classical histories, she'd know how to behave in a convincing manner after suddenly becoming affianced.

To a very attractive, well-dressed, extremely nice-smelling, completely baffling man.

It oughtn't feel like a tug beneath her skin to walk away from him, yet it did.

"I don't know what could have come over you," Aunt Giles exclaimed once they were safely in her uncle's carriage, a coach of truly antique distinction that ever smelled of horse, old leather, and, no matter what Lillian did to freshen the upholstery, mildew. "I hardly know what to think! What on earth did you do to wrangle an offer from Westrop?"

Lillian leaned her head back against the leather. Hester held her hand, clutching it in a far less affectionate but no less desperate manner than Westrop had. This was Lillian's lot in life: to hold other people up. She waved her fan to give Hester air.

Her stomach refused to unclench. Of course, her aunt would not be amazed, or approving, or appreciative. There was no possible scenario in which Lillian might have attracted Westrop on her own merits, ergo, there was some logic that could explain this outrageous circumstance. Aunt knew this, and Lillian knew this, too.

"I went to the library, like I told you, Aunt. I found an interesting book. The next thing I knew, Westrop walked in. His mother found us conversing. I suppose she thought it unseemly that we had been alone together, so he felt obliged to propose."

Aunt Giles pounced. "I never would have thought you so clever, Lillian. He'll be the heir of Waringford! Well done, child. Oh, *finely* done. And here I thought you and your books were going to be the death of me."

"I'm not going to hold him to it, Aunt," Lillian said with a sigh. "I refuse to marry a man who offers for me on any basis other than affection."

"If that isn't the most absurd thing I ever heard." Even in the shadowed confines of the coach, Lillian detected exasperation in her aunt's stare. "You most certainly will not decline the hand of a Westrop. As if you'll get a better offer." They pondered this a moment, then her aunt went ahead and said what they were both thinking. "As if you'll receive *any* offer."

Lillian lifted her head. She didn't know where this streak of rebellion reared from; she *never* talked back. "It could happen, Aunt. Some distant day, in some better, kinder world, a man could be moved to offer for me out of admiration alone."

Aunt Giles had clearly noted and adopted the disapproving-lady-of-quality sniff. "Well, if that's how you feel about it, we might as well give him to Hester. What do you think, my lamb?

Would you like to marry the big, handsome, well-connected, possibly very rich Mr. Westrop?"

Hester shook her head, a twist to her mouth. "Where's that chamber pot Uncle keeps under the cushion? Those pastilles are coming straight back up."

CHAPTER FOUR

G ower House stood on the busy thoroughfare of High Holborn, one of a line of stately mansions built in the age of the Tudors on what had then been the fringes of London. The solemn brick edifice had escaped the ravages of the Great Fire and now stood like an old sage looking down on neoclassical upstarts like Westrop House, which sported the Palladian façade popular in the current century and stood in a newer square.

The Waringfords were of long provenance; they'd established themselves around the Highworth area during Saxon times. But during the interminable lecture his mother had read Leo last night about shaming the name, lowering their family, and bringing scandal down upon them, she'd mentioned that these Gowers came from Wales. They might have watched the Roman armies of the Emperor Claudius land on their shores.

Miss Lillian Gower wasn't a lesser creature; she was something entirely different. And somehow, he had to convince her to go through with his wild scheme.

Perhaps, though she seemed out of the run of ordinary

young ladies, she could be beguiled and flattered, teased and courted as much as the rest of them.

He hoped so, when this woman he hadn't known a day ago suddenly held the key to his future. Leo tugged at the neckcloth strangling his throat.

He rapped on the door with his walking stick, and a harried-looking maid opened the portal. Interesting that Sir Lloyd did not keep a butler or porter. Leo hadn't had a chance to ask around at his club for information, but after his surprising announcement and the alarmingly swift departure of his would-be bride, he'd been informed that Sir Lloyd was a reliable fixture at every botanical lecture and exhibit in London and could be counted on to take a subscription to any forthcoming volume pertaining to the vegetative world.

The maid squinted at his card in a fashion that suggested she neither knew, nor cared, what the print said. "Oo don't want the missus and 'er gel, do'o? For they ain't 'ome."

"I am in quest of Miss Gower," Leo replied, taking off his hat as he stepped indoors.

"Aight, then, thas upstairs, tha is." The maid wandered off with a shrug, leaving Leo to find his own way.

The house was laid out in the Tudor plan, a tidy square with a central staircase and a cupola high above admitting the gray late morning light. Reception rooms lay to his right, drafty and dull without fires to dispel the gloom, while from the left came the sound of busy offices, kitchens and other work. There wasn't the same separation of servants as prevailed in the Westrop townhome. No doubt in Gower House, dishes came to the table still warm.

Leo climbed the wooden staircase with its carved balustrade. Oil paintings hung heavy on the walls, dark and cracked with age. Every one was a landscape, with human figures, if any, far in the distance. He surfaced onto the first-floor landing and found two doors leading to what he would guess were bedchambers, and two doors ahead of him standing open to admit the drift of a pleasant female voice.

"Parkinson's *Theatrum Botanicum*. Shall I put it next to his *Terrestrial Paradise*, or do you wish it with the *Hortus Floridus?*"

With no one to announce him, Leo made his own way into the room, then stopped inside the doorway, astonished. He'd stepped back into Duke Humfrey's Library at the Bodleian in Oxford, a place that in his years of study had provided solace, stimulation, and the silence he'd needed to balance a tumultuous family life and his high-spirited friends. It was as if he'd emerged from a narrow London alley into a quiet garden paradise full of gently flowing water and chirping birds.

"With the *Floridus,* I think," a man replied. "Under Pliny the Elder, and on a shelf I can reach. I'm fond of that one."

An older man stood in one corner of the room, which spanned the full front of the house. Every space of wall that was not a window, doorway, or fireplace held shelves of books, sturdy oak shelves that reached to the ceiling. They flanked the room like soldiers in formation, and in a curved niche atop each sat a plaster bust in the classical Roman style, looking down at the room with expressions of boredom, superiority, or disdain.

Miss Gower moved to a bay that held pride of place between two of the tall, sashed windows, letting in light that had grown considerably brighter since he last looked. Pliny the Elder watched with pained disinterest as she placed the large folio on a shelf next to a few other thick companions, then patted the leather-bound spine with affection.

"You ought to get a glass case to display this one, Uncle. The frontispiece alone is a work of art."

She wore a simple cotton gown caught up with a ribbon around the high waist, gathering the loose folds in a way that brought out the lovely curve of her breasts and hips. The subtle pattern of greenery and flowers along the white cotton appeared to shimmer. A green bandeau caught up the mushroom coils of hair pinned into large, soft-looking loops. She looked like a wild-flower come to life, and he entertained the sudden desire to touch her silken petals and press his nose into her subtle, heady scent.

He shook himself free of the distracting thought. The man in the antique white bag wig, dark breeches, and coat with the large skirts and enormous cuffs could only be the baronet. Leo cleared his throat.

"I'm not familiar with Parkinson's work. I daresay that's a loss on my part."

Miss Gower turned to him with one hand lifted in the air as if she held a theatrical pose. She had lovely arms, as nicely curved as the rest of her, though the proper sleeves came down to her elbow. She wasn't wearing gloves, and her hands were soft and round.

"Mr. Westrop." Her voice sounded breathy. Dare he hope that was a blush on her cheeks? He oughtn't feel pleased if he'd unsettled her, just because the sight of her was so unsettling to his own logical processes.

She moved to the bell pull in the corner of the room, as if this were the move she'd intended all along, and made use of it. "Uncle, do you know Mr. Westrop? Mr. Westrop, this is my uncle, Sir Lloyd Gower, Baronet Gower of Gileston."

Gileston. Leo made a note to look it up as soon as he got home. There were maps in the room, one on display on a heavy oak table near where the baronet stood, and a globe on its stand before one bay, but this was hardly the time to explore the family ancestry.

Actually, since he had proposed *marriage* to the girl, perhaps it was.

"Westrop." The baronet dipped his chin and regarded Leo over the rim of his spectacles. "Waringford's nephew?"

Leo nodded in assent. He would only, ever and always, be identified in relationship to his family. Where he stood in the line of descent and, more importantly, the line of succession. He might never be known for any achievements or accomplishments or contributions of his own labor or intellect; only his name would matter and, if he were so unlucky as to inherit it, the title.

He refrained from looking at Miss Gower, afraid he might see the same calculation on her face.

"Didn't see you at the latest lecture of the Linnean Society," the baronet remarked.

"No, sir." Leo sorted through his mental bank of London societies: ah, the botanical one. "I am not a member."

"Don't need to be to attend the lectures. Monthly. Panton Square. Last one was Smith on the botanical history of the *Mentha exigua.*"

"Er. How fascinating," Leo said.

"Lillian didn't like it." With a harrumph, the baronet turned back to examining the tiny print of the book he held.

Miss Gower's merry smile brought out the apples of her cheeks and pressed her eyes into little half-moons. "*Mentha exigua* is wild mint. Sir James spent far too much time on a discussion of taxonomy rather than the plant's more interesting properties."

"You enjoy botanical lectures, Miss Gower?"

"Yes, for the most part. Sir James did tell a funny story about being briefly taken in by an American mint he found growing in a friend's garden in Ipswich. It is not often he will admit a mistake."

Leo wondered what Miss Gower—Lillian—would think of a lecture by the Society of Antiquaries. He'd like to take her, if it would make her eyes sparkle in the same fashion. Of course, Leo was not a member of that society, either. He would have to make a significant contribution to this field in order to be considered for a nomination, and so far, he had contributed nothing.

"Lillian is an eccentric," the baronet said. "We used to call them bluestockings."

"That is not quite true. I am not equipped to converse on a wide variety of subjects. Only a few." She lowered her gaze to a table covered with neat stacks of books, her merry smile gone.

He shouldn't take that crestfallen look so to heart, Leo told himself. He was going to be responsible for driving a great deal more discomfort her way. He'd dug a pit trap before her feet last night, and she'd blithely stepped into it. Now he had to extricate them both, and he didn't know how.

The maid who'd answered the front door appeared in the door frame. "What, then?" she said. "That bell's a gone off like Christmas."

"Sarey," Miss Gower said, "when you receive a guest, you are to ask their name and show them to the parlor. Then you are to come find one of us—my aunt, preferably, if she is at home, me if you cannot."

"Well, he dint say 'is name, didee?" The maid cast Leo a baleful glare.

"Next time, you may ask. Now, if you would be so kind as to run to the kitchen and ask Cook for that tray for our nuncheon. Sir Lloyd has been working for hours and is quite famished, and we might offer Mr. Westrop tea, at the least."

"But I've the polishing in the parlor to finish," the maid complained. "Now I've to fetch for ye too?"

"It *is* part of the position we arranged for you to take, Sarey."

"I reckon I might go back to Dark Lane," Sarey grumbled, dragging herself from the room. "Least there I got to do my work lying down."

Leo stared at Miss Gower, wondering if he'd heard correctly. Miss Gower must be too innocent to understand what sort of business he guessed the maid referred to, for she hadn't a blush about her as she went back to the table.

He closed his mouth, deciding it was not his place to correct the behavior of her servants, particularly if Miss Gower remained unflustered as she picked up another folio and flipped open the heavy cover. "I beg your pardon for intruding on your morning," he said instead.

"Not at all, only I hope you do not mind if Uncle and I carry on. If we do not get these titles sorted, Uncle will forget his organizing principles, and we shall have to begin again."

Leo did mind, as a matter of fact. How could she be so calm when he had just ruined her life?

"Mrs. Merian's *Metamorphosis* of the insects in Surinam," Miss Gower said. "With *The Aurelian*, which is mostly moths and butterflies, or with *Terrestrial Paradise*, because of the prints?"

"Put her under Varro," the baronet replied. "High up, since I won't be likely to read it."

"Uncle, for shame. Mrs. Merian is the reason we know insects have a reproduction cycle and aren't simply spontaneously generated by mud. Her engravings are a work of art." She traced one with a loving finger.

"It's insects, and its Surinam. A place I am very unlikely to visit, and a subject of inquiry I am very disinclined to care about."

"Very well." She headed for the ladder leaning against one case.

Leo leapt to be of service, appalled that her uncle should leave a woman to clamber about the shelves on her own. "Allow me to place the book for you, Miss Gower."

The corners of her mouth dimpled as she regarded him.

Lord help him, those dimples were going to be the death of him. They were like tiny elf darts pricking beneath the skin, driving him to distraction.

"He'll want it between Sowerby's colored figures of mushrooms and d'Ardène's treatise on hyacinths. Are you familiar with those works?"

Leo surveyed the shelf. "I can blunder my way through Latin titles, Miss Gower. Third in classics at Wadham College, if my fame has not preceded me."

"How is your Dutch, Italian, German, and French?"

He regarded her with surprise. "You read all of those languages?"

"Bluestocking," the baronet called from his corner. "Let the girl have her head."

"And her ladder, apparently." Leo placed the wooden apparatus where she directed. "Hold this for you, shall I?"

"If you must. I suppose assisting in libraries is all in the round of your usual morning calls?"

Leo braced the ladder as she stepped onto it, and a cluster of sensations smacked him in the face. The gleam of delicate skin along her neck and throat. The scent of geraniums floating like a cloud, beneath it the fresh, clean cut of soap. The gentle brush of fabric against his hand as she climbed inches from his face. He was lucky the ladder wasn't high enough that he'd have the chance to see up her skirt. He'd come undone.

"Very rarely do my morning calls involve interesting employment," Leo replied.

"Yes, well, I need some project to occupy me while my parents are gone. Now if Uncle puts the books back where we've placed them, I'll be satisfied."

"Curtis's last volume of the *Flora Londinensis* has an index, praise the man." The baronet snapped shut the book in his hands. "Where did we put the other five?"

"Under Tacitus," Miss Gower called. "Third shelf."

The baronet turned to the wall behind him. "I don't see it."

"They're—*oh!*" She leaned to point, and her shoe slipped off the rung of the ladder. Without thinking, Leo shot up a hand to keep her from falling. His palm closed around the soft, round globe of her bottom, nestled in glossy cotton.

Warm, yielding woman. A bolt of lust shot through his gut, exploding like a firework in his nether regions, clouding his brain.

"I'm fine," she said breathlessly. "I have my feet."

He blinked. She was indeed secure on the ladder. Quickly she shoved the book into place and began to back down.

Move your hand, man. He slid his palm over her backside, up to the small of her back. The chivalrous thing to do. Make sure she didn't topple as she clambered down. The scent of geraniums pulled all thought from his upper stories.

She gained her footing on the floor and glanced up at him, her face mere inches from his.

"I'm fine," she whispered.

Put your hand down. Stop touching her. It took conscious effort for him to lift his hand from the smooth, warm slope of her back, to resist sliding that hand around her hip or up to her breast. Leo was a man known for his control, but Lillian Gower tempted him in a way he hadn't been tempted in a long time.

Last night, he'd funneled every bit of his desperation into his gaze, firing his urgent plea at her from across the room.

And she'd answered, as if she understood his dilemma. She'd said yes.

Now, with that rose blooming in her cheeks again, he couldn't think of practical solutions to untie the Gordian knot he'd created. He wanted to find where else that blush showed, and what more he might do to cause it.

No. He had to stop noting Miss Gower's blushes and

dimples, and sparkling eyes, and fearsome intelligence. Because all of these added up to indications of a perfectly fascinating and innocent young woman whose future he had just smashed under his boot, because he had made a proposal that was going to ruin her.

Lusting after her would make everything else supremely difficult.

"We must discuss our...arrangement," Leo said, reality dousing the fire of fantasy.

She stiffened. He needed that, and the sense of something tearing when she stepped away, taking her heat with her.

"Must we? Here's Sarey with a tray, and Uncle needs his nuncheon. You are welcome to sit with us, but I see no reason to trouble him with Banbury stories."

With lies and untruths? A tight knot cinched his throat. "I was under the impression that you accepted my offer."

"And I was under the impression that we were getting up a play. Put the tray on this table, Sarey. Uncle, come take your tea, and while you're about it, decide whether you want Woodville's *Medical Botany* next to Gerard's *Herball* or the *De Materia Medica*."

He wouldn't call it sharpness, because there wasn't a single sharp thing about her, but there was a defined edge in her voice. If she were a battle maiden with a shield, she'd be raising it and pointing her spear at him.

She'd taken his outstretched hand last night. She must know they couldn't avoid the consequences.

"I wasn't acting." The words, laced with desperation, tumbled out of him like rocks down a hillside.

She had a jaw as sweetly rounded as the rest of her, but he detected a stubborn tilt to her chin. "I was."

She swept to the table where Sarey had banged over a glass frame holding a delicate pressed plant as she struggled with the tea tray. Leo followed, feeling like a shark in shallow waters, cruising after its prey. She was so tender, so exposed, it was cruel of him to strike. "What do you mean?"

"I gather that your mother tried to invent a betrothal for you, and you invented one of your own. It's not real. I imagine everyone there understood that."

"There will be talk. There *is* talk." Quite a lot of it, last night after she left, and a continuing harangue from his mother.

She waved away Sarey, who listened with wide and fascinated eyes to their conversation, then sat beside the tea tray like a young lady who had been trained to her duty and would do it, steel in her backbone, fire in her eyes.

"I think it should be clear to everyone that it was a preposterous suggestion. If there was any interest in the beginning, I'm sure it's already blown away like seeds on the wind."

Leo stood like a prisoner at the executioner's block whom the priest had visited and left, taking hope with him.

She didn't want him.

It was absurd. This shouldn't be what sliced into him, not with everything else at stake. But her easy dismissal of him, of what he'd offered, stunned him like a blow to the head.

"I need you to playact a bit longer," he said.

He wanted, for the sake of his crumbling pride, to be enough to tempt Miss Lillian Gower. Without the title, without any accomplishments to his name, he wanted her to look at him and be tempted.

But to what?

"You've tied your garter now, girl!" came a shrill voice from the hall. The disagreeable-looking woman who had been with her last night charged into the room, waving a sheet of paper as if she were drying the ink.

"Hello, Aunt Giles," Miss Gower said, her tone calm, but her hand trembled as she cut the tart. "What is the matter?"

"It's in the *Morning Post.*" The older woman slapped the paper down on the nearest table. "Every piece of it." She cast a spiteful glance at her niece. "Including a bit about how your headgear was not quite *à la mode.* And that his mother is more surprised than anyone. And you were stuffing your face with a treat—I am so mortified!—while the future Marquess of Waringford proposed to you."

"Eh? What's this?" The baronet, in the process of dragging chairs to the table, looked up. "Lil's got an offer?"

The aunt registered Leo's presence without a flicker of an eyelash. "Yes, indeed, sir. Your grandniece is engaged to marry *him.*" She stabbed a finger into the newsprint. "It's in the paper. So there's no getting out of it, girl, despite what you think."

Miss Gower's profile resembled the wooden prow of a sailing ship, expression serene, face lifted in determination as she met the advancing army, breasts rising on a wave as she drew a long breath.

"*The Morning Post?* That is unfortunate. Nevertheless, I am sure we can deal with the one or two people who will prove curious."

Leo saw at a glance what she meant to do. She intended to put it about that, in the light of day and free from the smoky candles and fortified wine, she and Leo had regretted their giddy moment and decided they would not suit. They meant to go their separate ways, no harm done. And he'd be right back where he began.

No, worse off, because she didn't want him.

Sarey staggered into the doorframe, cheeks flushed, cap askew as if she'd been tugging it. She clutched a dusting cloth to her bosom, her eyes round as shillings.

"Miss, they's a whole flock of fancy morts bunching up the doorstep, and I know I ain't gonn'ta member a one of their names. Where'm I to put'em all, then?"

Comprehension dawned over Miss Gower's features the way some ancient Trojan scout must have looked when he saw the Greek ships pulled up on the beach before Troy: the army had come, and it could destroy them.

If she yet realized all she stood to lose, because of him.

He didn't have the right, but Leo clasped her hand and tugged her to her feet.

"Come with me. We need to talk."

CHAPTER FIVE

———

Green spaces were a refuge for Lillian, and always had been. The color steadied and calmed her. Her spirits lifted at the sight of flowers in bloom, whether they were stately cultivars lining a parterre or a hedge of spreading bellflower back home. The linden and wych elm around her family's cottage had been, in summers, the castles she hid beneath as she drew and dreamed of the places she'd travel as a botanist of note.

She liked best when the whole Vale of Glamorgan lay in its emerald cloak before her, and a whole day with nothing but her boots and her bonnet, her notebook and pencil, a bun and a piece of fruit in her pocket and the occasional scoop of water from a laughing stream. But even an herb garden would do in a pinch, when she needed a breath of real air.

Her uncle's garden behind Gower House was a pocket of life-giving green carved from the countryside and guarded as the city sprang up like mushrooms all around. Lillian knew the disposition of every plant—had placed a number of them herself, in the newer beds—and the orderliness was a balm to her nerves.

Less so the man walking the small brick path with her. Westrop was taller than she, like most men, and unobtrusively elegant in a blue superfine coat, gray pantaloons, and boots. The fall of his cravat said that either he couldn't be bothered with such things, or that he had spent patient hours arranging his neckcloth to communicate careless ease with his own attractions.

These attractions were many. She looked away.

"You expect this reaction from everyone?" Lillian asked.

They'd left her aunt to gloat over a stream of callers of more quantity and greater note than she was accustomed to accommodating. Lillian worried what story Aunt Giles would spin to explain Westrop's sudden and fantastical proposal. Lillian herself couldn't bear to sit there nibbling pound cake while London's most notorious gossips demanded to know what she had done to enchant Waringford's nephew.

She couldn't explain the circumstances herself, other than that she moved through some delirious waking dream. For here was this splendid-looking man beside her, strolling through the garden, and though London's gray-blue sky vaulted above her, she couldn't seem to find enough air to draw a proper breath.

"You uncle didn't seem perturbed by news of our betrothal." Westrop rubbed the saw-toothed lobe of a tansy leaf, then sniffed his glove. "When, by rights, he ought to have had some warning of my intentions, in your father's stead."

Lillian laughed as he wrinkled his nose. "My uncle, bless his heart, has little regard for gossip. He cares for no one's opinion but his own."

"Admirable. Why is your aunt not pleased by my offer?"

She liked his voice, a pleasant tenor. It put her in mind of her favorite dessert, roasted pears swimming in shrub, a kind of brandy wine that their housekeeper back in St. Athan made.

She paused to pull a tansy that had forayed into the wall

germander. "Little I do pleases my Aunt Giles." Now she smelled as he did: bright, medicinal. The scent would keep away pests.

"Does she want better prospects for you?" He regarded her curiously.

What could be a better prospect than him? Lillian decided she didn't care to catalogue her defects for this man. Let him detect them on his own, as did others.

"Rather she expects I shall have no prospects. She disapproves of my eccentricities, which my uncle encourages, as you've seen. She was hoping, I think, that you might think twice about me and decide to offer for Hester." Lillian glanced down the tidy garden paths, paved with brick. "Hex, are you out here?"

"Not listening." Her cousin's voice drifted from behind the dwarf peach in an opposite corner of the garden. "Mama sent me out here to make sure he doesn't take liberties. That sounds like something I'd prefer not to see."

"We won't offend your sensibilities, dear."

Westrop raised his brows. "Your aunt simply assumed I might transfer my affections?"

Lillian raised her brows in return. "I imagine it's quite clear that no one's affections are engaged in this scenario."

He resumed walking, brushing past a tulip tree in bloom, the yellow blossoms opening like cupped hands. "You won't entertain the possibility that I saw you in my library and fell head over spurs at the sight of you."

Lillian snorted. She'd been admonished time and again by her aunt not to make this sound in company, but the occasion warranted. "Pray do not give that out as your reason."

"We could. I perceived your abundant attractions, and I acted impetuously. Anyone who detects the same charms will commiserate."

"That you acted impetuously, I can acknowledge."

"But do not approve," he noted.

"I cannot blame you. You were about to be affianced against your will to Miss Ponsonby, who likely doesn't know a long barrow from a cursus."

He stared. "If *you* know the difference between a long barrow and a cursus, Miss Gower, no one of my acquaintance will be surprised by my pursuit of you."

She faltered, her shoe turning on a brick that had heaved itself up from the path. The notion of *pursuit* struck her as dangerous. Particularly by him.

"I was raised by antiquarians, Mr. Westrop."

"And I hope to become one. What a marvelous fit I will make for your family." He grinned at her, unabashed, the rogue.

"We are not affianced," Lillian reminded him. She had disturbed the border of sweet William and the scent rose to her nose, cinnamon spice.

She assumed he'd come to cry off, lay out the reasons, already clear to her, why it was absurd to consider a man like Westrop would harbor any interest in unremarkable Lillian Gower. She wasn't a woman men courted. She was a girl a boy might steal away for furtive touches, pressing himself against her through her skirts when he could lure her into a dark corner, then ignoring her when the rest of the excavating team was about.

She'd never felt a man's touch like Westrop's hand on her bottom. The move had been nothing more than a reflex, yet the shape of his palm, firm, long-fingered, branded her flesh, her brain. The heat girdling her hips was not embarrassment.

Westrop clasped his hands behind his back as he walked. This broadened his shoulders beneath his coat, bringing attention to the circumference of his upper arms. She knew men could pad the shoulders of their coats, but the arms? Of course, a man of the upper classes, who no doubt ate well and lifted nothing heavier than a full glass of drink to his lips at dinner, might well be rounded. *Well*-rounded. Lillian sniggered at her own joke.

"You accepted my hand before the company last night. I recall a distinctly resigned 'very well.' I admit, not the breathless excitement a man hopes to elicit from his bride, but one must work with the tools one has."

She squinted her eyes at him. "You may very well elicit such a response from the woman you choose to make your bride, sir. But we both know our engagement is a ruse."

His gaze moved over her face, taking in every line, as if he were memorizing her features. Or attempting to peer beneath her surface.

Lillian felt more bricks rolling beneath her feet. His hair was a deep russet, dark and thick, but his eyes were pale green. The contrast was rather striking.

"What if it were not a ruse?" he asked softly.

Her cheeks burned like a harvest bonfire. "An engagement in truth? What would that gain us?"

He couldn't intend an actual engagement, with an actual wedding at the end of it. She knew nothing of his nature and little of his circumstances. Marriage would disrupt her plans for her life. She meant to spend the summer focusing on her publication, getting her pages in order and finding a publisher. Come winter, she would be helping her parents catalogue and publish their findings about Stonehenge, then preparing for the next excursion, and she sincerely hoped they would take her with them this time.

Lillian was not made to be a hostess, like her Aunt Giles, though that would be required from the wife of a Westrop. She knew basic housekeeping, due to the simple fact that her mother didn't, and somebody had to supervise their small staff. She knew a great deal about the latest botanical publications, and the process of making botanical engravings.

She knew next to nothing of conjugal relations. The kind that took place between a man and a woman after the marriage vows had been sealed. Her heart rapped inside her chest, her breath halting at the notion of such intimacies. With him.

He broke the eye contact that had held for far too long and looked about him. "This is a very interesting garden."

He was not ready to reveal his reasons, then. Or giving himself time to invent some.

"Uncle is very proud of it. We have plants from all over the world."

She pointed out each section. "There, where we came in, with the tansy and cypress, that is the Italian garden. Next is the German garden, the Spanish garden, and the Dutch. Over here we have the English garden, the Oriental garden, and the Americas, North and South. He is considering a place for Australia, though I don't know where we'll put it."

She clasped her hands together so she stopped looking like a windmill, arms twirling. "That is why you found me with Forster's volume. My uncle only has the quarto, but your uncle purchased the folio, where the engravings are much larger, and I can get a better sense of the plants."

"Are you a gardener, Miss Gower? A budding apothecary?"

That twitch to his lips was fascinating. She *must* stop looking at his mouth.

"Nothing so practical. I am merely interested in the construction of a plant, and its artistry. I leave it to others to define their properties and functions."

"An artist." She detected politeness. It was for men to have the challenging discussions about taxonomy and definition. It was for women to furnish lovely watercolors that could occupy a space on the wall.

She gave him a decisive nod. She was a botanical artist, and he had best know this about her. "Yes."

"Is that a glasshouse?" In repose, his face was comely, cast in classical lines. Kindled with delight, his features were arresting.

"My uncle's design. He took inspiration from Mary Eleanor Bowes's orangery at Gibside. He also took many cuttings and seeds from her, including that dwarf peach sheltering Hester."

"May I see inside?"

His tone, his look, his very attention were a seductive combination. Lillian was not accustomed to men taking an interest in anything of hers beyond her bosom. She had shown the house to friends in town, female friends, but had not realized how tiny the space was until Westrop stepped into it with her.

She reminded herself she was not seducible. Not anymore.

"This must be a terrible indulgence, with the glass tax." He surveyed the plants lining the wooden walls with their large windows on all sides.

"The roof is glazed glass as well." Lillian pointed.

"How do you keep it so warm?"

He took off his hat and wiped a bead of sweat pearling on his forehead. He had a broad, intelligent brow, his hair sweeping back from a slight widow's peak, and the trace of slight lines suggested that brow was often wrinkled in thought. Lillian resisted the urge to wipe away a bead he had missed. Was she taking leave of her senses?

"A hypocaust system. Braziers of charcoal beneath the floor, and basins of water to create steam for moisture."

"That's a good amount of work for someone."

She was surprised he would think of it. "We have a boy who is mostly employed to fetch water for the house and garden, keep the braziers stocked on cold days, and keep the paths trimmed and swept. The one we have now seems to like the work."

And having a place to sleep. She wouldn't discuss the circumstances in which she had found the child, not with a gentleman of Westrop's stature. It was Lillian's experience that gentlemen of his stature made it a point not to acquaint themselves with the problems of the lower classes.

He fingered the sunburst of a grape leaf, one of the vines clambering along the northern exposure.

"Bacchus," Lillian offered. "One of Uncle's favorite wines. He says if he produces his own, he won't have to pay a wine merchant to adulterate his drink."

"I sympathize. Is that pineapple?"

"Uncle adores them. This is my pet." She showed him the dwarf olive in its wheeled wooden tub.

"You enjoy olives?"

"Enjoy is a mild term. I am greedy about them. This is a Manzanilla that Uncle had brought from Seville just for me. The thing flowered madly a few weeks ago, but I have yet to see drupes. It may be it won't fruit in a container, which would be a pity."

"You would have to move to a sunny clime to enjoy your olives then," he agreed.

"Perhaps I could persuade my parents to excavate at Pompeii. It would be a dream of theirs to go."

His eyelid twitched in response to this notion, but he diverted his gaze to the worktable. "What are you working on?"

"Cuttings of Uncle's Brunswick fig. It bears well, and the fruit is quite tasty. He gifts plants to his favorites."

Suddenly Westrop was quite close. He was not so tall that she couldn't fall into his gaze, intent, assessing. Moisture prickled across her skin. It *was* hot in the glasshouse.

"I want a cutting."

Her heart gulped. "You shall have to become a favorite, then."

What a fool she was. A handsome man stepped close to her, silver flame in his eyes, and every thought left her head. She couldn't have come up with her own name if asked.

"We are betrothed. That ought to qualify me."

"You haven't persuaded me why we ought to proceed with our supposed engagement." Her heart staggered inside her chest, a goat trying to find its feet on a rockfall.

His breath touched her cheek, and tiny hairs on her nape lifted. He smelled wonderful, the herbal tang of the tansy with something beneath that she couldn't identify but found enormously heady. Bars of silver stood out against the light green of his eyes.

"Might I kiss you?"

The breath whooshed from her body. "Absolutely not. Hester could see. My aunt would learn of it."

It would give him an unfair advantage. His lips looked delicious, the top lip with a firm and decided slant, the lower soft and full. Both sides turned up at the corners.

"We are alone, Miss Gower. *Most* compromising. Unless we are affianced."

"For what purpose?"

He leaned back and she sighed, light-headed. Alarm receded that this potent man might actually kiss her, the first real kiss of her life. In its place came a twinge of disappointment, which she quickly shoved away.

"To quell the gossip, first and foremost, that we stirred up with our performance last evening." He nodded in the direction of the house.

"It is only gossip. The judgment of others can have little impact on your prospects."

His prospects, at least. It was a different matter for her. She wondered if that reality had touched his mind.

"You shall guard me from the advances of Ponsonbys, junior and senior. You shall be my shield maiden. My aegis."

Any other woman could serve those purposes. He had no particular interest in *her*. Lillian turned toward the table and its fragmented plants.

"And what are the advantages to me in acquiring a betrothed?"

"Hmm." He stepped closer. She had nowhere to back away from the effects of his nearness. Warmth. Heady scents. That intensifying prickle beneath her skin.

"The usual things gentlemen afford ladies when they are courting. Someone to hold your parasol while we stroll in the park."

"I visit the park with my sketchbook and a bag to carry any interesting specimens. I rarely carry a parasol."

"Then you have need of me. What else? A partner for dancing and suppers."

"We do not venture out to very many entertainments. Hester—" She changed tack. "I find too many events in a week overwhelming."

"I shall protect you from all the unwanted suitors throwing themselves at you in *your* library."

She snorted again, the sound erupting before she could contain herself. "Are you fit for the task? There are a great many so inclined."

He grinned, and the effect was devastating. "I shall enjoy the exercise."

He was delighted to have made her laugh. That disarmed her as nothing else could.

"You must be serious, sir. You made a desperate appeal, and I could not let you drown. But I imagined you would call on me today to explain why we are both best advised to continue in our separate ways, and I would agree."

That considering glance again, too close an appraisal of her upswept hair, her face, her neck. The evaluation moved down her figure, then back up, and it was that—the return journey—that made her feel undressed.

Her nipples hardened beneath her stays. He had asked to *kiss* her.

"I made a public offer," he said softly. "I cannot jilt you now. It would injure my claim to be a gentleman."

She swallowed through a suddenly dry mouth. "I can do the jilting."

Her reputation might not survive the blow, but then again, she was not in search of a husband. In some future, distant time, if anyone materialized into that role, they could laugh together about that time in her reckless youth when she had, as a pretense, accepted the suit of a marquess-in-waiting.

"Miss Gower. What would persuade you to accept my hand? Or, at the least, a betrothal of some duration?"

She drew a deep breath, watched as his eyes dipped to her bodice before he wrenched his gaze back to hers. "You might help me publish my *florilegium*," she blurted.

He tilted his head. "Your—"

"A florilegium is a collection of flower illustrations—"

"Yes, I know."

"And I have made a study of the *Cypripedioideae*. You would know them as the lady's slipper orchids. My favorite is the genus *Cypripedium*."

His expression turned into a polite mask, calculation behind it. "Indeed?"

"You haven't seen one? It's a very elegant plant. Linnaeus himself classified it. And Richard Salisbury discussed four of the species in a talk he gave to the Linnean Society. It's printed in the *Transactions*, but the text is in Latin, and the ink drawings, while very fine, are not colored. My book is in English and has colored plates. It could be enjoyed by far more people."

He stared at her, and a tight loop pulled around her middle, like an ill-fitting gown. "There are many people researching orchids, I know. They hold an ancient fascination. Some think they are magical." She licked her lips, her mouth dry again. "I've made a close study of the plants around my home. All I need to finish my collection is to confirm a few facts about the *Cypripedium calceolus*, and..."

And that was all. She had this one thing to contribute. This single dream.

"Why would you require my assistance to publish?"

Sweat rolled down the back of her neck. "My uncle has agreed to help sponsor my publication, but all the printers I have approached want to publish under his name."

"And?"

Of course she would have to explain it to him. He was a man.

"I want to publish under my own."

He cocked his head to the other side. "Why haven't your parents made this happen already?"

"I don't expect to see them until the winter season sets in. Besides, they publish their works in the *Archaeologia*, the journal of the—"

"Society of Antiquaries. I know it."

"My parents have no printing contacts, certainly not in London."

"And you suppose I do?" His mouth curled, but it wasn't derision. He looked at her as if she'd removed a mask and he was seeing her face for the first time.

She twisted her hands together to keep from waving them in the air. "You are a Westrop. You are related to Marquess of Waringford. People will at least listen to you."

His eyelids tensed, fine lines fanning from their corners. He didn't like the reminder of his status. Well, if it appeared she was being calculating, she was. She'd seen the way people approached him last evening. He was presumed heir to a marquessate, his family was an old and established one, and he no doubt had wealth piled in every room of the ancestral home back in—Wiltshire, she had heard. A printer who saw this man strolling into his shop would prepare a far different reception from the one that met plain Miss Lillian Gower, daughter and heir of no one.

"And if I assist you in your endeavor, you will agree to pretend we are engaged?"

She swallowed the several objections that swelled to her tongue. How long he expected this to carry on. What it would require of her. What would happen to her when it ended.

What would happen to her if she had more of these mad, fleeting wishes that his interest in her could be *real*.

"I will consent."

He gave her a slight bow. "Miss Gower, this sounds a worthy enterprise. I would support your endeavor were I not your intended, but since I have that honor, I will do everything in my power."

"Thank you."

She could only explain what came next by the fact that she was giddy. The relief, the excitement, the sheer *hope* made her lose her head. Those must be the reasons her inhibitions so thoroughly deserted her.

She rose on her toes and kissed him.

A fast, firm kiss, like the peck of a bird. She wasn't at all certain how to go about it. The one boy who'd touched her had not paid any attention to her lips, but she had seen her father swoop a kiss to her mother's cheek or mouth plenty of times when he thought no one was looking, and the mechanics of it weren't difficult. A lift to her tiptoes, a quick press of her closed mouth against his.

A jolt like a knock on the noggin, the contact surprising, searing. She jammed back on her heels, certain her eyes were as wide with surprise as his.

"Thank you," she said again. How breathless she sounded, her voice misting from her mouth.

His shoulders bunched, and he forced his hands to his sides. She wondered if that meant she was atrocious at kissing.

"It is I who must thank you," he said softly.

Embarrassment crept up her neck. She already knew she blushed the color of the dogwood blooming in the English garden.

"We ought to emerge. Hester will be worried."

"Worried that my attentions will stay firmly affixed to you?"

She paused outside the door to look back at him. He would be near Hester for extended periods for the foreseeable future. "Hester is not interested in men. She is—special."

His eyebrows rose. "A sapphist?"

She didn't know what that was. "She is young in heart and, well, mind. Her sensibility is not that of a girl her age, and we don't know if she shall ever mature in that respect. But we—I— completely adore her, and I won't have her hurt or made fun of."

This was where another man would demand further explanation and exhibit scorn or ridicule. He would suggest something they could do, or hadn't done, as if her cousin were a problem to be fixed. He would thereafter treat Hester as if she did not understand English, speaking in a loud and exaggerated manner to her, and he would take care to use bewildering vocabulary and make references she wouldn't understand, enjoying himself at her expense.

Lillian's heart nose-dived into her house slippers, which she hadn't thought to change before she came outside, and now they were no doubt soiled.

"Excellent," Westrop said. "Another way I might prove useful to you—as your cousin's champion." He lifted his voice to direct it over Lillian's head. "Miss Giles, I can swear I have taken no liberties. Are you ready to rejoin the company?"

Hester stepped out of the path leading to South America. "I saw five bees on the peach blossoms," she reported.

"Did you?" Lillian jumped at the chance to turn away from Westrop. "That one hasn't produced fruit yet. I've been waiting to see if the plant is self-fertile, or if I need to breed it with the nectarine in the Spanish garden."

Westrop caught her gloved hand in his. "Miss Gower, I beg you to desist. If you are to continue talking of fertilization and fruiting, I cannot be responsible for what I might do."

"Of course. I'm boring you." She sensed the dogwood blush spreading to her ears. She had been mistaken to think he shared her interests simply because he had been curious about the glasshouse. Men wanted women to be demure and dimpled, and they did not want to hear about species and genus. Aunt Giles had told her this a thousand times.

A vein of rebellion rose within her. She was tired of restraining herself to try to attract a man. He had insisted she proceed with a spurious betrothal; he might as well understand what he had bound himself to.

"Linnaeus defined the *Prunus* family, you know, but it was Mr. Philip Miller, who was chief gardener at the Chelsea Physic Garden, who settled on the genus *persica*, since the plants were first cultivated in Persia and brought to Greece by Alexander the Great. For that reason Uncle placed it in the Oriental garden, but I proposed moving it to Spain because if indeed it requires a second tree to reproduce, then—"

She stopped when Westrop tugged her close. Close enough

that she could detect the dark spots of stubble along his jaw. His breath smelled of mint. She'd noticed that when she kissed him.

"Miss Gower, I warned you."

Was he going to kiss her now? She panicked.

"You're standing too close. Mother won't like it," Hester remarked. "Do you mean we'll have peaches this year?"

"If we're fortunate." Lillian stood dazed as Westrop stepped away. She grasped for her thoughts, suddenly scattered. "*Prunus persica* literally means Persian plum, which is amusing because the Romans, I understand, called the peach the Persian apple. The French called it *péche*, hence the English word. I wonder when they were first brought to England, since Miller mentions them in his *Gardener's Dictionary*. I shall have to sketch the flowers while they are in bloom."

"And hope we have peaches," Hester said. "Cook could create her own recipes. Persian apple compote. Persian apple tart."

"Persian apple flummery," Westrop said, holding Lillian's hand.

Hester countered him without missing a beat. "Persian apple cake."

"Persian apple pastille."

Hester pulled a face. "No pastilles. Persian apple fritters, perhaps."

"Persian apple preserves."

"Persian apple custard?" Lillian tried to enter the game.

"Outrage," Westrop reproved at the same time Hester wrinkled her face.

"Disgusting. You're eating that yourself."

"Persian apple cream, I will consider." He pretended to look down his nose, and Lillian couldn't help it. She dissolved into laughter.

She stopped when Westrop pulled her close again and held

her while Hester proceeded into the house, singing to herself, "Persian apple biscuit, Persian apple fluff."

Lillian sobered completely when Westrop leaned toward her and, with the same swift pecking motion with which she had kissed him, buried his nose briefly in her hair.

In her *hair*. Lillian held perfectly still while something swooped and dove in her belly, wings fluttering like a bat's.

"I consider myself a gentleman," he muttered. "But you, Miss Gower, are going to push me to the bounds of my restraint."

That must be a terrible thing, yet it didn't sound terrible. It sounded exciting.

This would not do. She was Lillian the steady, Lillian the prop, Lillian the balm that helped everyone else in the family go along in their course. She could not be that for her family if she lost her head over a man and an attachment that had no basis in reality, was merely fabricated to save him from the machinations of mothers and Ponsonbys.

Whatever sounder, deeper reasons he had for fixing on her, he had not yet found it in him to reveal.

Yet here she was, not pulling away from him, rather walking unsteadily toward her own doom, singing like a martyr of old.

"I suppose you ought to call me Lillian, as we are pretending to be affianced."

"And you must call me Leo." He gazed into her face with a combination of gentleness and wonder, and she couldn't bear it.

"Leo?" The name suited him perfectly. Strong, magnificent, a king among men. "I thought your name was Gideon."

"My first name. My second given name is Leonidas, after a different progenitor. I prefer it."

"Gideon was successful," Lillian argued as she led him into the house. "Leonidas died."

"Ah, but his sacrifice was heroic. Gideon killed for spite, as I see it. Leonidas protected his home, and he sacrificed himself for his men."

"Gideon lived to old age and fathered seventy sons. Leonidas had his corpse beheaded. An outrageous insult."

"And the death of Leonidas inspired the Athenians to fight more fiercely. Thus there was a Greece for Alexander to bring his Persian apples into, rather than it being Persia already. You *must* stop speaking of reproduction."

"It isn't ladylike, I know. But you'll find little about me is."

His gaze dropped to her bosom, but not in the furtive, lascivious way so many men looked at her. Nor was his gaze drawn against his will. He was making a point.

She laughed, and was gratified to see his eyes flare as her bosom moved. She only hoped he could not see how his perusal had made a steel band spring up around her chest, pressing her in. "That is the only part, I'm afraid."

His brows rose mischievously. "Not the *only* part."

This conversation was terribly indelicate. Heat rushed downward to her belly and legs, to another part of her she knew was incontrovertibly associated with the female sex.

This would *not* do.

"I was speaking of your lips," he said sanguinely. "Are you going to kiss me again?"

"No."

He nodded. "Later, then."

The heat spread to her cheeks. "Not at all. It was highly improper of me. I won't abuse your person again." One swift graze had made her want to kiss him again. She would not give in again to a man's fevered needs. She could not set her foot in that snare.

"Miss Gower. My Lillian." He raised the hand he held and placed it against his chest, above his heart. There were several layers of fabric there, his shirt, his very well-fitting waistcoat, his beautifully cut coat. But she absorbed heat and firmness and pure masculine strength. The top of her head floated away.

"If you are going to rend my heart by jilting me when you are finished with me and your florilegium, then I have but one request. Kiss me as often as you can before you kill me. Abuse me utterly—ravish me well and thoroughly, I beg of you—before you cast me away."

"Oh, do not be absurd." She ducked her head and strode down the hall to the parlor where her aunt still entertained her guests, all of them wanting to know what axis of the world had tilted to make a man like Mr. Westrop offer for a girl like Lillian Gower.

She'd be dragged through the brush over this, she saw already, and be lucky to come out on the other end with her dignity intact. There would be no succumbing to the man's temptations. She had made a bargain for her florilegium; that was all.

She could not afford for this man to change the fabric of the life she had carefully constructed. Her safe, quiet, harmonious life.

But with the touch of his lips still tingling hers, Lillian feared something had already worked its way within her, some alchemy changing her on the inside, and it might already be impossible to go back to what she had been.

CHAPTER SIX

Leo considered pulling his hair as he regarded the papers before him, but having cut it in the Titus style, he settled with raking his fingers over his scalp, trying to settle his rushing brain.

Everything was happening at once. In mere days, plans which had been stalled for months had suddenly tumbled into place.

Suppliers he'd not heard from in weeks had suddenly sent the last of his shipments, completing the list of equipment he needed. Contacts who had worked before in Uffington and the Vale of the White Horse sent lists of names of reliable local men they'd hired. Members of the Society of Antiquaries wrote or called on him to share techniques, advice, recommendations, and stories. The solicitor finally answered his letter promising to inquire about premises to let in Ashbury or Compton Beauchamp while Leo worked.

He knew what was happening. It wasn't that his ruling planets had suddenly aligned in a benign aspect or the ancient gods were smiling on him. Rumor had spread on its winged boots that Leo Westrop, aspiring antiquarian, had engaged to marry one of *those* Gowers.

Peter Gower had cut his teeth on excavations at Pompeii, learning from military engineers running disciplined digs. Alida Gower knew more about early Christian churches in Wales than anyone else writing on them. With this wealth of expertise supposedly at his disposal, Leo was finally being taken seriously, and everyone was willing to back his plans.

He'd been so busy organizing his operation and handling correspondence that he hadn't seen Lillian Gower in nearly a week. And instead of diminishing in his memory, the need to see her again kept growing. Had he completely lost his head over a pair of blue eyes, dimples, and exquisite breasts? Had he really instructed the girl to *ravish* him?

He'd promised himself he could call on her when the big pieces of his plans were in place, but one enormous element was still missing. He didn't have permission to excavate.

The summer season was upon them. The spring rains were over and the frost was out of the ground. He should have had his dig plotted and the first layer of soil up already, with an assistant hired to catalogue his finds. His trunks were packed and waiting. He only needed the landowner's permission, and then his enterprise could begin—the first dig he'd planned and would oversee on his own, the first step in what he hoped would be a long and respectable career and his entry into the Society of Antiquaries.

Barrington said he'd be happy if Leo dug up whatever he wanted, only splitting with him if he found a cache of Roman coins or a Saxon hoard, but Craven owned the land around Wayland Smith's Cave. Craven hadn't responded to his letters, and before he could go pining after beautiful botanists, Leo needed to run the baron to ground.

Abuse me utterly, he'd implored her. He was the Westrop

who prided himself on discipline and restraint. *What* had he been thinking?

His mother swept into the library, nose in the air, a fold of embroidery in her hand. Lady Mary rarely went about without some task to which she could apply herself while she fretted over what the servants were or were not doing, or how her sons had disappointed her this time.

"You haven't answered a single invitation." She eyed the stack of cards and vellum the butler kept delivering.

Society also wondered what Leo had been thinking, given the number of people who now wanted him at their soirees, evenings of dinner or cards, musical performances, or garden parties. He'd been a wonder when Rupert's sudden, shocking death left him in line for the Waringford title. Now, watching one of the Season's most promising heirs attach himself to a woman of no great family, wealth, or beauty was better entertainment than Astley's Circus for the *haut ton*.

His mother made no secret that she thought he'd taken leave of his senses. His family already feared he wouldn't amount to anything, given his decision to steer away from the military and the law and his utter unfitness for the clergy—he couldn't reconcile himself to the doctrine. Leo was a heathen, as near a pagan as they came, his only religion the stoicism of the early Romans and the love of proper proportions held by the early Greeks. His brother Joshua, who *was* entering the clergy, harbored no ambition either, having firmly declared his aspirations to be a quiet country rector and read books all day.

"I have been otherwise occupied." Leo pushed the invitations aside.

"I knew it," his mother huffed. "You chose that girl only to vex me."

"Of course not," Leo said. "I chose her on her own merits."

His mother sank into a chair—the one Lillian had occupied

the night he found her in his library. "What *merits* can you possibly detect?"

Those eyes the color of forget-me-nots, as if he could forget her, now. The smirk of that satiny mouth. The wildflower allure of her, the taste of lemon on his lips after that kiss, as brief as a butterfly's touch. The mushroom blonde hair that was as soft as silk against his skin. Her breasts—sweet heaven, her breasts. Just the thought of her shape made him glad he sat behind the large desk. How many times he'd traced in his mind's eye the serpentine curve of her bosom and waist and hips. How many times he'd imagined tracing that path with his hands. And his mouth. She'd taste sweet as a Persian apple.

God have mercy, his mother was in the room.

"She's quite intelligent."

If she knew the languages she'd teased him about knowing, she was far ahead of the common run of female. If she could read Latin—and he suspected she could make out a title or two —she was top of a class of gentleman's daughters generally not taught more than would make them ornamental wives, agreeable hostesses, and capable mothers.

If she had prepared a publication, she was in a class all her own. Even if it was nothing more than an insipid collection of the average floral watercolors that young women of genteel breeding were expected to paint.

He had agreed to help her publish to secure her hand, or the pretense of claiming her hand, to protect him from exactly this: his mother's predatory plans. It wasn't the bargain he'd expected her to drive, but he'd agreed.

How soon could he ask what he wanted of her in return?

"I'd say intelligence hardly recommends her. It's not a generally admired quality in a female." Lady Mary pursed her lips in a frown. "I've asked around, Gideon. There's no money in that family."

"Her uncle, great-uncle, is a baronet."

"Who lives off a tiny farm or two on the fringes of Wales. You've made a terrible mistake. Miss Ponsonby—"

"Would be an even worse mistake."

He flushed. Was he admitting Lillian was a mistake? No. She'd be ruined when she jilted him, of course. Even if it was the lady's idea, society was unkind to those who broke their engagements, especially if the match had seemed to offer her nothing but inconceivable advantages.

But she'd agreed to extend the ruse, and she'd agreed to do the jilting. As if she didn't fear in the least the slings and arrows that might be thrown at her. She was not in the common run of females at all.

"She'll shame you. Poor, plain, nothing to recommend her." His mother waved at the stack of invitations. "Best you haven't accepted any. They only want to laugh at you."

Heat prickled his neck at the thought of anyone laughing at Miss Gower. Lillian, with her sparkling eyes, the authoritative way she mapped out her uncle's garden and organized his library. Her taste for olives and her knowledge of how to propagate Brunswick figs.

The innocent way she'd talked of breeding and reproduction and fertilization. Her breasts had brushed his chest when she rose up to kiss him—she must have noticed, too—and the contact felled him like a tree. He'd been a struck flint, at attention over one brief kiss and the brush of those exquisite breasts. As if he were a green boy.

He was trying hard not to live in those moments when only a few layers of cotton had separated her bottom from his face. He had too much work to do.

He focused on Barrington's letter, open on his desk. "I won't have anyone laughing at her."

His mother raised one brow in that supercilious manner he

hated. "Indeed? So you don't think our friends won't find it amusing when you offer for a girl, then leave her for months to dig in the dirt and ghastly tombs. While she dangles after you here, and everyone asks her how she persuaded the presumptive heir to a marquess to lower himself to court an antiquarian's daughter."

That was exactly what he'd asked her to agree to, a selfish request. The kind thing would be to free her from their agreement before he left.

And watch his association with the Gowers, which had smoothed his path so significantly, go away.

His mother wasn't finished. "I won't give you any money for your frivolous endeavors, you know. Not a groat. And I'm sure that your uncle feels the same."

"I will supply my own funding, madame."

Though what he would do when his savings ran out, Leo didn't know. He didn't have reliable income of his own. He lived off a tiny annuity that his father had not managed to squander before he died, because his canny mother had tied it up in funds that made it impossible for her wastrel husband to spend it on gambling debts. Leo typically had just enough to pay his tailor and the fee for his clubs. He'd saved some by lodging at Westrop House instead of finding bachelor quarters, which would have afforded him a degree of independence from his mother's iron-fisted control.

There was also the negligible allowance from his uncle. How irritating it was to be a gentleman and not permitted to turn his hand to trade. If he married an heiress, as his grandfather and uncle had done, he'd have endless reserves from which to supply his expeditions.

Lillian wasn't an heiress. But if the Gowers were seen to be backing his expedition, credit would easily be extended to him.

"I see nothing lowering in my association with Lillian," Leo said.

His mother rose, crumpling her embroidery in her fist. "You will. And when you are caught in the trap of your own making, I can only say I told you so."

AFTER THAT EXCHANGE, Leo had no inclination to dine at home. With Joshua deciding to stay in Oxford for the summer with his tutor and access to the libraries, a solitary dinner with his mother would be as comfortable as the inquisition interviewing a heretic. Westrop House was a gloomy place now that his uncle had removed his family to Waringford Hall, using the excuse of his bereavement to leave his seat in Lords before the closing of Parliament. His lordship needed time to absorb the shock that Rupert, the dashing soldier and the nephew he'd admired, had been stolen away by the cruel hand of fate, leaving for his heirs the issue of Leo's father, the brother whom the marquess had least liked.

Leo was not sure anyone had liked Gideon Westrop, excepting the man himself and, at various times, his many mistresses.

It was too late to accept an invitation to dine elsewhere, and far too late to stroll over to Gower House to see what progress Lillian had made in cataloguing her uncle's library, how she was getting on with her fig cuttings, or whether her trees were bearing fruit. Leo should be tracking down Craven, not dancing attendance on a female. He was a man of sense and discipline. He needed to act it.

Brooks it would be then. The Society of Dilettanti still tended to congregate at the club, and there he could find like-minded friends to engage in conversation, and who might give him some manly advice.

He hired a chair to take him to St. James Street and admired the many layers of London as they passed before him. Leo preferred the neoclassical style to the thick, gloomy bricks of the medieval, but his favorite parts of London were where one could see the bones of the older city beneath.

He liked Tower Hill and walking the remnant of the Roman wall that had surrounded Londinium. It fascinated him to think what lay beneath the medieval outlines of the city. Camden, the great antiquarian of the Elizabethan age, claimed there had been a temple to Diana on the high ground of St. Paul's, but Leo imagined an even earlier monument, built by the people who had lived here before the Romans came. Legends said they had been giants, given the size of the standing stones they erected and the enormous mounds they left behind.

What might be concealed within those ancient hills? His hands itched to dig beneath the centuries of commerce and industry, find a window into the lives of humans in earlier times. They could tell stories of a history that went back further than anyone knew. He just had to get *inside*.

His chair weaved through the crowd in Seven Dials, where the famous sundial column had been removed and every building fronting the six crossing streets boasted a pub. The place hadn't become what its builders had hoped, another Covent Garden to bring the wealthy and their money; instead the Dials seemed to be dwindling into a slum. Leo in his brushed, tailored clothing would make a prime target for pickpockets, though the most expensive item on him was his coat.

He might be a man about town, but he was not a man of means. The Westrop family had an ancient lineage but not ancient fortunes. He had a feeling Lillian Gower would not care, but many other a girl who'd been targeting him might have reconsidered if she knew the state of his pockets.

His chair hurried him down St. Martin's Lane, past the

rebuilt church with its spire piercing the sky, and Charing with its Eleanor Cross, crumbling beneath the weight of five centuries of wear. Leo knew the story from chat among the antiquarians: Edward Longshanks had built a series of crosses to mark the places where his beloved wife's funeral procession rested as she was brought back to Westminster Abbey. Leo generally looked past such monuments; they were nothing but effusions of sentiment, and he was interested in more robust representations of human life, the battle for day-to-day existence, and the philosophies that kept humans clinging to their fragile thread of existence.

But Eleanor of Castile, Leo recalled, had been her husband Edward I's constant companion throughout his reign, all his progresses and challenges and trials. What must that be like, to have a wife who was not just the keeper of the domestic flame, a petulant goddess a man must placate with gifts and occasional pats of affection, but a true helpmeet in all one's endeavors? He'd never met such a woman, had never imagined one existed.

For a moment a vision touched Leo's mind. A canvas tent on the British hillside, sheltering his trunks of tools. Lillian standing beside him at a folding table, peering at a find as he dusted off the dirt, her expression of wonder matching his own. Her hair shining in a shaft of sunlight, her eyes as light and vast as the sky. Her lips soft and yielding beneath his as he bent to kiss her.

He shook his head as his chair turned onto Pall Mall. Someone hailed him as he passed Carlton House, Prince George's opulent palace.

"Yoo hoo! Mr. Westrop! But is Miss Gower not with you?"

Leo waved in acknowledgement to the matron, trying to remember the name of the daughter she'd thrust under his nose. By the saints, was he expected to dance attendance on his fiancée at every moment? His arrangement with Lillian was supposed to buy him liberty, not steal it.

The chair stopped before Brooks, a Palladian edifice of yellow brick and Portland stone with columns harkening back to a civilization that was ancient before the Romans had conquered it. He paid his fare and ascended the staircase to the first floor.

Men sat grouped around several of the green-covered tables in the Grand Subscription Room, but Leo declined the invitations to join a hand of whist or the circle ringing the hazard table. He didn't have money to gamble away, and his father's example had taught him that cards, or betting of any kind, was not a reliable way to put money in his purse. He made his way through the grand room with its patterned carpet, red velvet curtains shielding noise from the street outside, and entered the drawing room beyond, where another fire burned in the fireplace and another crystal chandelier dangled from the vaulted ceiling, twin to the one in the next room. Slouched in one of the armchairs was the top of a tousled head of curls that he recognized.

"It's in the book. Ten pounds that she'll jilt me by Midsummer," Daniel Rowland said gloomily. "That's still a month away yet. Want to put down twelve she'll do it sooner?"

"You haven't come round to the idea of the match?" Leo seated himself in the chair opposite his friend.

Daniel tossed the newspaper he held to the small table between them. "The more my mother praises it, the less inclined I find myself to put my leg in the shackle. Suppose that makes me an unfilial bastard."

Leo tried to call to mind the features of Daniel's intended. Her grandfather was a perfumier; her father had used the proceeds to buy himself a gentleman's estate. Daniel was studying to be a barrister, but he came from a distinguished line of clerics. His interests were medieval, so later than Leo's, but he was a good bloke all the same. At twenty, however, he simply wasn't ready to fall in line with his mother's matrimonial schemes.

"You'll be a rich bastard do you marry her, which I imagine is your mother's chief aim," Leo said.

"At least your mother was lining up comely ones for you." Daniel squinted at him, which told Leo his friend might be several drinks into his wallowing. "Until you pitched them all over for someone plain, just to spite her." He grinned. "Have to hand it to you, old man. You spiked her wheels but good. Wish I'd thought of it."

Leo twitched. Lillian wasn't plain; did his friend require spectacles? She was a luscious Venus in a crowd of starveling nymphets. It was the hand of providence that had her standing next to the refreshment table when his panicked gaze swept his mother's drawing room. He couldn't think of anyone he'd be better pleased to have foisted a falsely motivated engagement on.

"Do you ever think about it, though?" Leo studied the shelf of books against the wall, wondering if anything interesting had been added to the inventory.

"Think about how to free myself of the yoke?"

"Think about putting your neck in it."

There was no point in entertaining fantasies. Leo hadn't the means to support a wife. There was no future with Lillian, not until he had established his career and had income and funding.

Or his uncle granted his new heir an estate, and an income to go with it. Leo pushed the thought away.

Daniel sighed. "A wife, buxom at bed and board, obliged to pay the marital debt? Would save having to woo the opera dancers. But then she'll produce children, and I'll have to support them, too."

An image flashed across Leo's mind of himself as a child, screaming with laughter as he was carried on the shoulders of his uncle. Not the marquess, but the brother next older than Leo's father, the laughing soldier who had produced Rupert and then gone away to the American colonies and, so it was said, produced more children with a native woman there.

A child of his own. A son to carry on his own shoulders, laughing. A small daughter gazing up at him with enormous Delft blue eyes. Lillian with her proper woman's curves, carrying a child on her hip as she peered into one of Leo's trenches. The idea lit a fire in his gullet.

Daniel picked up his empty glass and peered into it. "Why *her*, though? Out of anyone."

"Why Lillian Gower?" Leo stretched out his legs. He could take Daniel into his confidence; though several years younger than Leo, the boy wasn't a teller of tales.

"Her parents are well-known antiquarians. They have excavated in Wiltshire before. They're at Stonehenge right now, with Cunnington. I hear Sir Richard Colt Hoare is funding that effort." Sir Richard, already a member of the Society of Antiquaries, was the one who had acquired Glastonbury Tor and was attempting to rebuild it. The things possible when one inherited a banking fortune.

"Sounds like they could pull some strings for you."

Leo pulled fingers through his hair. "I might ask them to. I need Craven's permission to dig around Uffington and the Vale of the White Horse. He owns all the land thereabout, including Ashdown. Don't suppose you know where his lordship is hiding himself these days?"

"Lord Craven? He was just made aide-de-camp to the king." Daniel set down his glass. "Suppose he's kicking his heels around London, at least until Parliament closes and the pomp and ceremony are done. Probably out tonight, at one of those dos all you big wigs go to."

Leo dug in his coat for the invitation his mother had pressed on him before he left. "I haven't responded that you're attending, but you ought to make an appearance, to stave off talk that you've gone mad," she'd said, peeved. "But do come home first to change into breeches. You can hardly show up to Highcastle House in pantaloons."

Portman Square lay in Mary-le-Bone; it would be a mile and a half back to Bloomsbury and Westrop House, then a mile and a half again in silk breeches and an evening cravat. Leo weighed the disgrace of showing up shabby against the risk of missing Craven. His mother would bring the London coach for her own comfort, so he would have transportation home.

It would be one more night of not seeing Lillian. Of not discussing how long this arrangement of theirs was supposed to last.

"Care to join me and the big wigs? No doubt the maidens would be happy for another young buck, especially if there's dancing."

Daniel brightened. "D'you suppose, if I do go and gallant about with others, it'll make Miss Lewton jilt me all the sooner?"

"Not too much gallanting, if you please. I'm already on the wrong foot with the Highcastles, and I need to make friends with Craven before I start digging holes in his monuments."

Daniel receded into his seat and repossessed himself of the discarded paper. "You're a bore, old man."

"So I've been told."

Would Lillian think so? Leo's restraint as an adult had been hard-won from a youth in which Leo feared he had the temperament that would lead him into his father's excesses. He would deny himself to the point of starvation—to the point of humorlessness, if need be—before he became so selfish not to care how his frivolity injured others.

Daniel clucked his tongue. "Still, I like your odds in the book a lot better than mine."

"What odds?"

Daniel jerked a thumb in the general direction of the betting book, which was kept in the subscription room. All the clubs had one, and the bets in the Brooks book, like those elsewhere, ranged from the ridiculous to the obscene.

"You've got less than a fortnight before she cuts you loose."

Leo located the book and a haze of panic clouded his vision as he read the bet, then the amendments that had been scribbled in below. That Miss Gower would end her betrothal to Mr. Westrop in a fortnight. That he would end things in ten days. That Miss Gower would jilt him in a sennight.

An entry from earlier that day conjectured that the entire arrangement was a farce, and all would become clear at the Highcastle soiree that night.

Leo clenched his hands into a fist, his palms sweating. She couldn't jilt him yet; he'd lose all the momentum he had gained in finally carrying out his plans. Without the Gower name to sanction his undertaking, he'd be right back to where he had been.

He couldn't let his time with Lillian end before it had even begun.

CHAPTER SEVEN

L eo claimed his hat, gloves, and stick from the porter. He would walk to Portman Square to wear off his ire and hope that London's fashionable West End streets would harbor fewer pickpockets or vendors trying to relieve him of his coin by honest means. He stalked past the famous bow window of White's club and turned up Berkley Street, passing the walled frontage of Devonshire House and the gardens that lay within. He wondered what Miss Gower would find to appreciate there, and in the gardens behind Landsdowne House, fronting Berkley Square.

He wondered what she would think of these bets.

He wondered what she thought of him, persuading her to a pretend betrothal, and then neglecting her for a week.

She was a sensible girl. She'd made no hint that she required his attention. She'd agreed, quite evenly, to be the jilt when the time came.

He didn't *want* to end it. Not yet. Not when things were finally going so well. And he couldn't take the time to attend her because it was possible he could locate Craven and secure the last intricate cog in his mechanism. Set his great dream into motion.

He would call on Lillian tomorrow and try to explain.

Explain what, he wasn't entirely certain. But somehow, she had become part of the dream.

"Mr. Westrop." The duchess greeted him with a thin smile at the top of the staircase twining up the grand, two-story entrance hall of Highcastle House. "How pleased we are that you should join us."

Leo raked his brain and remembered: the Highcastles had young unmarried daughters, though there'd been some scandal a few years earlier about the eldest running away with a lesser son with absolutely nothing to recommend him. Love—or at least passion—winning out over the plots of coldly strategic mamas.

"Your affianced is here somewhere," the duchess went on. "Likely next to a table of refreshments. That seems to be where she likes to establish herself."

Leo blinked through the sudden and irrational tide of sensation that rose within him at the duchesses' words. Was she cutting Lillian's shape? Lillian Gower had the most divine figure he had ever seen on a woman.

"I was hoping to run into Lord Craven. Have you seen him?"

"The baron is here somewhere as well. In fact he may be among the crowd besieging your affianced." The duchess frowned. "You haven't done that girl any favors by making her the center of attention, Westrop. It won't work to her benefit, in the end."

The remark sank into his skin beside the needle his mother had stabbed in him earlier. Neither of these women could see Lillian's merits—only that he was toying with her and would hurt her in the end.

His chest pinched. He couldn't allow Lillian to be hurt.

And she was *here*. Craven could damn well wait another moment. Leo stalked through the reception rooms, all high ceilinged, painted in jewel-like tones, and crammed from floor to ceiling with expensive furniture, enormous paintings, and art.

Lillian stood in the sapphire room, beside a statue of a helmed Minerva, gloomily regarding a sideboard of small yellow cakes.

His heart leapt at the sight of her, and he caught it immediately in an iron cuff. He would *not* be a dolt. Not before the crowd of people surrounding her. And certainly not when she looked an ancient goddess come to life in her shimmering white robe.

Her hair was coiled on her head like a heap of old gold, her headdress sporting white flowers of flax and narcissus that he had seen blooming in the Spanish garden at her uncle's. Their peppery scent kicked his senses to high alert.

Hester stood next to her cousin, munching a cake and listening as a man Leo didn't recognize spoke to Lillian, gesturing wildly with his arms. He was a handsome fellow, straight of bearing, dressed finely but not fussily in a gold silk waistcoat beneath a dark cutaway, his hair a cap of gleaming black curls.

"Blood red flower, on a tall stalk. Grows on the trees." He drew a shape in the air.

Lillian nodded, nibbling on a cake. "It does sound like an orchid."

"Have my sister bring you one when she visits next. She's a collector."

"My uncle would be pleased to make a space in his garden. Have you given samples to Sir Joseph Banks at Kew?"

Leo couldn't stop himself from butting in. "Good evening, Miss Gower."

"Oh. Mr. Westrop." Her eyes flared in the most gratifying

way—at least, he hoped that was interest, and not alarm. A sharp breath lifted her bosom, where the embroidered neckline of her bodice skimmed the tops of her breasts. He fastened his eyes to her face. Yes, that was a blush of rose in her cheek, but was it distress or pleasure?

"Have you met?" She gestured toward her companion. "This is Mr. Hyperion Falstead, the brother of—"

"The Marquess of Arendale. How do you do." Leo nodded his head in acknowledgement.

"Half-brother, properly speaking," Falstead said with a faint smile. He must be accustomed to explaining himself, for the Marquess of Arendale was undoubtedly descended from pale northern climes, while Falstead's features suggested African descent.

Leo sorted through his memory. Arendale's father's second wife, it was said, had been an African. The marquess and his marchioness had introduced his several siblings to Society in turn, and Society had embraced them as they embraced everything that was rich, important, and held a whiff of the exotic. The boy couldn't be more than eighteen—he wasn't courting Lillian, was he?

"Are you a botanist, Falstead?" Leo asked.

"My interests are more historical, sir, but one of my sisters is a great traveler and explorer. I was just telling Miss Gower about some of the plants she's found."

Leo managed to get rid of Falstead only to find Lillian's attention taken up by the Honourable Charles Greville, son of the Earl of Warwick. The man had to be at least fifty years of age, and he had the dubious honor of having made Emma Hart, as she was once known, both the darling of Society and the wife of his uncle, William Hamilton, after cultivating her for several years as his mistress. Guessing that Greville had a taste for voluptuous young women who looked and smelled like a damascene rose, Leo knew that he had to get Lillian away as soon as possible.

"—one of your uncle's Brunswick figs," Greville was saying with a self-satisfied grin. He directed an appreciative smile at Lillian's bosom. "I ought to have you to my home in Paddington Green to supervise me in the planting of it. You might enjoy a tour of my glasshouses. I have quite a selection of tropical plants —Lloyd can tell you."

"Then she has no need to see them in person, does she?" Leo took Lillian's arm. "Good to see you, Greville. Give my regards to your uncle."

Hamilton was a renowned antiquarian, and his collection of Italian artifacts was legendary, as was his careful cataloguing of them. Leo couldn't afford to make an adversary of either man, but neither did he wish to see Lillian fall into Greville's clutches.

Lillian narrowed her eyes. "I would adore seeing Mr. Greville's tropical plants," she said, and Leo sensed he was swimming into dangerous waters.

"Then I should be happy to escort you. Greville, you might send your direction to me at Westrop House, and I can arrange for Miss Gower to view your—collection."

Greville chortled, unfazed by Leo's near snarl. "At least mine's acceptable for viewing by young women, eh? Unlike some others in that society of yours." Still chuckling, Greville moved away, and Lillian turned on Leo in a quiet fury.

"You'll escort me? You appear all at once and insist on meddling in my affairs?"

His fingers tightened against his will. He held her arm above her glove, below the short puff of a muslin sleeve, and her arm was so soft, his mind blanked.

"I am your betrothed," he managed to say.

She arched a brow at him, singular. He didn't like the contempt suggested in that gesture. "Are you? I confess I'd forgotten."

"I did not call on you," he said, his voice low and grating, "as I was otherwise occupied."

She tried to pull her arm free, without it appearing to anyone who might be observing them that ought was amiss. "So was I."

Like a cad, he didn't let go of her but tucked her arm around his own, drawing her close to him. That was a mistake. Some long tunic-like garment floated about her, the embroidery matching that on the hem and bodice of her white round gown, and beneath that fabric lay her warm curves. She smelled of narcissus and rich, sweet earth. He wanted to bury his nose in the curve where her shoulder sloped up to her neck.

"Tell me what has been occupying you." The words came out as a growl. He was clenching his teeth, in fact every tendon in his neck, trying not to bend his head toward her. The urge to touch his lips to her, anywhere—hair, eyelashes, lips, skin—was well-nigh irresistible.

"You tell me," she said coolly, turning away. "Good evening, Mr. Delaval, how do you do?"

Leo scowled. This was getting worse and worse. Ned Delaval was a notorious scoundrel and ne'er-do-well, bastard son of the last Duke of Hunsdon, and as far as Leo could tell he lived off the current duke and duchess with nothing to recommend him but an allowance he promptly spent at the gambling tables, a reputation for keeping company with beautiful and lively women of the demimonde, and looks too handsome for his own good, not at all coarsened by his dissipated lifestyle, as they ought to be.

"Enjoyed *The Stranger*, did you, Miss Gower?" Delaval

asked with an engaging grin. "Suppose you were there to swoon over Kemble, with all his mechanical perfection and that noble Roman nose."

"He was very fine as the Stranger, but Hester and I were most moved by Mrs. Siddons as Mrs. Haller. Such remorse she displayed! I found the reconciliation at the end very touching."

Delaval chuckled. "Caught the Siddons fever, have you? I thought the woman next to our box was going into hysterics."

"We did not have the paroxysms, but Hester fairly jumped out of her seat during the *Bluebeard* afterpiece, when her father prevented Fatima and Selim from eloping and carried Fatima away. We were convinced Selim would not come in time to save her, and it would all end a tragedy."

"I enjoyed that one myself. Would rather have good rollicking music than the striding and declaiming." He turned to Leo. "Didn't see you at Drury Lane, Westrop."

"He was otherwise occupied," Lillian said.

Delaval, drat the rogue, raised a brow. "Too busy to squire one's betrothed to the theatre? I hope I never suffer that circumstance."

"Not all of us can devote ourselves to leisure, I'm afraid," Leo retorted. "I am currently organizing an archaeological expedition. Miss Gower knows that."

"Well. Should you need an escort to the theatre while this one's out expeditioning, just send round a note, Miss Gower. I'll take you to see something that's rowdy good fun. I hear *She's Eloped!* will be back on the playbill as soon as the lead is no longer indisposed."

Leo fairly rippled with rage. This scoundrel would not be escorting Lillian anywhere.

"Or perhaps you too, Delaval, will discover something more productive to do with your time than while away hours in a theatre box, following fantasy lives instead of living your own," Leo said, trying and failing to curb his sneer.

Delaval simply raised both brows. "Ah, a moralist. Suppose a man needs to do something with his time while the allowance rolls in and he waits for the transfer of titles, eh? I wouldn't know what it's like to have such expectations, 'course."

A trace of bitterness laced the older man's tone, and Leo raked his mind again as the rogue made his bow to Lillian and then moved away. Delaval had been born a duke's son and raised as the spare until a surprising development revealed he was in fact a bastard, the product of a bigamous marriage. The gossip was old, but the taint would never escape him, not in a social world so carefully stratified by blood and pedigree.

Leo flushed. He was *not* sitting on his thumbs waiting for his uncle's allowance to appear. He'd never expected to be the heir. He'd never asked for it. Rupert would still be wearing that mantle if a stray French shell hadn't knocked him from one life to the next.

He faced Lillian's cool, clear gaze. The blue was an ocean he could get lost in.

"I am not a moralist," Leo said, in answer to her silent accusation.

He wasn't humorless, either. But he adamantly refused to become licentious like his father, with the name of a new woman associated with his each season, a history of debts and bad wagers at the gaming table, and a worse history of semi-illicit schemes meant to produce the money to pay off his debts. If not for his uncle and his mother's cold thrift, Leo would likely have grown up in a debtor's prison while his father diced away their food and clothing to the guards.

"When did you go to Drury Lane?" he wanted to know. He'd imagined her safe and secure in her library and garden, peacefully going about her work, and she'd been out gallivanting in fashionable places where any rogue could leer and gawk at her.

"Two nights ago. Lady Cranbury sent Aunt Giles an invitation, and my aunt, who *is* a moralist, sacrificed her sensibilities to a tale of adultery and deception so that she, and I, might be seen in the Cranbury box." She popped a tiny cake into her mouth. "We've any number of invitations flowing in. All thanks to you."

"And how many rogues and fortune hunters taking note of you?" He had to master himself. He had no right to complain of the company she kept while he was absent. Not when he had no hold on her affections, and no real claim to her otherwise.

She licked her lips. "A great many."

That simple roll of her tongue over the red stain of her lips destroyed his composure. His mind bowed under the crowding impressions of silk and softness, gleaming surfaces, and warm, sweet spaces he wanted to explore.

He *wanted* a claim on her.

"Well, don't do it any longer," he said roughly.

"What? Accept invitations?"

She touched a finger to the side of her mouth, searching for a stray crumb. He battled the overwhelming urge to lean forward and absorb that mouth into his own. Stake his claim in the most primal way possible. She was *his,* damn it. Other men couldn't come along courting and casting out lures simply because Leo had pulled back the curtain and brought her enchantments to public notice.

He realized he was pulling her toward him, too close for propriety, far too close for comfort. Her gown whispered across his pantaloons. Her heat fevered his brain.

She wasn't resisting. She floated near, nearer, responding to his pull. Her breath quickened, and a dusty rose flushed her cheeks. Her eyes sparkled, wide with interest, curiosity. Desire arced through him like summer lightning flashing through the sky over Berkshire Downs.

"What archaeological expedition are you organizing?" she asked, her voice breathless.

Lust crashed up against the barricade of good sense, normally a fortress that surrounded him entirely. He was supposed to be here setting his future in order, and he was instead using every bit of his iron willpower not to stare down the front of Lillian's frock.

"I want to excavate at Wayland Smith's Cave, near the White Horse in Uffington. I'm convinced it's a barrow. I've been going round and round as to who owns the land, and Barrington says Craven owns it. I'm told that Craven was just made aide-de-camp to the king and is in London for the season. I was hoping to find him here."

Her eyelids flickered. He'd all but said he wasn't here for her. He rubbed his thumb over the bare skin of her arm and was gratified to feel gooseflesh rise beneath his touch.

"That's the reason I've neglected you. I've been getting my dig in order." Thanks to her. And her parents. And her agreeing to be associated with him.

She pulled her lip with her teeth. "I know William. That is, I knew him before his father died and he became the baron. My parents spent time at his family's estate in Hamstead Marshall one summer, digging around the remains of the old Norman castles."

"I thought your parents preferred prehistoric remains." It was the reason she'd caught his notice. There were few antiquarians interested in pre-Roman Britain; most preferred the impressive monuments of civilization, not the ancient remnants that whispered of forgotten beliefs and lost ways of life.

She considered the fingertips of her gloves. "It was one of those compromises my parents made—my mother likes the ancient monuments, and my father prefers the classical, though he'll take the medieval if he must. He won the coin toss that summer, I recollect."

"They took you with them?"

"They have every year. Until this one." Her brows drew together, her lips turning down. He wanted to coax forth those dimples.

"Perhaps you could point him out to me. The baron." Then he could keep hold of her. Then he wouldn't have to leave her here, the focus of a parade of rogues and scoundrels who wanted to see what Leo had seen, who wanted to know why Lillian Gower had been paid the addresses of a marquess-to-be. Such types would lure her away if they could, proving that Leo hadn't valued her enough and didn't deserve her in the first place.

His fingers refused to unclasp from her arm. She was strong as the stem that held water lilies to the bottom of a lake, anchoring them in any wind.

"Hex." Lillian glanced at her cousin. "We're going to promenade through the rooms, Mr. Westrop and I. Would you wish to come with us, or would you rather find your mother?"

Hester brightened as she observed Leo. "Persian apple pudding," she said.

He stared at her a moment, then let his lips twitch upward. "Persian apple pie."

She rolled her eyes. "That was too easy."

"I will endeavor to improve myself," Leo replied gravely.

He couldn't bear to look in Lillian's eyes at that moment. Something soft shimmered in those blue depths, as if she were blinking back tears.

"Come," she said, and led the way.

They ran their quarry to ground in the peridot drawing room, done up in the rococo style of Louis XIV of France.

Craven, the seventh baron of his title, stood beneath a large oil of Charles II, chatting with one of the Highcastle sons.

Craven was not yet thirty, around Leo's age, but unlike Leo he had distinguished himself in his career and served as a major in the 84th Regiment of Foot, besides his position as assistant to the king. He too had his dark hair cut short in the Titus style, and he had the same bold, prepossessing nose as the actor Lillian admired. Leo cursed his own nose, straight but respectably sized, certainly nothing to arrest the gaze. Craven's dark eyes were sharp and full of intelligence, and he had an enviable physique, shoulders broad beneath his well-fitting coat, strong legs filling out his evening breeches and hose. He had taken the time to don evening attire for the duchess's soiree.

Leo shared a similar physique, but he didn't have Craven's military bearing or a title of his own. Lillian would be bound to note his deficiencies in comparison.

His companion, in the first coquettish move Leo had seen from her, slid open her fan and flirted it before her face. "Lord Craven. You won't remember me, but I lived on a cottage on your property one summer while my parents explored the castle mottes at Hamstead Marshall."

Craven smiled as he straightened and faced her. "I do remember you," he said in a deep voice. His gaze swept over her shoulders, the shelf of her breasts, then back to her eyes. "The little lisping girl who followed me about calling me Wim Wim. How could I forget someone so adorable?"

"I'm sure you have any number of lisping females trailing you about at all times, milord," Lillian said dryly. "If I made an impression, I don't expect it was endearing."

His smile tilted to one side of his lordship's mouth. "You read me a lecture on the difference between southern marsh orchid and field cow-wheat when I confused them. I hope you know I have retained the lesson."

Damn the man, he was handsome. Leo forgot to smooth away his scowl as Lillian cleared her throat and directed attention to him. "Do you know Mr. Westrop? He too has antiquarian interests."

Craven's sharp gaze scanned his face, and Leo guessed the man had placed in a moment Leo's family, pedigree, new status as heir presumptive, and complete lack of accomplishments.

"Shame about Rupert," Craven said. "My condolences, Westrop. We were all quite shocked at his loss."

The mention nearly undid him. Leo clenched his teeth and nodded curtly. "No one more than I."

"Antiquarian, are you? How interesting." Craven said this in the polite tone of a man who believed all that was relevant in the world was the here and now, present decisions to be made, wars to be won.

Leo's Uncle Waringford was the same. The marquess truly could not comprehend how Leo was drawn to the past, or how he believed the answers to be found there could be illuminating. To such men Leo was merely a dilettante, pursuing idle pleasures, while they were the robust, vital men who shaped the workings of the world.

"I'm interested in some features on your Uffington property," Leo said anyway. "Particularly Wayland Smith's Cave near the White Horse. I've been hoping to look inside the mound and see if there's—"

"A secret hoard of treasure, buried with a Viking king? By all means, dig away if you wish," Craven said. "Write my steward. He'll supply what you require."

Leo blinked. Could it be that easy? He felt like a bull pacing his enclosure only to find the gate suddenly swinging open.

He almost didn't dare go through. When had the Fates simply handed him what he wanted?

"Thank you," he managed.

Craven nodded in Lillian's direction. "If you're anything like her group, you'll have a care, you won't bother the farmers, and you'll have things tidied up when you leave. Don't see any reason someone shouldn't have a crack at it. Though if you do find a Viking hoard, you'll recall that it's my property, eh?"

"Of course," Leo hastened to say. "Though it's likely that any barrow predates the Vikings and even the Saxons, and was more likely a construction by the tribes the Romans found when they—"

"I say, there's Prinny, swanning about the gallery," Craven said. "Forgive me, Westrop, I need to talk to him about the uprising in Ireland. I'll direct my steward to furnish whatever you need. Miss Gower, I expect an invitation to your wedding." He clicked his heels in a bow, then strode away.

"My goodness," Lillian murmured. "Prince George is here? Lady Jersey must be in attendance. Aunt Giles will be in transports if she gets a glimpse of either of them."

Leo stood stunned. "I've been trying to get permission to dig at Wayland Smith's Cave for over a year," he said. "And you... you simply walk up and smile from behind your fan, and Craven grants your request out of hand."

"Your request," she reminded him. "I merely made the introduction. What do you hope to find?"

He gazed into her face, so lovely. "Answers. You have smoothed my way yet again, Miss Gower. How might I repay you?"

He wanted to spread his hand alongside her face, touch that damask skin, and kiss her. Her lips parted on a soft breath, as if she wanted him to.

"My florilegium," she said. "Once I have the plates in my hand, I will consider your part of the bargain discharged."

And she would have no further use for him. Leo's heart gave a frantic jerk. The jesters who had entered their bets in the book at Brooks would be collecting their wagers, all because he didn't know how to woo.

"Are you free tomorrow?"

"Tomorrow I've arranged a visit to the Chelsea Physic Garden, where I'm told they have a calceolus. It should be in bloom right now, which will be to my benefit."

"I will escort you."

"There's no need."

"I insist."

"You have an excavation to prepare for."

Yes, thanks to her. And the occupation would take him away from her for weeks, if not months. Meanwhile, other men, rogues and scoundrels, would be circling her, sniffing with interest. Unless he could persuade her to remain engaged to him.

But when he returned—what then? What would he have to offer her? He had no right to ask her to wait for him.

But he wanted her to. He wanted *her*.

He leaned closer without knowing he did so. His breath stirred the tiny hairs curling above her ear. "I made a promise, Lillian."

Her eyelids lowered, and her lips parted on an exhaled breath. He *felt* the tendril inside her unfurling, reaching toward him.

"Oh, very well then," she said.

He took his leave of her before he lost his hold on himself completely and found a shadowed corner to press her against the wall with his body and commence the exploration he wanted to make of her mouth, and her other secret places. He had what he'd come for: Craven's permission to excavate the barrow. He couldn't debauch a gently bred young woman that he didn't intend to marry. If he were discovered devouring Lillian Gower in one of the Duchess of Highcastle's rococo drawing rooms, there would be no hope of her quietly jilting him.

He had to remain the sensible one, the Westrop with a head on his shoulders. He had to prove he hadn't inherited his father's blood or propensities. He had to show he was diligent, dedicated, and could focus on the mission.

The mission that was going to tear a piece of his heart from him when he left Lillian Gower behind.

CHAPTER EIGHT

Westrop's face when Lillian entered the drawing room of Gower House confirmed something she both longed for and feared.

He no longer looked at her as if she were the float that would save him from sinking, a means to an end. He regarded her as if he *saw* her. As a person. As a woman.

It would not do for her to harbor fantastical notions of an attachment growing between them. She need only look at the man, the firm oval of his face and the flare of his jaw, those lips that had been so soft when she kissed him—good heavens, had she gone daft that day? His eyes gleamed like peridots above the olive-green redingote with its velvet lapels. In buff pantaloons and tall boots, he was tall, commanding, powerful, beautiful. The very image of a gentleman of fashion.

Such gentlemen existed far from the realms inhabited by plain Lillian Gower.

Once this farce of an engagement was over, she'd never see him again. The thought brought a pang of jealous loss, and she scolded herself as he made his bows to her aunt. She would *not* be a goose. She would not throw her heart on a string after him, to be left dangling when he cut rope. She had seen the number of young ladies—and older ones, too—casting admiring glances at him last night, hoping to catch his eye. Pudding knees might be an affliction many women suffered in the presence of Leo Westrop.

She wanted her florilegium. She wanted to remain steady, calm Lillian, the eye of the storm. She did not want to find the edges of herself floating away, melted by his attention, seduced by his charm. She would cling to her sense of self-preservation.

"Shall we, my dear?"

She lifted her chin. The endearment was doing it too brown. He needn't perform before her aunt, who'd said more than once that Lillian had no business being wife to a would-be marquess, having no family lineage, no wealth, no beauty to recommend her, and certainly no great talents of her own.

But she *was* a rather good botanical artist. Good enough to be published. Lillian tucked the leather bag holding her sketchbook against her chest like a shield between her and the uncaring world.

"I am ready."

He held out his arm, and she hesitated.

This would be easier if he were one of those men who couldn't see past her breasts. She knew how to hold her guard against a man's lust.

The problem was the pudding. Being near him made her feel as if she'd eaten something peppery and her head and belly were departing her body at the same time, in different directions.

Oh, she would *not* be a goose. Lillian grasped his arm like the handle of a pan she meant to take out of the oven. "Hex?"

Hester rose and shook out the skirts of her simple round gown. She looked adorable and young in a short, fitted jacket, with a straw capote shaping her head.

"Persian apple pasty," she said to Westrop, her lips in a solemn line.

He regarded her with equal solemnity. "Persian apple—perfume."

He grinned as Hester broke into laughter, and Lillian felt something even more treacherous than desire. His kindness to Hex removed one of the glass panes shielding her heart. Worse than feeling attracted would be *liking* the man. When she knew he wasn't hers, and never would be.

He drove his curricle down Drury Lane, past the theatre where she'd enjoyed the plays and most certainly had not been wondering where Westrop was, if he were thinking of her. They circled St. Mary le Strand, with its stacked steeple and round portico, and Westrop drove them through the colonnaded gates into the grand yard of Somerset House. Lillian stared at the palatial building, a vast expanse of arches and windows, entablatures and new brick, a bastion of knowledge and progress and order.

"The Society of Antiquaries meets here," Westrop said. "I hope to become a member. Perhaps if I find something of note at Wayland Smith's Cave, I'll be nominated."

"The Royal Academy of Arts has its rooms here also, does it not? My uncle brought me once to see Mary Lawrence's botanical illustrations," Lillian said. "I should love to exhibit at the Academy one day."

Dismounting, he turned to help her, then Hester, out of the curricle. "I should like to see your drawings, Miss Gower."

His hands were firm, capable hands. This close, her senses filled with him: the trace of citrus in his scent, the way his sideburns shaped his strong jaw, the way his height made her feel both safe and bold.

An unholy glow appeared in his eyes as he looked down at

her. As if he were recalling that brief kiss in the glasshouse, just as she was.

"When my florilegium is published, you may purchase a copy, Mr. Westrop."

She fanned herself, glad for the high neckline of her round gown, the protection of the buttercup yellow half-robe that covered her shoulders and flowed down her back. A matching yellow cap completed her walking costume. She'd dressed considering the weather in the garden, with the breezes off the Thames. Now her costume was a guard against Westrop's too-knowing gaze. Hiding the flush of her skin when that gaze moved over her, as if he were absorbing every detail, the way she'd imprinted her mind with him.

"Why are we leaving the carriage here?" Hester asked.

"Because I trust these mews to guard my rig and not sell my vehicle, nor my cattle, while we're away." Westrop led them around the massive south wing to the terrace, past the fashionable people on promenade, then down the stone stairs that descended straight into the river, where they were met by the smell of wet and mud and fish.

There were all manner of boats pulled up near the stairs, with watermen hawking the open boats and ferrymen hustling their patrons into the hired craft. Some were veritable pleasure barges, with cabins and a roof, but Westrop pointed to one of the sleek, open wherries. "There."

Hester widened her eyes. "Oh."

Westrop raised his brows. "You don't like boats?"

"She's never been on one," Lillian said.

"You live in London."

"We live in South Wales, sir," Lillian retorted.

"Which is surrounded by an even greater water."

"Wading in the water is quite different than riding upon it."

She met his gaze with a challenge. This was where he

proved what sort of man he was. The arrogant sort who would tell Hex how to feel about things and would insist on his own convenience. The sort who would wheedle until he got his way. The sort who would throw a tantrum and rail against female whims and obstinacy.

Westrop met her stare. His eyes reflected the murky gray green of the river, with what looked like a dark blue rim around the iris. Strange, changeable eyes, yet she had the suspicion there was nothing erratic or unpredictable about him. He seemed a man steady as clockwork, reliable as the sun.

He nodded. "Very well. It's a fair sight longer to go by road, but I could take you through St. James Park, past Buckingham House."

"I want to try the boat," Hester decided.

Lillian took her cousin's hand. "Hex. Are you certain?"

"Will it rock?"

"A fair bit, I'm sure."

"And will it smell like fish the whole way?"

"Most assuredly," Westrop affirmed. "And there's a great whoosh when you go beneath Westminster Bridge at certain times. Nothing like the currents around Battersea, I'm told, but a ride all the same."

Hester's eyes flared, and she tugged Lillian's hand. "Lil. I want to whoosh."

Lillian bit her lip. "Hex—"

"We can stop and get out at any time," Westrop said gently, as if he were reading her thoughts. "There are stairs all along the river, and a great stretch of wharves. You forget the Thames was the first and is still the most important highway in London."

"The first?" Hester asked, looking over the boats with new interest.

Westrop beckoned one of the watermen watching them. "Why do you suppose the Tower of London was situated where it is? The Romans built Londinium on the river, but I'd wager gold they built atop a city that already existed. You've got a great tidal river that can ferry goods out as well as bring people in, and it lies in a great fertile belt of land. I imagine that if you could pluck up all the buildings of the old City, you'd find mounds and forts beneath that are older than history."

Hester watched him with interest. "I like your job," she said.

"Thank you, I think."

"Better than Lil's," Hester added. "All she talks about is plants. Buildings are much more interesting."

"I beg your pardon," Lillian said, but the matter was finished. Westrop, with his chatter, had managed to quell Hester's nervousness, while arranging their fare at the same time. He took Lillian's hand to help her into the small wooden boat.

"We'll sit at the bow, and Miss Giles can sit behind us. There will be less movement closer to the middle." He winked. "And we can persuade her otherwise if she decides she wants to swim."

Hester wrinkled her nose. "I'm not going to swim in *that*. There are dead things in it. And garbage. And fish."

One of their watermen, the one who'd spoken with Westrop, had red hair and tanned, freckled skin. The other had dark brown skin and curly hair. He gave a polite nod in response to Lillian's greeting. After the passengers had seated themselves, the watermen took their place at the oars and, in a well-rehearsed movement, shot their boat out of the throng into the center of the river. Lillian, thrilled and alarmed, grabbed for the nearest solid surface. It happened to be Westrop.

He grinned down at her, evidencing no concern that she had placed her hands on his person. "I won't let you fall in," he said.

"I don't expect I will. It's only—it's been an age since I've been boating. How are you, Hex?"

"Grand," Hester said, twisting about to look in every direction at once. "I can see St. Paul's."

"You'll see more," Westrop promised. "We'll go past the Adelphi Terrace and Whitehall, and then, after the bridge, you'll see Westminster Hall and Lambeth Palace, where the Archbishop of Canterbury lives."

"And I'm not sick at all," Hester marveled. "Yet."

The watermen kept up some stream of chatter between them, a language Lillian guessed was English, but riddled with so much dialect as to be nearly incomprehensible. "And they say Welsh is a strange language," she whispered to Westrop.

"Do you speak it?"

"No, but some of my uncle's tenants do, and many of the older villagers of St. Athan. I know the names of a few flowers, but little more."

"Plants," Westrop said, with a smile that was decidedly smug. "So much less interesting than buildings. I win."

She laughed, then did something she could only explain by being overcome with gratitude. She squeezed his arm against her bosom, as if she were a delighted child cradling a cat.

He hadn't been high-handed with Hex, nor selfish, nor petulant. He hadn't made cutting remarks about female unsteadiness or tried to shame her with exhortations to act her age. He'd simply offered her a way out.

Leo held very still, and Lillian grew conscious of how she clutched him. His gaze didn't drop to her breasts, though she was intensely aware of that part of her body, which suddenly felt hot and full, her nipples aching. His gaze roamed over her cheekbones, ears, and jaw, then lingered on her lips.

Heat coiled in her belly, stretching taut as ivy.

She let go of his arm.

Hester shrieked with laughter and clamped her hat to her head as the boatmen lined them up and they whooshed through one of the arches beneath Westminster Bridge, just as Leo promised. They regarded in somber reverence the medieval turrets of Westminster Hall, seat of British justice, with the spires of the great Abbey rising behind, keeping watch over its illustrious dead.

"Gothic monstrosity," Lillian whispered, and was gratified to see Leo's grin in response. That grin tugged at her belly as if there were a string attached between them.

Hester saw a flash of a red cassock on the balcony of Lambeth Palace and swore it was the archbishop. Leo agreed he must be out for a morning constitutional. They floated past the broad stretch of Tothill Fields, and Leo pointed out the landing for Vauxhall.

"Have you been? I should think you'd enjoy investigating the gardens."

"Aunt won't take us. She says the entertainments are frivolous, and you cannot be sure what, or who, you might stumble across."

"Your aunt would not last long on an archaeological expedition, would she?" Leo guessed, and Lillian shook her head with a rueful laugh.

"Are those the Neat Houses?" she asked, pointing across the opposite bank. "I'm told their produce supplies most of London."

"Have you an interest in seeing them? I could arrange it," Leo said. "If your interests extend to useful plants, and not merely the decorative sort."

"I beg your pardon, but that distinction is a mistake," Lillian answered. "Most plants combine beauty and function. They are both decorative *and* useful."

Lillian blushed again as he studied her. As if he wanted to

see beneath her skin, to her heart and mind and the passions stirring deep within.

"I suppose that is true of only some people," he said. "It is the rare specimen who can lay claim to both qualities."

Was that admiration in his tone? Perhaps she wanted too much to see it.

"Though one should be wary," she said, "as the function of plants can extend to both benefit and bane, at the same time. Very often a plant with healing properties can possess poisonous properties as well. Or the very essence that proves useful can become toxic, in too large of doses."

"That is true of some people as well. Toxic, in too large a dose. Yet I fancy there are some whose properties are wholly useful, besides being beautiful."

He was *flirting* with her. She didn't quite know what to do about it.

"Is that Ranelagh?" Lillian nodded toward the lines of trees with a rotunda showing between the foliage. "Aunt said she might be persuaded to take us there. She heard the entertainments are a bit more respectable, though the admission is higher."

"I shall take you whenever you wish."

"You'll be busy," Lillian retorted. "This must be Chelsea Hospital."

"Designed by Christopher Wren," Leo replied. "You must concede the beauty of a fine building."

"I concede that the gardens are very fine," Lillian replied. "A building may house the body, sir, but a garden nourishes the soul."

He chuckled, and the sound unseated something within her. It was quite unfair that his every gesture should make such an impression on her. She *must* not become a goose.

"I like that house." Hester pointed.

"Gough House, I believe. Belonged to the Baron Calthorpe, who died this spring, God rest him. Currently let by some nabob with the East India Company."

"I should like to live in a house that fine," Hester announced.

"Waringford Hall is finer, and you may visit anytime when your cousin marries me," Leo replied.

Hester's eyes widened. "Oh, how splendid. I shall do that." She turned to Lillian. "I should like to stay in a room that has pink paper, and have a sip of sherry before dinner, just like Mama."

"I can promise nothing, darling, as my *marriage* is a prospect far, far on the horizon."

Lillian shot daggers from her eyes at Westrop as the boatman rowed them toward a stair leading down from the riverbank. How dare he lead her cousin on in such a fashion? Lillian would be the one to break her heart with news that they wouldn't be invited to Waringford, not even as guests, once Lillian jilted Mr. Westrop.

As casually as if he didn't intend to crush both their hopes, Leo led the women up the stairs and through the black wrought iron gate set into a brick wall. Lillian caught her breath at her first sight of the garden.

Four cedar trees marked the corners of a small reflecting pool, shading a network of gravel paths dividing neat plots of green. In the center of the garden reared a statue of the man who had bought the Manor of Chelsea and leased it in perpetuity to the Worshipful Society of Apothecaries for the modest sum of five pounds a year, thus ensuring the gardens would always have a home.

"Who is that?" Hester tipped her head back to regard the statue, smiling beneficently down upon them.

"Sir Hans Sloane, physician and collector," Leo said. "He

sold his very extensive collection to the government on his death, for far less than what it was worth, on the condition that anyone, of any class level, should be able to view his curiosities."

"You know how you like hot milk in your chocolate, Hex?" Lillian turned slow circles as she took in the bounty surrounding her, overlooked by the blocky Tudor manor house and its glass wings. "Sir Hans is credited with that recipe."

"He learned it from the Jamaicans when he was there," Hester replied. "He didn't *invent* chocolate milk." She stared with some disapproval at the statue.

"Ah, Jamaica. Sloane described over eight hundred new species in his *Catalogue of Jamaican Plants*. Carl Linnaeus was so impressed he named a genus of flowering plants after Sloane. The *Sloanea*. Uncle has a copy of the Jamaican catalogue in his library."

"Sir Hans didn't *discover* them," Hester said fiercely. "They were already there. Just new to him."

"That is true." Lillian paused to replace a curl that the wind teased free of her hat.

"And his wife was rich from sugar plantations that enslaved Africans," Hester reported. "He wrote about the incredible cruelties that were inflicted on them. So that is where the money to buy all his wonderful things came from."

Soberly, all three of them regarded the statue. The waves of the river slapped against the stair, carrying the smells of mud and fish and the low voices of their boatmen, waiting in the shade. Birds called and twittered as they flitted about the cedar trees, which shed their delicious scent into the air, and insects droned in their early summer chorus. Sloane's expression had taken on a decidedly smug slant, the master of all he looked upon.

"I think of my tombs, and how we have no idea what lies within them, because whoever built them left no record," Leo remarked. "The Romans, if they didn't eradicate the earlier peoples, built over their monuments. Then the Saxons, then the Normans, and I am forgetting the Danes. The victors take the spoils and write the history, calling themselves discoverers and explorers, and the conquered—who speaks for them?"

Lillian swallowed. And now he was a thoughtful man, philosophical, attentive to the plight of others. She had to stop learning more about Westrop. It was a danger to her peace.

Hester turned to him. "I knew you had an interesting job," she said.

"I speak for the plants," Lillian protested. "Isn't that interesting?"

"Not really," Hester said.

Mr. John Fairbairn, the head gardener, hailed them with a smile, and Lillian soon gleaned that Leo had arranged for a personal tour. Fairbairn led them through the various garden plots, each with their separate function: the medicinal plants, ordered alphabetically; the beds of annuals and biennials; the perennial plants; the wilderness; the frames that sheltered the tender exotics. He showed them the bark stoves that warmed the plants from hotter climes and the glass case that housed the succulents.

In one corner, sheltered by the high brick walls, stood a tree only a few meters tall, its slender bole branching into graceful limbs bearing narrow, light green leaves. Lillian's mouth watered.

"The only fruiting olive tree in Britain is to be found here, in the Mediterranean garden," Fairbairn said with pride.

"The *only?*" Lillian tried to hide her dismay.

He nodded. "Don't seem to like containers, they don't. Prefer their roots in deep soil. In a pot, they'll flower, but they won't bear drupes."

Leo moved close to murmur in her ear. "We shall have to find a way to plant your olive tree, Miss Gower."

She shivered at the low, confiding tone in his voice. There was no *we* about this. There was no reason for him to recall her affection for olives, or her ambitions to cultivate her own tree. He was, after all, so *busy*.

He was only having this potent effect on her senses now because she'd spent the past week wondering where he was. Why he'd drawn her into a spurious engagement, then left her to face the gossip alone. He hadn't come to Highcastle House looking for her; he wanted Lord Craven. He was only here today because he'd made a bargain to help her publish her florilegium. Everything with him was about his expedition.

She refused to go weak in the knees over a man who was going to leave her. Damn his breathtaking, changeable eyes and steadfast, single-focused soul.

Lillian listened with one ear as Fairbairn showed them what he called the seminary for the young exotic plants. She had grown up playing second fiddle to antiquarian forays. She'd spent every birthday of her life on one dig or another. She wasn't high-born enough to be invited to a Queen's drawing room for her presentation, but she could have had a debut among some small society, perhaps Cardiff, or Bath, or Cheltenham, if her parents hadn't been so absorbed with poking about the ancient stones of Tinkinswood and St. Lythans.

She loved her parents, and she didn't regret a moment of her unconventional childhood, for it had made her a mature, self-reliant, sensible young woman, with a head full of knowledge, a backbone as firm as the rocks her father loved to clamber over, and a spirit as resilient as a young tree.

But she would not give herself to a future where she stood in the shadow of a husband's passions. If she ever acquired a husband—and to be truthful, such a possibility seemed distantly remote—he would cherish her. He would love her. He would build a life with her around their shared interests, rather than regarding her as a lovely and talented assistant.

As likely to find such a man as to get her olive tree to flower.

At long last, Fairbairn led them to the bulbous rooted flowers. "This is the one in which you have a special interest, Miss Gower? The Cypripedium calceolus." He chuckled. "I thought it was an *Epipactis* before it flowered. A hellebore. But now, there's no mistaking it."

"The largest flowering terrestrial orchid, at least in Britain." Lillian cooed in appreciation. "This is a fine one, nearly two feet tall."

"Oh," Hester said in delight, "it does look exactly like a lady's slipper! If the lady has a rather puffy foot."

"That is the labellum, and how Linneas named the species. *Cypri*, for Aphrodite, the Lady of Cyprus, and *pedium*, for foot. Isn't it lovely?" Lillian sank to her knees. "Ovate leaves, resupinated flowers. And look." She slipped a careful finger beneath the lip of one petal. "This is what I wanted to confirm. Two stamens—it's diandrous."

"You don't say." Fairbairn peered over her shoulder. "Two anthers? Not like the other orchids, then."

"And both fertile, from my observation," Lillian confirmed.

Leo made a small, muffled noise beside her, and she wondered why talk of reproduction dismayed him so. He didn't seem precious about other conversational topics, and for heaven's sake, the man had put a hand on her bottom to keep her from falling off a ladder.

She must not think about *that*. She focused on the flower.

"But this one has not propagated? She should spread via rhizome. That is what I have seen in the wild." Lillian pulled out her sketchbook and flipped through the pages.

"She?" Leo inquired.

"She is undoubtedly a lady, dainty yet powerful. Sure of her beauty, but not eager to divulge all her secrets." Lillian came to the page she wanted and pulled out her crayon.

"I'm told it may take a few years before she reproduces," Fairbairn said. "I've tried capturing the seeds, but with no success."

"I never had any luck propagating from seeds either," Lillian murmured. "I thank you for allowing me this chance to see one in flower, Mr. Fairbairn. I discussed my work with Mr. Bauer at Kew and he expressed doubt about the two stamens, which made me think I ought to revisit my drawings."

"Well, he is Austrian, so perhaps that's all he knows." Fairbairn watched her sketch. "You've a fair dab hand, Miss Gower."

Leo caught a handful of pages that slipped free of her notebook. "Lil—Miss Gower. These are strikingly well executed."

She looked up. "You sound surprised."

A smile pulled one corner of his mouth. "Shame on me if I am. I ought never have doubted you."

"But you did." Lillian narrowed her eyes at him, then went back to refining her sketch. "Never mind. Somehow, *I* am not surprised."

He studied the drawings in his hands while Lillian sketched, peered at the flower, sketched some more, and Fairbairn courteously escorted Hester while she wandered the gravel paths, pointing at whatever took her fancy.

"Lillian," Leo said at length. "These are *quite* good."

"Good enough to be published?" she challenged him. "These are only my base sketches. The ones for the book I've painted in full color, and I will need a quality engraver to capture all the details correctly."

"How long have you been studying orchids?"

"All my life." She moved to a new position to sketch from a different angle, extracting herself from his distracting heat.

"Like me and my barrows."

He sat regarding her, not the flower, and her concentration unraveled beneath his intent gaze. "I can't draw with you *watching* me," she said finally.

"I am observing the orchid. She is as beautiful as you say. Strong, dignified, graceful. Seductively elegant, yet she commands respect. There is nothing else to match her."

Lillian lifted her head to stare at him. His eyes glinted in the afternoon light, and the breeze from the river ruffled his neck-cloth. He had knelt in the path as carelessly as she, and he stayed with her, rather than wandering about on his own, becoming bored because no one was paying attention to him, making noise to draw attention to himself, as other gentlemen would.

He was also not studying the plant.

"She is unusual because of her size, but also her delicacy," Lillian said. "She is a complicated flower. The contrast of deep purple and bright gold is striking, but I adore the dots of color on her staminode—that is the part that looks like an upper lip. Those spots make her seem so demure."

His gaze lingered on Lillian's face. "Unusual indeed. But if she seems demure, I imagine that is what she wants us to see. She is a clever bloom. Hiding secrets."

Lillian dropped her attention to her sketchpad. Her hands felt unsteady. What was he *doing* to her? "I think you give her too much credit, sir."

"And I think you do not give her credit enough."

Hester's shoes appeared in the periphery of Lillian's vision. "I'm hungry."

"I'm almost done." Lillian jotted a few labels of the flower's organs and closed her sketchbook. "I've seen what I needed to see, thanks to the generosity of Mr. Fairbairn."

"And Mr. Westrop, who brought us here," Hester said.

"I am merely the agent to help Miss Gower realize her ambitions to publish." Leo rose in one movement, graceful and lithe as the cat he was named for. "I suspect her florilegium is art that demands to be seen." He held out her pages.

"You're relieved my book may be of passable quality," Lillian said dryly. "Since you entered our bargain quite blind, without being able to look in the horse's mouth."

"It's a fine, healthy horse, and I am increasingly realizing what an advantageous bargain I made. I see more and more benefits accruing to me."

"Why are you speaking of horses?" Hester asked. "There aren't any here."

"That is true." Leo turned her way. "What does your hunger require, Miss Giles? I see no Persian apples about."

She grinned at him. "I want ice cream."

"Persian apple ice cream?"

"Ice cream of any flavor." Hester chuckled. She was relaxed with Westrop, as she never was with strange men.

Lillian felt the bottom drop out of her stomach, as if she were hungry, too. It wasn't too much to ask that her cousin be treated with basic courtesy by her new acquaintances, yet all too often, basic courtesy seemed beyond them. But not Leo—Westrop.

Mr. Fairbairn took his leave and wandered off, with the request to have a copy of Lillian's florilegium once it was published. One of the boatmen escorted Hester down the stairs and settled her in the wherry.

Lillian paused beneath a cedar tree to tuck her pages into her sketchbook, then snug her sketchbook into her bag. The last thing she needed was for her work to be scattered along the Thames.

The scent of cedar intensified, and she looked up to find Westrop standing before her. A prickly heat ran along her neck beneath the layers of her gown and half-robe. The shade heightened the severe lines of his features, the slash of his cheekbones, the square jut of his jaw. More unsettling was the intensity of his gaze.

"I believe you have purposefully misled me, Miss Gower," he said.

His voice was a deep tenor, resonant, and hearing it struck an answering chord in her, as if she were a plucked string.

"I cannot imagine what you mean, Mr. Westrop."

"You let me believe you were an ordinary young lady with an interest in pretty flowers."

She positioned the strap of her bag across her breasts. "And so I am."

"You are a talented artist."

"It is not talent to draw something true to life."

"Yes, it is. I could not draw a figure if my life depended on the task."

She walked to the next cedar. A pied wagtail called from the riverbank with its distinctive *chirrup*, as if reminding her to hold up her chin.

"Is it my fault if a man sees only what he expects to see?"

"Are you accustomed to being underestimated?" He sounded stern.

"No. Usually, no one makes any estimation of me at all."

He drew closer. A shadow cloaked his jaw, the fine beginning of stubble. His lips were a shade a lady would envy. His breath smelled of wild mint.

He placed a finger alongside her jaw. Her skin wanted to lift away.

"I think you should kiss me again."

"Not *here*," Lillian squeaked.

"Then you must run away directly, because if you stand here a moment longer, I will kiss you, and I do not care who sees."

But there was no one to see them. The boatmen were settling Hester. The other boats passing on the river were too far away for the passengers to see them distinctly. Fairbairn had disappeared. They were Adam and Eve in the first garden, the only two people in existence, and she wanted his kiss more than she wanted her next breath.

She didn't answer. But she didn't pull away.

He stroked her jaw, tipping up her chin, and then he kissed her.

His lips were like a flower petal at first, cool and silky smooth. Breath escaped her at the gentle, fluttering touch. But heat rose instantly as his mouth opened against hers, and she found herself being devoured. Hers had been a chaste kiss pressed to his lips, the brief landing of a butterfly. His mouth was a well of pleasure, and she tumbled straight in.

She clung to his shoulders, sagging against him, and he took the invitation to press deeper. His tongue slid inside her mouth, and she nearly bit down in surprise. Instead she clamped her tongue around his, shocked, and his groan traveled from his chest directly to hers, the consequence of her arching against him, as close as she could possibly be. He stroked his tongue in her mouth in a rhythm that made her head cloud and her body tremble, a bright arrow of heat plunging from her mouth to her breasts to her belly, and lower still. This was possession, and she ached for more.

His mouth left hers. Lillian gasped for breath, then eventually, as the fog in her brain receded, opened her eyes.

He smiled at her, but there was something feral in his smile, and equally dazed, and triumphant, and hungry.

"You surprise me all over again, Lillian," he whispered.

She was about to ask what he meant when Hester's voice floated up from the riverside. "There's no ice cream here," she called.

Lillian blinked at him, trying to collect herself. She'd crossed some threshold, and now what she'd seen could never be unknown. "You," she floundered.

He offered her his arm. He was so solid and large and strong. "Yes."

"That," she tried again.

"Yes."

"We mustn't." She tried to sound firm as he escorted her down the stairs.

She focused on the steps so she didn't slip, then focused on not tipping over as she climbed into the wherry, so awash was she in dazed wonder. With the buzz in her head, she might have imagined the words he dropped in her ear as he took his seat next to her.

"Oh, my dear. But we *will*."

CHAPTER NINE

All Leo could think about was kissing Lillian Gower.

This was getting ridiculous.

As he checked off his list of supplies, he caught himself staring off in his library at the chair where she'd risen like a nymph from a river, a nimbus of golden light cast upon her hair and skin.

As he sat with other Dilettanti in Brooks, chatting with fellow antiquarians about their findings and methods, he saw Lillian in his mind's eye, kneeling in a bed of blooms, drawing the reproductive apparatus of orchids.

When he called at Gower House with his list of potential printers and found her glowing in her uncle's library, book in hand, the urge to draw her close was well-nigh irresistible. He wanted to press his palm against her soft, round bottom. He craved the intoxicating taste of her mouth, sherry and citrus.

Every time he smelled geraniums, blood rushed to his groin. This was intolerable.

The only solution was to get his campaign underway. Leave and let the bets in the book be damned. He couldn't sacrifice this opportunity to make something of himself, to make a find that would establish his career.

Besides, Lillian didn't want him.

No: she'd kissed him back. She wanted him, at least in that way.

But beyond *that*, she had no interest in him. She was simply waiting until she'd turned her work over to a printer, then she meant to jilt him and go about her life.

And he had no right to stop her. He had nothing to offer a woman of genteel status—nothing like what she deserved—and he oughtn't trifle with her affections, either. He'd uphold his end of their bargain—he couldn't think of himself as a gentleman if he did not—and then he must remove himself, and pine from afar, and curse, for the thousandth time, the profligacy of his father and other forebears who had left him with little but a distinguished name, which he would again drag through the mud of London gossip when Lillian jilted him.

He wouldn't add to the insult by making himself a fool.

London held over a hundred registered printers, Leo had discovered. Then there were those who ran their own presses, as Horace Walpole did at Strawberry Hill. Two publishers whom Lillian admired, Sowerby and Curtis, worked from their own premises, Sowerby from a room behind his house where he kept a shop of natural history curiosities, and Curtis from St. George's Crescent, whence the *Botanical Magazine* was issued. But they were too busy with their own publications to take on additional work.

And as Lillian had not the means to purchase a press, nor make her own copper-plate engravings, she required a printer. None were willing to take a risk on an unknown female.

But a great many, it turned out, were willing to enter discussions with Mr. Westrop, presumed heir to the Marquess of Waringford.

For this reason, Lillian wore a scowl on her face as they stood in Queen's Head Passage in the afternoon, with the shops of Paternoster Row behind them, the noise of the City all around them, and the majestic dome of St. Paul's looming at the end of the alley. Lillian looked very smart in her redingote, the color of a nectarine, with ribbons threading her bonnet and her bag with its precious pages clutched in her kid gloves.

She studied the shop window, lined with books for sale and the occasional broadside. "I've heard of this place."

"The Moor's bookshop," Leo said. "One can find the rarest of manuscripts here, as well as the highest quality prints. He is selective in the works he acquires, with an impeccable reputation."

"He works with the Duchess of Hunsdon and helps supply her antiquarian bookshop." Lillian anchored her bonnet against the wind. "She helped me procure a copy of Besler's book on the gardens of Eichstätt for Uncle's collection."

Leo wondered if the duchess's bookshop was where Lillian had run across that scoundrel Ned Delaval.

"Shall we go in? If you don't like this one, I'll find others."

Spending days with her was playing hell with Leo's intentions to behave with restraint. He was Odysseus chained to the mast of his mission, but Lillian Gower was a powerful siren's call. The velvet lappets crossing the bodice of her gown lifted in the breeze, and Leo fought the urge to grasp one and pull her to him, stealing a kiss from those raspberry lips.

He could not forget himself again. It would mean pain for both of them if he did.

She gazed at him with earnest eyes. "I appreciate this, Mr. Westrop. Very much."

The softness in her tone reeled him closer. "I vowed to find a publisher for your florilegium, and I shall."

"It is kind of you. Particularly when I know you are engaged with preparations for your expedition."

She asked frequent questions about his plans, showing real interest, and Leo enjoyed sharing his ideas with her. Very often she mentioned something her parents had done, or packed, that had him revising his mental list. She'd taken him to a shop that supplied her parents and the proprietor, recognizing her, had abandoned his other customers to show Leo the back room where he stored the best equipment.

Pretending he meant to marry Miss Gower was, so far, the cleverest thing Leo had ever done.

It was also the most dangerous to his mortal soul.

Her face was close as he looked down on her. Close enough that he could drop a kiss on her damask cheek. He considered it.

"You might call me Leo, you know."

He toppled into her eyes, those pools of blue, clear and vast as the sky of a Berkshire summer. "And you would call me Lillian?"

"It seems appropriate for those who are affianced."

She shook her head. "You and I both know the truth of that."

So much for his brief fantasy. Leo pushed open the door under the wooden placard advertising the Sign of the Scroll and with, a musical chime, ushered her inside.

The shop was tidy and well-kept. Light filtered through tall windows, motes of dust twirling in the golden shafts. Books piled and spilled over tall wooden shelves, with scrolls of parchment tucked neat as a beehive below. The shopkeeper, Mr. Masoud Karim, was tall, with a dignified bearing. Strands of silver shone in the dark hair showing beneath his turban. He wore a long cotton tunic with loose trousers beneath, attire recalling the traditional dress of his birthplace in Morocco, with comfortable leather slippers enclosing his feet. He nodded politely to Leo but advanced on Lillian with a broad smile.

"Miss Gower. I am delighted that Her Grace the Duchess of Hunsdon referred you to me. I saw the drawings you included with the baronet's treatise on starry stonewort, printed in the *Proceedings of the Linnean Society*. Beautiful detail."

"Thank you. They were only woodblock prints, and I thought my renderings rather rough, but they illustrated my uncle's points."

A becoming blush pinkened Lillian's cheek. She glanced at Leo, and he wondered if the low growl in his mind had emerged from his throat.

"You did not tell me you were previously published," he said.

"Under the aegis of my uncle only, which has made it difficult to strike out in my own name," Lillian replied. "That and the sad fact of my femaleness, I think."

"That did not stop Elizabeth Blackwell from publishing her *Herbal*." Karim nodded toward Lillian's bag, which she clutched to her like a shield. "May I see?"

"Mrs. Blackwell engraved her copper plates herself," Lillian murmured. "And then hand-colored them. I am not quite so brave or talented as to attempt intaglio printing myself, though I expect to add the colors at the end."

"After printing, but before binding," Mr. Karim agreed, holding out his hand for her leather-bound folio. With some hesitation, Lillian handed it over.

Mr. Karim then had the great fortune of being the first man to view Lillian's completed sketches. Leo envied him the privilege. He had asked to see her work, and she had shown him some pages but not the entire book—did she not trust him?

Or perhaps she did not think Leo able to appropriately judge the quality of her undertaking. The full florilegium was an honor reserved for Mr. Karim himself. The bookseller thumbed through the pages while Lillian held her breath, watching his face.

Leo wondered what *he* needed to do to win Lillian's riveted attention. He'd had it when he kissed her, but otherwise? He wanted to know where he stood with her.

"This is the most splendid depiction of the Cypripedioideae that I have seen, Miss Gower."

"You know your orchids," she breathed.

Karim chuckled. "I studied up only to impress you, after the duchess mentioned your work to me. Have you thought of examining the entire Orchidaceae?"

"That would be an immense undertaking. A life's work. I would adore it," Lillian said, and a note of sadness, or hesitation, threaded her honey voice. She gave the lappets of her redingote a nervous twist. "To be honest, I thought of beginning only with the calceolus, but my uncle encouraged me to branch out further. It is only a small book, I know, but I did not undertake the printing myself as I...I am not confident I would do it up right."

This hesitation did not at all match the young woman Leo knew her to be, who went toe to toe with him in their discussions and didn't back down from a challenge. He would have said, before they stepped into this shop, that Lillian Gower had a backbone of tempered steel. Whence this doubt in her own abilities, particularly concerning something he knew she loved?

He wanted to draw her aside and question her, but now was not the place. And he wasn't certain he had the right.

But *didn't* he have the right, as someone who cared for her?

Yes, he was coming to care for her. Very much. And it had to do with far more than the wildflower look of her, or her luscious shape, or the way that, even when she was standing in perfect innocence conversing with a shop owner, he wanted to kiss her.

"I can engrave the copper plates," Karim said confidently. "My son is learning a new technique called chromolithography, which would add the colors in layers, but I believe the superior approach would be to do engravings and have you color the pages yourself, Miss Gower. This is exquisite work."

The pink circled her collarbones and moved lower. "Thank you."

"I said as much myself," Leo put in, but she did not spare an admiring glance for him.

Soon the matter was settled with great satisfaction on both sides: Mr. Karim would proceed with the engravings and printing, then return the pages to Lillian for coloring, and he would then send the whole out for binding. Lillian handed over a pouch of coins—Leo had offered to help fund the project, but she refused—and once more they stood in Queen's Head Passage, with Lillian's scowl transformed to a beatific smile.

Leo held out his arm for her and was gratified when she took it, though Paternoster Row, where they had left his curricle, was only a few steps away.

"Lillian—Miss Gower. You are an exquisite artist. Even I can see that, with my untrained eye. Why have you no faith in your accomplishments?"

She fiddled with those velvety lappets once more. Leo had the strongest urge to draw one end across her skin and see what she would do.

"My accomplishments are not remarkable, in the grand scale of things."

He frowned in puzzlement. "You know a great deal about botany. You organized your uncle's library with authority."

"Authority over a very small realm." She faced the street. "Will that be your carriage? Your tiger is very dashing in his livery, for all that he is young. Wherever did you find him?"

He recognized she was firmly steering the conversation

away from herself. "It is more like he found me. I was kicking about Somerset House one day after a friend in the Society of Antiquaries admitted me to their rooms to use the library. We went to a new restaurant in Maiden Lane, Rules, as my friend had a taste for oysters. I walked home through Covent Garden, and this one insisted on being my link boy to light my way and protect me from thieves."

He lifted a hand to beckon the boy over. The lad complied straightaway, guiding the marquess's bay gelding, Atlas, in his traces.

"I wasn't so certain he wouldn't cut my pockets himself," Leo admitted, "but I made it home safe and sound, and apparently, he liked my payment because he was at the kitchen door the next morning looking for any work I could give him. I believe he likes being my tiger best. How old are you, Augustus? The lady wants to know."

"Ten and three years, sir, if me mother is honest, which I believe her to be, sir." Augustus patted the nose of the horse. "He likes me, sir, which makes me the man for this position, now don't it?"

Lillian smiled, no doubt at the swagger of this boy referring to himself as a man. "How do you do, Augustus." She held out her hand for the tiger to help her onto the high step of the curricle.

Leo was pleased to see that she didn't ignore the lad, as some ladies might a servant, or a boy with clear African roots, or both. Leo vaulted into the seat beside her and took the ribbons, and with pride in a job well done puffing out his striped waistcoat, Augustus clambered to his seat in the back.

Lillian twisted to address the boy. "Do you have family in town, Augustus?"

"Aye that, mum. M'father works at Gun Dock and m'mother at the brewhouse. The others do as they might."

"How many others?"

"Five brothers and sisters, mum. A good round half dozen, m'mother says."

"And what do they say about your employment with Mr. Westrop?"

"Don't bite 'im, don't cloy the lour, and don't knuckle to any ill treatment," Augustus said promptly.

"All excellent advice, I am sure." She turned to Leo with a smile. "Where are you taking us, Mr. Westrop?"

Leo cleared his throat, touched and a bit ashamed. He'd been guarding his fobs and pockets, not yet convinced his new tiger didn't mean to rob him. In less than a minute, Lillian had drawn out the boy's history and laid all fear to rest. A boy whose mother would advise him not to cheat or steal from his employer, nor tolerate abuse, was a boy Leo would choose to trust.

"Our direction is for you to decide, Miss Gower. We might go up Newgate Street and past the prisons, in which Augustus has expressed interest, or we might travel through the Churchyard to Fleet Street and perhaps find a book seller or coffee shop we wish to patronize. Or we might visit Lincoln's Inn Fields and enjoy the air."

It was as good as saying he didn't want to take her home yet, because he wanted the afternoon to spin out as long as possible. Now that printing of her florilegium had been arranged, he had no further excuse to dally in London.

She had no further reason to remain his betrothed.

Augustus leaned forward, eyes wide. "Lincoln's Inn? 'Sthat where the mumpers and rufflers work? I hear the beggars pretend they's crippled, then knock you down with their crutch and nip your bung."

Leo tucked away a smile at the boy's cant. "Half a century ago I believe you risked your life, or at least your pocketbook, to traverse the square, but since the rails have been put up, it's quite safe for us to take Miss Gower for a turn or two. A pity Miss Giles isn't with us today. There are some impressive buildings about the square that she could admire."

"Aunt Giles wanted her at home to take calls. She believes she can yet interest Hester in the social round. I ought to be there to support her." Lillian tucked her lower lip beneath her teeth, fingers worrying at her empty bag. "You needn't spend your time in frivolities with me, Mr. Westrop. I understand you have matters to attend to."

There was nothing he wanted more than to spend time with Lillian. Wasn't that an interesting realization.

"Surely you indulge the occasional impulse toward frivolity," Leo replied. "I should think you of an age to be properly disposed to all manner of wantonness, play, and complete absurdity."

"Perhaps that is true of my age, sir. But not me."

As Leo navigated the snarl of traffic thronging St. Paul's Churchyard—tradesmen, carters, visitors out to admire the great monument—Lillian leaned over and made a quick transaction with a young costermonger in her distinctive neckerchief and boots, calling out her singsong patter as she cradled a basket on her hip. Lillian straightened holding a twist of paper, which she opened to reveal pickled walnuts. She passed one to Augustus, then to Leo, and with some surprise, he took it.

"That was not a frivolous move?"

"Not at all, for now we have a treat to enjoy on our travels." She bit into a nut and made a face. "I've never had one. Aunt would not approve of simply buying wares off the street, and particularly an indulgence."

"Ah. So your aunt is the reason you are not frivolous."

"It is more that my parents—" She took another bite of her

walnut. "I do not know how to explain without sounding ungrateful."

"They do not condone frivolity? You may speak freely with me, Lillian. I am not a teller of tales."

She nibbled her nut as he steered them up Ludgate Street, then onto Ludgate Hill, passing the busy innyard of the Belle Sauvage and the looming hulk of Fleet Prison. She twisted to glance behind them at the dome of St. Paul's rising from the end of the street, like the eye of God always upon them, and her elbow brushed Leo's arm. She did not flinch or pull away at the contact, which he hoped was a signal of deepening trust.

"My parents." She passed another nut to Augustus, who crunched it eagerly. "Are not very practical people. Or rather, they are extremely sensible about their realm of interests, and have little regard for what lies outside that realm. I am an eminently practical person, so it has often fallen to me to look after things, you might say."

"I understand that feeling," Leo murmured.

She regarded him with wide eyes. "Do you?"

"There is Fleet Market, if you require any more fruits and vegetables. Or perhaps corn? I am not very daring, either," Leo said.

She handed him the last of the pickled walnuts. "You are organizing an archaeological expedition to study a legendary, nay, mythical place that has never before been explored. I can think of little that is more daring."

He spared a glance at her, though the traffic commanded his attention, Fleet Street being full of coaches, wagons, carts, sedan chairs, and pedestrians crossing where they would. "Using your own funds to finance printing of a treatise about a unique and very beautiful set of plants, for the edification of the masses?"

"Hardly daring," she scoffed. "Anyone with a pencil and colors, and access to a printing press, can create such a book."

"But not the contents. That comes from your own expertise, which it may be many others do not share. You ought to take the occasion to celebrate. You could be as known as the next Elizabeth Blackwell." Leo had never seen her *Herbal*, but he could ask Lillian if her uncle had the book, and therefore seize an excuse to call upon her one last time before he left.

The last time. A claw of something unfamiliar dug into Leo's chest.

"As Mr. Karim noted, my treatise is rather on the slender side." Lillian chewed her thumb and studied the passing shops, a lively assemblage of booksellers, printers, stationers, newspapers, taverns, and coffee houses, one sign advertising Ye Olde Cheshire Cheese, rebuilt 1667. "A proper florilegium would have more illustrations on offer, more subjects of study. Mrs. Blackwell's *Herbal* has five hundred plates. Perhaps I should not have been so eager to see mine in print. I could have done more."

"Or you can regard this as well begun, and do as much more as you wish at a later date," Leo said. "For now, you should revel in your victory."

"Perhaps." She was noncommittal in her answer, and he was reluctant to probe her silence. He had no right to know her secrets, and yet, he wanted to. He wanted to know every dimension of her, the veins of light and the veins of dark, the sunny gardens and the shadowed temples.

The man who won, truly won, Lillian Gower would be a lucky devil indeed.

They passed St. Dunstan-in-the-West, with its mechanized figures chiming the hour on the great clock, giants beating out the time with their clubs. He saw his time with her shrinking, shrinking.

What happened next was a blur. A dog darted from the pavement into the traffic thronging the intersection with Fleet

Street and Chancery Lane. A cart horse shied and thrashed in its traces, overturning the wagon attached, which crashed into a passing sedan chair and assorted pedestrians. Atlas, the bay gelding, reared with a scream of outrage, and suddenly the curricle tilted in the wrong direction. Leo dropped the ribbons and threw his arms around Lillian, certain that in a moment they would be thrown to the ground and crushed beneath a tangle of wheels, hooves, and feet.

Faster than Leo's eye could follow, Augustus was on the ground and at the horse's head, snatching his bridle to steady him. The horse regained his feet, and the curricle righted. The roaring in his ears receded. Leo comprehended that he had clenched Lillian to him, tighter than a prayer, and beneath his arm her heart pounded as swiftly as his own.

"Shh. It's all right. You're safe." Her hair smelled of lemons and apples, earthy and delicious.

"That was—what a tangle." Her voice shook as she surveyed the chaos, people shouting, dogs barking, horses bellowing and stamping, while people scrambled to right themselves and thieves swarmed the wagon's fallen wares, carrying away what they could despite the driver's shouted threats.

Augustus handed the ribbons up, his brown eyes wide with excitement. "Best take him up Chancery Lane, guv, and out of this hubbub. Lor, but we near had a tipup!"

"We would have, without your quick thinking. Thank you, Augustus."

Leo turned the curricle up Chancery Lane, where congestion was thicker, and the road needed improvement. Here the medieval character of the town was more in evidence, timbered buildings with their overhangs facing smooth edifices of brick. It was a tumultuous place, where the office of a rich solicitor might have a ladybird standing on his stoop, making her own solicitations to passersby. A pub reverberating with Whig rhetoric about freedom and man's rights might stand beside a coffee house catering to the Tory conservatives clinging to the ancient law and the *noblesse oblige* of the aristocrat.

The red brick rectangle of Lincoln's Inn appeared on their left, distinct in its Flemish bond facing and windows dressed in pale stone, and Leo slowed. The arched wooden doors to the courtyard of the Hall were shut tight, so he drove to the gate where the new Stone Buildings had gone up, majestic creamy brick and arched windows. Leo drew them to a halt, and Augustus jumped down to hold Atlas steady while Leo circled the curricle to help Lillian down. She felt firm and warm in his hands, a sure, solid weight in the world.

He wished he didn't have to let go.

"Leo," she breathed, staring at the gardens. "Mr. Westrop. This is lovely. Why are we here?"

"Do call me Leo. I need to steady my nerves and thought we could take a turn about the sights before I deliver you home. Come, we will look at the buildings first, then the gardens, and you might rule on which is the most impressive."

Leaving Augustus with instructions to walk Atlas about the square, as boy and horse were likely safe from tampering inside the enclave of one of London's oldest and most respected legal schools, Leo led Lillian toward the chapel. It felt natural to match his strides to hers, and she fit beside his body as if the space had been purposefully carved for her, her nose reaching his shoulder. She'd stopped shaking, and her face wore an expression of open wonder as she looked about them.

"Do not tell me you have an affection for this place," she teased. "Your old barrows and ditches must be far superior works to any place so excessively modern."

"Certainly. Behold the Stone Building. Scarcely decades old —such newfangledness. The chapel is practically new as well, built in 1620, if that stone is not there to mislead us. Did you know that when John Donne gave a sermon here, such a crowd came to see him that two people died in the crush?"

She shuddered. "I thought he was a love poet. Something about a flea? Or his mistress's clothes."

"You read the racy poems, then. He has some properly poetic lines. 'If ever any beauty I did see, which I desired, and got, 'twas but a dream of thee...'"

That was dangerously romantic. It sounded as if he were wooing her.

She appeared not to notice. "Why did you choose this place to stop?"

"I'm fond of it. I considered pursuing the law merely to spend time here. It feels—serene."

"Is the chapel *above* us?" she asked with some surprise as he led her through a brick archway into the cool, shadowed corridors of stone.

"So is the ceiling. Look up."

He held her arm while she craned her neck, and a small gasp escaped her. The sound had the same effect as a breath of air on a small flame. His awareness of her heightened, and he felt extraordinarily pleased to have pleased her. He ought to have learned his lesson about exerting himself to please others, yet Lillian's delight was as heady as fine wine.

"That's beautiful. It's so flowing, like the knots of fabric on a gown, yet made of stone. Remarkable."

"And below your boots, the bones of the hallowed dead who have made a contribution to this institution. Look."

She swept her skirts to the side, peering at the quilted pattern of stones under their feet. "It's a graveyard?"

"Do bones bother you?"

"I was raised by archaeologists, Mr. Westrop."

"But they do not always deal with human remains." He paused. "Do you...have plans to see your parents anytime soon?"

"Nothing certain." She glanced about the cool, quiet interior of the undercroft. "Could this entire building *fall* on us at any time?"

"Of course not. It's stood for nearly two centuries, and will likely stand for centuries more. Does this mean I oughtn't invite you to go digging about in barrows with me? They may turn out to be tombs. The tombs of great kings, full of treasure, but also, very likely, skeletons."

"You see why I prefer gardens." She tugged him toward one of the open archways and a patch of green beyond. "Broad, open spaces. Nothing to fall on your head save the occasional bird droppings."

"Miss Gower, you scandalize me."

"Well, it *is* a danger. Are these the gardens you promised?"

"There's a lovely walk this way, in the North Gardens. Nothing but gravel that way, in New Square, where the obelisk stands. And beyond are the Fields, which I hear are home to— what did he call them? Mumpers and rufflers? Thieves and pickpockets?"

"And beggars who are feigning their wounds, I hear." A smile puckered her lips at the corner, flashing those delicious dimples. "He is delightful, Lee—Mr. Westrop. What will you do with him while you are gone?"

"Pay him a retainer to resume my service when I return, I suppose. I expect to be gone the summer."

She was quiet at this, but followed as he led them up a tree-lined path through what had once been the kitchen gardens of the Inns. Another thing to Lillian's credit: she did not disdain walking. A healthy glow came to her cheeks at the exertion, but she made no complaint, merely kept pace with him, nodding at the other passersby who greeted them, students and teachers of the court going about their business, all of them, Leo didn't doubt, envying him his fair companion.

He tried to remember why he had never considered finding a companion for his life. Why he had been so certain he was not made for marriage. Happy marriages seemed rare, it was true, so was that why he had put the thought so far from his mind? Yet other people achieved such things in life. A home. A family. The company of a charming and sensible woman. Children who inherited their mother's dimples and blue eyes.

He caught Lillian's quick glance up at him, though she looked away at once. "What did you mean when you said you understood?" she asked shyly. "About my parents, that is."

"Ah." He swallowed the taste of pickled walnut, threatening to rise in his gorge. All at once the happy dream he'd begun spinning grew transparent and wafted away like the illusion it was. *This was why*, he reminded himself. This was the reason that fancies of happy husband hood and lifelong companionship were not for him.

CHAPTER TEN

Leo held Lillian's arm to him as they promenaded through the stand of stately English oaks. He knew, once he told her the truth, she'd see him differently. People always did. He couldn't escape the sins of his father any more than he could escape being the nephew and presumed heir of the Marquess of Waringford.

Their time together was ending anyway. He saw the gate ahead, looming like a dark tunnel in his path, an end to the light-filled, airy avenue they trod together.

"My father was not...what you would call a sober fellow," Leo said.

Few of the Westrop men were, at least in Leo's experience. A firstborn uncle, who died young, and his heir, who died even younger, might have matured into steady, respectable men, but one would never know now. The marquess was the model for a man of his class, losing no more than his pockets could bear at the gaming tables, never squiring a mistress where his wife or his wife's friends would see her. He provided his daughters with pin money and a coach of their own to share and ensured that men with less than respectable intentions, lineages, or fortunes never so much as looked at them, which perhaps explained why all three were yet unwed.

But Rupert's father had proved light-heeled when news reached them of a second family in the Americas. And Leo's father had been a notorious scoundrel, his reputation preceding him across several counties. That was enough to make Leo fear there was such a thing as bad blood, and he might have inherited it.

Rupert was their standout; Rupert went against the grain. He'd been loyal, brave, high-minded, if a bit of a hound for glory, but Rupert was gone, wasn't he. And that left Leo and his brother, Joshua, to steer the family toward respectable waters in hopes of eventually buffing out the stains on the Westrop name and, in time, contributing to the family coffers.

Only time would tell if Leo indeed bore the same strain of fickleness that seemed bequeathed through the Westrop blood.

"You seem to be." Lillian's Delft blue eyes were clear of contempt or condescension as she regarded him. "Sober, that is. Save for that wild momentary freak where you asked a complete stranger to marry you. Yet if your mother intended to force your hand, no one can blame you for arranging your own noose, as it were."

"You are not a noose." He squeezed her arm against his side, studying the quiet lane and the pocket of calm inside busy London. Lillian was like that, too: a deep pool of calm in a rushing world.

"My mother holds a great deal of sway over me, and she knows it. My father was, through most of my childhood, absent on...pursuits of his own." Pursuits that had brought nothing but indignity and debt to their family, but that was not worth saying. "I tried to supply what support for my mother I could. As a consequence, she became very closely involved in my life, even when I went away to Oxford. She feels she still has the right to govern me, as though I were yet in leading strings."

She paced alongside him, her skirts a quiet rustle, like the leaves swaying in the trees. "And you have not yet been able to establish your independence, even as an adult," she observed.

"That would require financial independence. My means come from my uncle, to some extent, and from my mother. Most of my resources go toward furthering my archaeological interests, which all in my family, save for my brother, think a complete waste of time. I had some trouble settling on a career, you might say, and so no one believes I am about anything useful in wishing to excavate in Uffington. They are all waiting to see what freak I take into my mind next."

"Is it a freak to you?" she asked softly.

"No. Rather I feel I've come across what I most want to do, and mean to keep at it, if I can. Given the resources and opportunity."

"Ah." They came to the end of the lane and, in unspoken agreement, turned about. "I have not established any independence from my family, either. As a woman, it is not expected that I would set up a household of my own."

"Do you wish to?"

"I am currently entertaining an offer of marriage," she said, with an arch look at him from beneath her cap. "But once that matter comes to its destined end, I shall have to give some thought to my future. I agreed to chaperone Hester during her debut season, but I hope my aunt will not press her to a second one. Which leaves me somewhat at loose ends, moving between the homes of my parents, my aunt, and my great-uncle, with no place of my own to land."

"Have you not thought about a husband? I thought it was the shared pursuit of damsels of a certain age. Perhaps the right shackle will give you the liberty to set up your household as you wish."

Not that *he* would be that shackle, of course. He knew he could not bear, ever, to fail another person the way his father had so repeatedly failed and disappointed him. Leo had long ago decided he would simply never put himself in that position.

"I do not think it is in the habit of husbands to be accommodating," Lillian remarked. "My father seems to be an exception in that, as in many things." They strolled through a patch of leafy shade, and she added, "They have written me. Happens that news of our engagement reached Wilshire. They invited me to join them whenever I wish, but said if I am too busy enjoying gadding about to pleasure gardens and parties with my betrothed, they will understand."

Leo wrestled with the tightening in his chest that accompanied this information, like grappling hooks tossed around his heart. He didn't know which line to pursue first. "Do you intend to join them?"

She frowned. "I want to, but I am concerned about leaving Hester. She doesn't enjoy the social activities my aunt forces on her. Taking her to the Physic Garden was such a treat for her, L —Westrop. Truly, it's the most delightful outing she's had in months. She said as much."

"I wonder what your parents think of *me*?" he couldn't stop himself asking.

She tucked her lips together, hiding a smile. The breeze stirred the curls peeking beneath her cap.

"They think I have reached awfully high, attaching myself to a Westrop."

"I suppose they too have wagers on when you will jilt me," he muttered. If Lillian were traveling to Wiltshire...her parents would not be coming to London, where he could speak to them, learn from them.

Prove himself worthy of the hand of their daughter.

She turned to him. "Put your own wager in the book, and I will ensure you win it."

He stared into her face—so innocent, so calculating. There were so many facets to this woman that kept emerging. So many depths.

"I believe that is cheating."

Her eyes gleamed with mischief. "And you won't presume to strip a coin or two from people who would make wagers on your heart? Very well. I respect the nobility of that sentiment." She resumed walking, steering him along.

"Would you," he began, and then fell silent. She arched a brow at him. "Would you like to see the Sardinian Embassy Chapel? I hear it is stuffed with silver plate and art from all those wealthy Catholics."

"And I hear the chapel is closed. Someone at the Highcastle soiree told me the Sardinian ambassador is trying to let the house."

Their last afternoon was slipping away. They'd walked the gardens. He'd shown her the chapel. Gower House was not far, a short jaunt down Holborn. Would she invite him to stay for tea once he took her home? Did she want *anything* from him?

But he had nothing to offer. There was nothing he could give her—including kisses—that wouldn't make him seem a rogue without a more substantial promise to follow. He didn't have the income to keep her in ease, and he didn't have the poetic bent that made him susceptible to falling in love and overlooking all the practical considerations. He couldn't risk becoming his father. If he hurt Lillian, the only woman he'd ever felt this kind of connection with—he'd do himself in first to prevent that ever happening.

Yet the thought of letting her go was agony.

He looked around for Augustus and saw the boy holding the

head of Atlas and chatting with a young man, an aspirant to the bar from the look of him, admiring the marquess's fine rig and cattle.

"Miss Gower. Lillian." Leo pulled her arm close to his body. Layers of fabric separated her flesh from his, and yet her nearness, the very *fact* of her beside him, toppled sense. "I don't suppose you would wait for me? Until I return from my dig. In the fall."

Two tiny lines appeared between her brows. "You mean... wait until autumn to sever our engagement?"

He let out a breath. "Yes."

"Why?"

"To...to thumb our noses at all the bets in the book saying our engagement isn't real."

"But it's not real."

She had warned him she was practical. Driven by good sense. He had not thought to find those admirable qualities so very frustrating.

"You have so very many other men lining up for your hand? Suitors you might rather consider?"

"No. Well...that is to say..."

He found himself drawn taut as a bow string, gripped with fury. "There is someone." Arendale's brother. That scoundrel Ned Delaval. Or Craven himself, good old Wim Wim, known to have an eye for a beautiful figure, the baronial bastard.

She glanced toward the brick building of the Hall, serene in its splendor and self-importance. "You have made me a curiosity. So many people want to know what might have possessed Mr. Westrop to offer for...someone like me."

"Someone like *what*, exactly? What is it you are presumed to be?"

"A very unlikely bride for a would-be marquess."

He set his teeth together. Her thoughts ran too much in line with his mother's dismissal of her, and there was that title again, casting an ominous shadow over his life.

"A couple's suitability is for the two of them to determine, wouldn't you say?"

"And for all their friends to wonder about, not to mention becoming a spectacle for society at large."

"I see. And you wish to cease being a spectacle."

She nodded, one brief tilt of her head. "There have been pleasant moments. I *do* wish to tour Charles Grenville's gardens at Paddington Green. I would very much like to see the orchid that Mr. Falstead's sister has discovered. But as for the rest of it, the attention, the scrutiny—it makes me very uncomfortable."

"So we simply go our separate ways." He still had a tight hold of her arm, he realized when she tried subtly to disentangle herself. Caught by a stubborn impulse, he refused to release her. He wanted her to *stay* with him, damn it.

"We are going our separate ways in any case, Mr. Westrop," she said gently. "You are engaged to oversee your dig, and I...I will go where my family needs me."

This was a facer, the neat, swift blow that severed a diseased limb or a gall from a tree.

She didn't want more time with him.

There was nothing to do after that but help her into the carriage, and Leo clung to the brief, warm press of her palm in his hand, savored the softness of her body beside his on the narrow seat as Atlas clipped the short distance down High Holborn. There was a danger in being near her. Lillian Gower threatened to reorient his priorities. She reordered what he wanted, channeling his desires into territory previously unknown. Like the way he could think of little but kissing her again, and what reason he might find to call upon her when he returned from his dig.

Months from now. When she might have forgotten about

him. Might already—the thought made his blood ice—have accepted a proposal, a real one this time, from someone else.

He opened the door of Gower House to shouting.

It was so unlike the generally placid atmosphere of the Tudor mansion that at first Leo thought he might have entered the wrong home. He considered shutting the portal and reopening it, save the urgency of the voices caught his attention. Lillian pushed past him, a fleeting impression of geraniums and warmth.

"What is the matter?" she called, alarm in her tone.

"In her own home! And this is the way he treats her." The housemaid, Sarey, held a broom and waved it in the direction of a short, corpulent man emerging from the small parlor where Mrs. Giles received her callers. He wore a harried, aggrieved expression, but it was nothing compared to Sarey's wrath.

"An innocent child. Only a cad would take such advantage." That must be the cook beside her, flapping a length of cloth near the gentleman's face. She had umber skin and warm, deep brown eyes currently snapping with anger beneath a delicate lace cap. "Begone with you."

"Mrs. Giles!" the man panted. His periwig was askew, and he tugged a flamboyant waistcoat over a pair of tight breeches that clung to every curve and roll of his sturdy frame. "Is this the treatment I am to expect in your house? After I was so kind to your daughter?"

"Kind?" Sarey screeched. "That ain't kindness! That's the sort of business as a man pays for, an you knows it."

"Git on with you!" The cook shooed him like a cat. "Not in this house, no sir, not from a lord or anybody."

"How dare you! Both of you! You'll be turned off without a character for behaving like this. Lord Bacon, I beg you will ignore this fracas." Mrs. Giles rushed out of the second family parlor, hands twisted in her apron. "But what of Hester, your lordship? You spoke of an offer—"

"She don't want what he's offerin'!" Sarey snarled. "It ain't decent."

"No thank you, no, sir," the cook barked, and together they drove the man toward the doorway. Leo stepped aside, snaking an arm around Lillian. She stood stiffly against him.

"What's happened?" she demanded. "What has he done to Hester?"

"I didn't touch the gel!" Bacon sputtered.

Leo had seen the man in Brooks: a minor baron who bragged about his cattle and the women he'd bedded, treating them as interchangeable. He was known for making vulgar wagers, then not paying out when he lost, and word was he'd been refused custom at more than one tailor and boot shop where he'd run up considerable debt. He was a terrible choice for Hester, and even the most desperate of mothers had to see it.

"Where is she?" Lillian's voice turned ominous. "Where is Hex?"

"Lord Bacon." Mrs. Giles rushed toward them as Bacon hustled down the hallway, grabbing his hat from the table and clapping it on his head.

"Allow me, Mrs. Giles." Leo released Lillian with a short, half-conscious squeeze of reassurance. Following Bacon outside, he stepped onto the small stone porch of the house, pulling the heavy wooden door shut behind them.

"What happened, man?"

Bacon wheezed with indignation. "Led me on, that's what! Promised me a willing gel, biddable wife, not half bad a price for the dowry, either. Only making sure the chit was as pliable as I was told. Ain't making an offer for a stubborn wench, one as won't take the bit." He rearranged his hat, pulling it firmly onto his head. His wig, Leo noted, was threadbare and badly in need of powder. Bacon would do well to leave it off and update his wardrobe. He was living in a past decade.

"Miss Giles is neither a chit, nor a wench, nor a horse you are inspecting for purchase," Leo said coldly. "What exactly would prove she was *pliable*?"

"See here." Bacon's bluster shifted to uncertainty, and he swept a nervous glance up and down the busy street. "You won't mention a word of this in Brooks, eh?"

"Have you done anything I'd need to call you out for?" Leo asked in a pleasant tone.

Bacon released a bark of laughter. "From *you*? The meek one, the Westrop with no gumption? That would be the—" He apprehended Leo's narrowed eyes and shifted tack. "Not a matter of honor, I assure you, Westrop. Nothing like it. Just—no need to say a thing in the clubs or thereabout, you know?"

"I won't." Leo maintained his pleasant tone, though the steadiest Westrop, the one with the least gumption, wanted to latch his fingers around the man's throat. "On the condition that Miss Giles never encounters you again. And," he added, adding a blow which he knew Hester would approve, "next time abolition of the slave trade comes up in Lords, you vote in favor."

This time Bacon's bark sounded agonized. "You can't mean that, man! My plantations depend on slaves. I'd have no profits otherwise."

"Then I suppose you'll have to find a way not to profit from human misery," Leo said. "Good day, Bacon."

The man tugged at his coat in irritation and stormed down to the street, shouting and muttering by turns. "Chair!" he bellowed, then, "Madness! As if I'd shackle m'self to—*Chair!*"

Leo opened the door to find Mrs. Giles filling the corridor with her wrath, all but breathing fire. "I suppose you've sent him away? Ruining Hester's chances for good."

"You don't want him for a son-in-law, believe you me," Leo retorted. "He's under the hatches."

She crossed her arms, still glaring. "He's a peer and a lord of the realm."

"With pockets to let. In debt everywhere," Leo clarified. "He would make Hester's life a misery."

"My daughter is not your concern!" the widow huffed. "She is—"

"Very much my concern, as she is Lillian's. Now."

He turned to the staff, who appeared to have been waiting for him, expecting him to resolve the manner. A mixed rush of apprehension and pride snaked through Leo. This was familiar territory: sorting out domestic messes, cleaning up after a selfish, irresponsible man, left to pick up the pieces and be the gentleman of the house, even when he'd been too young for the burden.

"Tell me what you saw," he said gently.

The cook pointed at Sarey, her face solemn. "She peeped 'im. I's just taking her part. Man like that won't listen to one woman, but two harpies, we can get him to shift his sticks." She smiled with pride. "An we did, dint we now."

"Very effectively. I must say I approve," Leo said.

"Well, I most certainly do not! The nerve of you two, and him a baron beside —"

"A lord who was not behaving like a gentleman." Leo sliced through the widow's protest. "You'd best hope Hester was spared more than indignity. What happened, Sarey?" He turned to the maid.

Sarey curled her fingers around her broom handle, nostrils flaring with indignation. "Sitting too close," she muttered. "All them sweet little words. Saw him take her hand and put it on his thigh, and I knew what he was about."

Leo had no doubt Sarey did, as she made reference to a man's thigh without turning a hair.

"I am glad you intervened, and I think Lill—Miss Gower will approve as well. Where is she?"

"They's both in the small parlor, sir."

"We are not at home to callers, *sir*," Mrs. Giles said icily, her eyes shooting fire at him.

"How fortunate, then, that I am practically family."

Setting his hat on the table Bacon had vacated, Leo strode down the hall and entered the parlor where he had taken many a dish of tea. The dark wooden paneling and timbered ceiling dated to the house's inception, as did the thick, intricately patterned rug, though the wooden chairs had been lately upholstered and new cushions occupied the bench beneath the windows.

Hester sat on the floor behind an occasional table, back against a carved wooden panel, hands over her ears and eyes screwed shut. Lillian sat beside her, her half boots poking out from beneath her skirts. Leo looked away from the shapely curve of her ankles and calves in their clocked stockings—now was not the time to be noting such things.

"I won't marry him," Hester said with great firmness.

"Of course you won't." Lillian snorted. "You'd be Lady Bacon."

Hester's shoulder quivered. After a moment, Lillian said, gently probing, "You didn't like how he—treated you?"

"Said he wanted a wife he could pet," Hester said, loosening her hands. "And who would pet him. Said he'd show me how."

Lillian met Leo's eyes, and he saw the fire raging in her. He felt the same roaring need to charge in, sword swinging, to protect the women. *His* woman.

The meek Westrop no longer, it would seem.

"Anything beyond petting, Hex?" Lillian asked carefully.

"No, because that was when Sarey barged in, and I am glad she did." Hester leaned her head on her cousin's shoulder. "Did she bring tea?"

"We can ring for it," Leo said. "And Persian apple plum cake, if you wish."

Hester fluttered open her eyes to regard him. "Peaches and plums?" She shook her head. "You'll never learn, Leo."

An indefinable warmth moved through him, curling and furling in the region of his chest. A region he'd so long kept hardened against affection, against trust, holding himself fast against the wishes and demands of others as he tried to find his own way.

Suddenly, it felt wonderful to be trusted. To be relied on. It didn't feel like a shackle around his ankles, dragging him down into the mire.

"Miss Giles calls me Leo," he said, very gravely, to Lillian.

"She's addled by the thought of your outrageous concoction. As are we all."

She smiled, and the curve of her mouth stamped that warm feeling into place, perhaps permanently, beneath his skin. Like the vessels that circulated blood and essential bodily fluids, but this was a channel only Lillian, and her smile, could fill.

"I want tea," Hester decided. "And I don't want a Season any longer. I don't like these men Mama wants me to meet."

"I have a solution." Lillian hadn't moved perceptibly, but Leo sharpened his gaze on her, alerted by the shift in her tone.

"We'll go visit my mother and father," Lillian said. "At Stonehenge. They've asked me to visit, and you can come with. Wouldn't you like to see the great standing stones, Hex?"

"I would, but you know what Mama will say about chaperones and so on." Hester rolled her eyes. "Besides, how would we get there?"

"I will take you," Leo said.

"How is Hester?" Leo asked as they strolled along the sun-warmed wall of the gardens, all that remained of the once-magnificent Basing House.

She seemed always to be walking in gardens with him these days, Lillian thought. And here in Basingstoke, a day's coach ride away from London, there was no one to observe and report to Aunt Giles or his mother or the London gossips just how the supposedly affianced Mr. Westrop and Miss Gower were conducting themselves. They were Adam and Eve again, the first couple, granted paradise and nothing to do but enjoy it.

"Hester is well now. I thank God we arrived when we did, and Bacon did not have time to...press his case any further. It helps that you have given us a day of pause in our travels. Too much time in a coach makes her sick to her stomach."

"I'm willing to do whatever you ask, Lillian. You need only say it." He squeezed her hand gently against his side.

Lillian bobbed her head, speechless. Her pleasure at his admission—and the use of her name—plunged through her like a stray bolt of sun disappearing behind the gathering clouds.

She had begun, in her heart, calling him Leo. Because he

was no longer the stern, distant Mr. Westrop, presumed heir to a marquess, who stood on a pedestal too far away for her to reach. He was the man who'd brought her lists of printers and smoothed her way to meet Mr. Karim. He was the man who, like a god of war, had chased Bacon from the house for terrorizing Hester.

He was the man who reached out to catch her when he thought her falling off a ladder in her uncle's library. Who had snaked a surreptitious arm around her as their wherry whisked along the Thames, as if he would keep her from tumbling over the side.

He had reached for her, at the risk of his own safety, when his horse reared and upset the curricle. She'd never felt as safe and whole, as secure and grounded, as she did in his arms. When he'd kissed her in the Physic Garden he'd made her world rise and fly apart into pieces, then settle and reform around a new want. A new dream. A new passion.

For him.

"Did her mother show any remorse?" Leo asked.

They strolled along the red brick wall holding back the tangle that Basing House garden had become when its masters withdrew. Lillian had given up trying to identify any of the plants. The only living things about them were the browsing sheep that kept the grass cropped around the ruins, and the occasional shrub that dared poke up across land that had once held one of the grandest homes in England.

Hester stood a short distance away atop the old ringwork, a banked wall of dirt and grass once the foundation of the castle. She held her hat against the wind and gazed down into the interior plain, a figure slender, determined, and alone.

Lillian felt a bit guilty that she had Leo's arm. It felt natural to be linked to him. Worse: she wanted to touch him. It didn't feel, here, like they were playacting on a stage. It felt like they might be any visiting party taking in the local sights.

It felt like this—the two of them together—might be something real.

A dangerous yearning, yet it didn't feel imprudent, this wish to confide in him. She'd never, besides Hester and the occasional friend, had someone who listened to her.

"Aunt spent the day before our departure scolding me for being impetuous and thick-headed, and for putting Hester at risk. I am, by turns, flighty, foolish, hasty, overnice, too quick to perceive a slight, and too dull to perceive the advantages of a situation." She glanced at him. "How, I ask you, can I be too quick and too dull at the same time?"

His jaw boasted a slight shadow, and a trace of red where he'd nicked himself shaving. Underneath his broad, flat black hat, with the brim jauntily rolled up on one side, his hair gleamed russet brown. He was both casually appealing and a blow to the senses, and it was becoming harder to steel herself against the effect he had on her.

He was not a large man, but he had an air of quiet command that drew respect. The landlord at the Angel Inn in Basingstoke tripped over himself to give Mr. Westrop the best accommodations, and to determine whether they would be staying long enough to attend a dance. A Westrop in his assembly rooms was something the landlord could brag about for months.

He was an easy companion in travel, too. They'd departed the previous morning from the Swan with Two Necks in Cheapside, their hastily packed luggage loaded on the rack and an antiquated post boy mounted on the near horse of the pair pulling their hired chaise. Whatever flurry Lillian had been in to prepare, Leo had had double the arrangements to make, for he had to finish the packing for his expedition and dispatch everything north.

He'd told her, as the yellow post chaise rattled along the turnpike, about his stroke of good fortune in discovering a second-in-command in the form of Augustus's father. The man had extensive digging experience and was willing to uproot the entire family at a moment's notice. Leo would deposit Lillian and Hester in Amesbury, then travel to Berkshire to meet his baggage train and crew and pursue the excavations he'd been planning for years.

He would have his dream, and she would have—the memory of him.

"I think you are neither," Leo decided, watching Hester dally along the rim of the ringwork.

"Not quick?"

"Not overquick to judge." His eyes appeared green, as if he had absorbed the colors of the countryside. "And you are certainly not too dull to comprehend what your aunt is about. She wants Hester married, and she thinks status will cover a great many personal failings in a husband."

Others might see his power, but Lillian had come to see his softness. The humor in the lips that had pressed against hers. The indent that appeared between his thick brows when something troubled him. The bleakness in his eyes as he spoke of his father and the low opinion the rest of his family held of him, as his father's son.

He was doing her a favor, like the gentleman he was—a man with a greater sense of nobility and integrity than most—but she would not confuse that with esteem for her. He thought of her as a convenience; that was why he had proposed extending their false engagement. She could still be his shield.

Which is why she'd declined. Best to make the cut fast, clean and sharp, and let the wound begin to heal.

Yet here they were. Exploring a site of vanished ruins, something between companions and friends. When the landlady had listed ways they could entertain themselves for the day, it hadn't taken but a moment for Lillian and Leo to agree they both wanted to see the site of Basing House, destroyed in the Civil War. Ruins and history drew them both—another element they held in common. Another gossamer tie that bound them.

"I do know Aunt has set herself against me now. But I cannot let her force Hex to marry someone odious," Lillian reflected.

But if she were Hester's self-appointed guardian, that changed Lillian's vague plans for her own future. She needed to think, and it was difficult to remain logical with handsome Leo Westrop pulling her thoughts toward him, like a flower turning toward the sun.

"What will your parents say when we descend upon them?" he asked.

"That it is predictable of me to act rashly, and I have always been a vexation to my aunt." She pursed her lips. "That I am ever reacting out of emotion, without thinking through the consequences, but they love me despite my silliness."

Leo's gaze held surprise. "You are not *silly*."

His firm declaration warmed her belly as if she'd eaten spicy food. "You do not agree it is a bit fanciful to spend one's days sketching a flower, and devote one's resources to publishing a book about a single family of plants?"

"Recall your audience, if you please. Many think it absurd, even morbid, to go poking about lumps of earth." He swept out a hand to indicate the quiet green expanse around them.

His heat against her body was having a strange effect. Her blood had turned sluggish, her mind a haze of mist. Was she falling ill?

"It's hard to imagine that, just over a century ago, one of England's grandest homes stood here," Lillian remarked. "Now there is nothing left but the gatehouse, a barn, and those earthworks that Hex finds so fascinating."

"The Marquess of Winchester took pride in building a palace as grand as Hampton Court," Leo said. "He played host to Henry VIII and Queen Elizabeth, which was no doubt a strain on a man even as rich as he was. But Winchester was a Royalist, and when Cromwell's troops took him after a great siege during the war, they left nothing behind of the house. I expect the villagers helped, carrying away the bricks and furnishings to supply their own homes."

"What happened to the marquess?"

"Tossed in jail, though pardoned before he could be executed for a traitor. His heir, now the Duke of Bolton, packed up and moved to Hackworth, a short distance away. The locals tell me he has impressive gardens, likely in better shape than these. We could go see them, if you'd like."

"Perhaps the nephew of a marquess might go about knocking on a duke's doors," Lillian said. "The niece of a Welsh baronet will inquire when the house is open to the public, and pay the housekeeper a tip for a peek inside."

"You could marry high." Leo patted her hand. "You could be a duchess opening her door to the curious masses on public days."

"Have the marquesses of Waringford ever been considered for a dukedom?" she asked, intending to deflect fruitless talk of marriage. "It seems the next step."

He tightened his hold on her arm. "Are you asking if *I* might make you a duchess, Miss Gower? That seems awfully ambitious of you."

She lifted her chin at his teasing tone. "A wise girl knows her prospects before she submits to the shackle."

"Touché. To answer your question, the recent lords Waringford have done nothing to distinguish themselves. They rose to the title the same time Bolton did, and for the same reason—supporting William of Orange in the Glorious Revolution. But my grandsire's single accomplishment was convincing an heiress to be his bride, and my uncle followed in those footsteps."

"You would have a great deal of influence, were you to become the marquess." Lillian didn't have to think about measuring her pace to keep step with him; they seemed to fall naturally into a rhythm, and when they reached the end of the garden wall, they turned as if they were a pair of horses who had been sharing the harness for years. "You would have a vote in the House of Lords. You would have livings to dispense, and appointments to make, and influence over members of Parliament. Your voice could add weight to any number of causes."

"Causes which are more worthy of my time, instead of digging about in the dirt with my nasty old tombs?"

She startled at the bitter edge in his tone. "And now I sound just like your mother, don't I? I only mean to say, as Waringford, you should have as much liberty as you like. You could have a place in the Society of Antiquaries *and* influence in government. If you wished."

They walked in quiet for a moment. Clouds fringed the horizon, threatening a gloomy dusk later, but the golden glow of late afternoon light broke through. The breeze carried the scent of loamy earth and grasses. A yellowhammer landed on the wall, voicing its rhythmic chirp, tail twitching. Lillian wondered if the bird had a nest nearby.

The business was so easy for birds and animals. One spent one's days foraging for food and finding shelter. When the time was right, one courted a partner, or let oneself be courted. One built a home and raised offspring. A simple, natural rhythm, as old as life itself.

She felt free, too, in this open space, in this meadow waving with blooms of campion and chicory. This could almost be a courtship as they walked together, learned about, confided in one another.

"The marquess, my uncle, thinks the hot blood of the Westrops must have failed in me and my brother," Leo said after a while. "He suggested my father spent all his vitality in his romps and pranks, leaving nothing to his sons. The whole family thinks I am both staid and fickle, at the same time, because I tried so many careers, and settled on one so unpromising. Even my mother's family has a low opinion of me—she is the daughter of an earl, as she will be the first to tell you. They wish me to be better. More like Rupert and less like..."

"Less like what?" she asked softly.

He rubbed his free hand along his jaw, then gestured into the air. "Do you know how many artifacts lie here about Basingstoke? There's Winklebury Ring, a hillfort built before the Romans came. A long barrow near Down Grange that's never been investigated. The town's been a wool market for centuries, and the old Roman road passed close by. But there's an even older track just south of town, they call it Harrow Way, which likely carried on the tin trade since prehistoric times. The Greeks wrote about it."

Lillian watched a blackcock and his greyhen pace through the tall grass edging the wall, the male keeping an eye on them from beneath his red brow. The greyhen tucked after her more splendid companion, content to be under his direction, submit to his whims.

"That is what interests me," Leo said finally. "Learning that history. It seems important to know. To get a longer view of the time we live in." He gave her a searching glance. "What will you do, once we have joined your parents?"

"I—I suppose I will join in their excavation. Endeavor to make myself useful." As she always did.

He smiled, the corners of his mouth lifting in a way that

lifted the corners of her stomach, as if the two were connected somehow.

"I look forward to meeting your parents. I imagine I could learn much from them."

There was something stiff in those words, something guarded. As if he sensed she meant to push, he deflected. "You are always attentive to the needs of others, Lillian. What is it you want for yourself?"

"What do you mean, what do I want?"

The question shook her. Lillian was often called upon to decide for others: the black lace cap or the bonnet to make calls, which wine to serve at dinner, which maid to hire for her uncle's home or her father's, which trunk to pack the trowels and brushes.

She was very seldom consulted on what she wanted for herself.

She felt her pocket, where she had stashed her sketchbook and a crayon for sketching. A nebulous hope was taking shape, and she dared not peer too closely at a new desire she would only be denied. Lillian wasn't Leo's pair, or his mate. It wasn't simple for them, like the birds.

"I want my parents to be happy, for Hester to be safe, for my publication to be well received. I suppose I simply want more of what I have already. But also..." She debated revealing so much. He had already removed, or seen through, so many of the glass panes set up around her heart.

"I want what you want, I suppose. To learn about what interests me and share that knowledge. Help others see the beauty all about us. And feel—oh, it sounds so silly to say it, but in the end—I want to have done something that matters."

He lifted his brows, those dark, thick brows that could make him seem so intimidating, and his eyes gleamed with the last peek of sun. The breeze stirred the hairs at the back of her neck.

"I do not mean to suggest that caring for others doesn't matter," she hurried to say. "That is perhaps the greatest contribution any one person can make. But I wish for what you said—to add to our knowledge about the world."

He watched her, and his face held an expression she couldn't decipher. The line of his lashes darkened his eyes and his mouth quirked on one side.

"There is something else I want," he murmured.

The low rumble of his voice scattered her breath. "What?"

He tugged her arm, and Lillian followed him around the far corner of the garden, out of the breeze, and out of sight of Hester. Valerian and betony drifted to her nose. Her heart seesawed, alarm and breathless hope in equal measure.

He slid his fingers along her jaw, palm cupping her neck, thumb grazing the curve of her ear. Thought buzzed away like the bees on the flowers.

"I want to kiss you again."

"Oh." She peered up at him, her blood forming lazy, hot pools beneath her skin. It was the open air making her so bold, the intoxicating scent of wildflowers swishing around her skirts. And the sense that if she did not seize this moment and kiss Leo Westrop, she might never have the chance to touch him again.

"Very well."

His lips were smiling as they descended to hers, which she turned up to him in eager greeting. He tasted as delicious as last time, mint and a hint of spice. The heat of his mouth called up a craving she hadn't known she carried, a hunger for his particular sweetness. A soft moan escaped her and disappeared on his lips as he savored, caressed, stroked. Then his tongue dove into her mouth and she fell into him, into the kiss, as if tumbling into a deep pool.

Shivers danced up her spine as his hand slid around her waist, stroking the small of her back. Her legs turned to flower stems, barely able to hold her upright. His other hand cupped her head, angling her mouth open for his plundering. Waves of dizzy heat circled down through her body, and she fastened her fingers to the lapels of his coat, delirious. Westrop. *Leo.* Kissing her. Kissing her as if he'd been hungry for her, famished.

She leaned against the wall behind her, as firm as the plane of his chest. He danced his tongue with hers and she rose to meet him like a cloud of heat and air and sun.

She tugged at his collar, another small whimper escaping her throat. Her breasts ached when he slid a hand up her waist and cupped his hand over one. Her nipple puckered inside her stays. A tension she'd never known sprang up between her breast and the space between her legs, like the string in a pianoforte, thick and vibrating. She felt wanton and abandoned and thrilled. Leo was touching her.

"Hell's teeth, Lillian," he groaned against her mouth. "I've dreamed of this."

His hand against her breast, cupping, stroking, made her delirium rise, an enchanted fog that furled around them both. She drew his tongue deeply into her mouth, wanting more touch, more sensation, more of *him*.

"Yes," she whispered. "Oh, Leo." His name on her tongue was a delicious sweet, as delicious as the heat of his mouth. She wanted to kiss him for days.

She sucked on his tongue, trying to pull him inside of her, and he answered her call, lowering his body against hers. Her breath whooshed away. She was butter between two slabs of hard bread. He dragged his other hand down her front, sweeping her collarbones, squeezing her breast, sliding to her waist and then her rear. With a firm hand on her bottom he hitched her hips toward him and her mind staggered, reeled, at the invasion, the fullness, the hardness, the—

Oh.

He stilled with her and lifted his head. His eyes were glassy, unfocused, his mouth gleaming with damp from her mouth.

"I hurt you?" His words were ragged, a hint of wildness. As if he were groping for a thread of control, of sense, just as she was. Her heart sang that they were in this together, both equally lost, and yet—his body was heavy against hers. A warning.

"No," she muttered.

"Too much. Too soon. I've—" He stammered, his fingers slackening, releasing her, and she sensed him about to move away. If he did, the beautiful, soaring feeling would be lost, and she would plummet to earth. She curled her hands in the fabric of his coat and held tight.

"You're perfect. I want this. To feel you." She spoke as if she had a fever, the words hot and rushed. "Only—it's different this time."

A shadow moved in his eyes, and his hand on her bottom flexed, as if he'd taken a blow. "You've been with someone else."

"No." She pressed her face into his neck, hiding the sting of humiliation. Wishing she could wash it all away in the clean sweep of his scent, in the heady goodness he made her feel.

"There was..." She licked her lips. "A boy, once. One summer, on a dig with my parents. I was young. He was a bit older. He...liked to touch me." She squeezed her eyes shut. "I thought I was in love."

Leo turned his face toward hers, his cheek brushing her cheek. He freed one hand to stroke her hair. "He hurt you?"

"No. It was..." She breathed hard, the images sharp against her eyelids, as painful as they had been those years ago when she realized the way of it. His rubbing, his groping, his squeezing, his heavy breath—he'd been using her body for his pleasure. A tool, no more than a warm object for him to press himself against. A fabric pillow. A sheep.

"It was like it didn't matter that it was *me*," she said finally. "I am ashamed of it now."

His breath ruffled the hair at her temple. "And you fear I will be the same way."

"No." The word wisped out of her. She opened her mouth against his neck, giving in to the temptation to taste him. Salty. Warm. A sinful treat.

He drew back his head and sucked in his breath as she licked him. His body pressed against hers, that male part of him against her legs—she felt his hardness through her skirts. Alarming, yet welcome. She nestled closer.

"It is—different with you. Like you are *with* me. If that makes any sense."

He touched his mouth to her shoulder, as if he would devour her in turn, yet the thrill was not fear. A flutter of excitement for the unknown.

"I want to be with you," he murmured. "I've dreamed of holding you. Longed for it."

She'd dreamed the same, she realized now. The reason she'd come awake in the deep of night, her skin tingling, an ache in her belly. She longed for him to be molded to her, just like this.

"What do you want, Lillian?" he whispered.

Him. More of this, the delirium, the flying, the sense that her body had become warm cake batter, ready to sink into any mold. Yet there was caution there, too. They were outside, for heaven's sake. He was a Westrop, a mighty oak. She was a Gower, a meadow weed. Yet he fit against her. So well. And his mouth—

"Will you kiss me again?" she asked shyly, skimming her finger along the fold where his neckcloth met his neck. How firm his skin was, how warm, with a scent rising from him like bread ready to take from the oven. She wanted to sink in her teeth.

"I will kiss you for days, darling," he muttered, and dragged his cheek across hers as he sought her lips. She tipped her mouth up for his onslaught, and the dizzy heat catapulted through her, familiar, a taste she was greedy for. Their mouths danced a rhythm of take and receive, give and hold, a pairing of salty and sweet.

The heat climbed her like ivy, a prickle between her legs, and she shifted her hips, seeking ease. She brushed against his hardness, not his thigh, and that—that was what she wanted. On a gasp, she drew his tongue deeper into her mouth, plunging her hips against him, helpless against the tide that caught her. A bright, hot star appeared at the center of her legs, an apex, and it pulsed when he groaned against her lips.

Her mouth went dry. Her breath stuttered. She didn't know precisely what she ached for, but she felt hollow, as if she were a window thrown open and she wanted something to fill her. Wind. Light. An answer to the tremorous, treacherous melting of her thighs.

Suddenly Leo froze and straightened, as if he'd been bolt-shot, and Lillian stilled. His hands opened. He lifted his head. Carefully, as if untangling himself from vines, he stepped away, setting her on her feet—she'd been cradled against him, kneading him like a cat. The look on his face was one of pain, and cold washed through her.

"Too much," he said hoarsely, his eyes glazed as if he'd taken a blow to the head.

"I'm sorry," she stuttered. "I—"

"Not here," he said. It was as if he were having the same trouble stringing words together as she was. She pressed her hands to her cheeks as if she could smooth away her embarrass-ment. *She* was too much.

"I'm sorry," she gasped again.

"No—there's no reason—it's not you who should be sorry."

Quickly he dropped a kiss against her lips, in reassurance, or as if he couldn't help himself. "I'm—I need to stop."

"Of course." Her cheeks heated her fingers like an open flame. What a fool she was. Of course he didn't want to be devoured. She's been rubbing herself against him like a wanton, using him the way Timkin had excited himself with her. She knew how that felt. She was crass, and careless, and this was *Leo*, and—

"Whatever you're thinking, it's not true," he growled.

"I—it's not?" He couldn't know what she was thinking. She couldn't meet his eyes, instead patting down her redingote as if she could smooth the creases from where she'd been crushed against him. Had crushed herself. She might have brick powder on her back, and how would *that* look when they returned to the inn?

He brushed his lips across her forehead this time, as if he couldn't meet her eyes, either. But he gripped his hands to her upper arms and inhaled, as if he were breathing her in, and she went still with wonder, the panic subsiding. Her heart circled a few times, then settled.

"If I keep kissing you, keep touching you," he whispered, "I'll spend in my pantaloons, and it will leave a stain, and I do not want to explain that to your cousin or anyone."

"Spend—*oh*." He meant pleasure. What happened to a man in the throes. What Timkin had been striving for, against Lillian's body, while she stood there embarrassed and wooden, wondering what she was supposed to do.

She hadn't felt a bit wooden with Leo. She felt as flexible as meadow grass when it sang as the wind moved through.

"Then I suppose we ought to stop," she said primly, though that bright star pulsing in the unnamable place between her legs throbbed, *Don't stop! Follow this! Finish!*

He chuckled and rubbed his hands over her arms, squeezing

gently. "I am the sober Westrop, you know." This time he met her eyes, and his were bright green gray, an open grassland, a yawning moor. "Even more sober than my clerical brother. I am not overset by anything. Especially not a woman."

"Oh." What did he mean—he did not *like* being affected? Would he never touch her again? Never have this, never *feel*—

"You overset me," he murmured. "But in the very best way."

"Thank you—I think?"

She'd crushed his neckcloth in pulling him to her, clawing him closer. She made a valiant attempt to neaten the twist. "You overset me as well," she whispered.

"I would say that is only fair."

It happened again, the lift of his lips tugging her stomach upward, and she stood staring at him like a little twit, adoration in her eyes.

"But I suppose we should not do this again." Regret swelled her voice before she could stop it.

He slid one hand down her arm, placed her hand on the crook of his elbow, her chivalrous escort once again, save for the mischief that danced in his eyes. "Oh, I hope we will, Lillian. Not here, but again. Soon. Somewhere better."

They both turned, and Lillian, still working her way back from the faraway land she'd sailed to, tried not to shriek at the sight of Hester watching them curiously.

"Those are liberties, I suppose? You're missing out on everything. There are cellars, and old fishponds, and a set of stairs in the ruins," Hester reported. "And a set of bones or two buried in the dungeons, I don't doubt. But I should like to see if the barn has bats in it, wouldn't you? Lil," she added with some concern, "why is your face so red?"

CHAPTER TWELVE

"Westrop!" Lillian's father advanced across the private parlor of the George and extended his hand to Leo, a smile bringing out white lines against the tanned skin of his face. "Of the Waringford Westrops? Sevenhampton, near Highworth?"

"The same."

"Have the henge at Avebury on our list of places we want to excavate." Peter Gower pumped Leo's hand. "Only a day's ride by horse from Highworth, isn't it? Lots of barrows around there, too."

"I've my eye on one Stukeley wrote about at West Kennet, one Aubrey marked as well. I'd be interested in digging there, after I'm done at Uffington," Leo said easily.

"Following the steps of the masters, I see. Good lad. Must talk to William while you're here—Cunnington, I mean. He's quite careful, sound methods. Not one of those who goes in and levels a place looking for novelties." Peter discarded his hat on a small table and ran his hands through his hair, which he'd cropped short. Lillian suspected her mother had been his barber.

"I should be happy to learn as much as I can from him, sir. And yourself. And Mrs. Gower," Leo added, as her mother finally released Lillian and came to shake Leo's hand.

Lillian smiled to see her parents so cordial with him—and with her, after showing up only a day after the letter warning of their arrival. Leo chose to meet them at the George, one of several coaching inns in the High Street of Amesbury, a rather severe old building showing its Elizabethan roots in narrow windows and a timbered ceiling. The Westrop name had commanded use of the private parlor, which was very convenient, and the party had already been promised a dinner of trout fried in anchovies, rump roast, and pickled eels if they stayed.

Leo wouldn't be staying. The thought was a sharp presence, like the flat of a knife against her skin. If she breathed too deeply, it would cut her.

Her mother, always bold, held Leo's hands too long and looked him up and down. He was impeccably dressed, his coat brushed and buttons polished, his neckcloth clean and as white as the ruffles of his shirt beneath. The buckskin of his pantaloons hadn't a crease despite the hours of sitting, or how, the day before, Lillian had pressed herself against his thighs and—

She *had* to stop letting that image creep into her mind at all hours. She wore a constant blush, as if she were marked by what had passed between them. She couldn't deny a new awareness of him, the way she was aware of the weather, or the scent of smoke in the air. Leo threatened to crowd all else out of her consciousness, and she would exist only to orbit him, like the rocky moon circling a life-giving Earth.

That would indeed make her a goose, and a sorry one when he went away.

"And you're the man who offered for our Lillian," Alida said. She was a handsome woman whose accent betrayed her northern roots. The gleam of silver in her dark hair and the network of lines around her blue eyes spoke to a life lived richly, with great enjoyment.

"And yet we hadn't detected that you two were acquainted," she added. "Lil never mentioned you in any of her letters, so I hope you will allow we were somewhat surprised at the suddenness of your offer."

"Bah, we don't want to hear about the wooing, my love," Peter chortled. "We want to hear what the man is up to at Uffington. Would love to scratch a bit about the White Horse myself. Don't hold a bit with Wise saying it was built by Alfred the Great."

Her father was, any observer would immediately see, the source of Lillian's looks. She had his square shoulders and bold nose, his hair the color of spring mushrooms, his bright eyes. Those eyes showed all his curiosity about the world and its workings, if less for the inner workings of its people.

He leaned over Hester, who sat with her spine as rigid as one of the wooden armchairs, which appeared to have sat in this parlor for two hundred years. Peter affectionately knuckled the girl beneath her chin, though his voice changed to the coo one might use with an infant. "No, we don't believe that for a moment, do we, Hex? Dear old Alfred the Great was too busy fighting off Danes to bother with carving silly horses into silly hillsides."

Hester gazed back at him thoughtfully, then blew out a stream of air that ruffled the tiny curls of her forehead, exactly as if she were a horse being released from the saddle.

"I was told there would be cakes," Hester said.

"Aubrey suggested the horse could have been carved by Hengist and Horsa." Leo glanced at Lillian. "Those are—"

"The Jutish kings whom Vortigern let into Britain, and thus led to the Angles and Saxons overrunning of the country, much to his dismay." Lillian unpinned her hat, a clever little straw capote that she had furbished with flowers. "Horsa means horse, in their language, so presumably the chalk outline is a monument to him. I've read my *Brut*, Leo."

"Have you now?" His gaze scanned her heavy coils of hair. The look was nearly a caress. She felt again his hand cupping her jaw yesterday when he kissed her, and there went that flush again, creeping into crevices in her body that she didn't want to be aware of in the company of her cousin or parents.

"Hasn't everyone?" she returned.

Hester frowned. "I haven't. Thank goodness, here's tea."

Leo cleared his throat and returned his gaze to Peter as a maid bustled into the room in a frilled white apron and cap, a large tray cradled before her.

"I am more inclined to support Aubrey's other hypothesis, that the White Horse was built by the Celtic tribes. However, the landmark that interests me is Wayland Smith's Cave, an old stone monument about a mile and a half away."

"Indeed? Tell me more," Peter said.

"A prehistoric monument? Tell us both more," her mother prompted. Side by side, her parents gazed at Leo in expectation, ignoring the tea tray toward which Hester cast a look of hopeful anticipation. With a sigh, Lillian rose and took her place behind the tray, releasing the maid, who left with a bobbed curtsy and a brief glance of admiration at Leo. He did cut a fine figure in his London-tailored clothes, and Lillian guessed fine-looking men were thin on the ground in a small town like Amesbury, as much as heirs to the higher nobility.

"The cave's not nearly as interesting as Stonehenge," Leo said. "Though there's an interesting theory that it was named after the mythical Norse smith, one known to the Saxons also. The track that runs past it, the Ridgeway, has been a road for thousands of years. Local legend has it that if your horse lost a shoe while traveling, you could leave the horse and a coin at the smith overnight and find that Wayland had shod your horse in the morning. Thank you," he added, accepting the dish of tea that Lillian passed to him. He took a self-conscious sip, and his eyes widened. "You remembered."

"How you take your tea? Aunt asked you enough times, I ought to recall. Have you ever had a horse shod by Wayland?"

"No, and I know no one who has. Yet the legend persists."

"As legends do." Alida took a dish of tea from Lillian's hands and passed it to her husband, who settled himself in another of the armchairs. "What interests you about the cave, Mr. Westrop?"

"I think it might be a barrow. There's a certain arrangement to the ditch around it that suggests the outline of such to me, and the way the passage leading into the cave has been blocked up seems indicative of a burial site."

"Fascinating." Peter sipped his tea. "We're looking for remains at the henge, don't you know. Seems like it ought to be a monument to a great king, for all Stukeley had to say about the solstice arrangement and such. Grand design for a tomb, much like the pyramids reported in Egypt. Or, at the very least, an ancient temple like the Acropolis, in which case we ought to find some interesting old bones, wouldn't you say, my love?"

"I leave the bones to you, dear," Alida said. She gazed over the rim of her cup at Leo, blowing softly on her tea. "Who do you have to help you? And where did you secure your funding?"

"I am responsible for my own funding, at present, and have arranged my own crew." Leo glanced at Lillian, scraping sugar from the loaf for Hester's cup. "But I won't go on about my plans. Surely you wish to hear what your daughter has been doing. She's preparing to publish her florilegium, did you know?"

"Can't really call it a florilegium when it's just a few flowers, can you?" Peter smiled fondly. "Still, I'm glad to hear you're doing something with your sketches, old girl. Knew my uncle would help you. Lloyd's a brick, for all that he's as eccentric as that seaweed he loves."

"Have a care, Hex, it's hot." Lillian carried her dish to Hester. "As a matter of fact, Papa, Mr. Westrop is the one who found a printer willing to take me on. Mr. Karim, who runs the Sign of the Scroll, will do the engravings. He works with the Duchess of Hunsdon, helping to supply her antiquarian book-shop. She's promised to carry my volume, if I'm pleased with how it turns out."

"Of course it will be lovely, dear," Alida said with a warm smile. "Mr. Westrop, have you done any excavating prior to this?"

"Nothing of mention. Did you know that Lillian received an invitation from Charles Grenville to tour his garden? And we were conducted around the Chelsea Physic Garden by the head gardener himself. He was impressed by Lillian's knowledge of the lady's slipper orchid. Asked her questions about propagation and everything."

"Did he now? How kind of him." Her mother looked at Lillian with new attention. "Now that Lil is here, my dear," she said to her husband, "we can have her do our sketches."

"Shouldn't we just!" her father exclaimed. "The Parkers are fine lads for the digging, but not for the drawing."

"Lillian is quite a talented artist," Leo said, and the fierce set to his face made her heart turn over like a puppy showing its belly. He seemed determined to make her parents praise or notice her. The dear man. He would learn.

"She's not half bad," her father agreed, and her mother smiled.

"You see through the eyes of love. I'm so glad, Mr. Westrop. Lil, darling, of course we're delighted you're here, but I'm not certain where we'll put you. We're staying at the Diana House, an old gatehouse to the grounds of Amesbury Abbey—the quaintest old place, you must see it. The Duke of Queensberry isn't in residence at the moment—we've been told he likes where he is in Piccadilly—but it's fine enough for our needs, if a bit small. You and Hex can share the trundle bed, I suppose?"

"Of course," Lillian said, and finally poured her own tea.

The Gowers announced they would take the new arrivals to see their site, and the group adjourned into the coaching yard to climb aboard the cart. While her parents tried to coax Hester into mounting another moving vehicle so soon after freeing herself from the last one, Leo drew to her side, and Lillian took the opportunity to grant him a reprieve.

"You needn't accompany us if you don't wish. My parents will talk of nothing but soil and sarsen stones. It will quickly grow tedious, if you don't have an interest."

His gaze roamed each feature of her face, spurring that blush again. She really *must* stop thinking of kissing him. She had to operate like a normal woman in the world.

"You can't possibly be suggesting I miss the opportunity to see Stonehenge. Nor could you forget, I have a particular interest in seeing how your parents and Cunnington have undertaken their excavations." Indeed, he seemed alight with pleasure, nearly thrumming in anticipation. Much the opposite of Hester, who was still arguing about why she must go along.

"Very well, then, come along, and do try to keep up," Lillian said with a prim tuck of her lips, and appreciated the crack of his smile. "Hex, it will be worth the discomfort. It's a heap of great, massive stones built by the ancient Druids, far bigger than any circle you've seen. Much more impressive than Harold's Stones, which we passed in Monmouth when we were traveling to London from Wales."

Hester folded her arms across her chest. A stray breeze

lifted her brown curls against her bonnet. "*How* much more impressive?"

"Vastly," Leo said. "Come, and there will be Persian apple punch after."

Hester's lip twitched. "Persian apple syllabub, and I'll go."

"You are an incorrigible creature," Leo replied. "I can't think of a dish more ghastly. Up with you, and sit toward the front by your uncle, so the motion won't jar you as badly."

Peter turned from the board where he sat with the ribbons in hand, Alida beside him. "Come along, Hex, there's a good girl. And you two lovebirds, let's not waste the light."

The heat, the solidity of Leo's hand as he helped her into the cart made Lillian's mind blank of all but the sensation of his lips pressed against her, his hands on her hips. Good heavens, this was becoming untenable. Her body was warm dough rising in the pan.

She took a seat near Hester on the wooden board that lined the inside of the cart, hoping he would settle himself opposite, a safe distance. Instead, Leo folded his long legs and sat beside Lillian, flipping the skirts of his tailcoat aside, draping his arm casually along the rim behind her back. Once again, her senses could take in nothing but him, as though she'd been splashed in the face with a bowl of cool water.

His knee gently bumped hers as the cart moved down High Street. His scent, cloves and tobacco, filled her head when he leaned forward to point at the church, a blocky medieval building of stern gray stone with a square Norman tower and high, narrow slits for windows. He curved his arm about her as the cart racketed over Queensberry Bridge, crossing the lazy Avon, then turned sharply down a hard-packed chalk lane that resembled nothing so much as a well-traveled sheep path.

How sweet it was to have Leo at her side, and how impossible that he would remain there. He was leaving soon, the next day or after, and all her besotted yearnings would diminish to intangible fantasies. Best that way.

She caught him watching her, not the approaching landscape. His eyes held the pooled gray of the sky. "Do your parents often treat you as if you were yet a child?"

She fiddled with her sketchbook, checking that it and her crayon were in place in her bag and that she had pages free for new work. "They are not the doting sort, but they want the best for me."

"They didn't inquire after your doings, or our engagement, or any of your plans for our wedding. And they didn't ask a single question about your book."

"Those things aren't likely to interest them, I'm afraid."

Lillian had long ago given up the futile wish that her parents might involve themselves in her life, at least not when they were in the midst of a project. Leo didn't know how much it meant that they'd left their dig for an hour or two to meet them at the inn.

"Their daughter's marriage doesn't interest them?" he inquired.

"They would come to my actual wedding, of course, and say all the proper things."

The cart caught a rut, and she put out a hand to steady herself. It landed on his leg. He was solid and warm. She pulled back as if she'd touched a live coal.

His brows shot together. "Did you tell him I proposed under duress? Do they think we are only pretending?"

"I didn't say a thing. But I doubt they are entertaining for a moment the thought I might truly marry a Westrop. It wouldn't surprise them to know our reasons, nor will it dismay them much when we call things off."

He opened his mouth, then paused. "Why wouldn't they believe you'd won my heart?"

"Leo, don't pretend to be obtuse. One has only to look at you, then at me, to understand the bets being laid at all the clubs."

He studied her features, and her heart knocked against her ribs, a curious nudge. She was enjoying this, the thrill that rushed through her at his nearness. But beneath was some pool of quiet tranquility she was beginning to feel in his presence, a pleasure that had deep springs. Beneath the shivers of infatuation, he sparked some calm radiance with her. He was so solid and steady at her side, and his steadiness steadied her.

"Then they do not see what I see," he said finally, turning his gaze to the hedged lane, with its glimpses of pasture beyond, which gave way to the gentle green swells of Salisbury Plain.

And that was an impossible thing to say, because Lillian wouldn't have the opportunity to discover what it was he saw in her. Foolish enough to sit beside him and savor his nearness when she knew they must part. The way her heart was beginning to behave around him, the sooner that parting took place, the better for her peace of mind.

CHAPTER THIRTEEN

Stonehenge captivated Lillian immediately with the magic that sang these great stones into place. The immensity of it was nearly absurd, the tall, hammered stones with their rough shapes jutting into the sky, standing scattered about as if they'd forgotten their purpose long ago. There was a weary, ancient sense to the place, with the fallen monoliths lying like enormous grey seals on the green turf, edges softened by time and weather.

Her parents occupied Leo with introductions to William Cunnington, fellow antiquarian, then busied him looking at this stone and that hole, staring for long lengths of time at humps in the scenery that meant nothing to Lillian. Hester peeled away to wander about. Lillian did the same, taking a seat on a smaller stone that sat apart from the rest, and pulled out her sketchbook and crayon.

A small, bright warmth bloomed high in her chest sometime later when she saw Leo stalking her way, hat swinging in his hand, wonder and satisfaction mingling on his face as he stared about him. He lowered himself to sit on the grass beside her, and the small bright place within her buzzed with contentment, like the bees murmuring in the flowers.

"What are you drawing?" he asked.

"Flowers, at first. I found some lovely specimens of meadow clary." She turned the page of her sketchbook toward him, realizing that she felt no hesitation in showing him her work. "Isn't she lovely? Look at the curl of those petals. I wish I had my watercolors to capture that purple. And I adore the fuzzy bits about the stem."

"That is lovely." His eyes traced the page, then lifted to her face, and for a moment she had the embarrassing fancy that he was referring to her. Something thumped in her chest. "What are you chewing?"

"A leaf. They're a touch bitter." She stripped a small oval leaf from a nearby plant and handed it to him.

Without a qualm he slipped the bit of green into his mouth, then made a face. "Tastes like medicine."

She grinned. "It is. Meadow sage, as it's otherwise called, has long been a staple of herbals and apothecary's stores."

He glanced at her lap. "And now you are drawing the stones. Or rather," he leaned forward, "your parents."

"I imagine tourists have sketched Stonehenge a thousand times. But my parents like to have records of their excavations. Did they tell you what they've found?"

"Nothing, yet. I gather your mother is a touch disappointed. Camden, when he excavated back in the time of Elizabeth, reported finding ash and burnt bones. The Duke of Buckingham made an enormous trench a few years later, looking for treasure. I imagine that's what Cunnington is hoping to find. There, where they're digging, is the base where that trilithon recently fell. Cunnington wanted to see if one of the legends is correct, and the stones mark burial places of the honored dead."

"And does it?"

"Seeing the place, I'm now inclined to believe Stukeley's claim that the entire ring is an astrological map of some kind. A way to chart the seasons and a ritual temple for the Druids. Inigo Jones said it was built by the Romans, like their roads and aqueducts and amphitheaters, but I think it is even older, and almost certainly holds some ceremonial value."

"How can you tell?"

He leaned on one elbow, the lord at his ease, his long, powerful body stretched out on the grass. With the low slopes of the plains and the cloud-stuffed sky behind him, the great stones of the henge at his feet, he seemed some ancient god come to life.

"Those mounds in the distance, there, and there? Tumuli. Burial chambers, if I had to guess. Aubrey speculated that the pits he found were for cremation burials—you can see the depressions outside the circle. But if there are no burials inside the circle, that suggests it was used for something else. See the ditch that surrounds the whole? I suppose a boundary of some kind."

She followed his pointing finger, squinting to see beyond. "What's over there—another barrow?"

"No, that is the cursus, a sort of long, smooth road. Stukeley thought the Romans might have built it to race their chariots. But it could be older, and have some other significance. A line of sight, a gathering place, an ancient trackway—I'd love to know."

Lillian sat back. "I don't see how we ever can."

"But we can learn as much as possible about a place, and form theories. That is the beauty. See that path, where it looks like the stones make a gate? Stukeley called that the Avenue. Possibly it runs down to the Avon, which the builders could have used to ferry the stones here from somewhere else. These sarsens are sandstone, and Salisbury Plain is chalk downs. Cunnington tells me there's another chalk horse over by Westbury, incidentally."

"He told me the Avebury circle is larger in size, but much

less is left standing. The Christian monks of the Dark Ages didn't like these pagan monuments and encouraged farmers to knock them down and cart away the stone. Perhaps that's what happened to some of the missing stones here."

"Or they just sank back into the earth, like that old giant wishes to do." Leo pointed to the weathered stone, taller than the others but listing to one side, as if weary of being the greatest and standing alone. "Or it's possible the circle was never finished. Ran out of stone, or the king ran out of money, or had to use his money to fight a war."

His enthusiasm lit a warm spark inside her. So did the easy way he conversed with her, as if he considered her an intellectual equal, the way her father regarded her mother.

"Perhaps it wasn't for religious purposes at all, but for entertainment," Lillian suggested. "A great dancing floor. Or an open-air theatre, like that of the ancient Greeks."

"Too tame," Leo teased. "You must be bloody minded, like these ancients. See that fallen stone, there? Jones called that the Altar Stone. And that other one, slightly reddish—the Slaughter Stone, where the victims were decapitated and then buried."

"You *are* bloody minded. And that one, standing apart, I suppose is where prisoners were chained."

"That is the Heel Stone, and if you stand there and watch, on the eve of the winter solstice, the sun will set exactly between those two sarsens." Leo leaned against her as he pointed, and Lillian's heart rapped against her ribs like a startled hare.

"Perhaps your smith's cave at Wayland will prove to be an astrological map as well," Lillian said. She must remind herself he was leaving; she must remember he was not hers. "Simply think of what you might discover."

"Enough to impress the Society of Antiquaries, I hope." He settled back on his elbow, at his ease with her. "I'm glad for the chance to talk with Cunnington—he's long been interested in these barrows. He's got a digging technique he wants to try, basically boring a hole straight down, and seeing what the layers reveal."

"It sounds exciting. A peek into the distant past."

He rolled the leaf along his lips, lost in thought. "You were right that we are alike in that. Both driven by curiosity to discover, and the wish to share our knowledge with others."

She met his gaze, steady, thoughtful, and that bright spot made large loops through her chest cavity, like a star in orbit. "Thank you for that," she said softly.

"For what?"

"For believing that I *can* add something. For believing in me." She smiled. "For not helping me publish my florilegium simply because a gentleman's oath compelled you."

Every piece of attire was in its proper place, yet his demeanor was so loose, relaxed, it lulled her into forgetting he was dangerous. "Your parents said you have never thought of marriage. Why not?"

She watched her parents moving about within the shadow of the immense stones. To the north, a shepherd boy grazed his sheep on the long grass, looking on curiously but without much concern.

"A dearth of suitors, first. Second, I have specific requirements. I think you have gathered that my parents have an unusual relationship."

He nodded. "She travels and works with him, rather than staying at home to tend the cookpot and her sewing."

Lillian snorted. "My mother can barely sew a button, but she can tell at a glance if a piece of bone she dug up was used as a digging implement, a brooch, or some other tool. My father doesn't permit her to come along out of affection. He relies on her."

"And?" He drew the leaf out of his mouth, tossing it aside, and Lillian told herself to stop staring at his lips, his white teeth.

She propped an elbow on her sketchbook and watched her parents as they stood side by side at the edge of a hole, supervising the diggers and addressing one another with an animation that told her they were having a productive disagreement about something. She hadn't put this feeling into so many words before, but here on this broad plain, with its enduring stones, she saw clearly what she wanted for her future.

"I don't know what man would want to tramp over the countryside with me and wait patiently while I sit and draw flowers. Moreover, I don't expect many men would share my father's feelings and regard their wife as a partner in their endeavors. But I don't want to be anything less than that."

"Surely," Leo said softly, "the man exists. You need only find him."

She sat back and fiddled with a few lines of her sketch. "I have cousins up north, from my mother's family," she finally said. "My mother has always spoken as if I'll end up wedding one of them eventually. My father will inherit the baronetcy after my Uncle Lloyd passes, may that day be far from us, and he will in turn want someone to pass it to. He hopes his legacy will be his antiquarian work, but at the same time, he doesn't want to be the end of the honors that his forefathers earned for the family. And Hester is not likely to marry and have children. So..."

"So it falls to you to continue the line and the title." A bitter flavor edged Leo's tone, like the bite of the leaf.

She met his gaze. "I imagine you know what that feels like."

His expression was vulnerable, soft, his eyes a well she could fall into and be lost in. He nodded slowly. "I would rather a title I earned myself. A modest little knighthood awarded for my discoveries, for contributions to the realm. Not an estate bought at the price of my cousin's life. And thank you for that," he added.

"For what?"

"For seeing me as more than the marquess's heir. It's all anyone has seen of me lately. Even—no, especially my own mother. I think that's one reason I've been so determined to arrange my own excavation. I want to be known as Leonidas Westrop, antiquarian. Not Leonidas Westrop, heir presumptive."

"Leonidas Westrop, benefactor of botanical publications," she said, rolling the name around on her tongue, savoring its full, spicy flavor as much as she savored the sight of him with his brocade coat, kerseymere pantaloons, and frank, open gaze. "You, as your own self, are very hard to overlook."

"I am very glad *you* think so."

She might have leaned toward him; he might have learned toward her. Or perhaps they met in the middle, for his face neared, close enough that she saw the stubble already sprouting along his jaw, the individual lashes that ringed his eyes, the crease in his lower lip. Then those lips touched hers, and she surrendered at once to the sensation, both familiar and new. A sweetness she recognized as belonging to him, laced with the sharp bite of the herb, the scent of meadow grass and chicory in her nostrils, and the buzzing of an entire beehive filling her ears.

He licked into her mouth, drawing her tongue into the dance she now knew, and a thick, warm syrup poured through her veins. She lifted a hand to his jaw to keep herself from toppling over. Her forehead might hinge open and all sense float away with the passing clouds. Leo kissing her was all she wanted in the world, all she ever wanted, now and always.

His hand settled on her side, above her waist, and the syrup bubbled and simmered. She met his kiss with a new urgency. She wanted this to continue, her mouth on his, but she also wanted something more. That thick, flowing stream wasn't filling her veins; it was hollowing her out, making her ache for something.

"Lillian!"

Her mother's bellow cut through the fog in her head. A sharp edge to Alida's tone made Lillian wonder how long she'd been calling. "Time to recollect yourself, dear. Come hither, we need you more than Mr. Westrop does."

Lillian opened her eyes and stared at Leo. It was a touch gratifying to realize he looked almost as bemused as she felt.

"I rather think my need is more urgent," he murmured.

Heat shot through her cheeks, and she slapped hands to her face in a feeble attempt to hide the blush. "I am kissing you in front of my *parents*, and William Cunnington, and that shepherd boy, and *everybody*."

"Kissing me very thoroughly." He squeezed her side, fingers pressing into her soft flesh, as if he couldn't help himself. "But you might say you are kissing your future husband, if anyone should scold."

Her mother's tone sounded more amused than disapproving as Lillian hastened over, sketchbook and crayon clutched in her hands. "We can all see you, you know," Alida chided, without taking her eyes from the pit where one of the Parker brothers scraped at something with the side of his trowel.

"I forgot myself. I'm so sorry."

Alida glanced back at Leo, who sat with hands on his knees as if he had nothing to do but watch Stonehenge gracefully weather and age. Her eyes narrowed. "Be on your guard, my girl," her mother murmured. "That man won't rest until he has you."

"Until he *has* me—how do you mean?"

"In the biblical sense. Carnal knowledge." Her mother slid Lillian a sidewise look.

The burn in her face intensified. "That is not where our—liaison is going," Lillian said.

"That is exactly where it is going, if you permit it." Alida did not seem terribly shocked or fretful. "Only remember, my dear, it is one thing in St. Athan for a housemaid to have a belly on her when she marries the butcher's boy. It is quite another for a niece of the Baronet Gileston to have a belly when she marries the nephew of a marquess."

"I won't be so foolish, Mother."

"Why wouldn't you be, when many a one among us has been as foolish before? A man like that is a heady spell, my darling. Keep your wits about you."

Lillian's father came to stand beside them. "What is it, John?" he asked the digger.

"Coin, I believe, sir." The young man kneeling in the pit held up his trowel. "Shall I pry it out?"

"Have Lil sketch it first. How many hands deep?"

The young man placed his palm horizontal to the side of the pit and measured downwards. "Four hands, sir."

"Good, good. Lil, my gel, get this in situ, will you, with the measurements in it. Can't tell you how much we've missed your sharp eye."

"So that is that why you sent for me." Lillian sat on a fallen stone, flipped to a fresh page in her sketchbook, and with a few strokes sketched the square of the pit. She'd forgotten how much she loved all this: the lazy hours of waiting and scraping the dirt, then the sudden, sharp thrill of a find. Those moments when her parents needed and wanted her.

Almost as dizzying as Leo wanting her.

"That, and my sister-in-law was eating herself into a fury over your behavior. Making an exhibition of yourself, kissing in public places, debasing the family, et cetera."

"How would I be debasing the family by putting a shackle

on the heir to a marquess?" Lillian held out her crayon and closed one eye, measuring the depth of the pit against her utensil, then applied those dimensions to her picture. "I would think she'd applaud me for setting my cap at him."

"Very precise measurements," a new voice said behind Lillian's shoulder. "Approve their methods, must say. Why I wanted them."

She craned her neck to see William Cunnington had joined them. In defiance of current fashion he wore a small wig, a waistcoat with a number of fobs and trinkets dangling on a chain, and sturdy breeches. He beamed at Lillian. "Drawings and everything."

Leo stood beside Cunnington. She hadn't realized the men were approaching.

She was quite sure, from the sudden, alert stillness in Leo's mien, that he had heard what she said about putting the shackle on the heir to a marquess.

She focused on her sketch, taking care to be fast but accurate. Her sketches were not only useful records for later, when her parents tried to reconstruct the setting, but might very well be included in their eventual publication.

He could guess she was being flippant. That she was using her aunt's language, not her own. He must know she hadn't *meant* it.

"Has anyone an eye on Hex?" she asked, self-conscious as everyone watched her work, including Leo.

"She's over petting the sheep," Leo reported. "I'll wager that will be the highlight of her day."

Lillian added a quick note to her sketch, marking the dimensions and the depth of the find. "Done."

With great eagerness, and great caution, her father pried the small object out of the wall of the pit. He dusted off the dirt, then gently blew. He lifted his face, meeting his wife's bright gaze as if everything else around them had fallen away.

"A coin," he said, handing it to her.

"Peter," Alida breathed. Lillian peered into her mother's hand as she examined the object, scrubbing away dirt and chalk embedded around the printing. "It's gold. And this is a Roman stamp, isn't it?"

"Gold." Peter nearly bumped his head to Lillian's as he strove for a look. "A solidus?"

"Lil. We need your eyes." Alida handed the treasure to Lillian.

Her palm tingled. She was holding something centuries old. The markings were surprisingly sharp and clear; the coin might have been dropped, or buried, while relatively new. And it was whole, not clipped, as one often saw, especially with later coins.

"D N MAGMA," she read around the head in profile with its diadem and noble nose. "XIMVS PF AVG. I don't know what that means."

"Some of it will be titles," her mother murmured, "and some will say where it was minted."

"Magnus Maximus?" Leo offered.

"By Jove." Peter took the coin and peered at it again, dazzled. "I'll bet that's it. And AVG might mean Augusta, which is what they called London for a time. What a find!"

"Magnus Maximus, the usurper?" Lillian frowned.

"Macsen Wledig to the Welsh, the soldier raised to emperor by the British troops," her father said. He looked at Leo. "He went on to challenge the sitting emperor—who was it?"

"Gratian was the one he had killed. But Valentinian, I believe, was the one who resisted. Went and recruited the eastern emperor—Theodosius, wasn't it?"

"I thought Theodosius was the count who defended the Saxon Shore," Lillian said.

Leo gave her a mock frown. "You told me you had read your *Brut*."

"All the names blur together after a while," she admitted.

"Heretic," Leo said. "You'd never confuse plants in that manner, no matter how similarly named."

"True," she agreed. She held Leo's gaze, both of them smiling foolishly at one another, caught up in the same heady thrill—the discovery, its import, and something else—being able to share the find with another, someone who understood.

She grew aware that, instead of conferring about the coin, her parents, and William Cunnington, and the Parker brothers, had all paused to watch her exchange with Leo.

"Aren't you two precious. Draw an impression for us, Lil." Alida pressed the coin back into Lillian's hand. "Just as you see it now. We'll clean it up later and write some letters of consultation."

"Of course, Mama." Lillian folded her legs beneath her and set to sketching the front, then obverse side of the coin.

"That is quite well-preserved. Do you suppose some Roman tourist dropped it?" Leo squatted beside her, watching her work, and that steady, bright hum within her carried on. The thrill of discovery lit his frame, as if he vibrated on the same frequency she did.

"Perhaps it fell out of his pocket while he was witnessing an execution."

"Or perhaps he paid the executioner for a nice, swift, clean blow."

"In that case we might expect to find his skull a bit further down. Please warn the Parkers."

"Would that upset you? Finding human remains."

She gave him a level look. "I prefer to find coins, or pottery, or tools, but again, you forget I was raised by these two. We've run across a human bone or ten."

"You enjoy this," he remarked.

She grinned back at him, catching his joy. "And so do you."

"Finely done, Lil." Alida appeared beside them, peering over Lillian's shoulder as the coin emerged, Maximus with his cuirassed bust and sharp, sloping nose. His profile reminded her a bit of Leo's with the strong brow and jaw.

"Who have you retained to make your drawings, Mr. Westrop?" Alida asked.

"Oh. Er. I hadn't thought to procure an artist."

Alida turned to him, her eyes widening. "But you must. It is part of proper methods and oversight. You must sketch where you found it in the setting, so you might identify the deposit in relation to the other artifacts. And then you will want a clear rendering for publication, later."

Leo blinked. "I—I didn't know. Where should I look?"

"Perhaps you might find a local near Uffington," Alida said. "We've relied on Lillian for years."

Lillian cleared her throat as an absurd thought leapt to mind. Wiser to push it away, but Leo was giving her that look again, the look that said, *Help me.* The look that said he needed her.

She *knew* that drawing close to him would be lowering her heart over a precipice, and she'd never get it back. She knew that this sense of companionship– of belonging, even—was an illusion conjured out of green spaces and seductive ruins and the freedom of open air.

She threw herself at the fence anyway, hoping the fall, when it came, wouldn't kill her.

"I suppose I might go with him," Lillian said.

CHAPTER FOURTEEN

Leo was brushing out the coat he'd worn to dinner—he'd declined to bring along a valet for the trip—when a timid knock came on the door to the accommodations he'd been given at the George.

"Nothing else is needed, thank you," he called. The innkeeper's wife, anxious to impress a high-ranking guest, had been wearing a path to his door with tea, then brandy, warm water for his washstand, fresh linens, and assurances that the bed hangings had been recently aired, the ropes of the bedstead recently tightened, and the feather mattress atop it all newly stuffed, but if there were anything else she could do to please his lordship, he was only to ask.

Lillian had been right. This was a precursor to what he could expect now that he had gone from being plain Leo Westrop of the Wiltshire Westrops to the next male in line for the Waringford title.

Lillian. An awareness prickled the back of his neck, as though he picked up on her presence before her voice floated through the wooden portal.

"Leo—it's me."

She sounded plaintive. He was swinging open the door before he considered the wisdom of bringing her into a room where they were alone, and there was a bed. Then he was wishing he could shut his eyes to the sight of her, but too late: the image was already seared into his brain. Lillian in dishabille, her hair unpinned and tumbling in golden sheaves over her shoulders, in the simple printed cotton gown she'd worn that day but without the neckerchief or apron to distract the eye from the shape of her.

He looked down. She was without stockings, a pair of velvet embroidered house slippers encasing her feet.

"You'll catch a draft." He curled his hand around her upper arm and pulled her into the room. "Lillian—what are you doing here?"

"Hex locked me out of the room." She held a hand to the bodice of her gown as if afraid it would fall off her.

"That can't be."

She nodded. He took her chamberstick, with its flickering candle, and set it on the small table beside its own. The two flames bowed and leaned toward one another, as if in cozy conversation.

"I went outside to use the necessary and splash my face in the tub. Mrs. Eyres says they keep it full of fresh water from the Avon for those who like a cold plunge for health purposes. I didn't plunge all the way, of course." Her teeth chattered lightly at this admission, but she didn't feel cold to his touch. Darker gold edged her hairline, as if with damp, and her cheeks bloomed a bright apple-red, but the arm he held was flushed with warmth. On the hot side, rather.

He knew he ought to let go of her. He didn't.

"Why would Hester lock the door?"

"She's nervous in public places. I told her I'd knock when I returned. But I think she fell asleep."

Leo stared, trying to force his brain into logical paths. His brain clung stubbornly to various observations that brought his mental machinery to a halt. The deep blue of her eyes in the candlelight. The smell of geraniums rising from her skin—her soap or toilet water, it must be. The frog orchid red of her lips, and the way her quick breaths made her breasts rise and fall. He couldn't look at her breasts. He'd come completely undone.

"Mrs. Eyres would have a key."

"Hex drew the latch on the inside."

"Then we must wake her up."

"I knocked as loud as I dared. She's a very sound sleeper." Lillian bit her lip, and he wanted to follow her teeth with his own. "This wouldn't have happened if I'd simply accepted my parents' offer to stay at the Diana House."

"They didn't have a bed for you. Or Hester." Leo had arranged their rooms at the George himself, feeling he'd won something by having Lillian near him. As if he could show her parents they had a rival now for her attention. Her affections.

He hadn't anticipated he would have her *with* him. Lust rose and circled like a sniffing dog.

"Do you want me to try and wake Hester?" Somehow, his hand was still anchored to her arm. And he'd begun drawing slow circles on her bare flesh with his thumb. She was soft and warm. The darkness at the edge of the room crept closer, encircling them.

She tipped up her face. "I...I suppose so."

She stood completely still, save for the rise and fall of her breath. She was as ensnared in the moment as he was.

His hand, he observed, was drawing her closer. His body obeyed an inevitable logic that his mind pretended not to see. Lillian needed to be close to him. That was all.

"Or." His voice didn't sound his own, a deep rumble, raw

with desire. "You could wait here, and we could try again in a few minutes."

"I suppose we could."

He raised a hand to her other arm, holding her in place, her breasts inches from his chest. His eyelids felt heavy. His entire body felt heavy, a thick heat pooling in his groin.

He could not ravish Lillian Gower in his chamber at the George. Even if it was a spacious chamber, with timber planks lining the high ceiling, the walls paneled with a warm, dark wood, the bed a shadowed alcove, beckoning. He must not seduce Lillian.

"Brandy?" His voice grated, painful, because it wasn't producing what his body wanted him to say.

Her teeth burrowed into her lip. "I am unaccustomed to spirits."

"It's a rhubarb brandy. Mrs. Eyres' own."

"Very well, then."

There was only one glass on the tray. Leo poured her a splash. Her fingers grazed his when he handed it to her, and a spark leapt up his arm, lighting a wildfire. He took a gulp straight from the bottle.

"Oh. This is delicious. Much like the shrub that our house-keeper in St. Athan makes."

There was nowhere to sit but on the bed, so she perched tentatively on the high mattress. Leo tore his eyes away. Lillian. On his *bed*.

"Tell me about St. Athan," he growled.

"My parents have a cottage in town. It's quite cozy, two floors, old stone and lovely carvings. The manor where my uncle lives is not far, so we see him often. Aunt Giles lives with him and keeps his house. Hester spends more time with us, usually."

"I have noticed you are practically sisters." He took another bracing swig. The brandy wasn't nearly strong enough to burn some sense into him. "Where will you live when you are married to this cousin?" Think of her married. Think of her as out of bounds. Belonging to another man.

No. His very being rebelled. Lillian belonged to *him.*

Her brows knit. "My presumed marriage, very far in the future? I suppose, in time, we will live in Gileston Manor. It would be most comfortable for Hester, and if my husband does become the baronet..." She made a face.

"Lucky bastard. Why don't you wish to be married sooner?"

She sipped her drink as if to draw strength from it. Her gaze touched and tangled with his, then veered away, as if she could sense his sinful thoughts. Could see he was, in his mind, stripping her gown and her shift from her, then grazing his mouth over all the soft, splendid skin beneath.

Her scowl turned fierce. "Because I want what any man is allowed to want. Liberty to pursue my interests. Work that engages me. Though there is the matter of how I support myself doing so, I suppose. At the moment we live on the generosity of my uncle."

"We are all of us dependent on another for our liberty," Leo said bitterly, and followed this with another draw from the bottle.

He lowered his hand to find her before him, a whisper of soft cotton, hair gleaming like silk. She took the bottle, fingers sliding over his, and poured herself another splash.

"Careful how you tipple," he warned. "You'll end up top-heavy."

"You'll be there first," she answered, her lips turned up at the corner.

Those dimples. Hell's teeth. He wanted to bite them, and her full, red lips.

Abruptly she sat on the bed. "Hester's angry with me."

"Why?"

"Because she wants to go with me—you—us—to Uffington." She tossed back a swallow of brandy like an experienced sailor, then covered her cough.

Leo turned this over in his head. Things were admittedly a bit fuzzy up there, furniture moving about. Lillian had a way of bending gravity so that his attention focused on her.

"Well, let her come with us."

She lowered the glass, her eyes huge. "You mean that?"

"Why not? She's not an infant. And you will require a chaperone. I can't simply cart a beautiful, unmarried woman into the midst of my camp and expect everyone to believe she's my assistant."

She scowled at him. "I *will* be your assistant. If you'll have me. I did put you rather on the spot, and if you don't want—"

"I want you," he said swiftly. "As my artist, that is. But see here, if I bring the woman I intend to marry—"

She narrowed her eyes. "An engagement formed and continued under false pretense."

"If I bring you under those conditions," Leo pressed on, "no one will believe I'm not also taking you to bed."

There it was, out in the open. What he wanted. Her, in his bed. Like this, except with less clothing, and more contact of skin to skin.

She sucked in a breath, and he tracked the rise and fall of those beautiful breasts. God, she was killing him.

"Very well. Hester will be pleased. And my parents. They wouldn't like to be expected to look after another person."

"Yes, you've said that is not their strength. Yet they certainly seemed to rely on your skills today."

"I learned from a very early age that if I were useful, I would merit their attention. I would be included in their endeavors."

"Do they support you in *your* endeavors?"

He knew the answer to that. She'd come to him, an utter stranger, for help in publishing her florilegium. Though her parents would certainly have the contacts, and ought to have the interest, she'd needed him.

If only she needed him in other ways.

Outrage rose within him, a slow burn like the brandy. They *ought* to take an interest. Their daughter was the most intelligent, self-possessed, clever woman he'd ever met, and she was so beautiful his eyes ached from looking at her.

She set her glass on the table beside her chamberstick. The light of the gentle flame kissed her cheek, as he longed to do.

"I ought to go back to Hex," she whispered.

He rose when she did. "You ought to," he agreed. "Because if you stay here, I am going to forget I am a gentleman."

"Indeed?" She searched his eyes. Her mouth parted, lips trembling slightly. "What will happen then?"

He lowered his head. She didn't draw away, merely tipped up her chin. Her eyelids drifted closed, and her trusting anticipation was so sweetly erotic that he felt his restraint pushed to the limit.

"Run. Run now, Lillian. Or you'll find out."

He whispered the words over her lips, and her shoulders shivered.

"Show me," she breathed, lifting her hands to his neck, and he was lost.

He'd forgotten why he wasn't supposed to touch her. She was here before him, and every thread of his body whispered that he had won her fairly and could claim her as his right.

He would only kiss her. He was certain she was an innocent. She had put herself into his hands, brought him a deliverance he didn't know he needed in offering to support his dig, and he would not spoil her for the life she wanted. When she left him and moved on to another— A growl rose in his throat.

He gave into temptation and fastened his teeth on that luscious lower lip of hers. The small, surprised sound she made drained blood from his head and sent it rushing to his nether regions.

"You are delicious," he muttered. "You taste like sugar."

"That's the brandy."

She met his kiss, practiced now, and the fit of their mouths teased his hunger to craving. Her gown was no barrier at all as he pulled her against him; he could feel every curve of supple flesh. She'd found him undressed, down to his shirt, his pantaloons half-unfastened; all he need do was open his falls and he could be inside her, what he'd been aching for since their kiss yesterday when she nearly rode him to climax against the wall of the Basing House garden. Inside her, where he'd wanted to be since that kiss in the Physic Garden. No, since the short peck she'd delivered in the glasshouse, the one that told him this woman lit a spark in him no one else had ever done.

He'd wanted her, on some deep, unacknowledged level, since she stood from the chair in his library, holding that book, rising like Venus from the sea and bringing love and pleasure into his life, beauty like he'd never known.

"Lillian." His breath was ragged, his heart pounding fiercely. Simply kissing her honed his need to a fierce edge. That, and the way her legs parted slightly beneath her gown so he could press against her softness as if she were ready to receive him. As if she wanted this.

He framed her face with kisses. "If you don't want this...if this isn't real..." If she were playing with him, letting him play with her, and didn't share this same ache—he'd rather she set him on fire and leave him to burn into ash. He didn't want to be alone in this, so helpless to the sensation of her in his arms, so desperate to have her that he couldn't form words.

"I want this," she whispered. Her breath touched his neck, a curl of heat. "I want *you*, Leo."

That unleashed him, and with a growl he pulled her day gown over her head. The soft fabric peeled from her like the cloth from a pudding, revealing the deliciousness beneath. Her eyes widened, and the reflexive clench of her thighs, the stiffening in her spine, told him not to yank her shift from her, not just yet. Not to raise the hem and drive straight into her, as the beast in him longed to do. Satisfaction was there, so close. He could take it. She would let him.

That would be gobbling the *pièce de resistance* without enjoying the *entrées* that came before. Like boring straight through to the heart of a barrow without observing the many layers of treasure on the way down. Leo pushed his hands into her hair, a glorious fall of silk, and kissed her until her body melted again to the buttery place she'd been. Until she leaned into him, ardently kissing him back, her soft mewl telling him she was hungry, too.

"I want to take you to bed, Lillian."

She lifted her face, her cheeks flushed, her lips reddened from his lips and teeth, and that light of unholy mischief entered her eyes, the one that told him she was about to be pert. "Then what?"

God, he loved this look on her. "I'll show you," he growled, and pushed her toward the bed.

Her neck tasted of almonds. Her collarbone and the delicate skin beneath, lemon paste. Her shift was fine white linen, with a low scoop to the neckline that bared the rise of her pale white breasts. Leo covered the exposed skin with kisses, dragged his tongue through the cleft between them. She squirmed, her breath coming faster.

"I've dreamed of this." He pushed the thin fabric aside and brought out the heavy globe of her breast, the nipple pink like the inside of a shell, pointed and hard with her desire. For him. Then he brought out the other and sat back on his heels, gazing in admiration.

"Perfect," he said. "Works of art. It's a crime to conceal these. You should walk about with them always exposed."

She squirmed again, the blush in her cheeks deepening, her eyes dark. "You're absurd. That would be vulgar."

"It would be a service to all mankind. God, Lillian. You're... you should be carved in stone and put in a public plaza, so everyone could look at you."

"Look at my bosom, you mean?"

He palmed her breasts, cupping one in each hand, interested in the way her nipples puckered further under his perusal. "I want a carving of you, a three-quarter bust that goes down to here." He touched a finger to her ribs. "And I will put you in my library to gaze upon when I can't look at you in life."

He slid his hands over the heavy globes, as reverent as if he handled an ancient masterpiece. Lillian's breasts were unparalleled perfection. The arrows of her nipples scraping his palms sent a bolt of lust to his groin so intense it was painful.

She tried to cover herself, and he grasped her hands and threaded her fingers through his. "I gave you a chance to run, and you didn't." He anchored her hands on either side of her body and leaned over her. "Now you must pay the price." And he did what he'd dreamed of for so long and set his mouth to Lillian's perfect breasts.

Her gasp made him lift his head, fearing he'd hurt her. "You wish me not to?"

She screwed her eyes shut, pulling her lip between her teeth. "You...may proceed. If you wish."

"I do wish. Fervently." He nibbled his way across the smooth, silken flesh, then traced paths with his tongue. Her heart picked up tempo; he felt the echo of it beneath his lips. He closed his mouth over a nipple and sucked, and she cried out.

"Am I hurting you?"

"No, it's..."

"How does it feel, Lillian?"

She bucked beneath him, twisting her hips as if she wanted to turn away, yet arching her back as if she might press her breasts further into his mouth. "I don't...I don't have words."

He sucked and licked and nibbled, feasting on her, surfeiting on her sweetness. Her soft moans and panted breaths inflamed him. She wanted him. His woman reveled in his touch, tossing on the same tempest of lust and pleasure that gripped him.

Her fingers sank into his shoulders, through the thin fabric of his shirt, tugging, pleading. He murmured around the nipple in his mouth, teasing with his tongue. "What do you want, my sweet?"

"I don't *know*," she moaned.

"I might."

He dragged a finger over the soft flesh covering her ribs, swept back and forth across the swell of her belly, squeezing gently. He loved how she filled his hands, her curves rich and full. Her breath hitched as he pulled the hem of her shift up her thigh. Her legs were as creamy as the rest of her, more meadows of sweet flesh he wanted to graze. He could, tormenting them both, but he was eager to reach her core. He pulled the hem up to her waist so he could gaze fully.

Her curls below were a darker gold, and he wanted to rub his face in them, see if they were as soft as the rest of her. She tensed her thighs as he ran his hand through the golden field.

"Can I touch here?"

She screwed her eyes shut, fingers clutching his shoulders,

body arching toward him. He loved her concentration, guessed how her entire focus had funneled to his fingers. "Yes."

"And here?" He slid his hand lower, where she was warm and slick and ready.

"Oh," she gasped, her eyes flying open. "*Oh.*"

He lapped at her breasts, not ready to leave them, while he explored with his fingers. So delicate. So lush. His cock throbbed in readiness, reaching toward her, toward bliss. "Tell me when I've got it right, darling."

He found the bud hidden within her silken petals, and her eyes drifted closed. "Oh. There."

"And now tell me what will please you," he whispered.

She pulled his head toward her breasts and squirmed around his hand. "Harder." Her voice was a wisp. "Faster. Oh, Leo, it feels so *good.*"

Her response maddened him, fanned the flames to a roaring inferno. He drew as much of her as he could into his mouth, sucking hard on her nipple. She begged and moaned and thrashed, gripping the bedclothes in her fists, pushing herself against his hand as she rode him. Her abandon was glorious to behold. He pressed his cock between the bed and her thigh so he felt every twist, every tremor as she climbed toward her climax, and when it broke over her, he nearly came too, so beautiful was her release, so deeply was he in tune with her body.

He popped her nipple free from his mouth and rubbed his hand across her belly, enjoying the flutter of her muscles. She opened her eyes, gazed with wonder into his face, and laughed aloud. He took himself in hand, certain he could come by her expression alone.

"You look so smug." She traced a finger along his cheek.

"You enjoyed that."

"I did." Her eyes drifted down his body, where his shirt hung loose, to his hand on his groin. "I—you didn't..."

"I enjoyed every moment along with you, darling. I assure you." He pulsed at the sight of her watching him, her fascinated look. A few strokes, and he'd be finished.

She reached out a hand. "I want to please you. It's your turn."

"There are no *turns*, darling. Only togetherness." At least with her, he was sure of this.

She turned on her side. "Let me touch you, Leo."

She pushed his hand away and regarded his member, which bobbed helpfully under her gaze, as if nodding at her to continue. "Yours is much larger than Timkin's. And prettier."

"*Pretty—*" He bit back a wave of furious jealousy. Hot rage stiffened him further. "Is he the one who—?"

She shook her head, then peeked up at him shyly. "I never wanted to touch *him*," she said.

His smugness deepened. He was her *first*. He would be her best, her most memorable.

Her only, if he could.

He let that thought melt away as she wrapped her hand around him. "Show me," she commanded.

He loved how bossy she was about what pleased her. She was *with* him, as attentive to his body as he was to hers. He clasped his hand around hers and led her in the rhythm he liked, and within a few heartbeats he was there, arching his back as he thrust into her hand, sucking in his breath at the relief of release. In the nick of time he caught a strip of linen from the washstand and spilled into it.

She watched with rapt attention as he quickly cleaned himself. "I thought there was more of a mess," she said.

Rage and jealousy speared through him again, spoiling the satisfaction. Until she reached out and lightly stroked his spent member, sending a fresh arrow of interest deep into his groin.

He tossed the cloth back on the stand. "Normally there is. If some time has passed. But I've been servicing myself regularly since our night at Highcastle House."

Rose bloomed in her cheeks as her lashes lifted and she met his gaze. "What?"

"All I need do is think of your breasts in that gown," he told her.

She blinked, the blush heightening, and he expected her to shy away, playing the maiden. But there was that devil in her eyes again. "Indeed," she said. "And what else do you think of when you—" She waved a hand toward his groin. "You know."

He laughed, fastening his falls and rolling toward her. She tugged down her shift, covering herself, and he smoothed a line from her ribs to waist to thigh, marveling at the lush landscape of her. "What do I imagine when I pleasure myself with thoughts of your body?" he purred in her ear.

She tensed, her voice breathless. "Yes."

"Let's save that for another time, or I'll find myself desiring you again."

She touched his face, and her expression sobered as her gaze traced his features, brow, nose, lingering on his mouth. "I'm afraid I will have that problem," she said. "Now that we've...I already thought about kissing you all the time. Now I'll think about *that*."

He pulled her against him. "About me pleasuring you?"

"About us pleasuring one another," she said shyly.

He turned his face into her hair, sinking his nose into the rich softness. He wanted to live and die with the scent of geraniums surrounding him.

"Do you need to go back to Hex?" he asked softly. "Or can you stay?" She hesitated, her brow furrowing, and he touched her lip. "For a bit."

She relaxed her frown. "I suppose I can stay for a bit."

He blew out the candles, then climbed into bed. She turned

toward him as he slid an arm about her, then pulled the coverlet over them both.

He pressed a kiss to her lips, overcome at the sense of completion. Lillian, pleasured, in his bed. His body hummed with satisfaction and a fierce, deep delight. He wanted her like this always, wrapped in his arms. He wanted to slide into her and stay there.

His cock stirred, interested at that idea, but he pushed the lust down and put a lid on it. He needed to proceed slowly with her. He couldn't devour her completely in one go, let her see the feral beast within him. He would lure her gently, one morsel at a time, until she came willingly and whole-heartedly into his arms. Choosing him. Wanting him more than she wanted anything else.

If only she would.

CHAPTER FIFTEEN

Lillian was proven right about one thing. After she had gone to bed with Leo, her desire for him was a wild colt that slipped its lead and roved everywhere, intruding on her thoughts in the rudest fashion.

When he strode across the mound of earth above Wayland Smith's Cave, helping his men cut back the shrubbery, she watched his shoulders flexing in the fustian jacket and remembered his body braced above hers. When he stripped off his hat and the sunlight picked out russet tones in his hair, the sight of his head at her breast flashed through her mind.

When he held her sketchbook, she studied his hands as they flipped through her pages and remembered his hot palms dragging along her skin, his hands cupping and shaping her breasts, his hand between her legs conjuring sensations she'd never felt. Want poked her like small demons with their pitchforks, inflaming her senses at the most inopportune moments, whisking her concentration apart like summer clouds.

She was a fallen woman—fallen far outside the bounds of sense. Now she knew why women were warned against giving themselves up to the pleasures of the flesh. But oh, such pleasure there was. She would turn and catch his eye on her, as she sat drawing, as she walked the embankment capturing its dimensions, or when she helped distribute luncheon to the workers, and blood rushed through her like a hare chased by a whippet.

Yet she could do nothing about it while they were surrounded by others at all times. Westrop had hired men from Ashbury, Kingstone Winslow and Kingstone Coombs, Idstone, even a carpenter from Compton Beauchamp. They were a competent handful, overseen by Claudius Caesar, Augustus' father, who had brought his family from London and who had become Leo's main source of support. The family, along with Hester, had also become Lillian's main social interactions in the week since they'd arrived from Amesbury.

Lillian put aside her sketchbook as she glimpsed Paulina Caesar driving the dogcart up the downs, coming to deliver food and drink. It being too far to go home for the midday meal, the men would otherwise not get their dinner until four or five of the clock, and Paulina had taken to bringing a nuncheon of cold meats and cheeses for the crew.

Her daughter Octavia, seventeen, sat in the back with her younger sister, Faustina, and Hester between them. Octavia was a graceful young woman, already showing herself the mistress of household skills and no doubt ready to run a home of her own as soon as she wished. She was Hester's age, but Hester had made fast friends with Faustina, eleven, and the two were thick as thieves, racketing about together with mischief in their eyes and whoops of laughter following in their wake. Lillian was gratified to see Hex enjoying herself so immensely, and even more gratified that Paulina had taken oversight of the domestic labor, allowing Lillian the freedom to join Leo, not missing a moment of this adventure.

Lillian came to the side of the cart and took the ribbons as the horse, a thick dappled gray, plodded to a stop under the dome of pearled clouds.

"You're just in time. I think a mid-day meal will be welcome." It boded rain later, and Leo had not permitted an idle moment for anyone, wanting to get as far as he could before the clouds opened.

"Any excitement today?" Paulina hopped down from the bench and shook out her white apron.

"They've gotten about a foot further in each of the three holes, but so far nothing, not even a potsherd."

"Mrs. Carter said Roman artifacts are always turning up in the fields west of Ashdown. Pottery, coins, once a brooch that caused a stir. I've her ale for now, though my own should be ready soon." Paulina passed a heavy ceramic jar to Lillian, who smiled at the weight of it.

"Paulina, if I've not said it before, I'll say it now: you have saved this expedition. We would have expired on the second day if I were in charge of procuring and preparing food."

Paulina nodded in acknowledgment, pushing a dark curl beneath her cap. "There's ham with the special cure they do in Calne, and a blue cheese, and lardy cakes. With nutmeg this time. And some pickled vegetables from the Berrycroft farm. Their gardens are better than the Manor's."

"Mutton?" Lillian asked.

"For dinner tonight, along with my own recipe for Marlborough pudding. The lady at the Rose and Crown told me how to make it. Octavia, my love, take your father his ale."

"Yes'm. Hallo, mum." Octavia nodded a greeting to Lillian, then set out to her father.

"Has Hex been behaving for you?"

"A perfect lamb, when my own little pigeon isn't stirring up something." Paulina smiled fondly as the two girls wriggled down from the cart and ran toward one of the stones that hedged the barrow, where they had discovered a nest of great bustard eggs. "Mind you don't disturb the babies, so they can hatch and grow to be the little bustards they're meant to be," she called in the fashion of mothers since the dawn of time.

"Bustard." Faustina slapped a hand over her mouth. "What a funny word."

"Bustard," Hester murmured, and the two collapsed in giggles.

"We want to see the eggs." The twins, Titus and Tiberius, popped out from the stand of beech trees and raced to join the girls. Paulina called out another warning, then sighed.

"Have the boys been underfoot too badly?" she asked her husband as he approached.

Both parents stood regarding their progeny, while Claudius sipped his jar of ale. He was a tall, solidly built man, with broad cheekbones and an angled jaw. Beside him, Paulina looked the female copy, with more refined lines to her oval face, long nose, and arched brows. They shared the same deep brown skin tone and jet-black hair, and Lillian was struck not only by their hand-someness as a couple but the way they seemed attuned to one another, following the other's thoughts.

Paulina had told her a bit of their story. Claudius had been a child brought in to serve as a houseboy in the home of a landowner on the island of St. Vincent when the British seized it from the French. He'd worked his way up to valet and had been brought to England when the gentleman fled the First Carib War. Hearing about the Somerset case, which declared that a former slave could not be transported from England against his will, Claudius liberated himself while the gentleman was in London and found work at the docks. He took the name he'd been given by masters as his surname and chose his own given name after the Roman emperor who had conquered Britain.

It took him two years of weekly visits to the brewhouse where Paulina worked for him to screw up the courage to woo and win her, and they had six children who had so far survived the illnesses and vagaries that plagued the lives of the young. Lillian had never before beheld what she would consider the model of a large, loving family, nor had she thought to encounter another couple as wrapped up in one another as were her parents, but when Claudius turned to regard his wife, he looked at her as if she were the sun and stars together, the heat and light of his world.

"Your ale's much better," he said, lifting the ceramic jug.

She nodded. "I know."

A small grunt came from the cart, accompanied by the thump of a heel hitting wood. Before either of his parents could move, Augustus, who was usually not more than a shadow's length from Leo's side, swooped into the back of the cart and picked up his brother, Anthony, not quite two. With great cere-mony the elder brother conducted the younger around the site, introducing him to everyone and everything, including a peek inside the cave, framed by its enormous gray stones.

Lillian plucked a jar from the basket along with one of the packets of oiled paper and made her way to Leo, who was striding in a circuit around his holes. He'd swapped his fine coats and pantaloons for a workman's fustian jacket and canvas trousers, with a kerchief knotted around his neck. He looked more like a pirate than an English gentleman, and Lillian battled the urge to grasp him by his kerchief and pull him toward her for a kiss.

"We've hit stone," he said by way of greeting.

He held out a hand for the food but didn't look at her or murmur thanks, too focused on the hole in the ground at his feet. A stray spring breeze flicked at his hair, carrying the scent of the hesperis flowering along the margins of the grove. Beech trees ringed the outer ditch surrounding the barrow, and their leaves shielded from sight the Vale of the White Horse, which would otherwise spread in green rolling splendor about them. A warbler called from a shrub, and a hobby sat in the branch of a tree, watching the flight of a dragonfly.

"What does that mean?" she asked.

"The stone? It might simply mean more of these sarsens, lying about as at Stonehenge, long since sunk into the earth. Or there could be chambers below, and the stones are a ceiling. To get a proper look, we'd have to uncover the entire mound. I've never heard of such a thing being done at a site, and I don't know if it's even possible to do in the time we have with a crew this size." He dragged a hand over his jaw in frustration, and Lillian flushed with the memory of how he held her jaw in his hand while he kissed her.

"The alternative is to go in through the cave." He, in contrast, didn't seem at all plagued by the memories that swirled around her like mayflies.

Lillian shuddered. "I'll draw what you bring out of the cave, but I don't care to go inside. Especially if a Norse elf still dwells here, as the residents of Ashbury would have us believe."

"Old stories. Folklore. Myth." He pressed the ham and cheese inside the slice of lardy cake and munched, studying the ground below them, sweeping his hand as he spoke. "If the ceiling is stone, the chamber could be relatively stable. A wooden platform, I'm not so sure. Timber posts could have rotted by now. In which case it would make more sense to come from above."

He handed her the oiled paper and took the jar of ale. "Mrs. Caesar's?"

"No, Carter's. Hers isn't ready yet."

Leo squatted and ran a hand through the silt at the bottom of the nearest hole. "Chalk. I have a hunch that if we cleared more of the shrubbery, we'd find a more impressive ditch than that at Stonehenge, or even Avebury. The earth on the mound had to come from somewhere."

He was sharing his thoughts with her, thinking aloud as her parents did to one another. She ought to appreciate this moment. Yet Lillian felt she wasn't *there* with him. She was merely the deliverer of his sustenance and the receiver of his speculations, a cart with legs instead of wheels.

She prickled with heat at his very nearness, a pleasant awareness that warmed her veins like brandy, and he hadn't even glanced her way, much less regarded her as if she were all the lights in the firmament.

She was being absurd. She was wishing he would behave with her like couples who had been building their lives together for years. Like people who were firmly and irrevocably in love. She was merely the woman he was pretending to marry, a woman he had taken to his bed, among who knew how many others.

She was the silly girl who had taken a gamble on being closer to him, volunteering to draw for his records, and he saw her as part of his expedition, not a companion. More fool she.

She turned away, intending to call to Hester and ensure she ate a bite, but Octavia had already spread a quilt on a cleared patch of ground and was handing around food to her siblings, Hex settled in among them like a fair-haired cuckoo in the nest.

Hester didn't need Lillian, either.

The neigh of a horse alerted them to visitors, and the draught horse lifted his head in his harness, looking with interest toward the Ridgeway, where a vehicle approached. Leo had told her what the villagers said, that the beaten track was a thoroughfare older than the Roman roads, as old as human habitation in these isles. Lillian tried to imagine what they had looked like, and what their lives had been like, these people who carved the White Horse and carried their dead to this tomb, if Leo was correct about its function. It was easy to believe giants had once lived on this land, with the size of the monuments they left.

A man with more silver than brown in his hair drove a light chaise toward them, pulled by a single horse. The top was pulled back to reveal his passenger, who bore a cloud of white-blonde hair beneath her cap, and who held a dainty parasol between her pale skin and the cloudy sky.

"Tourists," Leo muttered. "They'll want to ask questions and poke around."

"You must allow it, Leo," Lillian chided. "The cave is a landmark that has been known for centuries. Of course visitors will be curious about it. And you yourself told me once the treasures of Britain should be open to all."

"But not while I'm excavating," Leo said, looking exactly like a sulky boy who didn't want to share his new hoop and stick with a fellow. "I'm not shoeing his horse, even if he offers me far more than a groat." It was custom, based on the old legends, for visitors to leave a groat or sometimes a half-farthing for the resident spirit, whether or not they required the services of a smith.

"I'll answer their questions. Call me if you find something worth drawing."

Lillian moved toward the new arrivals with a friendly smile, recognizing that she was doing what she'd always done: trying to make herself useful. Taking over the tasks another disliked, so they might feel fondly toward her because of it. Smoothing the way of someone she cared about, so they might show care for her in return.

She faltered as she approached the chaise. Did she care for Leo? Had he wormed his way, that quickly, into the list of people she would sacrifice for?

She chanced a glance behind her to see him squatting above

one of the bore holes with Claudius, conferring and pointing. Her chest grew tight as if drawn by a net. She'd come to the point where the mere sight of him made her insides feel they'd been stirred into a pudding. The landscape around her shifted with him in it. He came to the foreground, and everything else receded.

That could not be wise.

"Hallo! Forgive us for descending on you, but we'd heard there was work being done at our favorite local monument, and we thought we must come pay our respects. I am the Reverend Woodfforde, and this is my sister, Temperance."

"How do you do." Temperance beamed a smile that transformed her from quite lovely to truly exquisite.

Lillian blinked. "How do you do." She introduced herself and Paulina as the other woman joined them. Temperance bestowed a smile of equal loveliness upon them all.

"We are so pleased to have new folk in Ashbury," Temperance said. "You cannot imagine how quiet it can be sometimes in our little village. You must come dine with us at Watercress Cottage. That is in Kingstone Winslow, just up the path from you, past the Upper Mill." Her blue eyes, a paler, more delicate shade than Lillian's own, scanned the knot of men standing above the cave. "We would be delighted to entertain Mr. Westrop, and you, Miss Gower, and you and your family as well, Mrs. Caesar."

Unless Lillian imagined it, the girl's gaze lingered on Leo, who now strode between the various holes, looking down into them and arguing with Claudius about something. That net around Lillian's chest grew tight, clenching her heart.

Temperance Woodfforde was, by any estimation, a beauty. And Leo was incredibly dashing. Of course she would take an interest.

He'd secured Lillian's promise to protect him from the

advances of other women so he could focus on his work. But what happened when he met a woman he didn't want defending from?

"You might join us for dinner at the Manor tonight, Reverend, Miss Woodfforde," Paulina said cordially. "It's a very modest table, only roast mutton and Marlborough pie, but we would be delighted to make friends in the area."

Lillian tried to catch her eye and nod furtively in Leo's direction. He was already impatient about the visitors. What would he say if he were called away from his digging to play the friendly host?

Host to a genial reverend and his very lovely sister. He might not mind in the least. Jealousy tanged bitter on her tongue, like raw comfrey leaf.

She'd followed Leo here because she wanted more time with him, as if within this ancient boundary they could spin out their stolen moments and belong entirely to one another.

She might have been enjoying an enchanted moment. But perhaps, for Leo, the spell was already over.

CHAPTER SIXTEEN

"I made the pudding," Hester announced, sliding into her chair at the long oak table occupying the old dining hall of Chapel Manor.

"Why, then I am sure to enjoy it." Reverend Woodfforde, standing behind his own carved wooden chair in deference to the ladies, winked at her. "I'm inclined to believe I would be impressed by anything from Mrs. Caesar's hands, but now I am doubly certain that pleasure awaits us."

Hester regarded him seriously, as if looking for the slant behind his words. Very often she sensed when others were mocking her, even if she didn't grasp the full import of the insult. But the reverend beamed at her in an avuncular fashion, and Temperance radiated her light over them all. Hester nodded, deciding to accept his remark as a compliment.

"Thank you. I hope you will not be disappointed. The recipe is quite simple, and Paulina helped, but apples are not in season, you know, and will not be for another month or more."

Leo's voice approached the dining chamber, and awareness rippled along Lillian's shoulders like a scarf drawn along her skin. The back of her neck heated. She was a maiden sitting in a medieval keep watching for her favorite knight, knowing she must share him with everyone else, when what she wished was for them to be alone.

She liked that version of the world, they two alone. She liked when she was the only thing his eyes lit upon, where his attention focused.

She liked it too much, she was coming to see.

She'd chosen the loveliest of her packed gowns, a simple round gown with puffed sleeves. The striped silk, sprigged with pale yellow flowers, shone a golden brown, a shade darker than her hair. With Faustina's aid she'd rolled her hair into a few coils pinned up and decorated with a clutch of lesser spearwort she'd found growing along the watercress bed. She regretted the simplicity of her attire when Leo strode into the room. She, Lillian Gower, who had never in her life dressed for the regard of a man, wanted the admiration of Leo Westrop.

He didn't glance at her, his head turned toward Claudius as he continued their conversation. "—anything yet, as I told him, and it won't speed our progress to have him ever poking in." Leo nodded at the reverend by way of greeting.

"Is there something the matter?" the reverend asked.

Lillian could not decide if the man was excessively cordial, or if a deeper motive lay behind his curiosity. He'd accepted Paulina's invitation to dine at once, which meant he was not otherwise engaged, which might mean there was simply a dearth of company to be found in Ashbury.

Or he was eager to get his sister inside the Manor, under the eye of the presumed heir to the Marquess of Waringford's titles and fortunes. His lovely sister, slender and shining like a sunny stem of toadflax. Lillian was a squat, round field mushroom beside her.

"It's Craven's steward, Peaty." Leo circled the table to seat Temperance while Claudius went to his wife. "He's been accommodating on other matters. Let us rent this pile, in fact, since he's in between tenants."

Temperance beamed at him and slipped into her seat like a butterfly folding its wings and alighting on a flower. Her hair had received careful attention, a puff of curls covered with a silken net dotted with pearls. The bodice of her dress was a demure V, and the shoulder puffs of her sleeves covered her upper arm, but there was no veiling her beauty. She smiled over her shoulder at him and Leo paused, staring. Lillian's throat ached.

"I wondered how you'd got this place," the reverend remarked, taking his seat. "Peaty's a good man. Exacting but thorough. Much admired by all who do business with him. But I'd expect no less from a man of Lord Craven's."

"He may be an exemplary steward, but he's not an antiquarian." Leo came to the foot of the table where Lillian stood, the only woman not yet seated. She had been taking the hostess's place out of habit but realized now what that would signal. The place she was trying to claim in Leo's life.

"Peaty thinks I should be hauling treasure out of the earth already, and if I'm not, I must be keeping something from him. Told me he'd be pleased to stop by and observe our operations any time it is convenient to me. How do I tell him no time is convenient?"

He'd related the steward's letter to Lillian yesterday while inspecting his mound for further places to dig. She'd been his partner then, his equal and sounding board as they discussed whether to bore down from above or come through the side. He'd talked to her the way her father tested ideas on her mother. She understood his eagerness to make progress, his frustration over any delays.

She was coming to understand much about him. His disposition, his tendencies, his preferences, his dislikes. She could predict his response to so many things.

How could she be so attuned to him, yet he did not seek her out when he entered a room? He didn't catch her eye or smile as she sat, though he'd stood struck by Temperance Woodfforde's aura of brilliance. When his hand grazed Lillian's arm, below her sleeve but above her glove, he jerked as if her skin had burned him.

A hot lump formed in her throat, as if she'd eaten a tart fresh from the oven.

"I would be happy to give Mr. Peaty a tour, Westrop," she said, her voice tight. "You've told me about your approach and your methods. I am sure I could accurately represent your work. Unless, of course, Mr. Caesar would prefer to apprise Mr. Peaty of your progress. Or if Peaty is the type to doubt the word of a woman."

Leo met her gaze, finally, and the tight line of his jaw softened, his mouth curving up.

"Any man would be a fool to doubt your capabilities, Miss Gower."

She flushed and pressed her shoulders against the back of her chair so she didn't lean toward him like some widgeon. It alarmed her, how much she craved his notice. His approval.

"Lord Craven must approve of you, Mr. Westrop, to give you the liberty of Chapel Manor," the reverend said. "This is a jewel of the area, you know. Been here for three hundred years, built shortly after the War of the Roses to please the Abbot of Glastonbury and lodge their monks traveling to and from Oxford. I imagine many a philosophical conversation taking place in this hall, and many a prayer uttered in the oratory over the porch."

The Chapel Manor, like Gower House, was of Tudor design, which was why Lillian supposed she felt comfortable here. A carved wooden screen partitioned the dining area from the formal parlor, but the chambers shared an elaborate vaulted ceiling, the heavy oak beams carved where they crossed with vines flowering into a Tudor rose. The transom windows, capped with a cinquefoil design, added to the air of age and stateliness.

Octavia and Hester sat straighter in their chairs, as if attuned to the grandeur. Only Leo looked immune, and Lillian wondered if that were because he had been reared in environs of greater luxury and historical pedigree, Waringford House in Sevenhampton, Westrop House in London, and no doubt half a dozen houses equally grand scattered over the marquessate.

"Certainly the monks never enjoyed such fine service." Temperance smiled at Augustus, who was playing butler that evening and supervising the twins in their matching footman's livery. Faustina was stationed in the kitchen, at the far side of the house, with instructions from her mother about which dishes to send in when, and within shouting distance should the need arise. Lillian didn't know where Paulina had fetched up the fine porcelain service or crisp white cloth for the table, but she suspected the resourceful landlady of the Rose and Crown might have had a hand in their accommodations.

"I am not certain Craven has any opinion of me." Leo sat back as Augustus placed the roast mutton before him for carving. "But he has a great fondness for Miss Gower, whom he considers a childhood friend. He offered the Manor at once when I wrote Mr. Peaty that a genteel lady would be joining my crew."

He winked at her, and Lillian's stomach closed like a night-blooming flower at dawn. If only she could be to him what that gesture portended, his partner. His companion. The one who knew his inmost feelings, who shared his quest.

She was sitting here tonight. She could pretend, if she wanted to.

"Tell us about yourself, Miss Gower," Temperance said. There was nothing besides wide-eyed innocence in her expression, but Lillian, like Hester, had been pricked too often by the sweetly poisoned barbs of the London haut ton not to be wary.

"Lillian is a fine artist," Leo said. "She's publishing a florilegium with a very respected printer in London, Karim and Son. We spent a week with her parents, who are excavating at Stonehenge, to train me up before we removed here. Lillian came to draw for me so I may have a proper record of our dig."

He could say all the pretty words, Lillian thought. So why could he not bear to touch her?

Temperance continued her sunny beam. "How accomplished you are, Miss Gower. I quite admire women of skill."

"Now, Temperance, my dove, do not rate yourself less simply because you have not published books," her brother admonished her. "To each his talent, as the Lord apportions, eh? Miss Hester, what is your talent, if I might ask?"

Lillian opened her mouth to tell him he might address Hester as Miss Giles, and to jump in if her cousin shied from the question. But to her astonishment, Hex, who normally disliked and ignored conversation with strangers, looked up with a serious air.

"I would say my talent is eating," she said. "And Mrs. Caesar's is preparing food, and Octavia's setting a beautiful table, so I think we make quite a happy trio."

The reverend laughed with more vigor than Lillian thought this observation deserved, but the others joined in, and even Leo seemed to lose some tension from his shoulders. The conversation grew merry after that. The reverend told lively stories of his former parishioners at St. Swithun's over in Compton Beauchamp. Augustus broke into the conversation to ask about the sarsen stones scattered around the churchyard of St. Mary's the Virgin, Ashbury's church, and far from reprimanding the boy for speaking out of turn, Woodfforde told him the common opinion was that the site had been holy well before the conquering Normans built their churches—perhaps even before the Romans brought their roads and their swords and the coins that farmers kept finding in the fields around Ashdown.

Lillian thought the reverend young to be retired from his calling, though he was a decade or two older than his sister, who could not be much older than Lillian herself. He was the most genial guest, describing to Claudius and Leo what little was known about the earthworks called Uffington Castle and, less than a mile away, Hardwell Castle as well. He drank with the men at a measured pace, but he didn't ignore the women. He made certain his sister sampled all the dishes, including the watercress salad and buttered asparagus; he praised Paulina extravagantly for her cooking and her beautiful children; and he drew out Octavia with questions about the local sights she had enjoyed so far, which she confessed to be the Manor's dovecote, complete with nesting doves.

He even spared kind words and avuncular winks to Titus and Tiberius, teasing them about the imperial namesakes, and gave Augustus a word of advice about how to spoon out the ramson soup without spilling a drop. He could not, Lillian thought, be so entirely kind; there must be some purpose to his concerted efforts to be conciliatory. Then she chided herself for her surly thoughts. Perhaps the Woodffordes simply *were* the most pleasant pair of siblings she could imagine existing, and Lillian was being churlish because she did not want Leo's appreciative gaze lingering on Temperance.

The reverend directed his kindliest smiles at Hester, to whom he turned with compliments as the Marlborough pudding passed round the table. "And I suppose, Miss Hester, that Mr. Westrop has already regaled you with the history of Wayland Smith, and how he came to inhabit this precise cave in Berkshire?"

Hester, savoring her pudding, sent an accusing look at Leo. "He has *not*," she declared.

"In my defense, the stories I hear keep changing." Leo wasn't willing to relinquish his status as Hester's new favorite, and particularly not to this newcomer. "Though perhaps the vicar here has a better grasp of the myth."

"Vicar no longer, I'm afraid, though I do find it difficult to put away the clerical collar, and even more difficult to put away my interest in pastoral care." Woodfforde winked at Hester before turning to Lillian. "The story is a bit distasteful at times— you know those Northmen were not genteel folk. But I assure you, Miss Gower, I shall not shock delicate sensibilities too badly."

Lillian could only nod, her throat filled with a thick, warm stew. The reverend's deference to her as their hostess, the lady of Leo's house, made her all too aware how much she longed for that distinction. How deeply she wished to be worthy of it.

She'd never had a table of her own to preside over, nor seen fare she'd helped prepare be so enjoyed, never entertained such a charmed circle of guests. It was very, very seductive. She wanted more of this.

"Mrs. Caesar or I will intervene if we find the story becomes questionable." Lillian hoped she sounded composed yet authoritative. Paulina instructed the boys to take away the covers and lay the table with sweets and cheeses. Leo leaned back in his chair, eyes shadowed, face studious, as the reverend turned to Hester with his tale.

"Wayland, as the Saxons called him, or Volund to the Old Norse, was a smith of prodigious skill. He could craft the most delicate jewelry to flatter a lady and hammer weapons of such strength they would never bend. The King of Sweden tried to woo Wayland with promises of money, but Wayland refused. He lived happily with his wife, the Swan Princess, in the far reaches of the north, where the ice made sculptures that inspired his craftsmanship."

The reverend's deep, warm voice wove a spell, and Lillian could see how he belonged in a pulpit. "The King of Sweden sent men to seize Wayland and kidnap his wife to force the smith to work for him. When the cunning Wayland built a weapon that could break him out of the king's prison and allow him to rescue his wife, the king ordered that Wayland be crippled, the tendons in his legs cut, so that he could not leave the king's service."

"What did Wayland do?" Hester eyes wide, took a sweet from the dish Woodfforde passed her. The good reverend had already apprehended that the way to Hester's heart was stories and sweets, and he clearly meant to use this to his advantage.

"Wayland worked and plotted. Then one day, the king's beautiful daughter came to Wayland seeking his talents. The princess was in love with the smith, you see, crippled and bitter though he was. She wanted him to set gems in a necklace her father had given her. She hoped with the project, Wayland would fall in love and marry her.

"She didn't realize the necklace was one Wayland had made for his wife, the Swan Princess. The necklace was how he wooed and won her, and the king stole this token of their love to give to his daughter. When Wayland learned that his wife had been commanded to marry another man, he did something truly wicked."

"We heard he killed the king's sons and gave the king jeweled goblets made out of their skulls." Titus, one of the twins, leaned his elbows on the back of his mother's chair. All three of the boys listened as raptly as the diners. Paulina pulled her son's ear to chide him for his ragged manners, and he straightened his back but didn't move away.

"I was going to leave out that bit, as I believe that is stolen straight from the ancient Greeks and the tale of Tantalus, who served his son to the gods in a stew," the reverend replied. "The tale is most unpalatable fare for ladies."

"I certainly would not wish to eat young boy, no matter how deliciously prepared," Temperance said.

She delivered the line so innocently that Lillian missed the jest until the boys broke into whoops of laughter. So, Miss Woodfforde was clever as well as exquisitely beautiful. Lillian shot a glance at Leo, who smiled with amusement, twirling his wineglass with long fingers.

Jealousy sunk in its talons and yanked. She felt as hamstrung as poor Wayland, unable to escape the spell cast upon her. Forced to watch in paralyzed agony, like the king's daughter, as the man she loved fought for and won another.

"What about the poor princess?" Hester demanded.

"Alas, she fared little better than her brothers. Wayland agreed to marry her, but he did not love her. He abandoned her and their growing babe, for you see, the project Wayland had been working on in secret all this time, the great wonder commanded by the king, was a pair of enormous metal wings. Wayland put them on and flew away, across the North Sea, and came to Berkshire. Here he built a new smith and, in mourning for his lost wife, told no one who he was. But travelers found his work was unsurpassed in quality, and to this day, if a rider on the Ridgeway leaves his—"

"Horse and a groat on the rock, and takes a quiet walk, he will return to find his horse properly shod," Augustus finished. "And every hundred years, the great white horse gallops off his hill and down to the cave so the smith can change his shoes. But is that all he can do? Shouldn't there be all manner of jewels and weapons and precious metals piled in his cave, and he's guarded them all this time?"

"Then Mr. Westrop will unearth them, I fancy, and hope he's not disturbing some ancient curse," Woodfforde said.

"What metal is it that let him fly?" Tiberius wanted to know.

"Iron, I'd wager," Leo said. "The Vikings used that more than anything."

Titus made a face. "Then there's only iron in the barrow?"

His twin elbowed him in the side. "But what if we find the wings?"

Their expressions transformed at the exact same time, and Leo anticipated the demand. "You'll be the first to try them, if your father approves."

Claudius grinned and shook his head. "What makes you think you'll be able to operate the wings? Wayland was a god to the Saxons."

"Until the light of the true faith came to the island with Augustine," the reverend put in. "Now we know Wayland could be naught but man. Not an elf, not a troll, not a wizard."

"What became of the princess?" Octavia asked.

"She married a man who loved her properly and raised her son to become the next King of Sweden," Lillian said.

"Or she became queen herself and ruled her people with wisdom and fairness for a good long age," Temperance retorted.

Everyone stared at her, including the boys.

"I fancy that ending for her," Paulina mused.

"Lively stories," Leo said, rising, "but none of them true. Wayland was borrowed from the old Norse by the Saxons, who never built with stone, and neither did the Danes, not even to bury their King Bagsecg, whom King Alfred defeated in the Battle of Ashdown. I have staked my reputation on the cave being a tomb even older than even the Romans, and if I'm fortunate, I'll find proof that will admit me into the Society of Antiquaries and help me equip expeditions far into the future. Reverend, Miss Woodfforde." He bowed slightly. "Forgive me if I don't stay to linger over port. I have to study my maps and plot our work for tomorrow."

He turned to Lillian. "Miss Gower. Will you join me when you can?"

Lillian nodded, her heart leaping around her ears. Leo wanted her.

"I will come to your study." No reason to appear eager. Or, before their friends and guests, too anxious.

"We also must be getting home," the reverend said in his genial manner. "We must pen up my sister's chickens for the night, and she will need to feed her little lamb."

Hester perked up. "You have a sheep?"

"I have an adorable little lambkin, and you must come visit and meet him," Temperance said with her unwearying smile. "I named him Puff."

"Yes, do come call on us at Watercress Cottage," said the reverend. "You will lighten our day. You and your lovely children as well, Mrs. Caesar."

"Though we understand how busy you are. Six children! You have been so blessed." Temperance held out her hand to Paulina, but the reverend turned away suddenly, and Lillian caught the pained expression that drew his face into bleak lines.

After waving their visitors off, with Augustus hitching the cart horse to their chaise, Lillian strapped a work apron over her gown and helped Octavia wash dishes in the scullery. Paulina dried and put away the porcelain service while the boys brushed out their borrowed livery, arguing over who had looked the finest and would end up serving in a great house. Lillian participated in the warm family chatter, so different from what she was accustomed to in the more somber Gower household, but the whole time her heart, like an untamed pony, tugged her toward the study at the back of the house, where an oil lamp spilled light through the doorway and Leo's footsteps sounded on the wooden floor.

She must not let him see her feelings so baldly. This was still a business arrangement to him.

She was the one who wanted it to become something more.

"Ought we call on the Woodffordes, do you think?" Lillian washed the goblets, recalling the dainty curl of Temperance Woodfforde's lips, the tips of her fingers on her glass. She was a delicate stem of lady's tresses beside Lillian's sturdy thistle. "They seem almost suspiciously eager to make friends of us."

Paulina paused with a cloth in hand and raised her brows. "You find kindness suspect?"

The reverend hadn't turned a hair at their unorthodox table arrangements, with their host's betrothed sitting in the lady's chair, his employees dining at table as his equals, and their serving staff participating in the conversation. Aunt Giles would have gone into fits at their shabby manners.

"He seems awfully interested in Hex." Lillian tilted her head toward the back door leading to the yard, where Hester and Faustina had taken a lamp and gone out to gather eggs for the morning.

Paulina put a platter on its shelf. "We can pay a return call at the least. You must realize, Lillian, that someone may take an interest in Hester. What if she wishes to marry and have a home of her own?"

Lillian shook her head. "I don't think she's fit for it. She needs looking after."

"And you're the only one who can do it?" Paulina cast an amused smile over her shoulder. "You've made certain she needs you. But do you also need her?"

"I care for her welfare." Lillian scrubbed at the pie plate, the clumps of congealed sugar.

"That's clear. But what are you doing about yours?"

"I don't know what you mean."

"Mr. Westrop."

That thickness rose in Lillian's throat again, and a warmth everywhere else.

Paulina smiled at her daughter as she took a rinsed plate from her hands. "Claud tell you I made him wait and work two years, wooing me?"

"Two long, desperate years, when he lived on hope and your smile," Lillian said.

Paulina rubbed a cloth over the serving plate, her face tender. "We needed to earn money to marry, like anyone. I'd have said yes that first night if I could. I knew, the way he looked at me—my heart was safe with that man."

Lillian swallowed hard. "Leo—Westrop doesn't look at me that way."

"You just don't see it. My word, you're worse than a cat on hot bricks. Go see what he wants."

"To discuss the excavation." Lillian untied her apron.

"Mmm-hmm. And he want more than that, you make him work to win you." Paulina hung the apron on its peg as Lillian melted through the door.

What more could Leo want from her? This was all she did, Lillian thought: offer her skills, her company, her quiet, uncomplaining support. Making herself available to another's needs so that they would want and appreciate her.

She didn't want to be merely useful to Leo. She wanted to be necessary.

She crossed the quiet, cavernous space of the great rooms toward the glow coming from Leo's workroom, where he and Claudius often conferred. The elder Caesar was currently out in the stable yard with Augustus, putting the animals to bed, and Leo was alone.

She didn't want him simply to look at her as he had before, as if she were a rare orchid he had discovered, and he meant to study every part until he knew her. Interest like that could so easily turn to someone else.

She wanted to be indispensable. Impossible to put aside. His partner, his helpmeet, his Paulina, the woman he built his life around.

They had made no promises. No vows to bind them. Only a false declaration to the world, and falsehood must out itself sometime.

She didn't know when it had happened, but she wanted this to be *real*.

She slid her hands over her skirts and entered the room.

CHAPTER SEVENTEEN

The room Leo had made his study shared the décor of the other rooms on the ground floor, with the oak-beam ceiling and chalk walls crossed with dark timbers. The lamp sent light dancing across the windows and its cinquefoil curves. Lillian was a medieval lady coming to her warrior knight, a Plantagenet queen given as a prize to her Tudor lord.

Or the hidden mistress of the abbot, sneaking time alone with him while the rest of the household looked away.

Leo stood at the oak worktable, covered with scrolls of parchment and rag paper. Lillian made out the maps and diagrams, anchored with a rough and unpolished chunk of rock, dark blue veined with layers of buttercream yellow. He held his hands clasped behind him over the plain back of his waistcoat, his coat discarded on a nearby chair. His hair looked as if he'd run his fingers through it several times.

"Your drawings are extraordinary, Lillian. Do you know how much you've helped me? It's as if, when I look, I can only see it in pieces, but your pictures help me see the whole."

He stared at a diagram she had made of the entrance, the

shelf of rough stone rearing up from the ground with its dark mouth open, the huge stones slumped to the side like fallen sentinels. She hadn't gotten the shading right, or the proportions —the trees in the background appeared too close—but the sense came through of ancient warning, as if a long-forgotten world with all its fears and dangers lay alongside the visible one.

Lillian shuddered. The reverend's story had hooked her as deeply as it had Hester, and she didn't know whom to pity more: Wayland, his legs crippled and his wife stolen to subject him to the king's will; the king's sons, helpless dupes to a tortured man's revenge; or the princess, the innocent maid tricked by her own longing heart and left in ruins. Such ravaged emptiness the smith must have felt, far from his native home, his wife and family lost to him, his prodigious talent turned to shoeing local farm horses. Such anger, such loss must be burned into the site where such a creature dwelled. How much of a taint would be carried by the things inside?

Without looking up, Leo reached his arm around her and pulled her to his body. He was warm and firm, and somehow his hard curves shaped around her softer ones, or she shaped herself to him.

"We'll have to go inside," Leo said. "I don't see a better way. We can bore a dozen more holes above and still come to the same result."

He smelled of nutmeg and citrus, like the pudding. She breathed him in. Wings in her belly opened and fluttered.

"What does Mr. Caesar think?"

"He agrees. If it's truly a barrow and they laid a roof of stone, then all we'll find coming from above is rock. We need to open the sealed entrance and see what lies beyond."

"Will Wayland allow you to disturb his resting place?"

Leo turned his head and pressed his nose into her hair. She

heard his inhaled breath. He was doing the same to her as she was to him: drinking him in with every sense. The flutter traveled outward, dancing along her limbs, up her spine.

"Did you believe the good reverend's story?" he asked.

"He was very persuasive. It's a memorable tale, if a sad one."

"But Wayland had his revenge, and he escaped the king's grasp to build a life on his own terms. I can't help but think he won in the end."

His body slowly angled toward hers, as if turned on a millstone. A mutter of satisfaction escaped him as her breasts came into contact with his chest.

The thought emerged in words before she could consider. "I found Temperance very lovely."

He nibbled along the curve of her ear. His breath across her cheek smelled of sherry. "Is she?"

"I've never seen lovelier, not even among the beauties of London," Lillian said honestly. Her eyelids lowered as he brushed his lips over the sensitive place beneath her ear. Her breath caught in the back of her throat.

"She smelled too sweet." He nibbled his way down her neck.

"Valerian," Lillian gasped. "I smelled it, too."

"I like your scent better." He put his mouth where her neck met her shoulder and bit, gently, at the soft flesh. Lillian dissolved. "Geraniums."

"But she is so...delicate. So graceful. Wouldn't any man want her?"

"All I could see was you, Lillian. Your enormous blue eyes." He lifted his head to look at her. He traced the curve of her cheek with a finger. "How delicious your skin looks in this gown. I wanted to lap you up, like cream." He bent his head again, dragging his tongue along her collarbone, and Lillian shivered. Her nipples tightened with delight. He moved over the crests of her breasts, nuzzling, nipping, licking where he'd nipped.

"All I wanted to taste were *these*." He squeezed her breasts through her gown, and the ache intensified. "May I taste you, Lillian?"

"I—I suppose you might," she gasped, clinging to his shoulders as her knees turned to jelly.

Deftly, as if he'd planned his attack, he unhooked her gown at the back, loosening the bodice. In a moment he lifted one globe from the nest of her stays. He steadied her with an arm across her back as he sucked along the heavy curves, then clamped his mouth over her clenched nipple. She arched into him, shaken by the pleasure that arrowed straight between her legs, by her body's instant, needy response.

"Oh, *please*, Leo."

"Please what, my darling? Kiss you here?" He kneaded the free breast with his hand while muttering with the other breast in his mouth. The arrows kept firing, building the sudden blaze at her core.

"Touch you here?" Suddenly his hand was beneath her skirt, sliding up her thigh, cupping and squeezing her bare bottom. She moaned with delight.

"Or here?" He slid his hand between her legs, his cool, callused hand against her sensitive flesh. She moaned and pressed against him, shameless as the flames lifted her. She'd craved him, longed for him, and now he was touching her at last, and she wanted him never to stop.

He slid a finger along her slit, parted the tender folds. With unerring precision he put his finger on the tight bud where all her need centered. "Perhaps here."

She bit back a moan. How did he *know*?

"Do you like that, my darling girl?" he purred.

She thrashed and clung to him, as if she could climb his body, find her way to release from this storm that swirled around and within her. He chuckled and slid both hands beneath her bottom, lifting her toward the table.

"Your maps," she gasped. "The papers—I won't be Empyrea." She swept a hand around her, trying to push the parchment aside so she didn't crush a precious diagram.

"Empyr—Ponsonby?" Leo raked his piles away as if they meant nothing to him in this moment. "You are far superior to Ponsonby, my dear."

"I notice I'm throwing myself across your desk in much the same way," Lillian observed as he perched her bottom on the edge of the table, skirts rucked about her hips, bodice gaping open. In the lamplight his face looked feral, fierce, the light in his eyes predatory. Yet his lips wore a wicked smile as he kissed her deeply, tangling his tongue with hers. She pulled his shoulders and wiggled, trying to press against him, and he chuckled against her lips.

"Thank God for that. *Lillian.*" He kissed his way down her neck again, his hands drawn to her breasts, fingers kneading, cupping. "Why haven't you come to my room?"

"I—I didn't know you wanted me to." She let her head fall back as he bent his mouth to her breasts, curling his tongue around a nipple. The pleasure was exquisite, the torment an ache close to pain.

"Oh, I want you. Every night, I hope I'll find you sliding into my bed. I dream of what I'll do to you."

"What will you do?" she gasped, trying to tug him closer to her.

"Kiss you everywhere. Here," he said, nuzzling her breasts. "Here quite especially. But also *here*—" He tossed up her skirts and his head was beneath them, his lips on the trembling flesh of her belly. "Here." Another kiss beneath her navel, above the thatch of hair. "And here." Gently he pushed her knees apart to blow on the sensitive, begging flesh, fanning the fire he'd lit within her. She gasped and nearly rose off the table.

"Spread your legs if I might kiss you, my darling Lillian," he said, on his knees before her. He slipped his arms beneath her thighs, supporting her legs, while he brought his hands to her tenderest place and opened her secret folds with gentle fingers. "If I'm doing it wrong, tell me."

"There?" Lillian squeaked, caught between need and agony. "I wouldn't know if—*oh.*"

He kissed her there, then swept his tongue as if he were indeed a cat lapping cream, and it was fortunate he held her legs because Lillian was falling, falling. She knew now the delirium she was falling toward and marveled as it built, a tall wave of pleasure that came from her toes and grew enormous, towering, all-encompassing, before it crashed down over her, cascading through every part of her body, sending liquid to every joint.

He rose with a smile of deep satisfaction and kissed each breast. "Apparently I did it right."

"You...that...what happened to me?" she panted. She curled her fingers into his hair and pulled his head toward hers, wanting to kiss him and never stop. "I want to please you," she muttered against his lips.

He groaned and she felt the hard outline through his pantaloons, pressing into her thigh. "Will you let me inside you, my beautiful Lillian? I promise I will pull away—before."

"Yes, please." She grappled with the buttons on his pantaloons, and he laughed and moved her hands away, releasing his falls. She palmed his cock as it sprang free and his eyelids went heavy, his breath a hiss.

"You want me," she said smugly. Her, plain, plump Lillian Gower. If only passing lust, and only now, this beautiful man wanted to be joined in the most intimate of ways to *her.*

"Hell's teeth, but I do."

He fit himself to her and hissed again as he sank inside in one long, smooth glide. *"Lillian."* He screwed his eyes shut, face tense, jaw working as if he were holding something back. When he had himself mastered, he opened his eyes and looked at her, that wicked glow in his gaze. "You want *me*," he said smugly.

"Yes," she whispered, drawing him close. "Yes, Leo, I do."

He felt wonderful, filling her, and his pleasure fired her own. He shifted and pumped against her, gripping his lip between his teeth, his expression nearly pained, all his focus on the place where their bodies joined, and as she rode him she didn't know if it were a new pleasure or echoes of the old, but the cascade came again, surrounding and lifting her, and she gave herself over to it, to him. When she opened her eyes she found his gaze locked on her face, studying her like one of his diagrams, soaking up every ounce of her pleasure.

"I want to join you," he muttered. "Press your legs together for me. Darling, beautiful—" He lost his words then as he pulled out of her and instead drove himself between her legs, one stroke, two, and then he was shuddering the way she had, pressing a hand beneath her, soft fabric brushing her bottom as he spent into it instead of her skirts.

She clasped her arms about him as he lay against her, cradling his weight, holding him while he slowly knit back together, just as she was doing. Words pushed to her lips that she caught just in time.

I love you.

Did she? Did she love a man she'd known only a few weeks? She could not say he was not toying with her. She could not vow this was more than a dalliance to him. He had not said a word of what she meant to him, or what he wanted from her, yet she was ready to cast her whole heart away on him, placing her future and her hopes in his hands like an offering left in the shadowed mouth of a cave, unsure what her sacrifice would achieve.

She swallowed the words. "That seems more of a mess than last time," she said instead.

He gave her a lazy, satisfied grin and threw the crumpled neckcloth to the floor. "I've been saving myself for you. Waiting in my room, night after night. Dreaming I could hold you like this."

He lifted her as if she didn't weigh as much as she did and settled them both in the chair. Likely he was crushing his expensive coat, and clearly he didn't care. He nestled her bottom onto his lap, draping her knees over the armrest, idly stroking the skin of her calf.

She rested against him, knowing what she risked to surrender. But his arms were so safe, so warm. His heart beat so steady and solid against her side. She went to tug her bodice over her breasts, and he tugged it down again so he could study the whole of her bosom.

"Too beautiful to disguise," he said.

"I can't walk about with my bosoms showing, Leo. Not even to satisfy you."

"Only show them to me, then." He kissed her temple, sweeping her hair aside with his lips.

"Paulina will know if I come to your room," she said after a moment. "Even though they have the steward's rooms on the other side of the passage. I suspect she knows we are up to something already."

"I expect she's caught me watching you like a besotted fool."

Had he been? She wanted to press, yet she couldn't bear if he returned a light-hearted answer. Not when her heart was so heavy with this new awareness.

"You are only besotted with your cave," she grumbled.

He looked over his worktable as if his mind were there

already, plotting how to break through the heavy stones blocking the back of the cave. But his hand wandered up her leg beneath her skirts, warm and possessive.

She wanted to be possessed. By him.

"You've fulfilled one dream of mine. Of lying you down upon my maps and taking you on the table."

One more prize to claim? Land to be conquered and won, or a monument to be explored and owned? Was that all she was to him?

She swatted his fingers away as he slid his hand between her thighs. She was replete, her body sensitized from the pleasure, yet in agony. This couldn't be all she meant to him, the way she held and won him. She had to be more.

"Better than taking me atop the barrow, I suppose, with everybody watching. Like some pagan ritual of olden times."

"Damn it, Lillian." He bent his lips to her neck. "Now I'll be dreaming of spreading you out on the barrow. And me between your legs, worshipping. I won't be able to get any work done." His hand came to her breast, and she pushed him away and rose.

It was all about the work for him, and the physical gratification she could offer. Her artistic knowledge, her archaeological expertise, her body: she'd offered freely, and he'd accepted freely, making no promises in return. And that made her a fool. She went to the table and started straightening his maps and papers.

An instant later a hard, hot wall pressed behind her, his arm snaking around her ribs to cup a breast. She felt his member pressing against her bottom, barely disguised by the thickness of her skirts.

"You're angry with me. Did I hurt you?"

Not in the way he might think. She closed her eyes and braced her hands on the table, wondering if she dared surrender. Every moment of pleasure was a golden cord binding her to him. Hamstringing her, like the tortured smith, so she couldn't leave.

He slid his flesh against hers, gently rocking, a question, asking if she was ready again. If she wanted him.

What more could she give him that would make him want her utterly? *Her,* and not simply what she offered?

"Once is enough, for now." The strangeness of it tunneled through her, the sensations of new discovery. She drew away, pulling up her bodice, pulling down her skirts. The wick in the lamp flared, sizzling, and she glimpsed some sober, quiet depths in his eyes when she looked up at him. He looked—regretful? Resigned?

"Are you sorry?" His voice was deep, rough, as if emerging from a cave.

"For this? No." She touched his chest. "I love—love being with you. Not just this, but all of it. When we talk about your dig. When you talk to me about anything." She picked up the heavy rock that anchored his larger map. "Like why you would carry a heavy rock in your luggage."

His face remained shadowed, his brow furrowed as he stroked the rough surface. He rested his other hand on her hip, as if he couldn't bear to let go.

"One time when my father was about, and sober, and had some money, he took my mother and brother and I to Derbyshire, to the Peak District. There's a cavern where they mine blue john—that's what stone this is."

"I've not heard of it," Lillian murmured.

"It's valuable, I believe. Makes lovely ornaments and jewelry. My father brought this rock away, swearing he'd have something fashioned for my mother. A piece she could show off. Something to make her proud of him."

Leo's face was terse and beautiful in the dancing shadows.

"When he left again, who knows where, I hid the rock in my chamber. I was fascinated with it, and angry at him because he hadn't kept his promise. And I wanted...I think I wanted a solid memory of that time when we'd all been together, and happy. He came looking for it to pay a debt, but I wouldn't tell him where it was, though he roared and nearly tore the house apart."

Lillian's eyes smarted with tears. She smoothed the lines of his brow with her fingers. "And you keep it still?"

He shrugged. "As a reminder, I suppose. Not to be again the foolish boy I was, trusting anyone, believing—*hoping*—my father would reform." He tapped a sharp edge of the mottled blue-gray stone. "But as a reminder also that what is rough on the outside may be valuable within. There can be treasures found in the unlikeliest places, if you know where to look."

"That is a valuable lesson." She swallowed the thick ache in her throat.

His gaze met hers, and she was caught. Good sense told her to move away, go to her room, climb into bed with Hester, not dream of Leo Westrop. Her heart was not at all in agreement with the agenda of her good sense. His face drew close to hers, his arms near enough to step into, and what would he do if she told him she was his completely?

"Lillian, I..."

"What?" she whispered, waiting. Aching to hear what she wanted to hear, dreading she'd hear something else.

The clock in the parlor chimed enough bells to tell them it was late. Leo blinked and stepped away. The spell was broken.

"I suppose you ought to go to bed."

"Yes, I suppose I ought."

He caught her hand and kissed it, and she leaned toward him like the dancing candle.

"Good night, my beautiful Lillian."

She nodded and withdrew, climbing the stairs to the chambers on the first floor. Hester lay in the bed, quietly breathing, while moonlight cast a glow through the window. Lillian laid aside her dress and crawled into bed in her shift, her body still charged, aglow.

It was too late for her to leave with her heart intact. Too late for this arrangement to end with anything but hurt. A hurt she was afraid would cleave her to the bone when they parted.

CHAPTER EIGHTEEN

"A re you ready to go back in?"

She glanced up from her sketchbook, and the familiar punch hit Leo's gut when Lillian's gaze locked on his. Her eyes were the blue the sky might have been, had clouds the color of dirty sheep not covered the Vale of the White Horse.

Lillian Gower grew more lovely each day, and increasingly, the bolt of pleasure that burrowed into his chest at the sight of her tapped into a desperate knot growing there—the knowledge of how much he would lose when she was done with him and returned to London.

She drew a deep, steadying breath, and the muslin neckerchief tucked at her bodice fluttered over her breasts. She dressed sensibly for their days of work, sturdy leather boots, today a printed cotton round gown covered with a thick apron, a cloth bonnet catching up her hair. His mind flashed greedily to the night before, that hair spread over his pillow, her blue eyes hazy with passion, those magnificent breasts flushed pink from his kisses. The way her back arched off the feather mattress when he brought her to the peak of pleasure, the way she choked back a sob-scream so she didn't wake the house.

Stow it, Westrop. He'd asked, all but begged her to come to his bed, and so she had, and now he was wild for her. Famished. She was a feast, and he could never be sated.

She was growing on him in so many ways, so many tendrils curling and rooting deep. Far too often he caught himself pausing while the men dug to look about, find her sitting on a sarsen or curb stone drawing the countryside, or wandering the vale beyond, studying a new flower. The days she was gone, visiting the Woodffordes or helping Paulina at the Manor, he chafed at her absence as if at an ill-fitting shoe. Those evenings, instead of sitting in the parlor with the others talking about their day or playing games with Augustus, he called her into the library and relished the quiet way she worked on her sketches while he read and jotted notes and studied his maps, the two of them knit together in the glow of the oil lamp, a world unto themselves.

He liked the Caesars immensely, but he liked being with Lillian more.

Best were the nights when she came to him with her chamberstick casting pale light on her skin and her hair in its braid over her shoulder and her feet in the cloth house slippers, muffling her steps. The touches and the pleasure—God, the pleasure, yes—but also when they lay together after, her drowsy in his arms, telling him stories about her life, listening to his. He could see in those tales how a fanciful, dreamy child had grown into a sensible, managing sort of woman, dauntless and determined, but he still caught glimpses of the imaginative, inquisitive girl beneath, raised on open air and freedom.

Her parents had treated her as a creature capable of reason, and she had become so, but she also had a generous, loyal heart along with her level head and keen mind. Leo had come in the past weeks to admire and respect her many talents, and to appreciate her occasional flaws—the stubborn streak a mile wide, like bedrock beneath a sweet burbling stream, and the way she agreed to something she didn't want to do if it would please another.

Like now. She hated going underground. But she'd gone once before into the small antechamber, at his request, to draw the site before they removed the chalk rubble filling up the passage. And she would go now, to draw what lay beyond, to be at his side as the first humans in hundreds of years to look upon the contents of the cave.

"What's in there?" she asked, rising to her feet. Jaw taut, fingers taut on her sketchbook, he could see her reluctance, yet she would do this for him, because he asked.

He wanted to pull her to him and wrap his arms tightly about her, pressing her against him until not a feather could fit between them. Until he felt her heart beating inside his body, and he had absorbed all her fear, all her aches, everything that had ever tormented her. What was he doing for her that could possibly repay all she gave him?

"I'm not certain what we'll find. But if I am correct and it is a barrow, Aubrey and Stukeley, the greatest antiquarians of their age, will spin in their graves."

He grinned at her, joyed by the mere shape of her face against the cloudy sky, the curves of that delicious body that yielded to him again and again, and at the thought of discovering something new, of proving his theory correct despite the pronouncements that others had made. She managed a smile in return and gave him her hand to help her descend the clump of fallen rock where she'd been sitting, sarsens that had long ago guarded the entrance to the cave, now passing their centuries in quiet slumber as time itself had forgotten their task. Her hand slid into his like a key in a lock, her eye to his hook, something necessary and belonging joined together at last.

"Tell me again why I am doing this." She clenched his hand

as they faced the square of dark leading into the mound of earth, the two sentinel rocks flanking it, one a sharp edge slanting away, the other a curved hump.

"Because the drawings, like your parents said, are crucial to the excavation. I will submit your sketches with my findings to *Archaeologia,* the journal of the Society of Antiquaries, and hopefully they will find my report substantial enough to merit my nomination into the Society."

He squeezed her fingers gently. "If my findings are of interest, I will have patrons who will be willing to help me fund other digs, the way Sir Richard Colt Hoare is funding Cunnington and your parents. Your sketches will help others see the site if they cannot travel on their own. And your name will be on the title page, right alongside mine. Drawings supplied by Miss Lillian Gower."

"My name until I marry," she said, her voice tense, and the thought tripped and tangled in Leo's mind. If she married him, she would be Mrs. Gideon Leonidas Westrop. She would have his name. She would *be* his.

He stood to gain so much, did she wed him. Her skills lent to their shared projects. Her trust in him, her care for him. Her by his side, like this, his sweet, laughing companion at work and at board, and in bed—the pleasures he'd discovered rose about him like a tidal river, swamping his senses. That pleasure like nothing else he'd known.

Married, she would be his to shelter and protect and cherish, all her days and his.

And she would gain—what?

A man with a questionable future, current resources spread thin, prospects unknown until his uncle decided on his heir. A man who had nothing to offer except his devotion and promises, and promises could not be spun into pin money, or meat on the table, or lodgings for her beautiful, clever head.

She deserved more.

She was worth more.

Her fingers gripped his so tightly that he was certain she had stopped up the blood. "Promise me there is not a troll in there," she said. "Or some wicked Norse elf or ancient god."

"There is no one, Lillian, my love. If I'm right, it's a tomb of the Celtic dead. If I'm wrong, it's nothing but a pile of rubble. If it is a barrow and there is a wraith, I will vanquish it for you."

"You had to bring up ghosts." She let go of his hand and slapped her sketchbook to her bosom as if it were the shield by which she would conquer or be carried home upon, like an ancient Spartan princess. "Very well, let us proceed."

Claudius stood just inside the square chamber, carrying the candle in its lamp. He beckoned them forward.

The floor was thin, hard chalk, the sides and ceiling slabs of great stone. The musty smell lifted Leo's head, made his chest inflate with a giddy rush; it was the scent of ancient earth, undisturbed. The antechamber had been picked clean ages ago, any treasures carried off in Roman times if not before, but the passage beyond—no one might have seen this since the ancient Celts closed it up with their final prayers and incantations.

It wasn't treasure he wanted or needed, even if it were the tomb of an ancient king. He wanted the discovery of something new. To be the first to find, and study, and share with the world.

A low passage, about six meters long, extended beyond the door the workers had cleared. The men knelt in a chain, passing wooden buckets of rubble back from the excavators working just ahead. Outside the cave the twins, with Augustus overseeing, poured the buckets onto the piles through which other workers sifted, looking for interesting items. The same chain passed the empty buckets forward along the line to be refilled. When a man grew too tired and cramped, he called for relief and crawled outside for a breath of fresh air, and the line closed around him.

The chip and scrape of the diggers' tools echoed off the great slabs of stone that lined the passage, where smaller, flat stones fit into the crevices to form a solid wall. The chamber was an ancient, underground processional, built by the same peoples who had erected the stone circles to commune with their gods. No Greek temple, no ziggurat of ancient Babylon could be more impressive.

"Westrop." She kept her voice a whisper, as if fearing they would be overheard by spirits. "This is truly astounding."

Carefully she touched the smoothed surface of a massive stone, and his heart swelled further, teasing at its seams. She understood. Claudius was a worthy partner, but he was interested in the engineering and mechanics of the excavation. Lillian had been raised among ruins and the ghosts of past civilizations; she knew what this *meant*.

"There's a transept ahead, with two more chambers on either side. We're not sure yet how far the passage goes."

"Imagine what it took to move these." She trailed her hand along the passage wall as if envisioning the crude tools that had hewn these megaliths from the shoulders of the earth, then transported them here to the chalky heaps of the Berkshire Downs.

Leo wanted to lift her hand and place it against his chest so she might slide her palm over him in the same way. He tamped down the impulse.

They reached the cross passage, with workers busy on either side clearing the doorways of rubble. Leo bent his head to keep from banging the stone roof of the passage as he peered forward. Two workers shifted dirt and rubble into buckets, then passed them back to the men in line.

"What have you got so far?"

"The end's blocked up, guv, with these great stones. I'll say that's the end of it, an' if there is another room beyond, no one wants us folk inside."

Claudius raised his lamp. "The terminus, do you think?"

"That means the chambers are in a cruciform shape," Leo said. "But this can't be early Christian. They built churches and single graves. Not barrows like this." He lifted a lamp from the floor to peer at the stone wall facing him, its secrets sealed. "Do you know of any appearances of the cruciform predating the Christian period, Lil—Miss Gower?"

She tilted her head to the side, like a little bird about to trill to its mate. "There are some records of ancient Babylonians using the shape for tombs and stele, or so I've read. But I cannot say what it meant to them."

"That would be interesting to pursue. But I think this design alone will interest the Antiquaries already, even if we find nothing—"

"Found somethin'," a worker reported, struggling to pull a heavy stone out of a pile of rubble.

Lillian dropped to her knees the same time Leo did, heedless of staining her gown on the dirt floor. He felt the same excitement pulsing from her.

"Weighty thing, this," the man panted.

Lillian yanked a pair of thick leather gloves from her apron —she'd sewn pockets into it where she stored her tools, a fashion he'd seen her mother sporting at Stonehenge. She helped the men brush the layer of dirt away, revealing a broad rock, large as a dinner plate but deep as a gravy boat, with a smooth depression in the middle.

"It's so heavy!"

"Too large to carry about easily—"

"It's been smoothed—look at the bowl in the middle."

"A statue of some kind? The beginning of a stone carving?" Leo wondered aloud.

"Naught but a rock," the worker said, baffled.

Leo sat back on his heels. "But here? What for? Why hide such a thing underground?"

Lillian laughed, and in the dim light, her eyes sparkled. "It's not simply a rock, gentlemen. I've seen something like this before. I'd wager this is a quern stone."

"A what now," said the digger.

"Quern, from the Old English term *cweorn*, the word for corn—never mind. It's a grindstone. Look for another stone that might go with it," Lillian instructed. "It may be a smaller rock, or cylindrical in shape. This would have been used to mill grain."

Leo stripped off a glove and rubbed the rounded surface. "Of course. This feels like millstone grit, much like the stones we use now. I should have realized at once."

"It not a wonder if you didn't. It would have been women's work." Her eyes fairly danced. She was as thrilled about this discovery as he was.

"But why household goods?" Leo wondered. "They wouldn't have lived in here. There's no sign of soot on the walls from fires, no sign of a midden heap for refuse. It could only be—"

"Grave goods," she said soberly, reaching the thought at the same time he did.

They both fell to digging. Eventually the workers, who had been toiling for some time, left with Claudius for a respite, and it was just him and Lillian, alone together. Leo scooped with his trowel while Lillian used her pick to pry out larger pieces, turning each over in her hands. He looked over when he heard her swift intake of breath.

"Leo—Look." She held out her palm and he stared.

He met her eyes. "Arrowhead."

They studied it together as he brought the lamp closer. "It's flint, but white—I've not seen that before. Flint is usually gray or black, I thought."

"And look at the brown speckles caught on some of the ridges. I do hope that's not dried blood."

"It's finely chipped. This might have been carved with a heavier stone—or maybe they used bone?"

"It's so oddly shaped. More a trapezoid than a triangle."

"It needs a barb to stay in the flesh." He winked at her horrified expression. "You're not an archer, I take it? Men's work."

He held his hands cupped around hers and her heat reached him, her scent deepened with a tangy note of sweat. His libido flared, as if his passion for her were twined now with his passion for exploration and discovery.

She licked her lips, leaving them wet and moist. Ready for his kiss. "There's no shaft."

"Likely rotted away. Unless the placement is ceremonial. Or accidental."

She placed the arrowhead on her sketchbook and turned with him to the pile, now considerably reduced, a small mound heaped against the back wall of the chamber. They worked in companionable silence, punctuated by the occasional murmur of interest, and a coo from Lillian when he found a piece of a potsherd, curved into a crescent moon.

Lillian took off her gloves and ran her fingers over the short grooves in the hard, dark-gray surface. "Look—it's decorated."

"I wonder how big the original pot was, and what it was used for."

"Cooking, perhaps? It looks as though it's been blackened."

"A jewel box for an ancient queen to store her baubles," he teased.

"Perhaps it is broken because the wife crowned her husband with it when he came home reeking of the pub."

"I hope your husband will never give you such cause for vexation."

She turned back to her digging, moving the lamp to illuminate her work area. He tended to his own pile, scooping and pouring, but his awareness of her tickled his skin, like a horse being brushed.

"I haven't properly thanked you for all you are doing for me," he said. "I hope your parents don't resent me for stealing you away. I suspect they rely on you a great deal."

"They would forget to eat if I didn't put meals in front of them, so there is that," Lillian said.

Her lightness tapped on a nerve. Her parents were clearly too wrapped up in their own world to appreciate their gem of a daughter.

The tickle on Leo's skin turned to a cold sweat. Would he do any better? He tended to get wrapped up in his own concerns as well. He'd never before been responsible for another human being. But with Lillian at his side, he could envision what his life might look like with a companion. She made him want that, if she were the woman at his side.

The silence spooled out, and he could not determine whether it was the companionable sort, or if she were cross with him.

"How is it you have not become an antiquarian as well, raised as you were?"

She regarded a lump of chalk in her hand. The chamber was not small, but it felt close and secret, as if the walls leaned inward, enclosing them.

"I've always been fascinated by plants. I'm intrigued by what man has built, and often impressed, but nature's beauty— that truly calls to me. The intricate and flawless design of an individual flower. How each species is so unique. Function and beauty, balanced together—the poetic ideal."

She set the clump alongside the other treasures on her sketchbook, her own little trove. "What of you? Were you an antiquarian from a young age?"

"I was. I suppose it was inevitable, given where we lived, so many odd ruins about, loaded with legend and history. Have you heard yet of the Blowing Stone, the sarsen over in Kingstone Lisle? It has perforations all the way through, and when you blow through it in the right way, it makes the most impressive sound. My childhood self was never able to produce it, but they say that's how King Alfred summoned his troops for the battle of Ashdown."

She threw him a smile. "The battle that killed the Danish king whom some say is buried here. With his quern stone."

Leo chuckled. "He would have an iron spear and sword, if this is King Bagsecg. Highworth has a long history as well—it's recorded in the Domesday book as a Saxon settlement, but I've had old gaffers show me traces of Roman artifacts they've discovered. It might have been a fort town before Julius Caesar first tried to subdue the Celtic tribes. It's frustrating that we know so little about them."

She looked up thoughtfully at the monumental stones enclosing them, a line between her brows. She hated being underground, yet she'd stayed with him for a great length of time—hours, or so it felt.

"Was that your interest, then? The peoples who lived here before the Romans came?"

"Not at first." He kept scooping, pouring, his mind tracing paths he hadn't visited in an age. "In my early days, I wanted to be a Saxon warrior or a Viking chieftain. Valiant and fierce. But I soon realized I wasn't actually interested in war and conquest. My cousins teased me about it, a great deal in fact—neither my brother nor I are the type of rowdy men that the Westrops typically produce."

"What happened?"

"To make my brother and I different?" His laugh was a short bark, lacking humor. "My father. But he gave me one thing, at least. He took me to the White Horse once, when he was traveling to Wantage on some business. I wasn't impressed by some chalk scraped out of the ground—I couldn't tell what shape it was meant to be, and told him so. But then he drove us by Uffington Castle, a huge mound of ramparts within its ditch, and I was entranced. I wanted to know who had built it, what it was for, what it might have looked like in its original state, and I was so baffled when my father could not answer these questions. How could we not know the purpose of something so immense?

"I wanted to know," he concluded. "And those questions drove me. I didn't even care when my cousins made fun, or my mother disapproved of my activities, or my father—" No need for the rest.

She sat back on her heels, scratching her hair beneath the cap. "I find it hard to believe your family isn't proud of you."

"To them, I haven't accomplished anything. Joshua, who wants to be a vicar, they can excuse; they imagine an archbishopric for him someday. But an antiquarian—it's a hobby, not a profession, and not an admirable one. Not virile or manly enough. No drama, no excitement. No service to God and country. Like Rupert."

His throat closed around a memory, a long-legged Rupert daring him to race across a field where the ram had been penned apart, Rupert leaping the stile like a red deer, then laughing when Leo caught his heel and fell on his face in the blooming meadow.

"I'd like to meet your brother," Lillian said softly.

Leo pried his trowel into a new pile and loosened the hard-packed dirt. "He's in Oxford for the summer and not likely to visit, as he enjoys our mother's management as little as I do. But you could meet the others, if you like. We've received an invitation to dine at Waringford Hall. Both of us."

Her eyes widened. "Your family seat? It's near here?"

He nodded. "A mile outside Highworth, in Sevenhampton. It's where I grew up, for the most part. My grandfather liked to have everyone under one roof, the better to supervise their affairs and dictate their actions. My mother has taken up that role now, after my aunt, the marchioness, passed away."

He felt her gaze brushing his face, like the wings of a butterfly. "They are so close, yet you have not visited already."

She didn't press or judge, instead waited until he was ready to explain himself. "They want to meet you, of course."

She dropped her gaze to the dirt before her. The candle in her lamp jerked on a sudden, invisible current.

"Oh." She picked at a lump of earth, something whitish and hard. More chalk, he supposed. "And I imagine your uncle wants to speak with you in particular. Are you ready?"

"No."

She took out her brush and began scraping, that slight frown on her face again. "What do you wish to happen?"

"In truth? I wish for Rupert to show up and laugh at us all for believing the report of his death. My uncle will kill the proverbial fatted calf in celebration, everyone will be relieved that the title will go to someone deserving, and only my mother will be left to fret about how I am frittering my life away in unmanly pursuits, and not marrying and building a family and fortune as I ought to be." He jabbed his trowel into the earth, though he could shatter something fragile with his spleen.

"And when Rupert does not appear?" she asked softly.

Leo closed his eyes, his forehead throbbing with a sudden pain. "I could see if Joshua wants to inherit. He can't take the title, not with me alive, but I could sign over the estates and the rest. He'd be more worthy of inheriting than I would."

"Leo," she said, and he sensed her question.

How could she find him worthy of her hand, when his family found him worthy of nothing?

"You have to understand. Every member of the Westrop family, as far as I can recall, has been a rakehell and a profligate, but a ne'er-do-well with one focus besides his own pleasure: to build the fortunes of the family. My grandfather earned the elevation to marquess and married an heiress, the daughter of an Oxfordshire drug merchant, quite rich. My uncle, when his elder brother died young, expanded the family fortunes by marrying the daughter of a London cheese merchant, also vastly wealthy.

"My great-aunt was a lady of the chamber to the Countess of Yarmouth, favorite mistress of the second George. My other uncle, Rupert's father, was a governor in the American colonies before the war. Only my father managed to tarnish, rather than enhance the reputation of the family. My father entered merrily, heedlessly, into one scheme after another, and each drained us of money and respect, rather than the opposite. I suppose that put me on the back foot from the beginning."

"Leo," she said, her tone changing.

"It's not self-pity. It's fact." He stabbed at the earth, as if he could strike back at his father, at the burden he had left for his wife and sons. "I don't believe for a moment my uncle would truly consider me as his heir. If he did, he'd have settled matters already, the instant the news about Rupert reached us. I imagine there's an entail of some sort, I don't know the terms, but my uncle could break it if he cared for the legal expense. Or he could cut me out by murdering me. I half expect, should we dine with them, my goblet will be poisoned, like the king's cup in *Hamlet*."

"Leo," Lillian said, "I found bones."

CHAPTER NINETEEN

Lillian kept quiet as Leo drove the borrowed chaise through the streets of Shrivenham, past the thatched-roof cottages and the Jacobean Manor House with its pointed gables and deep windows. She looked like a nymph of the dusk in a gown she'd borrowed from Temperance Woodfforde, her hair worked into elegant coils by the combined labors of Octavia and Faustina, whose giggles had drifted from her room as they prepared.

She also looked very serious.

"Farthing for your thoughts," he said lightly.

She graced him with a smile, and there was that dimple that never failed to make his heart hitch.

"I'm astonished that Hester agreed to stay with the Woodf-fordes overnight. I thought she would fuss about us leaving her with the Caesars while we went to dinner without her. She's never slept away from her family before." She hesitated. "You don't suppose..."

"That there will be a repeat of what happened with Bacon?" He guessed the line of her thoughts from the twist to her lovely lips. "No fear in the slightest. The reverend dotes upon your cousin even more than Temperance does. They will spoil her thoroughly and do everything to ensure her comfort."

"I've never quite trusted anyone else to look after her properly. Including her mother," she murmured.

"But tonight you are free to be young and frivolous."

That dimple again. "I cannot recall when I was last frivolous."

"When you threw caution to the wind and kissed a complete stranger after you lured him into your glasshouse," he reminded her.

A shell pink blush traced the curve of her cheekbone. "There is that."

"I believe that is a fault we share. Too little time spent being frivolous."

Along the road to Highworth, the shops and cottages gave way to flat lawns of pasture rimmed with the occasional hedgerow to mark a field or border. The chesty, long-legged Wiltshire sheep, with their horns curling back from noble Roman noses, floated across the sea of green like a fleet of tiny galleons, sleek after their spring moulting. Lillian smiled as she watched the lambs gambol about the feet of their elders, butting one another and the occasional dam, who would raise her regal head and stare complacently until the youthful antics subsided.

"I beg your pardon," Lillian said. "I am frequently frivolous. I spend my time sketching plants, don't you know. What could possibly be more destructive to my prospects of securing a respectable husband and setting up a household of my own, than daydreaming and drawing when I ought to be improving my embroidery and my housewifery skills. And my posture," she added, and he heard her Aunt Giles in her words. "And my topics of conversation. And my—very *me*-ness, really."

Leo clicked his tongue as the horse, sensing laxness, bent his head to nip at a clump of thistles. "We are alike in that as well. Our families wishing we were more a credit to the name."

"I still cannot believe your relatives would find anything lacking in you, Leo Westrop." Lillian canted her shoulders toward him, careful not to crush her dress. "Have you told them of your discovery?"

"*You* made the discovery," he felt compelled to point out.

"I found the first set by pure luck," she answered. "We were working together."

His heart did something strange in his chest just then, shifted and settled like a dog circling in its bed. His mind had been taken up for most of the past few days by contemplation of his find, what to do with the bones, how to report to Craven, how to build a convincing theory for his peers.

Part of his mind had also been preoccupied with worrying about this dinner, Lillian's first encounter with the Westrop family and Waringford Hall. She would see where he had been brought up, and she would see how his family regarded him. He worried she would see their view of matters and think less of him.

Or worse: she would look at Waringford Hall and see more. That the marquessate would be the lure that would make her want him, stay with him, be his in truth.

He didn't want her to be another Empyrea, pursuing him for his possible future.

He didn't see what else he had to offer.

But this was Lillian, who was as entranced by his antiquarian work as he was. She worked side by side with him, discussing options, making decisions. When he'd wanted to unearth the bones immediately to identify what animal they belonged to, Lillian insisted on brushing away the dirt, layer by careful layer, and drawing the bones in situ. She hadn't fainted with horror when Claudius determined that the bones were human, that the skulls of the two seeming adults showed cracks, that one set appeared to have belonged to a child.

Lillian Gower was the perfect archaeological assistant, accomplice, and amanuensis. And he suspected the fit of her in his life accounted for the heights of pleasure he found in her arms. He could service himself, or hire a companion for the night, and it wouldn't be close to the same. The pleasure was from being with *her*.

How could he make her want him, and him alone?

"My mother will be shocked that I've been handling bones at all." He might as well prepare her for the evening to come. He turned off the Highworth road onto the rutted lane that led through the fields of the home farm and the rear approach to Waringford Hall. "You have met my mother, so you see what a stickler she is. In her prayers every night, I believe she thanks God for making her daughter to the Earl of Fossey so she may be addressed as Lady Mary. Calling her nieces by a courtesy title higher than her own would have eaten her alive."

Lillian tucked in a smile. "If only you were reaching as high for yourself. It must be killing her that you lighted on a lowly baronet's grandniece, a plain old miss. She tried so hard with you."

"The epitaph we might carve on her tomb, in a day I hope is yet far in the future," Leo said.

A reed bunting flared up from his hiding place in a buckthorn, a male with his black throat and white collar. His plainer missus joined him a second later, as if reluctant to abandon a nest. Even the plainest bird of field and meadow had his mate. A home, a family.

Lillian traced the golden embroidery on the silk of her robe, the panels a darker purple than the dog violet that bloomed beneath the hedgerow. "And the others I'm to meet?"

"My uncle the marquess will want to know every detail

about the bones. He thrives on the morbid. He'll talk at length about Rupert, about all the horrible ways he might have died— I'll warn you now."

"I understand he is grieving," she murmured.

"Cursed, more like. The heirs to Waringford seem to meet horrible fates. My grandfather inherited after he lost two brothers. One died of malaria on his grand tour. The second died on the hunt. Pursuing a deer into the night, determined to catch it, for which he was thrown from his horse and drowned in the pond. They say you can hear the hoofbeats of his horse on certain nights as his ghost thunders down the drive, still in pursuit of that prized buck."

"Terrible accidents," Lillian observed.

"And that was the previous generation. My eldest uncle died in a duel. Over a woman. Not the respectable lady he was pledged to marry the next day, but the mistress he refused to give up, and whom an acquaintance reportedly slandered as he was gaming one night, deep in his cups."

"He died the night before his wedding? In a duel over his mistress?"

"A tale belonging to a previous century, I know," Leo agreed. "Not our enlightened age. Aunt Dorinda remains unmarried. Says she's never found a man who interested her as much as coursing hares. It's a wonder she hasn't fallen from a horse and broken her neck, but she's so disobliging she'd argue with the devil when he came to take her.

"Rupert's father died in the Americas years ago, and my own father threw off his mortal coil in the most disagreeable circumstances at least a decade since. My uncle's wife passed with great dignity and little lament two years ago, and that leaves my three cousins, all daughters, for whom I expect my uncle is madly planning weddings to avoid the detestable circumstance of having Waringford pass to me."

"He cannot dislike you that much?"

"But his lifelong dislike for my father can spill over onto my brother and me."

"Are you close with your cousins?"

"I grew up around them, you might say. They were girls, you see, and Rupert and I weren't about to include them. Lucy, who is twenty-four, could beat us at most games if we let her. She was born to be a blacksmith or a metal worker—she has a fascination with old weapons. Catherine is twenty and in two seasons turned down every offer because she refuses to marry a man who knows less about ancient languages and civilizations than she does. Annibel is—hmmm, sixteen? She likes animals better than people."

He glanced at Lillian. "Those chummy dinners we have with the Caesars at the manor? Please do not expect any charm from the Westrops. We are more a Greek tragedy than a romantic farce."

But she would endure that, wouldn't she, if she wanted badly enough to become a marchioness.

Lillian gazed around them as Leo pulled through a small wood and turned down a lane bordering a vast green park that had been landscaped to resemble a natural setting. Trees with full canopies bowed over the green swales like graceful ladies in court dress. A small river meandered to a quiet pool, complete with foot bridge and a pair of mute swans sailing the placid water. A small folly sat tucked beneath the drape of a massive willow. Leo had spent many an afternoon of his childhood splashing in that pool, making reed whistles, catching fish and tadpoles, sifting for favorite possessions that Rupert had stolen and tossed into the water.

An enormous neoclassical edifice sprawled before them, slashed with over a dozen bays of windows, each with its own cornice and pediment in white brick that contrasted with the flint-gray stone of the exterior. Lillian swiveled her head to stare as they traveled along the lane that circled to the outbuildings clustered to the south of the hall, including the stable yard and carriage house.

"You didn't prepare me for how very large Waringford Hall is," she said quietly.

Leo's chest tightened. The Hall tended to inspire awe.

"I don't know how to warn people it's the size of a small hamlet. They wouldn't believe me. The original hall was much smaller, that central section that you see. My grandfather extended the house on each side. My uncle built the parallel wings. You can go for days in that house and not see the other people who live there."

"I'm not dressed for this." Her voice faint, she gathered the folds of her traveling cloak tightly about her. "Leo—they are going to detest me."

He wanted to gather her in his arms and assure her that his family would adore her. But as he turned the horse onto the gravel drive and pulled into the shadow of the house, Leo feared he'd made a terrible miscalculation. When had his family valued anything Leo deemed important?

An iron railing had been added along the top of the porch, creating a balcony accessible from the first floor, the room his grandmother had made over to a morning room. Leo wondered what else had changed in his time living in Oxford, then London. Waringford Hall wasn't his home any longer.

One of the double doors smacked open and a young woman spilled onto the porch, cradling her apron. By the time he brought the vehicle to a halt, a phalanx of people stood with her, his family ranged beneath the white portico, the servants flanking them in formation. He was getting the formal welcome.

Lillian *was* underdressed, by the look of them. Her silk robe was elegant enough, a simple round gown with side and back panels of royal purple, embroidered with gold thread, and a front panel of cream silk embroidered in purple. But her neck and hands were bare of jewels, while the Westrop women fair dripped with them, and their hair looked as if they'd sat getting their heads dressed for the better part of the day, while Lillian had nothing but a simple knot of purple flowers anchored in her coils.

The delicate scent surrounded her. The Westrop women looked stately and useless, flowers bred in a glasshouse for show. Lillian, like a medicinal flower of the meadow, was useful in every part.

He gripped her hand firmly as he helped her descend the chaise and sent off a quick prayer to every higher power he could think of. "If they see what I see, Lillian—" what he had glimpsed in her that very first night in his library, in fact— "every Westrop will be at your feet, as you deserve."

Which would smooth her way to a higher position, were that what she wanted of him.

Leo scanned the front of the house, looking for a friendly welcome. The servants stood woodenly, his family composed and expressionless. He went down the receiving line, only recognizing one face among the male servants, the butler who seemed an aged pillar when Leo was young. He wore breeches and white hose, a dark cutaway coat and a periwig.

"Haskins," Leo greeted him. "You look—" Haggard. Aged. "As dignified as ever."

"Welcome home, sir." Haskins tilted his chin in a formal nod.

"Annibel." Leo greeted the youngest female. "Is that a hedgehog in your apron?"

"Of course." She lifted a mutinous jaw. "An innocent, fat little hedgehog. What else could it be?"

"Oh, how adorable. I've always wanted one for a pet."

Lillian reached out a hand, and Annibel twisted the cradle of her arms in the opposite direction.

"Watch out, he bites."

Lillian dropped her hand but retained her forced smile. "I do believe she's holding a stoat," she whispered to Leo.

Catherine dipped her knees in a tiny curtsy. "*Kalispera,* cousin."

"Still speaking Greek, I see," Leo murmured. "Good afternoon to you, too."

His cousin leaned close to whisper. "*Kali dunami.*"

Lillian stared curiously. "She wished me good strength for my coming ordeal," Leo said for her benefit.

Lucy looked him up and down. "You don't look any more distinguished. Shouldn't you?"

Leo kissed her cheek and tried not to bristle at her insolence. "Should you?"

She sniffed. "I suppose you haven't actually done anything distinguished." She gave Lillian the same frank stare. "Except attach yourself, finally. Good day to you, Miss Gower. Aunt Dorinda is in fits that you haven't chosen an heiress, Giddy. She thinks if you couldn't have gone for breeding, you could at least have gone for wealth."

Leo fit his teeth together. "Is that why she isn't here? Hiding out in a pet?"

"No, she went back to Leiden with Aunt Winifred. Swanning through the canals and picking tulips as we speak, I'm sure."

"Dorinda is the aunt I told you about, the one who does nothing but course hares, and Aunt Winifred is Rupert's mother," Leo explained to Lillian. "Consoled herself with a count from the Low Countries after my uncle died in the war with the American colonies."

"Leiden is home to the Hortus Botanicus. One of the oldest

horticultural gardens in Europe, and one of the most impressive. Perhaps your aunts will have the good fortune to see it." Lillian remained unruffled in the face of his family's rudeness. Did that mean she was not desperate for their approval? Or was she playing a longer game?

Leo's mother bristled like an upright arrow beside the marquess, telling him who of the household women had won the battle to declare herself hostess and erstwhile lady of the house. "Hello, Mother."

She offered a cold cheek to be kissed. "Gideon. Your hair needs a trimming. And you brought her, I see."

"You remember Miss Gower." Leo linked his arm through Lillian's, who curtsied.

"Lady Mary."

"We'd have had a better moon if you'd accepted our invitation when we sent it," his mother said to Leo. "You'll barely have enough light to find your way home tonight."

"We'll manage. Thank you for your concern."

His uncle had aged also, and not well. He seemed a stone heavier than when Leo had departed for Oxford, and leaned on an ebony walking stick with a curved gold handle carved with intricate floral designs.

"Gideon," he said, his voice the same slow rumble. He wore an antique powdered wig and silk breeches, and spared a disdainful assessment of Leo's gray pantaloons and somber dark blue coat. "Couldn't be bothered to turn yourself out for your family, I see. Nor call on us when you first arrived, though your mother tells me you've been in Ashbury for nearly a month."

"I wasn't certain of my reception here, sir. And you of course are welcome to call upon me at any time. Lillian, this is my uncle, the Marquess of Waringford, Earl of Highworth, Baron Hannington, and the Baronet Westrop of Redlands.

Uncle, this is Miss Gower, niece to Sir Lloyd, the Baronet Gower of Gileston."

"Never heard of the place," the marquess said by way of greeting.

Leo squeezed her arm. "They're usually more polite," he told her. "I am sure, were you on your own, they could manage to show basic courtesy to you."

The marquess narrowed his dark eyes. "I'll show you regard when you've earned it. Well, come in. Haskins, tell Cooksey to send up the first course before everything goes over cold."

"Yes, milord." Haskins bowed and disappeared in the direction of the servant's stair while the marquess led the procession into the house.

Lillian drew in a breath as they stepped into the vast entry hall, her eyes widening at the grandeur. The two-storied space evoked a temple of ancient Greece, with arched doorways and carved entablatures above the pillars lining the wall. The busts, vases, and full-length marble statues were none of them antiques, many of them commissioned by the marquess's extravagant older brother, who'd had a love for all things classical. Their shoes tapped over the black-and-white marble tiles, echoing off the carved ceiling. It was an austere room, empty and cold, and he'd never noticed how devoid of color the room was until Lillian, with her vibrancy, stepped inside of it.

"It gets better," he bent to murmur in her ear.

Her shoulders rippled, as if his voice, his breath, moved through her. "Define better," she murmured back.

Instead of the formal dining room, his uncle, with Leo's mother on his arm, led them to one of the smaller dining rooms, the one Leo thought of as the blood-orange room due to the color scheme of the papered walls and draperies lining the tall, narrow windows. In the center of the Axminster rug stood a small mahogany dining table, its drop leaves extended, laid not with the Sèvres set his mother preferred but the plainer Worcester porcelain, patterned in orange and blue. Candles glimmered from the crystal chandelier and the tapers lining the table.

"We thought a simple, intimate family dinner, Gideon," his mother said with a bland smile. "As we didn't want to overwhelm your guest."

Your guest, not *our*. They were determined to make Lillian feel unwelcome.

He debated whether to object to the slight. How much did he want Lillian to feel at home? As if someday, all this could be hers?

"How kind of you to arrange for a cozy family gathering, Lady Mary." Lillian smiled sweetly. "Leo and I have been rather rustic of late, living at the manor house in Ashbury. We should feel quite overwhelmed by anything too grand. How clever of you to realize."

His mother had moved out with a pawn, and Lillian had brought out her knight. His darling girl had teeth. Leo wanted to squeeze her and laugh when he saw the sour twist to his mother's mouth as her jab was deflected.

"Haven't set foot in the Chapel Manor in an age," said a new voice, drawing Leo's attention to the divan against the far wall. "Any headless monks roaming the place? Ghost of an old abbot, roaring in his cups?"

"Hello, Aunt Melina." Leo gently tugged Lillian across the room toward the elegant woman sitting amid yards of silk done up in the style of three decades past. "I've brought you a treat. Miss Lillian Gower, botanist and floral illustrator, who I think is the first person who might match you in your love for orchids. Lillian, this is my formidable aunt, Lady Melina. She's the one who was a lady of the chamber for the late Queen Caroline, then waited on the favorite mistress of the second George. None of us are certain why she gave up running the country to live a quiet life among her flowers, but here we are."

"That's *orchis mascula* in your hair, girl," Aunt Melina said. Her bright eyes gleamed from a finely boned face layered in delicate wrinkles. "Don't try wearing it after it's fertilized, it will stink to high heaven."

"Early purple orchid? I'm aware. Is that red helleborine in your posy?" Lillian indicated the knot of purple and pink flowers pinned to Melina's bodice. "I'd love to know where you found it."

"My glasshouse, of course. I've got *Anacamptis morio* and *Orchia purpurea* as well. That's green-winged and lady orchid for you dolts that don't know," she said to Leo, gripping her walking stick and holding out her free hand so he might help her stand. "I'll show you my collection if you persuade me you've the sense to appreciate them."

"Do you have a ghost orchid?" Lillian asked. "I've been looking for a specimen to study."

"*Epipogium aphyllum?* Mine haven't flowered in a few years." Melina transferred herself to Lillian's arm and hauled her toward the table, ignoring the others. "Now, girl, if you can tell an *Ophrys sphegodes* from an *insectifera*, I'll believe you're worth something."

Lillian guided the older woman to her preferred chair and helped seat her. "I really can't tell the early spider apart from the fly orchids until they flower," she said apologetically. "My lady, it is truly impressive that you can recall all the Linnaean names."

"Only my orchids," Melina chuckled, "and only because I wanted to frighten you. Leo told me about your book, so I studied up. You'll give me a copy of your florilegium when it's published, of course. Mary, stop looking like you ate a sour twist, I let you have the foot of the table." She gestured toward the hostess's customary seat. "You can trouble yourself about what everyone is eating, and I'll talk to this intelligent young woman."

"If I knew flower names instead of animals, you'd call *me* intelligent," Annibel grumbled, sliding into a chair on her great-aunt's other side.

"You won't be interesting for another five years, chit," Melina retorted. "And if you dare bring a stoat to the table, I'll put it in the dish with the veal."

"Oh, very well." Annibel, with a yank of her ties, pulled off the delicate muslin apron and handed the bundle to the footman beside her, who had just delivered himself of a platter of turbot dressed with smelts, lemon, and barberries, and what smelled like a lobster sauce.

Eyes widening, the footman sent a look of appeal at Haskins, who was placing the haunch of venison before his lordship. A twitch of Haskins' brow indicated the footman was to take the animal and say nothing of it. The footman hurried from the room, holding the apron away from him in stiff arms, as if it were old fish.

Lady Mary closed her eyes and drew a deep breath, nostrils flaring. Leo, taking his own chair after seating his mother and cousins, caught the glance Lillian snuck across the table at him and grinned.

She was marvelous. He was almost glad his family was behaving abominably. It made Lillian take Leo's side all the more.

"So, Gideon," the marquess said as he carved the venison, "don't suppose you've found anything interesting. It's nothing but an old cave, after all, and everyone told you so."

"I am sure our findings wouldn't be of interest to you, sir," Leo said blandly.

Lillian raised her brows, her astonishment clear. "My

mother won't wish me to talk of human remains at the table," Leo explained.

Lucy's fork clattered on her plate. "Bones? You found human bones?"

Leo nodded. "It's a barrow after all. My theory has been confirmed."

He knew his face mirrored Lillian's broad, pleased grin. She'd shared every moment of their discovery with him, from his elation to his doubt about what to do with their findings and worry about how his write-up would be received.

"Who? The Danish king they say is buried there?" Catherine demanded.

"Nothing so grand. All we found with the remains were a flint arrow and a quern stone. Lillian identified the quern stone," he added. "If there were any grave goods, they were likely carted off centuries ago by clever thieves. Or perhaps the people buried there were not rich, but the fact that they had their own chamber suggests a position of some importance. We suspect they might have been some kind of royal family—a king, his queen, and their little prince." Lillian had proposed it was a family burial, and that made as much sense as anything, given how little they knew.

"How do you know they're human bones?" Annibel asked, pushing aside the turnips and carrots to get at the harrico of mutton.

"The shape of them, and the skulls." Leo flicked a glance toward Lillian, who was addressing a veal cutlet garnished with lemon peel and a Seville orange. "I have friends who belong to the Society of Antiquaries who I hope will be able to tell me more. The Ashbury coroner was out to look at them already, which was Miss Gower's idea."

Lillian nodded. "That is the procedure my parents always

follow, as sometimes the coroner can identify the cause of death. They'll be quite envious of you, Leo."

"That's right, your parents are antiquarians as well." The marquess scowled. "Would have thought a baronet's nephew would require a real trade to support himself."

"Archaeology *is* a profession to my father, milord. He is fortunate to have benefactors who support his work."

Leo saw his mother recoil at the discussion of trade and income at her table. Lillian, unaware, scooped pea soup from the tureen. "My parents are excavating with Mr. William Cunnington at Stonehenge this summer. They have been digging around one of the fallen trilithons. Their theory is there is a cache or grave beneath that displaced the soil, and that is why the stones fall."

Annibel straightened in her chair. "I should like to see Stonehenge."

"And you ought—there's no other stone circle quite like it in Britain, or on the Continent, from what I've read," Lillian said. "But the rings at Avebury are nearer, and larger, if you are interested in that sort of thing. Your cousin ought to take you sometime." She winked at Leo, who shook his head with a rueful smile.

"Can see why Leo wants to marry you," Aunt Melina remarked, forking up French beans. "You like the same old things."

"I suppose it helps," Lillian agreed, adding a slice of lamb pie to the older woman's dinner plate.

Leo dropped his eyes to his slice of roast chicken, slathered in parsley butter sauce. He hoped Lillian never learned that what brought them together—what made him mark her, apart from her angelic interference with his mother's Ponsonby scheme—was that he'd known of and admired her parents. He sensed that, in the way of women's vanity, she would not appreciate this knowledge.

"Such a distasteful hobby, Gideon." His mother shuddered. "You've made me quite lose my appetite, going on about old bones. But I suppose we saw it coming, with how much time you spent as a child, digging about the old earthworks in Sevenhampton when you ought to have been at your lessons."

"Those are the remnants of a medieval village, from how Leo described them to me," Lillian said, her voice animated. "And he found a Saxon belt buckle made of bronze and a glass bead. Such a discovery has made many a young lad into an antiquarian, I would wager."

Lillian's approval warmed Leo, sliding down his chest like warm butter sauce.

"Father says mucking about England's mounds won't yield anything useful," Catherine said. "If Gideon wanted to make anything of himself, he'd go work at important sites, like Herculaneum or Pompeii."

"Those would certainly be fascinating excavations," Lillian said in her steady, mild tone. "But I should think it also necessary to illuminate the British past. Think of what is buried beneath the earth all around us, right here."

Quiet ensued, as if the diners were contemplating this possibility. Suddenly Lucy roared and lifted her arms, her fingers shaped into claws. "What's beneath *us*, right now, are the bones of old giants slain by Brutus. If they ever rise, they'll shake down the walls of this house Father is so proud of, and the ghosts will eat us all in our beds!"

Annibel recoiled and emitted a tiny shriek. Catherine shook her head. "Ghosts don't eat people, Lucy."

"But vampyres do."

"Vampyres don't exist. Voltaire said so in his encyclopedia.

You really ought to read it sometime, though you'll have to improve your French if you wish to—"

"Gideon," his mother said sharply, "look what you've begun. This is the influence you have on your cousins?"

"His cousins are silly enough on their own," Aunt Melina remarked. "Can't blame Leo's influence. Vampyres, children? Piffle."

"His name is Gideon." His mother frowned.

"I prefer Leo."

"Gideon was your father's name. You should be proud to bear it, despite—"

"We will not discuss my brother at this table," the marquess said through tight lips. "Talk of human remains and vampyres are gruesome enough. You'll turn my appetite, and I'm ready for the next course."

On the word Haskins signaled for action and the footmen removed the first course, bringing in the second: turkey poults, roasted rabbits, and fricassee of lamb. Lillian's eyes widened at the sight of the lobsters; Leo knew she had a fondness for them.

"So, Miss Gower." His mother turned her attention to Lillian. "Your accomplishments are to know a bit about flowers?"

"A bit, ma'am. My specialty is the yellow lady's slipper orchid. The *Cypripedium calceolus*," she said with a wink to Melina, who grinned around her apricot puff.

"Are we to be impressed?" Lady Mary sniffed and turned to Leo. "Empyrea Ponsonby is accomplished at watercolors, music, dancing, drawing, and embroidery, and her French is flawless."

"Lillian knows French, German, Italian, Latin, and Dutch, and she can organize a library," Leo replied. "A useful, rather than decorative skill."

"Your father stands to inherit the baronetcy, I suppose." The marquess turned his attention to Lillian as well. "But where will it go next, if he has no son?"

"It might pass to my husband, and my son, should I have one," Lillian answered.

The marquess gave Leo a glittering stare. "He'd hardly know what do with your paltry Welsh title, did he inherit all of mine."

Lillian watched Leo herd his peas about his plate, and he realized she was anxious for him. The apricot tones of the room looked as if blood had been let there many times before, and left to stain.

"Gileston Hall is a respectable house, sir, and the farms are productive, the tenants loyal," Lillian said. "I believe my uncle has been a good landlord, though he doesn't speak a word of Welsh and spends a great deal of time in London. He attends as many meetings of the Linnean society as he can."

"And where were you raised?" Lady Mary inquired. "What about your education?"

"My mother saw to my learning, ma'am. I believe she made a very good governess."

"You think so?" Lady Mary showed her dismay. "A Welsh woman, raised at the fringes of society, thinking she can breed a girl up to sit at a marquess's table? Those are very lofty ambitions indeed. I associate with the Levenson-Gowers, you know. They don't acknowledge your branch of the family at all. Your great-uncle must have done something hideous, or the baronet before him, to be expelled so abjectly from the family line."

Lillian visibly swallowed; he watched her slender throat work. "My mother is not Welsh, mum. She's from Galloway, so, Scottish. Or Norse-Gaelic, if you wish to go further back."

"The Westrops were here before the Normans came," Catherine said helpfully. "Or the Danes. At least, the town was.

It's a Saxon word meaning west village. We were probably bakers or something. Common, like the Gowers."

"Is your mother's family of any note?" Lady Mary demanded, talking over her niece.

"Not as distinguished as the Westrops, mum. Or the family of the Earl of Fossey," Lillian said, and Leo thought the lilt in her voice was not meekness. She turned to Catherine. "Fossa is a Latin word, is it not?"

"A pit or cavity, like Gid—Leo and his barrows," Catherine replied. "Aunt Mary's family doesn't go back as far as ours, though. I know, because she's applied to the college of heralds at least a dozen times to find something older in her ancestry."

"Lady Catherine," Mary said with set teeth, "I believe our family history needs no justification. I would be interested to hear more of Miss Gower's breeding."

"You mean lack of breeding when you use that tone," Annibel said, wide-eyed. "Are you going to make a comment about the size of her slice of cherry tart? You are always telling me to watch my waistline or men won't ask me to dance, yet you haven't made a single comment about her plate, and she's plumper than Lucy."

"I'm not plump, I'm robust," Lucy replied. "Sturdy. Miss Gower is simply...ample."

"That is one way to put it," Lillian agreed, with a beet color rushing to her cheeks.

Leo nearly choked on his turkey. He knew it fell to him to defend Lillian, but he was trapped. A gentleman didn't comment on a lady's shape, and he didn't know whether to acknowledge his family's rudeness or ignore it. What had gotten into the girls? Lucy was prone to speaking her mind—it was one of the things he most liked about her, actually—but he'd never known his cousins to be cruel. They were far too aware of their own eccentricities, individually and as a collective, to find it in them to hold forth in judgment over others.

This must be his mother's influence. Why couldn't his family simply be cordial to Lillian, as the Gowers had been to Leo?

He glared at his mother, but she had Lillian in her sights still. "And what about the rest of your family? The woman who was with you at Westrop House, the widow—she is your aunt?"

"My father's sister, madam."

"And your grandfather married his cousin, did he not? Another Gower. So perhaps the inbreeding would account for why your cousin is simple."

Lillian went as still as if she were posing for a portrait. "There is nothing wrong with my cousin Hester."

"Oh, is there not? Forgive me, I had heard talk that she is a bit—what is the kind way to say it? Slow."

"Innocent?" Lucy proposed.

"Not entirely innocent, for I hear there's a reverend in Kingstone Winslow who is pursuing her quite determinedly. Though a girl can be simple and sly together, I suppose—the two aren't exclusive."

"Hester doesn't have a sly bone in her body," Leo exclaimed.

"Hester, is it?" His mother's cutting gaze swung to Leo. "Not Miss Giles? You two must have become intimately acquainted."

"Not intimately." Leo bristled.

"There is nothing going on between Hester and Reverend Woodfforde," Lillian said, though Leo heard the doubt creeping into her tone. "He has simply been kind. His sister loaned me this gown for dinner as I had nothing appropriate in my luggage, and no way to find anything in Ashbury on short notice."

"I can see how that gown would belong to a reverend's sister. So Gideon did not tell you we invited you to dinner weeks ago?" Mary murmured. "How odd. I would have thought he would give his intended time to prepare to meet us. Given that he is asking us to accept a girl we know nothing of—who never moved in our social circles, who had no background and breeding to speak of—into our family."

"I have been busy with the excavation, Mother. I didn't intend a slight. Besides, you just saw me in London."

"But you didn't bring Miss Gower to the house once to meet us then, either," his mother pointed out. "It's almost as if you were ashamed of her. Embarrassed by a decision made in haste, the kind of thing you might now regret but not know how to free yourself."

Aunt Melina chewed her cherry tart. "I can still see the gel —she's right here. Is she invisible to the rest of you?" She turned toward Lillian with a rustle of silk and lace. "In my day, we wouldn't say ample, we'd call the girl effulgent."

"With emphasis on *full,*" Lillian murmured. "Rather clever."

"I offered for Lillian on her own merits," Leo said, hoping the others couldn't hear the grinding of his teeth. Lillian hadn't touched her lobster; in fact, she'd put down her fork entirely. It was an outrage that she should be served foods she loved, then shamed into not touching them.

"You did not know Miss Gower existed until that night I introduced you to Empyrea Ponsonby," Lady Mary retorted. "When, much to my surprise—and yours, I'd wager—we found her lurking in your library. Almost as if she were planning something."

The marquess lifted his head from his apricot puff. "Eh, what's this? When was the betrothal announced, Mary?"

"June the second, sir," Mary said primly.

"How convenient. Shortly after we learned Rupert had been killed in battle at Îles Saint-Marcouf."

The room went entirely silent, save for the scrape of Aunt Melina's fork on her plate as she calmly consumed the last of her tart. Everyone else stared at Leo's uncle, then at Lillian. The candlelight hollowed her cheekbones and made her eyes shine like brilliants.

"You are not," Leo said quietly, "suggesting what it might seem you are suggesting, sir."

"That she didn't know a thing about you until you stood in line for a marquessate?" Waringford shot back.

It couldn't be true; he wouldn't entertain the thought. "Lillian came to my library—your library, Uncle—looking for a book you'd purchased. The last thing she cares about is whether I have a title." He hoped. This was the opportunity to test that truth, wasn't it? "I beg you will forfeit the title back to the Crown if you think I'm so unworthy. Or marry off Lucy and get her breeding as quickly as possible."

He wanted to see what Lillian would do if it were clear the title would *not* pass to him. Would she stay with him, choose him anyway?

"I beg you will leave me out of this," Lucy retorted. "I already hear it enough from your mother, if you please. *I'm* not about to throw myself on a man simply because I think a title is in the offing."

"Yet you believe Lillian would." Leo laid his knife beside his plate; he had the regrettable urge to curl his fingers around the handle. "Have me declared unfit and give everything to Joshua, Uncle. I don't want anything from you."

"Joshua can't bear the weight of the responsibility, and you know it," the marquess said, his voice sharp as a whetted blade. "And that would be your fault as well, wouldn't it?"

"I am not the reason Joshua is as he is," Leo said, his jaw aching with the force with which he clenched his teeth.

"We all know that's balderdash," his marquess said.

"Though you'll never admit your part, will you? Too busy holding yourself apart and above the rest of us. Thinking yourself so much better than your own blood. Can't say I blame you, given *her* influence, but I don't like it one bit, you insolent pup." He stabbed a utensil in the air, indicating the foot of the table, where Mary gasped and went pale.

"I beg your pardon, Waringford. *My* influence?"

"Think you're better than us as well," Waringford barreled on, raising his voice. "You drove your husband to half his antics. Most of them, come to that. He might have settled some of his wildness if you weren't always preaching to him about respectability and trying to curtail his actions. Any man of blood would have broken his traces, tight as you held them. And now you've gone and ruined your sons, both of them. Turned them into simpering nanny goats."

"Gideon is not a nanny goat," his mother cried, her face spotting red.

"You said so yourself! Not enough man to tell when he had a real find before him, and fool enough to shackle himself to the worst possible match. All to thumb his nose at you, Mary, and me as well. And now I've lost all my heirs but these two? What's a man to do?"

"If this isn't the most vulgar discussion I ever heard." Melina wiped her fingers on the table linen and grabbed the handle of her walking stick. "Get a hold of yourself, Cornelius, you're turning into a boor. And you're raising your daughters to be so as well. I declare, I thought the king's whores the cattiest women I'd ever meet, but you surpass them all." She turned to Lillian. "Shall I send a footman to light a lamp and I'll show you my glasshouse, gel?"

"That won't be necessary tonight, Aunt Melina." Leo rose from his chair. "Lillian and I will be taking our leave."

"Oh, don't drive at night, Giddy," Lucy exclaimed. "That's unwise."

"Why not? There's a moon. We're not going to encounter robbers between here and Ashbury."

"What if your horse steps in a hole? What if it throws a shoe?" Annibel demanded. "Think about your animal, at least."

"We really have been beastly, haven't we? After I told Father we didn't want to." Catherine's eyes filled with tears.

"This is just like you, Gideon," his mother said in a strained voice, half-rising and pressing a hand to her bosom. "To leave in a sulk and not listen to sense—"

"I won't listen to insults, not for myself nor for the woman I love. Come, Lillian." He held out his hand, and she placed her palm against his as if she were accepting an invitation to dance.

"Are you certain you want to leave in this fashion?" she murmured, leaning close. "Not stay and make amends?"

"I'm not in any state of mind to make amends. We can be home in two hours without risking our necks. Say you'll come with me?"

He curled his fingers around hers, drowning in her deep blue gaze. A shadow moved across her face, more than the moving light of the candle, but her expression was steady and clear. Trusting.

"I cannot say no as I have no transport otherwise," she said dryly, "but I'll go whither thou goest, Leo."

Haskins had Lillian's wrap and Leo's hat ready at the door, along with his gloves, caped coat, and driving whip. Leo thought he detected a flicker in the butler's expression—disdain? Wistfulness? It was impossible to guess what Haskins was feeling.

"I hope we'll be seeing more of you, Mr. Westrop," the butler said.

"I am less and less certain that my future lies in this direction, Haskins," Leo said dryly. "Do look after yourself, and Aunt Melina."

"I shall do so, sir."

Leo took Lillian's arm and stepped off the porch to the chaise and horse, held by a yawning stableboy. A heavy load fell away with each stride. The weight of expectation was a tangible burden leaving his shoulders as he helped Lillian up into the carriage. And as he drove away from the vast expanse of Waringford Hall, he didn't look back to see which rooms had light at the window or try to guess who might be peering out.

He'd always known he didn't fit with his family, that he'd never live up to what they expected of him. He'd dreaded the thought of a final break, the tear that would leave him alone and unsupported in the world.

But he had Lillian beside him. She didn't want the marquess to be. Just plain Leo Westrop, antiquarian. And that was all he needed.

CHAPTER TWENTY

The ride home was a test of endurance such as Lillian had never known. She had spent weeks of rain battened under a canvas tent when her parents refused to leave a dig, when the chill damp crept through her coat and into her bones. She had been caught in weather when she tramped too far on a plant-drawing expedition and had to lie on a hillside praying lightning would not strike her, or forge through lashing rain toward the last cottage she had seen, hours before, seeking shelter.

She had stood for hours of interminable chat at soirees and parties during the Season, and she had sat for hours more of gossip and false kindness, shoving her mouth full of sweets to keep from saying something untoward during calls and visits. But every jounce of the chaise on the rutted road back to Ashbury was a question of how many blows she would take for Leo. Another? And another? And one more?

"You are determined to press on to the manor tonight?" she asked as they crossed the mill bridge into Shrivenham. Leo wheeled the carriage around the stately Beckett Hall, seat of the Barrington family, and she thought longingly of the feather mattress on her bed, the brocade coverlet curling softly about her, the pillow stuffed with down easing her aching head. If they ever reached that refuge, she would sink into the comfort and forget the hours just passed.

"Another hour," he said tersely. "I can slow Boreas to a walk if you're tired of being jolted."

At least he recognized the trot was jarring her bones, not to mention increasing the chances that the horse could injure himself on the road. There was no one about, it being darkest night and all humble folk sound asleep in their beds, resting for a day of productive labor on the morn. The moon sailed a pond of translucent cloud, its outline clear and cuttingly bright against the star-battered sky.

"Are there demons chasing us?" she asked mildly. "Or will the demons be with you wherever you arrive?"

"My family behaved abominably tonight. I cannot begin to apologize for their treatment of you."

"They were as horrible to you. Saving your aunt, Lady Melina. I quite like her." It seemed necessary to salvage some good from the inquisition.

"I delayed accepting the invitation because I feared they would demean me and everything I've accomplished. But I never anticipated they would be so cruel to you. I have been too long under your influence, around people who are kind and good at heart. I forgot how they could be. And my uncle the worst among them."

"He is grieving, Leo. It is plain to see your cousin's death has shattered him, and not just because he needs a new heir. I gather Rupert was beloved of you all."

"A far superior man in every way."

She touched his hand, rigid through the driving glove. "Not to you. You are not less. Just...a different person. With qualities that, regrettably, it does not seem your mother and uncle place much value upon."

"Nor does the world, I'm afraid."

"Why..." She hesitated, for it was not her place to ask. But what she and Leo meant to each other had no conventional label, not in the polite language she'd been taught.

"Why do they think your brother could not handle the estate?"

His jaw tightened, his knuckles gripping the ribbons, his shoulders one solid plane. Lillian was about to retract and say he must disregard her prying when he answered.

"The matter is less one of deserving than of being capable. You said you've always known, from a baby, that Hester was different. She was born..."

"Simple, as they said," Lillian said quietly. "That is how people refer to her."

"Joshua was quiet, but he was otherwise no different from other boys. Sweet, deliberate, slow to anger. He would do anything anyone asked of him, if he thought it made them happy. Hester has that quality as well."

The horse flicked its ears, as if catching the current beneath his words.

Lillian nodded. "It is wonderful, that obliging temperament. Up to the point when people try to take advantage."

"As they did of Joshua. I knew this. I am the older brother. I ought to have protected him. But he liked to fish and I didn't, so I would leave him went I went digging, and sometimes I left him alone for a long time. We knew not to let him have coin, he would simply give it away, always believing the person who asked deserved it more than he did. But he did have his treasures that he always carried about, and those he would not part with. The only way to agitate him was to try to take away one of his little artifacts."

"Valuables?"

"Not even close. A stone he found in a river. A coin I gave him from one of my digs. Small bits and bobs that meant something only to him. But he would guard them so fiercely, and these older boys, not from our estate but from Highworth, took it into their head that Joshua's things were valuable. We avoided them as much as we could. But I saw them one day when I was exploring the ruins I told you about, the remains of the old medieval village. I should have known they were headed to the lake where Joshua liked to fish. I should have known that they might...hurt him."

"Badly?" Fear laced her tone, her throat tight and hot. She recalled, against her will, the image of Lord Bacon putting Hester's hand on his leg. A bully who knew he could bend the girl's will to his, and Hester had not the presence of mind, nor the physical strength, to resist him.

"Bad enough. One of them bashed him on the head with a rock, hard enough to black him out. I brought him home and our nurse tended to him. And when he came to his senses...he was not the same boy any longer."

"Like Hester?" she asked quietly.

"In some ways, yes. He struggled to learn after that. He has a hard time remembering something you told him five minutes ago. He simply cannot pay attention—there was no hope of him attending a boy's school. He managed to pass university with the help of his tutor, because he is not unintelligent. But he is easily upset. Sensitive to certain things that never used to bother him. He is skittish in new environments. I think being a curate is the only job he is fit for, as he still loves to read and is as sweet-natured as ever. But he would never be able to handle very great demands. In some ways he will be a child all his life."

"That is not your fault, Leo. The blame lies with his injuries, and the boys who hurt him."

"Yet that attack never might have happened if I were there. Or had returned sooner."

He would always blame himself, Lillian saw, because he loved his brother. She grabbed the wooden side of the chaise as a sudden tilt of the wheel threw her toward Leo. His body was warm and firm, hard and unyielding. He was a man who had been carved by blows, hammered into form like the flint arrowhead they found in the cave, and yet his heart had not become hard, and his character had not been twisted into bitterness.

She wanted that body next to her. She wanted to hold him in her arms until all his sorrow fled.

She let herself slide against him, fitted to his form, and leaned into him, placing one hand on his arm.

"Take us home, Leo," she whispered.

By the time they reached the ivy-clad walls of the Manor House, with its windows dark like sleeping eyes and only the moon to light their way to the stable, Lillian was bread dough that had been punched all over, left to rise, and then punched all over again. An exhaustion of the spirit pulled at her, so many confused emotions slithering in her chest, like eels. She hung up the harness while Leo brushed the horse, which they would return the next day, then left Boreas with his head in a bucket of oats. Leo climbed the stair beside her as she held the chamberstick, candle flickering against the carved wooden ceiling, and paused at the door to her room.

"Hester is not here," he reminded her. With his low voice, his undone cravat, the hair that needed barbering curling over his brow, he was a dark incubus, the force of seduction luring her to surrender.

He had never been in her bed; she always went to his.

Some dormant sense of self-preservation that she had tamped down all this time teased a wagging finger in the back of Lillian's mind. What was she to him? What was *this*? This dinner had brought to her attention, with painful clarity, the writing on the wall she'd been pretending not to see.

She wasn't a woman who could stand boldly at his side in the eyes of society, claiming a station equal to his. She was the woman he brought to his bed in secret, and in the daylight they drew the pretense of their betrothal around them like a sheer muslin veil that could disintegrate in a sharp wind.

She could never be his companion. His wife.

"It has been a trying day," she said, searching for the way to resist, to protect herself.

"I hurt you, taking you there. I all but tossed you to the wolves." A haunted shadow lurked in his eyes, and it was that, more than the warm, heavy hand he slid around the back of her neck, that made her weaken. With his thumb he rubbed the aching base of her skull, and that need for self-preservation subsided at once, curling and settling in its bed with a sigh.

"Let me make it up to you," he whispered.

It was easier to surrender, and it was what she wanted. She didn't want to lose him, not yet. He must know, too, all the reasons a marriage between them was impossible. They were too different in station, in expectation, in wealth, in pedigree. She would always be the lagging horse, not pulling her weight, the subject of speculation and gossip that would follow him wherever he went, the arbiters of society wondering why a Westrop and the presumptive heir to a marquessate would bind himself to an antiquarian's daughter.

He pulled the round gown from her and let her hang it on its peg while his hands skimmed the skin he had uncovered. She closed her eyes in bliss as he unclasped her stays and rubbed the flesh beneath, freed to resume its natural shape. He did so adore her breasts. It was the one weapon she had to remedy their inequality; she would be able to win any argument with him, all their lives, simply by flaunting her bosoms.

"They are not wrong, your family," she informed him as he lay her on the bed and pushed up the hem of her shift so he might unroll her stockings. "I am unfit."

He paused to meet her eyes, his catching the shadows that flitted and lilted about the room in the light of the dancing flame. Her skin trembled where he had kissed, and where he had yet to kiss.

"You fit me very well, Lillian, and you know that." The brush of his erection against the inside of her leg left no question of what he referred to.

"The very shape of me is an abomination." She let her head find the pillow as he resumed his task of examination, touching and kissing every inch of her.

"I dote on the shape of you. Every inch of you is perfect. At least, what I have seen so far. Let me explore the rest and I will make my final pronouncement."

He meant to take his time with her tonight, and she let him. His touch, his kisses, the light sweeps of his tongue soothed the inward hurts, drew her mind away from the knowledge that was taking shape inside her, like a barrister marshaling his arguments. He ended his survey of her body between her legs and she rose at once to the pleasure, eager, familiar, yet devastating each time, razing her to the ground. When he entered her he took his time again, his strokes long and slow, and she shivered with delight as she swept her hands over his back and buttocks. So much man, so much brilliance, and all hers for this moment in time.

"Leo." Her pleasure burrowed deep, bright and fierce, desperate.

"Do I have you?" He watched her face so carefully, like a man on his grand tour studying the art, eyes opened to the splendors of another world. She squeezed her eyelids together, afraid to be so bare to him, so needful.

He had her. That was the painful beauty of it all. He moved in her, with her, as if nothing mattered more than her pleasure, than bringing her to this new place, and when she tumbled over the edge into a place brighter, further than she had ever gone before, she was alone, because he pulled out to spend in his hand, his body shuddering alongside, but not *with* her.

"It isn't fair," she said drowsily as her body drifted back to earth, as he curved his body around hers and nuzzled his lips in her hair. "I get to enjoy everything, and you…"

"Could ask for nothing more, Lillian. Being with you is a pleasure greater than anything I've known."

"Not *anything*," she demurred, because she wanted honesty between them, finally. He was a man. She knew something, pieces overheard here and there, dark hints from her aunt about the way of the world. "Surely there have been others."

Though there hadn't been for her, and wouldn't be, later. She knew quite firmly and clearly, as if it were a lesson spelled out on a slate, that Leo Westrop was the only man she would find *this* with. The man who had awakened her and the man who would hold all her memories when he left. There would be no other after him.

He tugged a hand through her hair, coming free from its pins. She would have a rat's nest to untangle in the morning. "There was only one other," he said finally. "And that barely counted."

"How can it not count?"

"It was arranged by my mates for my eighteenth birthday. I was away at university. I was the only one of my friends who hadn't…well. They saw this as a problem to rectify and arranged a night with a woman. Paid her well, I hope. She was very accommodating, but so…" He shook his head, burying his face in her hair. She wondered if his shudder was from laughter or revulsion. "I could tell by how very encouraging she was that I was doing everything wrong. It was an embarrassment all around. I deduced after that, from the way my mates talked, that there was something...different about me. I need to be fond of a woman before I have any interest in intimacies."

"I had thought you much more practiced."

He smiled, a sleepy, satisfied curve of his lips. "Perhaps you mistake eagerness for skill. You are very lovely, Lillian."

Not to anyone else, she wanted to tell him. Leo was the only man who found her beautiful.

Her heart clenched, a string pulled tight as the mouth of a purse. "You said—tonight, at dinner—you said, the woman I love."

He stilled. A long lock of hair fell from his fingers, like folding silk. "I did, didn't I?"

A hot rush, the need to retreat. "If you only said it to rile them—"

"What if you married me, Lil?"

The hot rush rolled over her and whisked away, taking her ability to breathe. "You—what?"

He slid a hand from her shoulder along the curve of her side. He knew she was too sensitive to tease, that her nerve endings were still raw and open, singed by the pinnacle she'd reached. Her mind was a calves foot jelly, shuddering.

He had called her Lil. Only her family could call her Lil. Only the people she most loved were allowed that intimacy, that access, that knowledge.

The candle threw its light, the flame diving into her, sweeping through.

She loved Leo Westrop. She hadn't been imagining or infatuated, before. She loved him true.

His lips brushed her temple as he whispered. "What if we made this real?"

A laugh shook from her, mortification, disbelief. He would ask this now? After the night they'd endured?

"We couldn't possibly. Didn't you see what your family thinks of me? For that reason alone, even if everyone else..."

A hot weight blocked her throat, and she couldn't swallow nor choke it up. He would eventually be accepted by his family if and when the marquessate passed to him. He, without her, could mend what had been frayed tonight. She couldn't be the source of such friction, or the reason she broke with his family. A couple couldn't survive in the cold, alone.

"It's not to be thought of, Leo, not now. The only way to save face is to jilt me." The thought was a sword through the chest. She blinked with surprise at the strength of the blow, waiting for the roaring pain to follow.

His voice was even, neutral. "I already said I wouldn't be the one to end things."

Of course, because he was a gentleman. He wouldn't sully his reputation in such a way. They'd agreed; she must be the jilt. The woman foolish enough to cut free the heir to a marquess.

The woman foolish enough to leave Leo Westrop.

"Very well." Her heavy breath scratched her throat. "The sooner I jilt you, the happier you'll all be."

His arm tensed around her, cradling her ribs. "*I* won't be happy."

Perhaps not at first, but he would be, in time. He'd come to his senses and know relief, might even mend things with his family without her crowding the way. It was only the pleasure they shared that had befuddled him. His first experience of bliss that disordered the senses, that made rational thought flee and crouch in the shadows like a mouse chased away by the light.

"I don't want to lose this," he muttered, and she agreed. *This* —the touching, the pleasure. She wanted it, too. She reveled in their bedsport as much as he did. But she wanted more from a marriage.

She wanted the impossible.

She wrapped her arms about him, tears seeping through her eyelids. "I won't leave just yet. This is...rather nice."

But no matter how she lingered, she was in the cart carrying her to the guillotine. She'd known from the beginning there would be an end to them, and the reasons had been made painfully clear. She could draw out the time until their parting, but leave him she must. And the blow, she already knew, would be unbearable.

CHAPTER TWENTY-ONE

"Ashdown House!" Paulina looked up from cutting the loaf cheese for their nuncheon. "That big fancy house south the road from us?"

"Lord Craven is in residence for a while, on a respite from his duties to the King. He invited Leo and I to dine with him." Lillian brushed dirt off the potsherd cradled in her work apron, trying to hide how nervous this invitation made her. At least she was working above ground again while Leo and Claudius delved the cave, clearing the rubble out of the second room, discussing what to do with the bones.

"That house was built by the first Earl Craven," Reverend Woodfforde remarked. He sat on a blanket a short distance away, Hester seated beside him making a cat's cradle with Temperance. A sunny day would have made for an ideal picnic, but, though cloudy, the day was warm and free of insects. A great tit called from a hazel some distance away, the sound rising and falling like a bubbling spring.

Faustina scampered over from the sarsen that sheltered the nest of eggs which the girls had been monitoring several times a day. "Bustard eggs still there," she reported as she climbed onto the blanket, taking a biscuit from the plate. "Whose palace is Miss Lillian visiting?"

"One built for Elizabeth, the Queen of Bohemia," the reverend said. "They called her the Winter Queen because she only reigned for a season. Craven loved her madly and built her a palace to match her beauty, but sadly, she died before she could ever take up residence."

"The palace," said Titus, darting in to nick a biscuit. "That's as has the field with the sheep the magician Merlin turned into stones?" He grabbed a second biscuit and whisked back to his twin. The boys had conceded to help others tell them apart by their neck scarves; Titus wore a red cloth, and Tiberius blue. Lillian didn't doubt they occasionally traded to mix everyone up, thrilled by their private joke.

"So they say." Woodfforde smiled at Hester. "Should you like me to build you a palace, Hester?"

Hester looked up from her cat's cradle, scanned the reverend's face with a considering gaze, then went back to her weaving. "I like your cottage better," she decided. "It's large enough for me."

"And you are welcome there whenever you wish. You shall be our own Hestia, goddess of the hearth."

Lillian noted the affectionate, amused way the reverend's gaze rested on her cousin. She told herself her guard was protectiveness, not jealousy. Woodfforde said that letting Hester go would tear the fabric of his and Temperance's lives, but he had only known Hester a handful of weeks. How could such a speedy affection be true? Leo had been with Lillian weeks more, and he never spoke of how their parting might affect him.

Since the night of their dinner at Waringford Hall—the night she'd realized she loved him—she'd done her best to show him that, all else aside, she was a worthy match. It was as if her spirit wouldn't accept what her mind told her, and she wanted him to see a way they could be together. They shared similar interests. They complemented the other's strengths. They brought out each other's best qualities and smoothed the other's rough edges.

Yet the ground between them felt as fragile as one of these pots buried in the earth for a hundred years. It could crumble at a harsh word, a careless touch.

"I invited Craven to come here." Leo folded himself to the ground beside Lillian, joining their conversation with ease.

A warm glow spread through the side of her body, as if she'd drawn close to a fire. Leo's attention never failed to make her nerves hum melodies, like a music box.

Temperance, too, sat up straighter, flicked a lock of hair over her shoulder, fluttered a quick gaze Leo's way. She wasn't flirting so much as newly self-conscious. Leo Westrop entered a conversation, and a woman became more focused, more aware.

He'd been careful and courteous to Lillian in the fortnight since the family visit. Letters came from Sevenhampton, but Lillian didn't see his replies. He treated her as if she were beaten gold, liable to dent or shatter at a forceful touch. His ardor hadn't cooled, but he hadn't spoken again of love. Or marriage.

But he'd been waiting for this: for Lord Craven's approval to carry forward with his dig, to plan further work, a project lasting well into the next year. And he sought a sponsor to nominate him into the Society of Antiquaries. He might be waiting until he knew what his future might look like before he could speak to Lillian as if she were more to him than stolen pleasure, a clasp of passion. As if she might truly become a partner for his life, a companion for his future, no matter what his family or the world might think.

"Doesn't William want to see the cave?" Lillian asked.

"He suggested we catch him up on our progress first.

Perhaps your Wim Wim is hoping to impress you with his lavish house and fine table."

"The lord fancies Miss Lillian?" Faustina peered into a basket beside her and pulled out a slender green stem with a spike of flowers, the petals shaped like butterfly wings. "This one."

"Ooh, green-winged orchid. This specimen has white flowers—I'm accustomed to seeing purple. You must show me where you found it." Lillian passed her potsherd to Augustus, who laid it on the cloth with the other fragments and fell to the task of attempting to piece the shards together. Faustina handed her the flower, and Lillian pulled her sketchbook out of the bag lying on the grass beside her.

"You shall have a second florilegium after this summer, Miss Gower," Leo remarked. "I wonder how Mr. Karim is doing on your book?"

"He confirms that the plates turned out beautifully and are ready for me to color, and Aunt Giles writes to say that he is cluttering up her drawing room with his packages and pages. I am eager to begin."

"But not eager to leave us, I hope," Leo said.

She paused her crayon to risk a glance at him. Always that strange warmth at the sight of him, as if she were melted wax and his nearness made an impression on her, every time.

"Or at least not leaving until after her sketches for us are complete." Claudius seated himself beside his wife and pulled back the shawl draped over the little bundle resting on the blanket beside her. His entire face softened at the sight of his young son, sleeping soundly, and his paternal pride sent a needle of sensation plunging into Lillian's chest.

She hurt at the very thought of leaving. She had come here with Hester and within scant weeks this group had become her circle, the Caesars accepting her at once, the Woodffordes slowly endearing themselves. Hester had blossomed with more people to love her, and Lillian had, too.

For the first time in memory, she'd been among people who took her exactly as she was and didn't dole out their affection or attention according to her usefulness to them. They allowed her to be entirely herself. And with that approval, she could be herself in greater measure, her mind expanding, her interests nourished. She laughed at least three times a day. She felt fulfilled, body and soul.

And she had done it all under the veil of a lie. These people, her new friends, this magical circle, all of it had come about because she was pretending she would marry Leo.

What if there were a way she could have him in truth?

Paulina tilted her head to the side. "Must Miss Lillian leave at all?"

"To the palace, you mean?" Hester looked around.

"I must return home sometime," Lillian said. The pang lacing her middle wasn't hunger at the sharp, rich smell of the cheese. Where *was* home now—Gower House, in London, with her uncle's library and glasshouse and garden? Gileston, the drafty manor her Aunt Giles managed with the attention of a keen-eyed kite? The tidy cottage in St. Athan where she'd been raised, but which felt small to her now, so remote and confining?

She was of an age to have a proper home of her own. And she didn't.

Home was how she felt with Leo. The sense of comfort and connection, like sliding on a house slipper that had taken on the exact conformation of her feet. That sense of unshakeable presence and belonging.

And she couldn't have it. Not unless she knew he felt the same.

Her skin prickled. She laid aside her sketchbook, with the flower upon it, and rose. "Is someone approaching?"

"That will be Octavia with the cart and the rest of our nuncheon," Paulina said. "And she should have a package for you, Miss Lillian."

Octavia pulled the horse to a halt and broke into a smile as Lillian stepped forward to meet her. "I brought it, Miss Lillian."

"What, to be opened upon the dust and dirt of the cave?" Lillian said lightly. "I can wait until we're back at the manor."

"But Miss Woodfforde will want to see it." It was Temperance who'd gifted the gown to Lillian—not loaned this time, but gifted—and Lillian didn't know how to begin to return her largesse. For one thing, she'd never owned anything so fine.

"I want to see it, too." Faustina pressed forward, basket forgotten.

Temperance watched with her benign, beaming smile as Octavia opened the box and drew back the tissue paper, revealing the alterations she'd made. Ribbons of gold satin twined the sleeves and hemmed the edges of the netted cotton tunic that fell away in a small train from the taffeta round gown beneath, the dark yellow of juniper flowers. More ribbons decorated the simple bodice, cut into an alluring V above the high waist.

The shopping excursion to Wantage to secure the ribbon had been another revelation, the women all going together, Hester engaged by the sights and sounds of the market, clinging more to Temperance than to Lillian as they wandered the festive stalls and shops spilling forth their small treasures. It was the first time Lillian had enjoyed an unabashedly feminine pursuit, and the company made it so.

"Take care his lordship don't steal her from you, Mr. Westrop," Paulina said, inspecting Octavia's stitchery and nodding her approval. "He'll see what a prize she is."

"I intend to do my best, Mrs. Caesar, though that gown,

combined with Craven's advantages, will make me exert myself to the utmost, I fear."

If only it would, Lillian thought. She hadn't chosen the gown to enchant Craven. Dinner at Waringford Hall had been a disaster, his family determined to show Leo every reason Lillian didn't suit. But if he saw her in a new place, dining at a lord's table, accepted in circles as high as his—perhaps everything could be different.

Perhaps. Lillian lifted her hand away from the gown, afraid she might crush the fabric. It was meant for a delicate woman, thin and lovely, graceful, well-born, accomplished. Someone worthy of being courted by a lord.

Not someone who would give her virtue away on a false promise, bartering her future for a handful of stars.

"If his lordship does spirit you off, Miss Gower, you'll leave Hester with us, eh?" the reverend said with a wink at Hester.

It was too much, suddenly, the pretense, the uncertainty. Lillian's insides twisted and her mouth tingled, as if she'd chewed on sneezeweed. She reminded herself that her role here as the excavation's artist, as part of Leo's crew, was as true as anything. The friendships she'd built were as true as her bond with Hester.

It was only everything else that was a lie.

"THAT IS the hill where King Alfred assembled his troops before the Battle of Ashdown, where he fought back the Danes." Leo pointed to the large rampart of banked earth in the distance as he turned down the lane leading to Ashdown House. "And these scattered stones, these are the sheep bespelled by Merlin, according to local legend. Some say Wayland made the sword Excalibur for King Arthur."

Lillian's nerves were strung as tight as the tangled cat's

cradle Hester had made, and she wondered if Leo's chatter disguised nerves as well. So much was riding on how Craven received their find. He could be outraged that they had desecrated an ancient grave and demand they cease at once. He could order Leo to change his tactics, and as it was Craven's land and monument, Leo would have to comply. He could decide to take a closer interest in the dig, and Leo would chafe at having to answer to another.

Or Craven could simply decide to bring in other workers who wouldn't follow Leo's careful methods, and who would take all the credit, in the end, for his discoveries.

She fingered the headdress of flowers that Faustina had woven for her, culled from the gardens clustered about the manor. Yellow hawkbit, corn marigold, and fleabane, with a few scarlet pimpernels added for color. She'd made herself as splendid as she could, wanting to fit the part of Leo Westrop's intended, even if no one felt she deserved that role.

As if she could, somehow, manage the leap from being an antiquarian's daughter to the wife of a marquess's heir.

As if she could be Leo's wife, in truth and surety. Not just a woman with whom he was temporarily amusing himself until the more pressing concerns of his work and his family called him away.

They drove the reverend's chaise and horse, and once again, Hester had let herself be deposited at Watercress Cottage for the evening. Hester seemed to regard the reverend's rented home as if it were already her own. Knowing how difficult Hester found it to adjust to new places, and how much familiarity meant to her, Lillian dreaded the hysterics bound to ensue when she took Hex away from Ashbury and her new friends.

"Just think if you could claim Wayland's cave was Arthur's tomb," Lillian said. "That you have discovered the bones of Arthur, Guinevere, and Mordred."

"And rival Glastonbury Abbey for that honor?" Leo replied. "Your Wim Wim might not appreciate the boost of traffic on his lands. Unless there were a way to make money from the visitors, more than the odd coin stuck into the stones as an offering to Wayland."

"He is not my Wim Wim," Lillian bristled. "Don't be absurd."

"I would imagine he's in line for an elevation of title, given his service to the king. You could have a sure bet instead of my doubtful future as a marquess."

So he *had* heard her vaunt to her mother weeks ago about putting a shackle on a marquess, and he returned it to her with a new layer of bitterness. Surely, by now, Leo must know her better than that. She turned her face toward the field dotted with stones, which truly looked as if they might have been grazing sheep, no discernible pattern to their distribution.

"You have not reconciled with your family, I take it?"

"If ever. You cannot have forgotten how rude they were to you."

"To protect you from a match they find unworthy of you, as you well know."

"That is the part I cannot forgive," Leo said. "My family's opinion of me is carved in stone, at this point. There is little I might do to redeem myself. But they did not even give you an opportunity to display all the reasons they might love you. They decided against you from the first."

Lillian swallowed against the burning sensation that suddenly throttled her. He was speaking once again of *love*. "Save for Lady Melina," she said. "I shall send her a copy of my florilegium, as promised, and we shall be great friends. She can teach me everything she knows about orchids."

The burning sensation crept downward, snaking through her belly. She couldn't contemplate the hole that would open in her life if she had to leave Leo. If there were any way to win his family's approval of her, surely winning over Lord Craven would be one step.

She'd lose, too, the esteem of the friends she'd made in Ashbury if they parted. The Caesars would take Leo's part, as his employees and friends. The Woodffordes would no doubt align themselves with the Westrops. And in London, why, she'd be cut by any number of acquaintances were she to jilt such a promising match as Leo Westrop. She would no longer be on the fringes of polite society; she'd be entirely cast out.

But if he wanted her to stay, what terms would he offer? What if their bond didn't mean to him what it meant to her?

The burning squeezed her heart, as if she'd taken foxglove. What if he didn't see the future for them that was beginning to take shape before her eyes?

Ashdown stood before them, a tall, narrow mansion in the Dutch fashion with its flanking lodges looming like a very elaborate gate. Behind it, the downs rose in gentle folds, here and there lined with trees, their rich green canopies catching the bronze light of the setting sun. Leo pulled the horse to a stop on the gravel drive.

He turned to her, his face with an expression she hadn't seen. "Lillian. I want you to know—"

The narrow front door opened and a tall man in a dark tailcoat and white breeches strode down the steps, the powerful lord at ease in his domain.

"Westrop!" he boomed. "Don't dally out here with your lady. I want to hear what news you two bring me. Peaty says you've found bones."

WILLIAM, Baron Craven, had no lady for his table, but his mother had, as he put it, trotted up the road from Benham Park for a visit. "And my sister Maria would like to meet you as well, Miss Gower, but she didn't want to leave the baby, Charles, who has developed a summer sniffle. Look her up when you're in town next, and she'll issue you vouchers to Almack's, if you want them."

As she followed him through the lovely, empty rooms of the house, marveling at the opulence, Lillian took a moment to understand: William's sister Maria, now married to the Earl of Sefton, was one of the patronesses of Almack's Assembly Rooms. Even Lillian knew the social cachet that a voucher at Almack's granted one. The King's court being considered too fusty, debutantes wanted to be seen at Almack's to be launched into hopes of an advantageous match.

"Aunt Giles will be overcome at the very notion," Lillian murmured, subdued by the haughty glowers from portraits lining the hallways.

William laughed. "The voucher is for you, my dear. Your aunt will be lucky to get a Stranger's Ticket. She's assumed quite a few airs over your putting the shackle on Westrop here. Behaves as if you lower yourself to marry into the family of a marquess. She told my sister Georgiana she would have thought you worthy of a royal duke, not an uninspired mister. You can imagine how well that went over, since my sister Elizabeth married an uninspiring mister and is happily raising a daughter with him in Kent."

"I am glad to hear of Elizabeth's happiness," Lillian answered. "I enjoyed meeting your sisters that summer, though you never let Georgiana play with us, and Elizabeth never wanted to. What can my aunt be thinking about royal dukes? They are exclusively interested in wedding widows and keeping mistresses."

William chuckled as they arrived at another tall, narrow door, which a butler opened to admit them into a formal drawing room. "You'll get on famously with Mother. You never met her that summer. She was already running around Europe with Alexander."

"Your brother?" Leo asked.

William raised an amused brow. "Her lover, whom she ran away with while my father was alive, and we were all quite young. Charles Alexander, Margrave of Brandenburg-Ansbach. He's not here—back at Benham, is he, madam?"

"Back in Hammersmith, fitting out Brandenburg House for my opera, *The Princess of Georgia.*"

A woman in a purple silk robe with long sleeves and elaborate trimmings sat on a damask sofa. She had a narrow nose, pinched lips, and bright, lively eyes that raked Lillian with an assessing gaze. Her hair was powder gray without, Lillian suspected, the use of powder, and the skin of her decolletage was smooth and lustrous with seeming youth. She looked formidable, and exactly the woman Lillian wanted to be at the same age.

"My Alexander has built a theatre for me attached to our house—can you imagine? He indulges me in every way." She held out a slender hand to Leo. "I'll answer to Lady Craven, but you may call me Margravine—everyone else does." She gave an airy laugh. "Until Francis grants me the title of Princess, which he's been hinting he might do."

"Francis II, the Holy Roman Emperor?" Lillian asked, awed.

"The same. William, we ought to go in at once. My chef was in spasms already at the state of your kitchens, and he'll fly into the boughs if we're late and ruin his meal. I don't know why you don't keep a staff here and visit more often."

"It's rather small," William said blandly. "A nice little hunting box, though not a great deal of hunting around here, I've found. Of course, it depends what you're looking for."

He winked as he took Lillian's arm and they processed into the dining parlor behind her ladyship, who had possessed herself of Leo. Craven's touch didn't inspire the same thrum of pleasure and awareness that Leo's did. Nor did his scent of citrus twine into her middle as did Leo's, though they wore the same Eau de Cologne.

Lillian made a point not to gape at the grandness of the room as they seated themselves at a mahogany dining table shimmering with porcelain and crystal. Where the dining parlor at Waringford Hall had been blood-orange, the scene of carnage, Ashdown was cool and clear as ice, and the conversation was as sharp and scintillating as the dishes were impressive. She was really here, Lillian reminded herself; that great and mysterious designer of life had arranged for her to have exactly this, dinner in what amounted to a palace with a woman the equivalent of a princess, a lord who had the ear of the king, and the heir to a powerful peer who was himself making unparalleled historical discoveries.

This was her life now, that seductive voice whispered in her ear. She could have this.

Yet the small cap sleeves of her splendid gown chafed her shoulders as she lifted a bit of salmon to her mouth, reminding her she sat in a gifted gown and she lived on borrowed time, a vivid respite carved from the mundane demands of her life. She was engaged in an elaborate performance, as staged and mannered as one of her ladyship's plays.

Lillian caught Leo's look and he smiled at her, his eyes crinkling. He was nervous, too, and the shared gaze seemed a relief to him. Warmth rushed through her then, confirming what she had come to suspect. It was only Leo Westrop who could move her, warm her. It was Leo who had cast snares around her heart.

It was Leo she wanted to be bound to. And she had no idea what came next for them.

"I'm not the least bit qualified to make an assessment about what you've found," William said sometime during the second course, after Leo gave a full accounting of the work at Wayland Smith's Cave. "But I'll recommend you to the Society of Antiquaries, if you haven't a patron already. I imagine unearthing old bones will make quite a stir in some circles. Perhaps I'll be able to raise the rents on the Chapel Manor if you make the area a famous site, like Stonehenge."

Leo looked every inch like a man who had just been handed his dearest dream, and looked wary of accepting it, as he knew full well the gods could be capricious. "Than—thank you, sir. I would be most appreciative of your support."

Craven nodded in Lillian's direction. "You made a smart choice procuring a Gower to help you. Lillian will have had plenty of experience, being raised on digs and all."

"That was purely coincidental," Lillian said, taking a slice of breast of veal in ragout. The chef had turned out a wonderful meal, and since none of her companions were monitoring her portions as Aunt Giles tended to do, Lillian meant to enjoy it. "Leo proposed to me quite on the spot, and out of the blue, you might say."

"A romantic story to tell others, but you can be honest with me." Craven snorted. "I ran into your friend, Westrop—the Methodist minister's grandson, Daniel Rowland. Been telling me about the Dilettanti, boasting of his collection."

"I had heard one of the pursuits of the Dilettanti is collecting erotic literature," Lady Craven remarked. "And art as well. I'm told they make a great show of viewing and comparing collections."

Leo's lips went tight. "That is a hobby for many, I understand. I myself have been led to collect different kinds of artifacts."

"There's no shame in a healthy interest in the erotic," Lady

Craven said. "And a lady can benefit from a man's knowledge, if he applies it correctly." She winked at Lillian, who promptly found that foxglove feeling returning.

"Mother, let us attempt to engage in our guests' interests, and not our own." Craven turned toward Lillian. "Certainly, Westrop's been benefiting from your knowledge. Your sketches are superb—feel like I'm there. And Rowland's right. It makes perfect sense Westrop would go after the daughter of antiquarians to help prop up his own reputation. A sensible match in all respects." He winked at her, the gesture oddly echoing his mother.

"If only the other Westrops felt so," Lillian said, but her response was perfunctory, her voice pushed across a great distance. Her mind was suddenly far away, back in the library of Westrop House and that very first meeting, when Leo Westrop, in the magnificent flesh, had been a spectacle she couldn't tear her eyes from.

One of those *Gowers?*

She'd thought he enjoined her to wait for him in the reception rooms because he'd been enjoying their conversation as much as she had. Of course, he had asked questions later about her parents, but it had never occurred to her that his interest in *her* had been due to *them*. She'd simply, naively believed that, as he cast his desperate eye about the drawing room of Westrop House, looking for a way to evade his mother's trap, his eye lit on Lillian as a likely deliverer because of their sudden if brief connection in the library.

When all along, he'd merely wanted access to her parents.

Not just her parents. To be fair, he'd also made use of Lillian's skills. After she had all but thrown herself upon him, because she'd longed so desperately to spend more time together. Offering herself, wholly, like an orchid unfurling its petals, a tender young shoot turning eagerly toward the sun.

How convenient for him.

She tried to catch Leo's gaze. It didn't matter why he'd first singled her out, did it? Not if what he felt now was sincere. If their time together had blossomed into something true and lasting that could bear fruit year after year. Not simply a showy annual that bloomed for a short season and then faded away.

He didn't seek her gaze in return, but looked at his dish and his slice of ox palate.

Suddenly Lillian hated nothing so much in all the world as she hated ox palate. She had the sudden nonsensical urge to shove her entire place setting to the floor.

But of course she didn't. She ate her meal, though it all tasted of stewed greens, and not the tasty kind but the bitter, overcooked variety. After dessert was concluded, which tasted like wet parchment to her, Lillian allowed herself to be led to one of the formal parlors and regaled with Lady Craven's with tales of the Continent, of life in Hammersmith now that she and her margrave had removed to England, of the musicians they had supported back in Ansbach and the reception of her various songs, pantomimes, and farces, though recently she had decided to enlarge her oeuvre and reach a different register with the opera of a troubled princess. Lillian smiled and nodded, nodded and smiled, and sipped her tea as if she were enjoying herself immensely and didn't feel like a pot left too long in the kiln, scorched to brittleness, ready to shatter at a strong touch.

Lady Craven set down her china cup and regarded Lillian as if she were studying a painting by an unknown.

"He is besotted with you, of course."

For one awful moment, blood draining from her fingers, Lillian thought she meant Craven. Her own cup rattled in its dish. "I—that is—"

"Westrop." Her ladyship tilted her head. "All the signs of it.

He cannot look anywhere but at you. He seeks your approval of everything he says. He is entranced."

Lillian carefully set down her dish on the table inlaid with a veined marble matching the fireplace. The gilt-edged mirror above the hearth reflected her own face back to her, pale and bewildered. She in her shades of yellow looked out of place in the room, toned in sea-foam blue and pale silver. She was a sturdy flower of the meadow popping up uninvited on a stately manicured lawn.

"Leo—Westrop and I are...we have not made firm plans about our future."

"You are engaged to be married, are you not?"

Lillian couldn't say what mad urge compelled her to confide in her ladyship. Perhaps she'd been addled of late by having female companionship, Paulina and Octavia and Temperance and Hex, when for too long she'd been without the ability to confide in or be guided by older women, save for the odd moments her mother spared her attention or her aunt set aside time to enumerate Lillian's long list of faults that required correction.

"In truth our betrothal was unexpected. Generated to extricate Westrop from being compelled to marry another young lady he had no affection for. Our agreement, from the beginning, is that I will cry off when things have run their course."

"But they haven't yet," Lady Craven said softly, her bright gaze roving every inch of Lillian's face. "Things have charted a new path. For you."

Lillian nodded. The tea burned on her tongue. "I cannot say if that is true for him also."

Her ladyship reclaimed her teacup, fingers pinched around the delicate handle. She regarded the room as if it were unfamiliar to her, as if she'd had no part in its furbishing and no stake in its continued welfare.

"I saw my future plotted out for me when I married William's father," she said. "I was sixteen and threw passionate fits, which my parents of course ignored. I am an earl's daughter, and he, though the son of a Shropshire vicar, was certain to inherit the title and estates from his uncle, which he did. I managed his homes and I gave him children, but there was no affection."

Lillian concerned herself with her own beverage, now cooling. What could she say? It was not her place to console, and Lady Craven only described what was true of the majority of aristocratic marriages, alliances of bloodline made to consolidate wealth and position.

That was precisely why the other Westrops objected so passionately to Lillian's attempting to enter their family. She had no lineage, no breeding, no fortune. She brought nothing to this alliance but a knowledge of various antiquarian practices and the features of assorted plants.

Her ladyship smiled, lost in a pleasant memory. "So I sought affection elsewhere. Many times. Do you know Charles Greville?"

Lillian blinked in surprise. "I have made his acquaintance. He invited me to view his gardens."

A bark of laughter met this confession. "He'll not have lost his eye for a shapely female, not at his age. He dropped me as soon as he laid eyes on that Emma Hart, or so she styled herself then—she's Emma Hamilton now. But then I met Alexander." Her eyes softened, her lips curving in a fond smile. "He built a villa on his property for me."

Lillian waited, trying to parse out the lesson in the story, if there was one. That she might find another after Leo lost interest? That arranged aristocratic marriages were destined not to be happy?

"I found love," her ladyship said simply. "I'd had many

affairs, and he'd had many mistresses, but we found one another. And that has been worth everything. Worth him giving up his principality to move to England with me so I might see what has become of my children. Worth a snub from Marie Antoinette, though she paid the price for her arrogance, didn't she. George won't have me at court, not the rigid moralist he is, but we are happy. Free to live as we wish, Alexander with his horses, me with my plays. Did I tell you he built me a theatre at Brandenburg House?"

Lillian nodded. "A true sign of esteem."

"So love redeems all." Her ladyship dipped her chin decisively. "It seems excessively romantic to say it, but of all the things one might live for, love is the best among them."

The wet paper of dessert had, Lillian found, formed a great clump in her throat. She couldn't swallow around it.

She loved Leo Westrop. A love she would harbor always.

Surely, surely that was enough of a foundation upon which to build a life together.

Her ladyship glanced around again. "The men will have left the dining parlor by now—William doesn't like to linger at table. He'll have taken his port, and no doubt your young man, into the library. Go along and join them, dear, and I'll be in presently. I've a need to visit the retiring room first."

A footman stood outside the parlor, as if he waited on her ladyship, and this saved Lillian the trouble of asking the direction of the library. This room was done up in browns and golds, and Craven and Leo stood before the fireplace, another massive marble frontage, but instead of a mirror, which would have reflected her to them, this mantelpiece held a series of plaster busts, carved in Classical style.

Lillian's heart lifted at the sight of Leo in his evening gear, his shoulders so broad beneath the wide lapels of his green velvet coat, his back firm and strong. How intimately she knew every muscle of that back, and of the buttocks tucked beneath the long tails of his coat, and the muscled thighs in his buff pantaloons. How generous, how careful he was with that strength when they lay in bed together, and how much she drew from the solid surety of his presence when they drove together, or worked side by side at the cave, or dined or—everything, really.

She *loved* him, and she couldn't wait to tell him. He was the most rare, the most precious, the most beautiful thing that ever existed. She wanted the privilege of leaning on Leo Westrop, looking at Leo Westrop, holding Leo Westrop, every day and every night of the rest of her life.

The air seemed filled with colored light, like bubbles of soap floating in the air. With them came the words of the men's conversation, as clear as cut glass.

"—but not marriage," Craven said, lifting a brow.

Leo drank deeply from the glass he held, a glimmer of red and amber. "I'm afraid my family will have made that impossible."

"Does she know?"

"She agreed to our arrangement from the beginning. And about its end."

"But you don't wish to end it."

"I don't."

Lillian's heart beat in her ears, so loudly she could barely hear. Foolish heart. She wanted very much to hear, to savor the words that came next. Leo loved her too. They had found it together, that fairy tale land of mutual adoration, that realm so unreachable for so many mortal lives. She almost giggled, buoyed by the airy delight rising inside her. That she, Lillian Gower, would have been blessed with this gift, this man—

"Will she agree to being your mistress?"

Leo inspected his glass, swirling the liquid with a heavy wrist. "I hope so. I can't offer anything else."

Her heart pounded, deep and slow. Then slower still, as if it might stop altogether.

"What happens when you do wed? She's a proud one, despite everything."

Leo shrugged, one shoulder rising then falling like the executioner's axe. "My mother's backed me into a corner. I never intended to marry, not in my position. But what else can I do?"

Craven nodded, his mouth lifting on one side. "She's a lush one, if that's your taste. You've already got the slip on her shoulder. You'd be a fool to let her go now."

Leo nodded, the side of his face tense. "Exactly."

"Westrop."

Lillian's voice cracked out of her. She was breaking, just as she'd feared might happen back in the dining parlor, or the sitting room. His words were the tap at her crown that was taking the whole careful edifice apart, and if she had not gone to pieces at Waringford Hall under the combined assault of the Westrop family, she could not, *would* not crumble here. Not simply because Craven had made Leo define what he really wanted from her: a continued affair.

That wasn't a bond of hearts and minds. That wasn't a future. That wasn't something she could take to bed at night and wake up beside in the morning.

"I am ready to go," she said.

Leo's head shot up, and the expression of horror on his face was almost comical, the exaggeration of a pantomime.

"Lil." He visibly recoiled. She saw the leap of his mind, trying to calculate how long she'd been standing there. "We were just—"

"I heard." She kept her tone very tight. She kept her fingers curled tightly too. Kept everything in her close together, held hard, as if she were the anchor on a balloon full of hot air and would lose the whole thing if she didn't keep a tight grip.

"I think it's time to end this. Don't you?"

"Of course. We should get back. There's not as much light tonight, and the Caesars are waiting."

He offered courtesies to Craven, the polite and customary noises about their gratitude for dinner and his continued patronage. Of course he must curry Craven's favor. Lillian needed to be out of this room, out of this house, before she shattered, because the pieces would not fall into a quiet heap: they would explode like the eruption of Mount Vesuvius so long ago, burying everything around her in hot lava and burning ash.

A groom brought their carriage to the gravel drive, lamps lit against the falling night. The moon that had seemed so lovely and magical outside her window now was a cold will-o'-the-wisp, laughing at her. Had it only been last night she'd held Leo in her arms and gazed out the window at that moon, making a wish on its potent magic?

So much for wishes.

Leo tried to take her arm to help her into the carriage, and she pulled away. He could not touch her. She would not allow him to touch her ever again.

She wrapped her arms around herself as they set into motion, the chaise rolling up the road toward Ashbury. Toward her bed that was no longer her refuge. Toward the lie that had come apart. She pulled her shawl around her shoulders, but nothing could shield her from the cold slicing her apart on the inside.

She'd known, hadn't she? She'd known all along. And yet, like a complete widgeon, she'd kept hoping for something different.

"This is what I've been waiting for, Lil," Leo said, his voice a low murmur in the shadows of the night, only the lamp on the carriage and a hazy half moon their guide. "Craven promised to support me. I have a patron, and an in with the Society of Antiquaries. People will read my publications. They will support my work. I have a future now."

"Then it is time to bring our agreement to an end," she said.

"Lillian. What you heard—"

"Doesn't matter." It did, it *did,* but she couldn't bear to hear him say again that what she had imagined as a deep affection between them, the kind of connection that could weather years of trials and only grow stronger, fonder, had been nothing but pleasure of the body for him. He wanted her as a *mistress,* but not a companion for life. She grasped at the edges of her fleeing control and pulled them to her, hard, as if she could stop flower petals from scattering on the breeze.

"You've achieved what you wanted. I held up my end of the bargain." More than her end. She'd given him everything. "I need to get back to London. My parents—my uncle—Hex." She couldn't seem to string words together. "My life is with them."

"*Lillian,*" he said raggedly. "I need you—"

"Faustina can keep records for you. I've taught her a few things. And Augustus can draw, come to that. You *don't* need me, not anymore." She drew a deep breath, hauling in air as if that could stop the cold, could tamp the gathering eruption. Hot or cold—what was she? She barely knew. Every sense was cauterized with agony.

She'd been wrong. So wrong.

"What do *you* need, Lillian?"

The question nearly severed her tight hold on everything, sent her sailing off into the dark. That he could ask that, think about what she needed, but not *love* her—that it was all passion and lust and convenience—and a chance to learn tricks of the trade from her parents, God help her—

She needed for this, all of this, to have been real. To have meant something. Not a pleasant diversion during a summer dig, but *real*.

"My florilegium is waiting for me," she said unsteadily. And her own life. Her empty, quiet life, which would be a vast cave of loneliness without him. She couldn't think of it now. She'd begin shrieking and howling, like some mythical spirit, and she might never recover her wits.

"My parents will need my help. My uncle can use my assistance." Aunt Giles wouldn't welcome her return. She wouldn't think of that, either. "And I think it is time I got Hex away from here."

He nodded. "Very well. I can pause the operation for a week or two, or put Claudius in charge. I can bring you to London, set things in order, check on your florilegium—"

"I do not think that is necessary, Westrop."

Dear heaven, something in that tea had left her lips numb. She could barely move them. "We agreed from the beginning that this would end, didn't we? And now it is time. Things have run their course."

He turned to her, his face full of shadows, and she caught only the downward curve of his lip. "Have they?"

"We agreed I would be the one to jilt you. Because you couldn't do it and be a *gentleman*."

He hadn't been a gentleman when he'd kissed her and stolen her sense away. He hadn't been a gentleman all those nights in her bed when he'd introduced her to a pleasure that had seared her bones, a pleasure she would never forget, never be free of. Damn him.

"So, this is it. My jilting."

She lifted her chin. Her mouth trembled. "I won't be your mistress, Leo." She would, in an instant, if she had only herself to think about. "My family might be lower than yours, but I won't shame them. Their reputation matters." *Her* reputation mattered. She wouldn't be allowed into the Linnean Society if she were a known courtesan. "As for marriage..." Her heart clenched, stopping her air. "That was never a real possibility. We knew that from the beginning, too."

His voice was as tight as hers, his face as solid and impassive as a sarsen stone in profile. "This is the end of it, then."

"Yes," she said, and managed to keep her voice from breaking as her heart fell into thick pieces, cleaved through. "I'm afraid it is."

CHAPTER TWENTY-TWO

"Marriage, Miss Gower," Reverend Woodfforde said. "Let me be clear. I am proposing marriage."

He sat across from Lillian in the wood-paneled parlor of Gower House, the gray of the London afternoon barely lightening the somber tones of the room. Lillian blinked, trying to wrap her mind around this revelation.

"You wish to marry Hester," she repeated.

She'd left Ashbury a fortnight ago. In that fortnight, Paulina had written twice, Octavia once. Augustus had sent her a piece of chalk he'd filched from the White Horse at Uffington, and Faustina had appended a note to her sister's missive informing Hester that the bustard eggs had hatched.

She'd heard nothing from Leo.

After she'd told him she wanted to end things, jilted him on that cold, endless drive from Ashdown and then retired to her room to sob in her bed, he'd watched in silence as she packed her things. He'd watched her quarrel with Hex about leaving, endure the pleas of the Caesars and Woodffordes to stay. He'd heard of her difficulty hiring a post chaise, for which she had to travel to Swindon.

He hadn't begged. He hadn't tried to explain himself, though she longed to hear a true explanation, for him to tell her she'd been wrong in what she heard, wrong about what he said to Lord Craven, wrong about what he intended for them. He'd merely promised that he would be sure to credit her name for the sketches if his findings on Wayland Smith's Cave were ever published. He'd watched her leave without once breaking his stoic, stony expression.

Her heart in tatters, Lillian went through the motions of each day. Conferring with the housekeeper about meals and accounts. Meeting the girls Sarey collected off the street or from Dark Lane, girls who wanted to leave their profession, agreeing to find them positions in the house and train them up to steady, safer work. Coloring her plates when she wasn't taking calls, and the calls were many. Far from shunning her as a jilt, everyone left in London wanted to know the particulars of how and why Lillian Gower had broken off with Westrop.

Thank goodness she had her florilegium. Inking plates, keeping the proper colors within their lines, was all she could manage at the moment. It helped her keep a handle on the world.

He had not followed to beg for her back.

The Reverend Woodfforde and his sister had followed; they traveled to London only days behind and had been calling on Hester morning and night. And now, a fortnight later, the Reverend had worked up the nerve to tell her why.

Lillian looked back and forth between the reverend's hopeful, nervous expression and Temperance's steady, bright beam. "I am sure you realize you will need my aunt's permission regarding Hester's hand."

Woodfforde nodded. "I am aware, but you seem to be— better informed about Hester's needs. So, we hoped to approach you first on the matter."

"I am very sorry to say this, but I do not think Hester is suited for marriage," Lillian said carefully. "For one thing, I do not think she has—any interest in supervising a household."

"She would have no responsibilities in our household," the reverend said. "Temperance sees to all those arrangements."

"But what if Temperance should marry and leave you?"

Temperance folded her hands in her lap, and for the first time, her smile slipped. "I am not likely to marry, Miss Gower."

"But why not? Forgive my being impertinent. My cousin's happiness is in question."

"And my happiness," Temperance said steadily, watching Lillian's face, "is in the companionship of my female friends. Select, dear female friends, fellow sapphists, like me. My brother condones these friendships, so long as I am discreet. Living in his household shields me from questions. Of course, my discretion would extend to keeping Hester unaware of— shall we say, the nature of my liaisons. Though I would like, now and again, to introduce her to my companions, I have no intention of setting up a household of my own. Hester would have the benefit of my oversight as well as my brother's devotion."

Lillian nodded. At least now she knew what a sapphist was.

"But I fear my cousin is—not equipped for the other demands of marriage, either. Motherhood, primarily."

"Ours would not be that sort of union," the reverend said.

Lillian lifted her brow. "Oh. You, too, have—other companions?"

The reverend raised his gaze to the ceiling, studying the intricate woodwork of the carved panels. Temperance readjusted her hands, folding them in opposite layers. "The illness that took his wife and children several years ago left my brother incapable of fathering more children," Temperance said steadily.

Lillian surveyed the reverend, who cleared his throat, blushing slightly. "I would never importune Hester if she did not wish for conjugal relations," he said. "I am happy to have her merely as a companion. But if she did wish for—more closeness, there will be no risk of offspring. Our union would be without issue."

Lillian's heart crumpled as if a trilithon had fallen upon it. A man could wish for a woman's companionship. He could simply long to be near her. Conjugal relations could be an addition to other affectionate bonds, an enhancement, so to speak, but not the whole substance.

If only Leo had felt the same. If only.

"Then why marry?" Lillian asked. "Why not simply visit her frequently, or host her as a favored guest?"

"As her husband, I could devote myself to her care and keeping," the reverend said. "I could bring her from her mother's house into my own. My primary concern in life would be her comfort. We understand she is a gentle creature, innocent in her ways. She will not...flourish in the typical situations. But I think, among us, my sister and I can offer a situation more or less ideal.

"There will be no demands on her, no responsibilities, other than to please herself and enjoy our company. When I lost my family, I thought I could never care again for another. Temperance saved me from despair. But we have long felt the house is so quiet with just the two of us, and Temperance's companions —well, none of them have expressed the desire to join a household with her doddering old brother."

Lillian smiled. The reverend was far from doddering. She guessed that his gentle, steady nature had been tempered by grief, forged by the fires of searing loss. And she could guess why he had stepped down from his position as vicar, and was not likely to take it back. Temperance would not have the same freedoms if her brother were in a position of public scrutiny.

"Hester is what we need to complete us," the reverend said simply. "We adore her. She has brought such joy to our lives. I see us going on quite well together. And if we are legally wed, I can leave her my property at my passing, to ensure she is financially secure." He cleared his throat again. "I mentioned the possibility of offering to her aunt, and she—ah, indicated that she would readily consider my suit, old as I am. We could even consider hosting Mrs. Giles for extended visits. We have a smaller cottage on the property that might suit her."

Nothing would suit her aunt but playing the lady of a great house, Lillian wanted to say, but it was Hester's future under discussion here. Hester had an offer of *marriage*.

Lillian had supposed, in what thoughts of her future she was able to piece together after the Great Shattering, that Hester would be her companion into her long spinsterhood. But now Hester was loved, and doted upon, and here was a man who wanted a future with her. Not because of what Hester could offer him in wealth or family or skills, but for the sheer delight of her presence.

"We should of course consult Hex in the matter," Lillian forced through a tight throat.

"Yes." Hester entered the room and plopped into the chair beside the reverend. She sent him a look of gentle fondness and stretched out her hand. He took it.

"I should like for you to be my husband, Matthew. And I shouldn't mind if there were a baby."

The reverend cleared his throat, and Lillian saw he was suffering the same knot of emotion that had visited her windpipe. "I am not quite prepared for a babe, my dear. But perhaps if we adopt a dog? A nice sweet-natured little spaniel who will sit in your lap or at your feet and romp with you through the garden."

Hester nodded. "I should like that, too. I do hope Mama says yes."

Lillian smoothed her apron over her skirt. Her apron didn't need smoothing, but it was something to do with her hands. She was suddenly at a loss, a great piece of her life shifting away. A wall guarding her heart had been knocked down, and all of a sudden there was an inrush of air and light, a disorienting change to the prospect.

"I might suggest you call again tomorrow," Lillian said. "Aunt Giles will be at home to callers, and Hex and I will have an opportunity to acquaint her with the idea."

The reverend nodded and rose, taking her hint. "And you are preparing for your lecture tonight, are you not? In that case we will not keep you. But I hope you do not mind that we both will attend. Temperance and I are not members of the Linnean Society, but we are told the meetings are open to anyone."

"I should be honored for your support," Lillian answered. "And please do take the liberty of retrieving me from the floor if I suffer nervous prostration."

Hester giggled. "Lil's never swooned in her life."

"There is a first time for everything, is there not?"

A first time for falling in love, and for discovering how overwhelming, how completely immersive passion could be with the right partner.

A first time for heartbreak, for becoming acquainted with the desolate, charred landscape that survived a lightning strike to one's heart.

There came also first times for the publication of one's florilegium, and the arrival of the first bound copies, the plates a beautiful showcase of years of study. Following that came an invitation to present her work at the monthly meeting of Linnean society, where Miss Lillian Gower was invited to give a talk on the unique features of the Cypripedium calceolus, with the possibility of future appearances should this talk be well received.

"You are certain you want to marry, Hex?"

Lillian took the opportunity to talk alone with Hester as her cousin helped her dress for the evening in the narrow attic bedroom allotted her at Gower House. "It will mean going to live at Watercress Cottage with the reverend and Miss Woodfforde."

"With Matthew and Temperance," Hester replied. She sorted through Lillian's hairpieces, discarding each on the dressing table. "We talked about it several times. I like them. I should like living with them more than I like living with Mama and Uncle Gower."

"But you might live with me, Hex. At some point I might set up a household of my own, and you will always be welcome there."

Hester sniffed at Lillian's bottle of eau de toilette, from which wafted the scent of geraniums. "Aren't you going to marry Leo?"

"No." Lillian's throat closed. "Not now."

"That is too bad. He wasn't the wrong sort. Why not?"

"We...Mr. Westrop and I...wanted different things from our future."

"Oh." Hester nodded. "That is the nice thing about Matthew and Temperance and I. We all want the same things. A nice quiet house, a few good friends to have for dinner, and a dog. Maybe the occasional explore, if we want to take the carriage out, but no London. No boring parties. No having to do anything but what we wish."

"That sounds...ideal, actually."

Hester tilted her head to the side. "And Mr. Westrop didn't want that?"

What *did* Leo want? A place in his profession, the respect of his peers. A companion to amuse him at table and in bed.

"I don't believe so. No."

He hadn't wanted *her*.

Or rather, he had wanted her, in the carnal way, but not in the pleasant companionship kind of way. Not sharing the more important things, like a home. Possibly children, if the carnal relations resulted in such.

There might be a time, years in the future, when the admission that Leo didn't want those things with her wasn't the ripping out of an organ, or a limb. The time might come.

"Try these flowers with that dress," Hester said. "I picked them from the Americas."

"Gaillardia," Lillian said. "I adore that flash of red around the center. Thank you, Hex."

Hester nodded. "I wish things had worked out with Mr. Westrop, since I am leaving you. You are always looking after everyone else, Lil. I should like someone to look after you for a change."

"TO CONCLUDE, I have found these points applying to all four species of the Cypripedium that I have studied," Lillian said.

She kept her gaze trained on her notes, because when she looked at the large room and all the faces turned her way, her mind went blank as the face of a chalk cliff, and every word swam away from her head. Her notes were an anchor, a place to find her footing.

"These include the *acaule*, the *calceolus*, the *reginae*, and the *candidum*, all of which I describe in my book."

Was it in poor taste to mention her book? She had brought copies to give to those of her uncle's friends who had been her early subscribers, but she would be happy to collect subscribers for a second printing. Mr. Karim had expressed his pleasure with how well the final copies had turned out, and Lillian herself could hardly believe that something like this existed in the world with her name on it, her small contribution to a great and increasing store of knowledge.

"Without seeming fanciful, I would like to suggest that its more seemingly primitive features contribute to the beauty and usefulness of this plant." She was almost done; if she only kept to her notes, then all that was left was to endure the questions, some no doubt meant to trap her.

"You will recall the slipper orchids are distinct in that their inflorescence is terminal, rather than branched, and their ovate leaves display parallel venation. The pouch-like labellum requires the pollinating insect to travel past the staminode, bees being the preferred method of delivery. And, as I mentioned, not least of its several unusual features is that the slipper orchid is diandrous, possessing two fertile anthers."

This raised another murmur, and she knew she would be challenged on this point. "But while it may not flower annually, the slipper orchid is a lovely addition to any collection, bringing the footprint of the Lady Aphrodite—if you will forgive me this bit of fanciful interpolation—to British soil. This concludes my prepared remarks. I will be happy to entertain questions."

She looked up, and the broad room narrowed to one singular point, the whole world becoming a cylinder of light focused on one subject. Leo Westrop stood near the back of the room.

Questions came at her, and she gave answers, but she hardly knew what she was saying. The lamps lining the walls of the room were too bright and hot yet too smoky and dark to see clearly, all at the same time. She broke out in a cold sweat beneath the sheer muslin scarf she'd tucked into the bodice of her round gown. One of her prettier gowns, the one she'd worn to Highcastle House, with the embroidery that made her feel like a flower.

Leo's intent, penetrating gaze, unswerving from its focal point on her, made her bloom like an orchid that had been dormant for seasons. Years.

He was here. Why was he here?

He raised his hand to indicate a question.

Lillian swallowed the burning pastille in her throat. "Yes. Mr. Westrop."

At the name—the name of the fiancé she'd jilted—every head in the room swiveled in his direction.

He advanced up the aisle between the rows of chairs. "Tell me, Miss Gower, since you have studied this flower in depth, particularly the *calceolus*. How does the lady propagate? The flower, I mean. The orchid."

The burning from her throat crept up her cheeks, scorching her eyes. He was *here*. He looked so splendid in the bottle green coat and pantaloons he'd worn the night he broke her heart. It was as though they'd never left that moment. It was as though the ache of the weeks without him fell away into some chasm of unremembering, and all she could recall was how it felt to be in his presence, because he was here.

I beg you will not talk of reproduction, he'd said. Because even then, he'd been longing for her, imagined being with her. But passion was all he'd wanted, not her in whole. Not the complete Lillian, uncontained, undainty creature that she was. She must remember that.

"It is very difficult to grow the Cypripedioideae from seed," she answered. "I know of no cases where a gardener has been successful at it. Cuttings also appear to be insufficient. I believe one must capture the plant at its rhizomes and make divisions at the root. My greatest success has been in transplants that replicate the plant's natural growing conditions as much as possible, including traces of original earth."

"That would suggest there is something in its natural element that is necessary to the plant's survival. Something in the air, the temperature, the exposure to light?"

"My theory is something in the soil," Lillian said. He drew closer, and her lungs contracted, laboring to draw in air as her heart expanded in her chest, taking up too much space. "Perhaps there is some specific mineral or nutrient that is necessary, the way a specific insect is required to pollinate."

"That's me," Leo said. "I'm an orchid."

"Do not be absurd, sir. You are a *Homo sapiens,* not a member of the Cypripedioideae."

"But I find there is a very specific element necessary to my survival," Leo said. "And if I lack it, I will die."

"That is a fanciful imagining."

"That is absolute truth." He neared the lectern where she stared down at him. His eyes were wide and the silver of mercury, his expression earnest, troubled, and—adoring. He wore a look of open adoration. Her knees loosened.

"Ask me what is necessary to my survival." His gaze didn't waver from her face. Her heart wavered, though. It looped in her chest like a bee whirring in circles.

Lillian couldn't speak. Her tongue was glued to the top of her mouth like the fused sepals of a Cypripedium.

"Ask him, Miss Gower," urged an audience member, a female voice.

"Say it's her!" Was that Temperance? She was normally so soft-spoken. "Go on, then, Mr. Westrop."

"It is you," Leo said simply. "My life is empty without you."

"That is factually untrue," Lillian said, her voice wobbling. She couldn't break her gaze from his stare; he had her hypnotized. How fortunate she had a lectern, because it, and her fingers gripping the wooden platform, were all that was holding her upright.

"It is metaphorical and spiritual truth," Leo said.

There, before the entire audience on the premises in Panton Square, he lowered himself to one knee like a knight of old kneeling before his lady. "I made a spectacle of you once in public, Lil—Miss Gower. I snared you into a ruse, a pretense of an engagement." Several gasps rose from the audience; this bit of gossip would be spreading before they left these rooms. "I won't pin you to an answer before all these people. But I am asking you again if you will be in my life—*be* my life—as my bride and wife in truth."

"For real this time?" Lillian asked weakly.

He nodded, and they stared at one another in silence. A church bell tolled, the bells of St. James, and it seemed the beginning of something. He was here, which should not be enough, but it *was*, and moreover, he was saying things that were so closely in line with the secret desires of her heart, she couldn't trust that she was hearing him speak them. She felt the same way she had when her brush moved aside dark earth to show the dull grayish white of human bone: a mystery, a secret, a truth revealed.

"Let us speak in private, you and I." Lillian turned toward one of the vestibules leading from the main room with its columns and carvings.

Distinct groans emanated from the audience. "This is what happens when you give females scientific training," a man muttered—it might have been Sir James.

"Their feminine sensibilities wither," another agreed. Was that Woodfforde, the traitor? Lillian didn't have time to consider. She stepped into a smaller, empty antechamber and immediately regretted how close the space demanded Leo stand to her. She couldn't reason with him so near; all she could think was how much she wanted to be in his arms. Scientific studies hadn't blunted her female sensibilities in the least.

"You told Craven you only wanted me as a mistress." That was the heart of it; that was the break, the defining point, the end of a season of plenty and the beginning of famine.

"I said it." He nodded. He stood close. He was larger than she remembered, more solid. He smelled wonderful, like fresh earth and herbs.

"It filled me with shame, but I said it. I said it because I did not want him, a stranger to me, to know the truth of my heart before you did."

"But you let me believe you meant it," she whispered. The flame in a lamp high on the wall danced in a draught of air, and her heart sidestepped with it like a spooked horse, wanting to come near the thing it desired, afraid of being captured if she did.

He looked around them. It was a short, narrow hallway, a long oaken table standing to one side, assorted busts in their niches. A place of temperance and learning, not a place for passionate declarations.

"You'll have noted that my family calls me Gideon, and I dislike the name."

"I've wondered why."

"Gideon was my father's name. Refusing to be called by his name was the way I could refuse him. Every peccadillo, every scandal, every insult to our family...every time he was elsewhere when we wanted him at home, and every insult he dealt us when he was home and I wished him gone—it was a way to repudiate him. If I did not use his name, I could not be anything like him."

"I do not think—"

"Let me say it, my love. When I saw what Craven saw, that I

had been dallying with you for my own amusement, abusing your heart...I saw my father. I saw myself doing exactly what my father would have done, and I hated myself for it. That is why I did not try to stop you when you left. I was ashamed that I had used you so badly. That I had not made my intentions clear from the first. I thought I deserved to have you jilt me, for behaving as I did."

"But you are not your father," Lillian said. He was close enough she could touch him. She anchored her hands at her middle. If she touched him now, something would alchemize and change inside her; she would become fused to him and might never be able to stand again on her own.

"Do the intentions matter, if the outcome is the same? I wanted you from that first night, Lillian. I left your uncle's home thinking what it would be like if we had a life together. I wanted to hold you, provide for you, keep you safe, make you happy. And I could not see how to do that, with what little I had to offer."

"All I want is to be loved," Lillian said, her voice treacherously unsteady. "Not as a mistress who can be set aside. Loved inside of marriage, where I am the cherished, and the first, and the only."

"I want that too." His eyes burned like fairy lights through fog, the green lights that came from swamps on a dark, magical night. "But how can that be enough? I depend on my family for my finances. What she could save my father from spending, my mother manages. My allowance from my uncle is small. I do not know how I could provide you a home or the life you deserve."

She swayed closer to him, not touching yet, but breathing his air. "Our home will be our latest expedition, your dig and my flower studies," she said.

"But how to finance such a life, my love? We must be practical. The sparrows and the lilies of the field may not need to toil, but a man must have income."

"We can live on my inheritance," Lillian said.

He drew closer—was she leaning toward him, like a climbing vine reaching for support? "I beg your pardon," he said.

"My mother's parents left me money," she said. "A small annuity, and a property in Galloway that brings in some rents. It is not large, and I have mostly been investing the proceeds of late, since I have so few expenses. That is how I paid Mr. Karim to print my florilegium."

"My wife," Leo said, "is an heiress?"

"By no means, or at least, not a grand one. But we wouldn't be destitute. I might find a way to draw an income from my sketching as well, like Mrs. Delany. That would not sully the Westrop name with trade. Though I doubt your family will accept me no matter what."

"If I may have you," Leo said, "I will say farewell to all of them, and good riddance."

"Not Aunt Melina," Lillian said. "I have yet to see her glasshouse."

He took her hands, and the contact made her shudder, as the earth must have shuddered when the great trilithon at Stonehenge fell, surrendering to the inevitable pull.

"That is how I will win you?" he asked softly. "With my Aunt Melina's glasshouse."

"And digs where I get to tramp about fields sketching flowers," she said. "You don't know how happy that makes me. I can think of few things that thrill me more."

He lifted his brows and she read his face, the sultry burn in his eyes.

"Well, *that,*" she said, her cheeks heating. "That part of our union is thrilling also. But I feared it was the only thing, for you. And I could not bear to mean so little."

"My darling Lillian." He gathered her to him. "You mean *everything* to me."

The door to the lecture room opened. The Marquess of Waringford stood there.

Lillian blinked. No, it was really him, not some apparition.

"Has Miss Gower accepted you yet?" the marquess demanded.

Leo kept his arm around her. He was citrus and open meadows and rich earth and everything she loved most in this world. She leaned against him and was not ashamed. Sometimes vines were not clinging; sometimes the symbiosis was mutual, and not parasitic.

"Not in so many words, but I will continue to assemble reasons to persuade her. I'll ask for your approval, uncle, but it will be a formality. I'll marry Lillian with or without your consent. And if you see fit to cut me out of the succession, please do so at once, so she is aware of how little comes with my hand."

The marquess studied Lillian. He appeared in better health than when she last saw him. Lines of strain fanned from his eyes and mouth, though, and his neck behind the cravat showed the tendons of his throat, the mark of a man who had left behind his robust prime to begin battling the infirmities of old age.

"You'd take him with nothing?" he demanded.

"Nothing but love," Lillian confirmed. "Though I intend that he will help me further my career, the way I intend to help further his, so there will be some benefit to me."

That, and passion. The flush stayed in her cheeks at the thought. She could not touch Leo without feeling all those other touches, the layers of their history forming, building, growing rich and deep.

"Come to dinner at Westrop House tonight," the marquess said abruptly. "We have one or two things to discuss."

"UNCLE INSTRUCTED us to be beastly to you," Catherine confided. "He wanted to scare you away if you were merely setting your cap at a future marquess."

The Westrops and their guests sat around the carved oak table that had been restored to the center of the dining parlor in Westrop House. Aunt Melina sat on Lillian's right, Leo to her left. Lady Mary sat in the hostess's chair at the foot, glowering at Lillian, but tonight, she was the only one doing so.

"To be clear," Lillian said as a footman set a dish before her, "you lot weren't what scared me back to London."

Lucy nodded. "Told Father you had more backbone than that, and you weren't digging for gold. Not from Leo, at any rate." She sliced into her fricassee of lamb.

"I do not generally bring pets to the table," Annibel said. "Tonight, for instance, my hedgehog is in the parlor. I shall be happy to make an introduction when the ladies withdraw, should you wish."

"I would like to meet him," said Hester, sitting across the table from Lillian. "I'm going to have a dog when I marry."

"I hope not to marry for many years," Annibel said. "Please tell my father that."

"Same for me," Catherine said immediately. "I want a good match, Father. Not just *any* match. I want a man who is as wild for me as Gid—Leo is for Lillian, though I wish for my husband to be a good deal more intelligent, and handsome, and rich."

"Best of luck in your search." Lucy snorted. "Will someone please tell Father that *if* or when I do marry, it shall be for myself and not to fulfill some line of succession."

The Westrops fell silent at this, and Lillian guessed from

Leo's face that the ghost of his cousin Rupert had entered the room, a grief still fresh.

"Ungrateful, irresponsible hoydens, without an ounce of dignity or sense of duty," the marquess said calmly, and without heat. "About the succession," he went on, attacking the roast. "You can have all the sons you want, Lucy, but the title goes to the next male heir, and my grandfather set up the entail to follow the title. Unless you do away with your cousin, you'll be calling him milord at my funeral, and his sons thereafter, should he have them."

Leo's hand was steady as he spooned his soup. "You could marry and sire a child yet, sir."

"Just to spite you?" The marquess shook his head. "I've no need for a wife, and no need for an heir if I've got one. I can see you're not following after your father, and an antiquarian won't shade the name if you turn out an Aubrey or a Stukeley."

"I shall do my best, sir."

His uncle nodded. "You can live here when you're in London, so long as you let the girls lodge with you while they find husbands. And I suppose your lady could manage Waring-ford Hall."

Lady Mary made a squawk of disapproval, seeing her terri-tory infringed upon. "And you mean to simply turn me off, Waringford? What, am I to live in a crofter's cottage? After all I endured with your brother?"

The marquess regarded her curiously. "Refuse to get on with your new daughter, eh? 'Spose Leo can put up at the Compton Beauchamp house, then, if he's to continue poking about that old cave."

Leo put down his spoon, staring. "That's one of yours?"

"And will be yours, eventually. It's part of the entail. Have to sit down and acquaint you with the estate."

"And you can see my glasshouse while he's at it," Lady

Melina informed Lillian. She turned back to Uncle Gower, on her other side, for whom she had ignored the rest of the table for most of dinner. "Got a ghost orchid, I have."

Sir Lloyd nodded, heartily devouring his collar of mutton. "Could be Lil's next project. Told her she should draw all the orchids. Do up a proper florilegium. She could focus on it now that she's not distracted by bringing this one up to scratch." He leaned forward to address Leo down the table. "Was going to drag my old bones up to Uffington if you didn't turn up, son," he said. "Got tired of my girl moping."

"I was not moping," Lillian said, mortified at Leo's grin.

"Were too. Why, the other day I asked her where she put the latest issue of Curtis's *Botanical Magazine*, and she brought me Cranke Andrews' *Botanical Repository*. And when I told her to fetch me a volume we'd filed under Pythagoras, I found her standing and staring at the shelf under Ptolemy!" He shook his head. "Was afraid you'd made her addlepated. Don't waste her good mind, lad, even if you've been taken in by those dimples."

"I love Lillian for more than her dimples," Leo said gravely. "Though I admit they were the first thing I found fetching about her, they are not her only fine quality." He winked at Lillian, who couldn't decide whether to scold or blush.

"Gideon always did have an eye for women built like Venus," Lady Mary said. "Though a woman with that shape needs to watch herself, or she'll grow round as a melon."

"Do you refer to your late husband, madam?" Lillian asked. "Because Leo and I intend to remain active in our respective professions, which I hope will prevent me from acquiring any shape you would disapprove of."

Lady Mary glared at her for having the presumption to correct her, while Lucy bit back a smile, Catherine grinned openly, and Annibel made no attempt to hide her giggle.

"That's my boy," Lady Melina crowed, slapping the table

beside her plate. "Found a girl with spirit. What we've always wanted for you, nephew. You've been serious for far too long."

"I anticipate nothing but a great deal of future happiness, Aunt," Leo said with a smile toward Lillian that made her feel she'd turned into a pudding. "More than I deserve, I suspect."

Under the table he reached for her hand and held it, and Lillian recalled that first night, the night of his astonishing proposal, when he held her hand as strangers congratulated them. She'd known then that something new was coming into being, something that would unalterably change her life.

Now she knew the shape of it, and it was beautiful. It was this man beside her, loving her till the end of his days, and her loving him in return.

And he'd brought her all this: a table full of family, her circle expanding like ripples from a stone thrown in a pool. This, too, was beautiful. More beauty than any one person deserved, perhaps, but she would enjoy it as long as she could.

With Leo, she knew this happiness was real.

Since archaeology wasn't a developed discipline in the late 18th century, people like Leo and the Gowers, who enjoyed studying the remains of previous civilizations, called themselves antiquarians. William Cunnington really did work at Stonehenge in the summer of 1798, employing the Parker brothers, but it would be many years until proper excavations were made at Wayland's Smithy, then known as Wayland Smith's Cave. I've relied on the excellent work of R.J.C. Atkinson and Stuart Piggott to create Leo and Lillian's findings; one of the burials in the barrow, which turns out to have been built in two stages, contained two adult skeletons and child-size bones. Any errors or inaccuracies must be attributed to my characters' more limited understanding of the features about them, and to my not being an archaeologist.

It was believed at the time that Stonehenge was built by the Druids. The theory of the three ages—Neolithic, Bronze Age, Iron Age—hadn't yet been developed. The tribes predating the Romans were referred to as Celts, because that's what the Romans called them, but theories about the civilizations before them were little more than legend and myth. I worked in my favorite theory, lifted from the medieval chronicle of legend and pseudo-history called the *Brut*: the earliest Britons must have been giants, because of the enormity of their stone circles, barrows, and other marks they left on the landscape.

Speaking of Stonehenge: the giant trilithon was leaning at the time Leo and Lillian would have seen it, and one of its companions had recently fallen, which spurred Cunnington's exploration. The discussions Leo and Lillian have about the monument reflect, to the best of my knowledge, current thinking at the time. The Romans had a mint at London during their rule of the isle, and the coin honoring Magnus Maximus is attested elsewhere, though I confess I planted one at Stonehenge to give Lillian a way to show off her skills.

The entrance to Wayland Smith's Cave would have been a tumble of stones when Leo found it. The magnificent structures we see now, at both Stonehenge and Wayland's Smithy, were reconstructions of the 20th century, meant to restore these impressive and ancient monuments to what we think their builders wanted us to see.

Lillian's favorite flower, the Cypripedium calceolus or yellow lady's slipper, was, after the Victorian wave of orchid fever, so critically endangered in Britain that for decades of the 20th century only one plant was known to exist in the wild. It had a bodyguard, and its location was kept secret. Thanks to the work of conservationists and biologists, these orchids have been reintroduced in gardens around Britain, but I couldn't resist the opportunity to draw attention to endangered species like the calceolus or the starry stonewort that Uncle Lloyd studies. Biologists now know that the lady's slipper requires a particular fungus in the soil in order to absorb nutrients; I gave Lillian, ahead of her time, some inkling of this, because the interdependence provided such a lovely metaphor for her relationship with Leo.

The botanical volumes in Sir Lloyd's library are all real books. So is the work of the women Lillian is so inspired by, including Mary Delany, Mary Bowes, and Elizabeth Blackwell. The dedicated historians, archaeologists, botanists, scientists, and scholars, of their time and ours, are the reason readers like you and I can explore their world and appreciate all its varied beauties. They are the giants in whose shadows we stand.

I hope you've enjoyed Leo and Lillian's story. Thanks for taking this journey with me,

Misty

ABOUT THE AUTHOR

Misty Urban fell in love with stories at an early age and has spent her life among books as a teacher, scholar, editor, writer, and bookseller. Her favorite stories take you new places, teach you new things, and end with a win. She especially likes romances about unconventional heroines who defy the odds and the unexpected heroes who woo them, so that's mostly what she writes. When she puts down the book she likes to take long walks, drag her family to new places, or hang out around water, dreaming up new stories.

Visit her at mistyurban.com
Join author's newsletter

ALSO BY MISTY URBAN

Ladies Least Likely

Viscount Overboard

The Forger and the Duke

The Painter Takes an Earl

The Mad Baron's Bride

Marry Me, Marquess

Contemporary Novels

My Day As Regan Forrester

My Thing with Timothy Kay

www.ingramcontent.com/pod-product-compliance
Lightning Source LLC
Chambersburg PA
CBHW050515110726
47899CB00005B/1468